D1521756

CALAVERAS

LISA MICHELLE

For the people of Calaveras County,
and to Chyann

PART ONE

A mother's love for her child is like nothing else in the
world. It knows no law, no pity, it dares all things and
crushes down remorselessly all that stand in its path
—AGATHA CHRISTIE

The moments before death were good. Dreaming of you and dinner in our new home. A fine home, with pictures on the walls. Furniture that matched. There was a long wooden table loaded with food. Surrounded by family and friends and children. Almost like some sort of celebration. But it wasn't. It was just the way dinners were meant to be, but never had been.

I was finally happy until you ripped me from that deep perfection where I wanted to live forever. Offensive barking filled me with dread as I sat up, my heart fully awake and kicking, but not me. Not yet.

In the dark, my eyes opened wide, I still couldn't see. There was no time to recall the place where sleep had taken over or why Huck was barking at you before the deafening crack. Pain in the back of my skull knocked me forward.

Past is present at the moment and I'll think of you for an eternity.

Time is precious. Don't know why I know this, but I do and fall onto my side. I can't see the shadow of my attacker as much as I can feel it smothering me.

You.

"I'm sorry." The urge to say that comes from deep in my soul and is impossible to stop. Sorry. I try again, but the words stick somewhere between my tongue and my mind. I shouldn't have lied.

I'm sorry—I have to say it before it's too late, but only a pathetic moan escapes.

Another crack, like the amplified boom of thunder. Breaking slowly. Rolling around inside my head. Pain like lightning surges, then dissipates just as fast.

The tangy scent of pine offers repose. Stars so close in the deep black it's as if I could easily reach out and take one. I try, but death is sudden. Unexpected.

Why?

ONE

A banner struggles to escape its tethers above the dark entrance. *Welcome to Calaveras County Fair and Jumping Frog Jubilee.* Colossal cement frogs flank the muddy road, grinning as headlights hit them. Remnants of cotton candy linger, as does the chill of a May night. Rows of American flag pennants snap and salute rodeo fans as they exit across a soggy pasture parking lot. Under a full moon, Gene Autry crackles "Happy Trails" through rusty speakers.

Behind the bucking chutes, Joe Quick, a lanky bullfighter ten years past his prime, pries a black Resistol off his dirty-blond head. Dried sweat crusts his red-white-and-blue clown cheeks as he limps by a dozen portable pens restraining bucking bulls and broncs. Popcorn mingles with manure. Joe stops. Looks at Spooky, voted bucking bull of the year. The massive black bull smacks his head against the metal rails and keeps it there until Joe rubs and scratches the sweet spot just below and between his banana horns.

"Are you the rodeo clown?"

Joe turns to see a girl missing her front teeth but smiling like she hasn't a care in the world. "I'm a bullfighter—not a clown. I save guys from getting hammered by a bull."

"What about girls? Do you save them too?" Her stringy brown hair flaps like wings under her cowboy hat.

"I would—just ain't that many girl bull riders around. I'm Joe. What's your name?" Joe holds out his hand.

"Chyann. I'm gonna be a bull rider. Or . . . maybe, a bullfighter like you." The girl pulls a marker from her back pocket. "Will you autograph my hat?"

"I'd be honored." Joe signs his name across the back brim and dumps the girl's hat back on her head.

"Thank you!" Chyann runs to her parents as they give Joe a wave of appreciation.

In the door of his flatbed, Joe finds his OxyContin and downs them with a perspiring can of Coors. A cell phone on the seat dings, and Joe grabs it: 10:15. He listens to the message from his wife. "Hi, hon. I'm going to bed, so don't call. That paint colt finally launched me like a lawn dart today. Counterfeit bugger even tried to kick me while I was down. Anyhoo, don't worry, I'm fine, just tired. Hurry up and get your butt home. I took rib eyes out for dinner tomorrow. Love ya."

"Love you too," Joe whispers and tosses the phone on the seat.

"Good work tonight." A corn-fed old cowboy rides toward Joe.

"Thanks, boss." Joe scrapes makeup from his cheeks with a dirty rag and looks in his side mirror. "Can you pay me in cash?"

"Pay you?" It sounds more like a statement than a

question. "Your pay's goin' toward what you owe me."

Joe stops scraping. "Can I get half?"

"Soon as I do."

Joe looks up with a smeared smile. "Me and Em's tryin' real hard to build a cabin."

"Keep tryin'." Boss spits a long stream of tobacco juice as he rides away.

Roper struts up looking like a young Elvis. "Dang! Boss Hog be gettin' fat as a tick on a tampon!"

Joe knocks back his beer and comes up for air. "You get the money?" He crawls onto the flatbed.

"Don't *even* get me started. Last night, at the dance, me and this biker dude, we totally hit it off right. *Really* hit it off." A sigh causes Roper's smile to stray. "After dinner, we sinned, and, you know. Long story short, I fell asleep and the fag stole my money." He unzips his Wranglers. "Does this look infected?" Digging in his underwear, Roper faces Joe. "No, seriously, look. Do I need *penis*-cillin?" Roper's laugh is more like a bray.

"Get back, just—if you ain't got the cash—" Joe can't avoid looking in Roper's direction. Peeking from his zipper is a roll of cash.

"Ha! I knew you'd look. Perv!"

Joe shakes his head and grins. "You fucking need therapy."

"Nope, hanging around a loser like you makes me feel much better about myself. These undies are cool, right?" Roper works the wad of bills back into the Velcro money pocket. "Found them online. I can get you a pair?" He zips up as Joe slides off the flatbed. "Got *your* money, honey?" Roper asks, crossing his arms.

"Yeah, but I had to earn mine, you trust fund bitch." Joe grabs a denim shirt from inside the cab.

"Don't be hatin'. I'm broke as you are. Had to borrow money from my Auntie."

An aching pain punches through Joe as he removes his Red Bull jersey, revealing a scar the size of a silver dollar below his sternum. A souvenir from Bushwacker—a bull that killed one rider and caused another to think like a third-grader. A horn had impaled Joe as he worked at freeing a rider's hand wedged in the bull rope. Saving the cowboy cost Joe two weeks in ICU and a season without pay. A fundraiser paid the bills for three months. Bankruptcy covered the rest.

"Let's go over this again, just in case. I can*not* lose this money. Bankruptcy is not an option for people with trust funds." Roper dips his hands into his jean pockets.

"Fuck you." Joe eyes Roper.

"I didn't mean because you filed—I just . . . forget it. Regular old five-card draw, right?"

"Maybe you shouldn't come with me." Joe closes only one of the three pearl snaps on his right cuff, leaving the two nearest his palm undone. "This ain't the game for beginners."

"I know how to play poker. Winner take all, right?" Roper pulls a new deck from his shirt pocket. "Hey, what if their cards are different than ours?"

"This ain't my first rodeo. In a few hours, that wad won't fit in your panties." Joe snags the deck from Roper, slides the cards out, and fans them like a sophisticated street magician.

"Handkerchief?"

Roper pops a white hanky from his vest pocket like a well-trained assistant. Gene Autry concludes "Happy Trails," and the night goes silent.

Joe folds two aces into the handkerchief and tucks it into his shirt pocket. He sneezes, pulls the handkerchief out and wipes his nose, then stuffs it back into his shirt pocket. Voila, the two aces are gone. Sliding his sleeve up, Joe exposes the cards. Bouncing like an excited pup, Roper claps. "Amen! I love you! I'm gonna enter every Podunk rodeo in the West."

"Me and Em have to start the cabin or I'm in deep shit." The arena lights pop off. "*Wooo*" and "*Yeeowww*" echo from drunk fans desperate for fun.

Angels Camp is a refurbished gold rush town complete with mercantile, three-story hotel, and corner saloon with a former brothel upstairs. Hanging from a clothesline above the deserted street, antique dresses, worn-out overalls, and torn flannel shirts float like ghosts. Vintage lamps line Main Street as frogs harmonize with Roper's spurs—clicking and clacking and croaking.

"Why the hell didn't you take your spurs off?" Joe asks.

"I forgot, okay?" Roper steps around painted frogs on the sidewalk. "Don't have a tizzy. Not like I flimflam people every day. I'm usually extremely ethical. I believe that—"

"Rope! It's fine."

They pass Utica Park—named for the Utica gold mine— burial site of seventeen men who perished when it collapsed. Entombed below a slide and row of swings. A bronze statue of Mark Twain glares down at them as they pass. Sprinklers kick on, hissing until they reach the dark end of Main Street. "You cannot fuck this up. Understand? Not one of these fuckers wants to lose at a winner-take-all game. Tell me again why this works," says Joe.

Balling his fists, Roper walks faster and faster. "Okay, okay . . . When the cards come to you for the third time, everyone will have a hand they *think* they can win with. They'll bet big. We do too. You sneeze—pull your hanky, slip the aces in, and we win."

Made of century-old pine and washed in white, Saint Joseph's church waits like a savior. Saint Financial Aid. Below the oxidized brass bell, a Roman-numeral clock reads midnight.

"Midnight mass. Last time I played with this gangbanger from Stockton. Father Ortega asked the dude if he'd been baptized. I don't know if the guy didn't hear him or what. But ole Ortega had one ear off and was whittlin' at the other before the bastard could even get up and run. Mexicans didn't touch him, that's how connected he is. He killed his brother for cheatin' on his wife—I heard he keeps him in the freezer and hacks off chunks to put in the beans."

"OMG." Roper comes to a halt. "He'll hate me, right?"

"Fuck yeah. Don't talk. Don't make eye contact. Just sit the fuck down and look at your cards." Joe gives the handkerchief in his shirt a final adjustment.

Darkness cloaks the rear of the church as Joe approaches a skinny back door. "Shit. He'll lock this. If *anything* goes wrong, you hit this door and you hit it hard as you can. It'll bust, and you run, keep running, don't look back no matter what." The old door bleats like a sacrificial lamb as Joe opens it. Roper follows. Down warped and narrow steps that lead to a dim glow. Creaking wood and clapping spurs amplify each step as the wail of an organ begins.

"This is all kinds of creepy, man." Roper puts his hand on Joe's shoulder. "Smells like something's burning."

"Simmering flesh—now shut the fuck up."

The organ trembles as they enter the dank basement. Burning votives and Virgin Mary veladoras crowd the cramped space, along with a folding hexagonal card table and three strangers. Father Ortega stands in a black floor-length cassock accented with a shoulder cape. At six-foot-five, he is an effigy of something sinister and looks down upon them with dark, wilting eyes. Roper grabs Joe's arm and squeezes.

"Donations?" Father Ortega's authoritative voice commands, his gnarled hands holding out a donation basket. Roper attempts to ignore the chains tattooed around Ortega's wrists, the Glock holstered under his arm, but an inappropriate laugh escapes.

Joe pulls a white envelope from his back pocket, _IN GOD WE TRUST_ written across the front in blue clown eyeliner. He places it in the basket.

Roper palms the wad of cash in his secret underwear. Looks up at the priest. "Is the bathroom, is, umm, there a bathroom?"

Ortega's razor-burnt chin clenches into his neck like a

closing fist. Nostrils flare. The heavy cassock swings as Ortega seems to float across the room. Stopping at the freezer, he sets the basket down. With a swift slap, Ortega stifles the organ music coming from a cassette player and roars, "And he shall lay his hand upon the head of his offering and *kill it* at the door of the tabernacle of the congregation!" He takes a calming breath and softens. "Leviticus."

Roper turns away, digging out his cash as fast as he can. Delicately, he lays ten thousand dollars in the donation basket. With eyes locked on Roper, Ortega flips through the curling bills like they're pages of a Bible.

At the card table, Joe sits between a bearded Brit and Luke, who wears a grizzled Afro and huge sunglasses. Miss Kitty takes the seat across from Joe. A pucker-faced woman in blue eye shadow and a lacquered auburn twist taps her long gold nails like claws practicing for a concerto. Ortega blesses Roper with the sign of the cross. "May the Lord be with you."

"Thank you. Thank you very much. You too, sir, Father." Roper stumbles into the seat next to Miss Kitty.

Ortega drops the deck in front of Roper. "Shuffle." He flips the cassette over, and organ music grinds as Roper shuffles. Miss Kitty lights a long brown cigarette and takes a deep drag while Ortega divides poker chips between players. "Ladies first." Ortega slides the deck to Miss Kitty. "I will watch over my flock." He raises his palms above his head and explodes, "And I will inflict the wrath of God upon the sinners!" Roper squirms in his chair as Miss Kitty deals the first hand.

By two a.m. smoke clouds the basement and a dozen brown cigarette butts litter a silver tray. Miss Kitty lights another as Joe sniffs and wipes his nose on his sleeve. Poker chips applaud as the Brit drags in another winning pile.

"Beans are ready." Ortega waits for a response. No one looks up. No one responds. Luke rubs under his glasses and pushes the deck to Joe. Joe sniffs, shuffles, and sniffs again as Ortega watches. "Coming down with something, my son?"

"Allergies. Happens every spring." Joe wipes his nose with his sleeve again and deals. The organ quits and Joe swallows hard. The Brit, smiling with everything except his lips, stares wide-eyed at his hand. Miss Kitty taps her nails a beat faster, and Luke remains cool behind his shades. Roper sneaks a peek at Ortega, who is now glaring at Joe.

"Would you like a tissue?" Ortega grins.

"Sure." Joe adjusts the cards in his hand.

Ortega rises—moves next to Joe. Leans in uncomfortably close. "Why?"

"Why what, Father?" Joe avoids eye contact.

Ortega jacks his gun and shoves it against Joe's nose. "Why go to all the trouble of carrying such a nice handkerchief and not make use of it?"

"I forgot I had the damn thing!" Joe tightens his brow and shuts his eyes.

"Well, then, give it a whirl, won't you?" Ortega insists.

The moment lingers before anyone moves, or speaks, or

breathes. Roper's palms press against the green felt table as Joe draws the handkerchief slowly—carefully—from his shirt and dabs his nose, then replaces it. Miss Kitty reaches across the table and snatches the handkerchief—freeing the aces to buck wildly through the air and land on the table. Joe shoves himself into Ortega and flips the table. "Run!"

Gunfire explodes. Screaming, Roper lunges for the stairs. Ears ringing, they take the steps two at a time, unable to escape the sour acrid smell of spent gunpowder. "Go, go, go!" Joe's muffled panic repeats. "Go!"

At the top of the stairs, Roper catapults himself through the locked door. Fragile wood cracks and antique hinges give. Another shot as Roper and the door crash against the gravel lot. Two more shots burst from the basement. Joe grabs Roper's arm and drags him across the lot then down an embankment. They drop into the creek behind the church.

"Move your ass!"

For a quarter mile, they splash between boulders and branches. Spiderwebs sticking. Swatting. Squealing. Stumbling over slick stones, Roper goes down. "Shit!"

"Come on! Up here." Joe cuts out of the creek. Up a steep bank on all fours. A barbwire fence stops them. Stepping on the bottom strand and pulling up on the next, Joe stretches the middle section of the fence wide open. "Hurry." Roper wiggles through, then reciprocates the process. Joe slips between the wires like a snake between stacked brush. They sprint under a full moon. Casting long demonic shadows across an overgrazed pasture—closing in on a dilapidated barn.

Weathered wood offers sanctuary. Joe steps through a missing plank, but Roper struggles. No tools, no tractor, no bales of hay, only fermenting earth, creosote, and feces stagnate the empty space. Joe sucks air through his open mouth as Roper heaves in the corner. "I—I kinda pooped my pants."

Joe laughs with lungs deprived of oxygen. He can't stop laughing, then doubles over holding his side.

"*So* not funny." Roper tugs and tugs until his wet boots and spurs release.

Joe's hysterics go on and on until, finally, a long silence fills the open space. "I promised Em I wouldn't play cards no more. She finds out I been gamblin' . . . lost this much money—she'll kill me." Joe puts his hand on Roper's shoulder. ".38 in my truck will fix this shit right now."

"Nope! *Not even* going back! Donation to staying alive! You don't get caught cheating and expect to get your money back. Not with that creepazoid. Oh God, do they know where you live?"

"They think I'm from Lodi. And run a vineyard there."

"We are so lucky." Roper plops onto the dirt floor. "Maybe I can write it off. What do I tell Auntie?"

"I'm fucked. I borrowed that cash from a guy in Vegas!" Joe blows a long breath and sits next to Roper.

"I'd float you a loan, but I don't get another check until fall."

"Sorry, Rope. Really. Sorry you ruined your fancy

underwear."

"It's not your fault." Roper unbuckles his belt. "I'd probably be dead if it weren't for you." He wiggles out of his soggy jeans. "You always got my back . . . I want you to know I appreciate it." He slides out of the secret-pocket undies.

Joe throws his hat against the ground and lies on his back. Clasps his arms over his forehead and stares at the speckled sky through the broken roof. "I'm such a fucking asshole."

"Yes, you are. But Em loves you, and so do I." Roper wipes and tosses the soiled undies into the corner. "She won't stop just 'cause you can't build the cabin"—he wiggles his legs into his jeans—"so you have to stay in the trailer a while longer—so what. It's not the end of the world."

"We could a been killed. Or shot." Joe grins and shakes his head. "Or worse . . . you fucking floppin' around the ER flirtin' with the doctor like last time."

Roper looks down at Joe and grins. "Amen, brother."

Sunday morning blossoms as church bells echo down Main Street. Joe climbs the blue steps of the white church that offers benevolence in the light of day. Sliding into the last pew, Joe sits next to a weathered man in jeans and a tan canvas coat. The faithful flock sit upfront.

Playing "Ave Maria" on the organ, Miss Kitty, in her Sunday best, sings and smiles at Joe. The weathered man slides closer. Pulls the _IN GOD WE TRUST_ envelope from his coat pocket and hands it to Joe with the same gnarled fingers and tattooed wrists of Father Ortega.

"Took three hundred from your cut. Have to pay my cousin for the door, and everyone said you should have left it unlocked. That cool?" The soft words sound nothing like the Father Ortega from last night.

Joe holds the envelope down near his knees and opens it. Without removing the one-hundred-dollar bills, he carefully counts his share. Finally, when he reaches seventy-seven, he closes the envelope. Folds it in half and tucks it deep into the inside pocket of his leather jacket.

"Thanks, Abe." Joe stands.

"You're not staying for the service?"

"Em's waitin'. Gotta get home." Joe pats Abe on the shoulder and the music stops.

"I'll pray for you."

Joe slips his hands in his jacket pockets and caresses the cash inside. His boots echo like flesh slapping hardwood. Out the door. Down the steps.

TWO

Johnny Cash plays through a dust-covered boom box, rattling the barn's tin roof. Unashamed of her incompetent pitch, Emma Lee sings too loud while loading the last shovelful of horse manure into a wheelbarrow. She leans the shovel against the log wall and sings, "Bound by wild desire—I fell into a ring of fire." With a quick pull, she tightens her tawny bobbed ponytail. Unsophisticated and wholesome, she's just short of beautiful. Twenty-eight years ago, Emma Lee Dunnigan was accidentally born in this barn, a story her mother loves repeating whenever Emma Lee leaves a door open. Muscles on her rangy arms strain under her Lynyrd Skynyrd tee as she fights the ornery wheelbarrow—pushing it along a dirt trail behind the barn. Hank, a decrepit border collie, and Huck, her year-old brindle rescue pup, follow.

The ranch is graced with seasonal creeks that grumble in spring—threading their way down acres of jade-colored hills, through a lush meadow, until finally reaching an impressive pond. Apple trees are heavy with soft pink petals that flutter and fall. A bold, sweet scent after a spring rain induces a sudden and inexplicable optimism. Cows watch their calves buck and play in pastures where spicy cedars and pines reach for the sky. Ancient oaks cast twisted shadows.

"Em?" Kate, a graying and wilting version of Em, shouts as she untangles herself from clean white sheets hanging on the clothesline behind her clean white house. "Made a pot of spaghetti."

"No, thanks, Mom. Joe's comin' home. Gonna cook him a steak," Em yells from the barn as she drops the empty wheelbarrow.

Cramped in the Airstream, Em washes her hands and face in a miniature bathroom sink. Nails chewed to the quick. A blast of deodorant under each arm. A dab of mascara, then peach lip gloss tidies her appearance. Overhead, a mischievous fly drones. She swats twice at the pest, then scrutinizes herself in the mirror duct-taped above the sink. Letting her hair down, she combs it to the side and considers it. Too boyish. She parts it down the middle, hoping for something trendy, then wraps the sides behind her ears, grunts, and pulls it back into a ponytail. The droning stops as the fly lands on the mirror and is exterminated with a smack. A wing, and specks of red and fluorescent yellow, smear Em's hand. The dismembered carcass lands on a pregnancy test stick resting on the counter.

Joe's Ford purrs up to the trailer, and Em bolts out the door, wiping wet hands on dirty jeans. She married Joe Quick four years ago during the National Finals Rodeo in Las Vegas. The previous year, Joe had fought bulls and

Emma Lee was Miss Rodeo California. Reluctantly, she primped and competed for the title of Miss Rodeo America. The winning queen would receive a twenty-thousand-dollar scholarship and give Em her shot at becoming a veterinarian. She won the horsemanship section of the competition, and an engraved silver buckle trimmed in imitation gold. The tarnished buckle sits next door, in her mom's house, on a shelf above the woodstove, covered in dust and ash, alongside two dozen others. Emma Lee finished third in the Miss Rodeo America competition and abandoned the pursuit of becoming a veterinarian in exchange for Joe, an Airstream on her mother's ranch, and part-time work as a vet tech at the Mother Lode Equine Clinic.

Joe kills the engine, climbs out of the truck as Em runs through dust and diesel fumes to him. Their attraction is magnetic—they fit together as if created that way. Joe cradles his wife's face in his hands, then smiles and tosses her over his shoulder like a sack of grain. "You got some ridin' to do, cowgirl." Up the Airstream steps, he attempts to squeeze through the narrow trailer door.

"Put me down! Really. I'm not kidding, Joe! You're squishin' him."

Joe stops. Backs off the steps, then slowly sets Em down. "Him?"

"I was gonna tell you after dinner."

His hazel eyes absorb her words. "I did it?"

"Yep." Em nods with an embarrassed grin, looks down, realizing her feet are bare.

"When? How pregnant are ya?"

"I'm thinking a few months, maybe. I missed my last two periods and—"

"You know it's a boy? For sure?"

"Got a feelin'."

"I gotta feelin' too. Feelin' our boy's gonna have his own room." Joe reaches into his back pocket and hands Em the _IN GOD WE TRUST_ envelope.

She looks inside. Sees the cash. "What's this?"

"Down payment on the cabin."

"You been playin' cards? Tell the truth."

"It's the money Harvey owed me for driving the water truck on the Butte Fire. I ran into him after the rodeo."

An intense, almost-orgasmic pleasure surges through her, like sliding into a warm bath on a cold day. She leaps on Joe, cinches her arms around his neck, her legs tight around his waist. "I love you." She kisses his neck. Bites his earlobe. "I love you." Another kiss.

"Baby, I love you more. Holy shit, we're gonna have a baby!" He rocks her side to side.

Kate, with her long graying braid pulled to one side, yells as she approaches from the path between her house and the Airstream. "Forest Service called." A warm apple pie cradled in hands thickened by a lifetime of weather. "Hi, Joey."

Joe sets Em down and hugs his mother-in-law, who doesn't attempt to hug him back. She never has been a people person, and the pie in her hands prevents the usual awkwardness that comes with polite affection. "You're the best, Kate." A bouquet of warm apples and cinnamon linger as she hands him the pie.

21

"Forest Service said two of our cows are up on Devil's Nose. They didn't see no calves."

Em crosses her arms. "That's a three-hour ride if you hurry."

"I'll see if I can find where they busted through the fence." Joe scoops out a hunk of pie with his fingers.

"Go in the morning." Kate presses her thinning lips together.

"I'll take that paint colt. Be good for that dumb son of a bitch, 'specially if we're gonna brand calves next week?" Joe fills his mouth.

"We have to. And Roper asked if he could bring his sister. I said she could run the nut bucket." A grin lifts Kate's face. Savannah carrying a bucket of calf testicles seems somehow artistic.

"Perfect job for that skank," Joe says around a mouthful of pie.

"Be nice," Kate and Em recommend in unison, then look at each other until no one speaks. The silence thickens. Turns awkward as Kate tries to wait them out.

"So . . . ?" She rocks back on her heels. Looks at Em with tired but knowing brown eyes. "Anything else?"

Almost smiling, Em bites her lower lip—focusing on her bare feet. "Nope." She shrugs and shakes her head with the innocence of a guilty child.

Kate clasps her hands behind her back and waits another long minute. "Oh, come *on*, you two! Just 'cause I'm gonna be a gramma don't mean I'm deaf."

Like most nights, Kate eats dinner standing over the kitchen sink with old Hank, the dog, staring at his bowl. Waiting for leftovers. Only, tonight, Kate opens a bottle of Pinot she'd been saving for a special occasion. Wine works wonders on a woman's truth. *Grandmother. Grandma. Granny.* None of them feels right. *Nana?* Hell no. Imagining being a grandparent brings a familiar mix of dread and optimism that came with the thought of ever dating. The dating was easy to excuse herself out of. It was always the same. *I can't make it. I have to fence to fix. You're welcome to come help?* It culled the slackers. Kate gulps the last of her third glass of wine and sets it on the counter. Dumps her leftover spaghetti in Hank's bowl and watches him gulp it without chewing.

"Sorry I overcooked the steak." Em clears the plates off the collapsible table, the Airstream still filled with smoke to spite the open windows and door.

"It was good." Joe rubs his jaw as he chews and chews the last hunk of meat. "My mastication muscles were getting soft."

"What? Your masturbation muscles?" Em dumps the burnt meat onto one plate and sets it outside the door for Huck.

"I said *mastication*. I been saving my masturbation muscle for you." Joe laughs, sweeping table crumbs into his hand.

"Good." Em leans against the sink. Smiles that sweet smile that she knows gets Joe every time. "I missed you."

"I missed you too." He's up and pressed against her. His hands gripping her ass, pulling her into him. "You're comin' with me to every rodeo from now on." His kisses are soft and short on her neck, then long and hard on her mouth. An overwhelming desire to feel his weight on top of her drives her to the couch. On her back, kicking off her flip-flops while Joe unzips her jeans. Kissing her stomach, then sliding his tongue into her bellybutton. She laughs and grabs his ears, not because it tickles, but because she is so happy.

"Is it okay? I can't hurt the baby, right?" Joe looks serious.

"Don't flatter yourself." Em arches and wiggles out of her jeans while Joe watches. Staring as if he truly appreciates her beauty.

He shakes his head in disbelief. "Holy shit."

"What?"

"I love you." He seems surprised and undresses as if it were a timed event. "I mean it, Em. I really, really, *love* you." His warmth inside her.

THREE

Fluorescent lights buzz and spill from the barn into the dark-blue dawn. A sorrel colt, cursed with white legs, eats at the feed manger as Joe pulls slack from leather straps and buckles down his bedroll—securing it behind his saddle. Heavy canvas saddlebags hang over the horse's flanks and stow enough provisions for two days. Perched on a shelf, above the tack room door, Joe stretches to reach a vintage aluminum tube, then forces it into the middle of his bedroll.

"You're takin' my dad's fly rod?" Em walks in, crossing her arms partly due to the cold but mostly due to the sentiment she has for her father's fly rod.

"Hey. Thought you wanted to sleep."

"Sleep when I get old." Em tests the tube's security with a twist and a push and a pull. "Suppose to be lookin' for cows, not trout."

"You're the best peanut-butter-and-jelly sandwich maker I know, but I need meat."

"Better bring some back for me and Mom."

"Yes, ma'am." After untying the colt, he kisses Em. "Love

you." He bends and kisses her belly. "Love you too."

Outside the barn, Joe's ass hits the saddle a little too hard. The colt flings and drops his head. He bucks like an oil derrick—up and down and up and down as if in slow motion. Joe pulls one rein and tips the colt's nose—forcing him into a tight circle. After a half dozen circles, Joe kicks the horse and sends him hopping through the apple orchard. They lope toward the rising sun as Joe glances back at Em with a confident smile. Huck barks and takes the lead.

"Be careful!" She waves and whispers, "With that rod, you goofball."

Flies cling to the frosty Airstream. Wilting yellow tulips rise as the promise of warmth wakes them. The trailer door bursts open—thumps against metal. An explosion of vomit drowns the flowers as Em folds. Groans and catches her breath, then heaves again. Spewing every bit of beefy bile from her stomach. She spits and spits, then wipes her mouth with her vet tech smock. "God dang." After a long, deep breath, she takes a seat in the doorway, then looks at her watch. Already an hour late. Another long, slow drag of breath, and a bit of color returns to her cheeks. She digs the cell phone from her pocket and dials.

"Hey, Brandi, it's Em. Still at home—I'm sick. I don't think I can come in today. Thanks. Yeah, I'll see you tomorrow. Bye." She lies back on the cool doorway floor and rests her hand on her forehead. Long, deep breaths over and over until dogs bark at a speeding vehicle rumbling through the pine and down the gravel drive. A new heavy-duty Chevy slides to a stop, and Roper jumps out.

"Hey, Rope." Em stands, but he doesn't greet her with the extra-long hug he's been greeting her with since they wore braces and cutoffs with matching cowboy boots. He's trembling.

"Where's Joe?" With a hand on his hip, he looks away, shaking his head as tears bloom.

"Getting cows off Devil's Nose, what's wrong?"

"I loved that guy, looked up to him like a fucking brother."

Em grabs Roper's arm. "What is it?"

"You deserve better than that sick piece of shit." Roper swallows with tears in his voice. "It's Savannah."

Em pushes her fists deep into her smock pockets. Her shoulders rising. Tensing without permission.

"He's been messin' with my little baby sister! Jesus Christ—she's only fourteen!"

"I know how old she is."

Hiding his face in his hands, he cries like a girl, "When's he gonna be back?"

She stalls. Taking it in. Shakes her head. "How do you know this? For sure, I mean. 'Cause, you know, I hate to say it, but your sister isn't the most honest person." Her muted tone doesn't hide her desperation.

"I love you, Em—" Roper drops his hands from his face. "Savanah's pregnant!"

"Bullshit." Em stumbles backward into the trailer and slams the door.

"Fourteen, Em! Not cool. Not cool at all! And also illegal.

My dad's reporting it to the sheriff. The fucker's going to jail unless I find him first." His voice seeps into the trailer through the open window. "He's corrupt, Em!"

No, he's not. Em sits on the edge of her bed—staring at a fly trying to escape a spiderweb. The back of her brain tingles with an intense itch that can't be scratched. As Roper's truck revs and tears away, a high-pitched buzz fractures Em's memory. Her vision blurs. She blinks. Faster and faster, then wipes her eyes with trembling fingers. Drags her palms down her face, again and again, wanting to clear the blur. Eyes shut tight, she finds the phone in her pocket and pulls it out.

Kate barges in. "Honey, Em, you okay?"

"You heard?" Em stands, but the overwhelming sensation of spinning sends her back down onto the bed.

"We'll figure this out." Kate forces calm as she squeezes Em's wrists.

"It's a lie. I know it. Why?" Em wipes her eyes. "Why is she doing this now?"

"Who knows. Just stay calm, and when Joe gets back—"

"He won't be back 'til tomorrow. He's gonna fish." Her heart is racing so hard it hurts. Her eyes sting. "What is wrong with Savannah? Roper's gone nuts. He said Joe's going to jail." Em scrubs her eyes with the base of her palms.

"Don't fool with your eyes, hon." *Goddamn it, don't start up with your eyes. Please.*

"Don't look," Em whispers—freeing her wrists. Scrubbing her eyes hard.

"Stop rubbin' your eyes! Listen to me—" Panic rising in Kate's voice.

"I should talk to Dad. I haven't even told him he's going to be a grandpa."

Kate's face collapses. Her rosy cheeks turn pale. "Honey, you *know* you can't do that."

"Out please." Em jumps up—forces Kate back, out the door, then locks it.

Flies that had clung to the outside of the trailer are alive and well and buzzing in Kate's face. With her back pressed against the locked door, panic fogs her thinking. She can't contemplate her next move. Ravens bark from a distant post. Mimicking the dogs. Distracting her. Why, Kate thinks. *Why are ravens always near? Always watching. Following. What the hell do they want?* If she had her gun, she just might shoot them.

Beeping tones of numbers being dialed on a cell sneak out the open slotted window. "Daddy, it's Em . . . I miss you too. Can you come home?" Em's warm words uncoil like a hissing snake. "You're gonna be a grandpa." Chills suck the air from Kate. She covers her mouth with both hands. Considers praying. It never helped before. Goddamn it. How has she reached middle age and knows less than she ever has?

Agony rushing her. Ripping the old wound wide open. The wound she thought Joe had healed. A strange invasion like rapid blood loss makes her weak. Shaking, she stumbles off the doorstep, then catches herself and sits. Reaching out for something to stabilize her. Reaching for something that isn't there. Quietly falling apart as she listens. "And . . . Joe. They're saying he did a real bad thing. I don't believe it, but

Roper said he got Savannah pregnant. They're gonna arrest him!"

Fraught with Em's long silence, Kate waits, still as a bird in a bush.

"Devil's Nose. We had some cows run off, and he went to get 'em." Kate doesn't breathe. A cold, dark terror passes through her like the sun just turned black.

FOUR

Neon pinks, violets, and blues light the back of Devil's Nose as darkness devours the day. In the meadow below, Joe's colt's front legs are bound by a set of burlap hobbles tied above his ankles. A mound of tender new grass tempts the colt. He stumbles forward and tears a mouthful. Campfire embers flitter up a wall of quaking aspen as Joe tosses in another log. Green cedar pops and hisses as Joe stares into the dancing flames. A twig snaps somewhere in the brush and rattles his senses. He spins around. Huck hoists his head off the bedroll, pricks his ears. A timid growl escapes. They listen. Crackling campfire, creek, and crickets all serenade a symphony accompanied by a west wind that kicks an essence of warm cedar through the damp meadow.

Joe swats Huck away from his bedroll, sits, and pulls his boots off. "I love you, Huck, but you best get used to playing second fiddle. I'm gonna be a daddy. You believe that?" Joe sinks into his bedroll, and Huck curls in next to him. Joe rubs the dog's soft ear. "There's gonna be a boy calling me Dad." He pulls the cover under his chin, crosses his arms under his head, and closes his eyes with a tearful grin. "Man, oh man, I already love him, and he ain't even here yet." The luxury of private weeping. "Thank you, Lord."

Stars sprout and earth rotates as night grows. The Milky Way spills across wide-open space, and below it all, Huck sleeps in a ball next to a few glowing coals as Joe snores. A silhouette emerges—approaches from behind the wall of white-barked aspens. Closing in on Joe. Tall. A cowboy hat cloaks a face. Huck's growl wakes Joe. Instinctively, he sits up from a deep sleep, but before he can remember where the hell he is, a rock cracks the back of his skull. Huck barks incessantly but isn't brave. With a feeble effort to turn toward his attacker, Joe collapses onto his side. Onto the crisp carpet of pine needles. Thought and movement paralyzed by his seizing brain. A pathetic moan encourages the killer to raise the granite rock with both hands and pop the cranium with a final blow to the right temple. Thin skin splits and craters with bone. Blood dribbles, then pools, as gloved hands slide Joe's bedroll away from him. An eye escapes its socket and comes to rest on the bridge of Joe's nose. His hazel iris dilates with death.

FIVE

In the dead of night, crickets go silent. Joe's colt snorts and tugs against the burlap hobbles tied around his front legs while the killer buckles down the saddlebags. Like a secret witness, Huck watches from a safe distance. Joe lies on his side as if watching the killer roll the bedroll and tie it to the back of the saddle.

A gloved hand works a cold bit into the horse's mouth. The frightened animal's hind legs jig and trample Joe before the killer can get the horse under control and close enough to the corpse. Joe's heavy leg is lifted. His boot shoved through the stirrup—up to the ankle. A serrated pocketknife saws through the burlap hobbles. The instant the horse's legs are free, he twists his head and sidesteps. Joe follows. With a snort, the colt backs, pinning his ears at the body following him. Joe's arms shift above his head as if he has decided to surrender.

"Heeyaw!" the killer screams, and the colt bolts—dragging and bouncing Joe across the meadow as Huck follows them up the ridge and out of sight. Crickets come to life. With both hands, the killer lifts the bloody granite and tosses the evidence into the fire. Cooling ash swarms like scavenging buzzards as Joe's murderer escapes the site of this tragic but accidental death toting the fly rod.

Morning at the ranch is consistent with most preceding mornings. Blue jays squawk. The crippled cat is curled on a stack of firewood on the porch. A frosty dew spreads under the apple orchard as tendrils of smoke climb from the stovepipe, twisting and turning like vines in the atmospheric pressure. The only flaw in this perfect portrait of the West is the green-and-white Calaveras County Sheriff's SUV parked in the driveway.

At the kitchen table, Kate refills Deputy Paul Lipinski's tin cup with coffee while he downs the last of a hearty piece of apple pie. A sticky crumb lingers on a single hair in his red mustache as if one of his many freckles has suddenly slipped out of place. He stands, says, "Thank you," and pats his belly as the radio on his hip squeals. He spins the volume down. "Mr. Rivera is adamant about pressing charges. Please contact me the minute Mr. Quick arrives." He hands Kate his card. "We'll need him to come in and give a statement."

"He need a lawyer?"

"I'm not at liberty to advise you, but I don't think it's necessary at this point. Just have him come in so we can start processing the pieces."

Kate slides the card into her back pocket as she escorts Lipinski to the door. "It'd be extremely helpful if you'd wake Emma Lee. I just need to ask—"

"Nope." Kate shakes her head like an ill-mannered pony.

"She was up all night bawlin' and throwin' up. Her and that baby need rest." She opens the front door. "I sure hope Roper didn't do somethin'. He was rantin' like a maniac, said he was gonna kill Joe."

"People make threats all the time, I wouldn't worry." He shakes her hand. "Thanks again for the pie, Ms. Dunnigan."

Kate watches Lipinski pull out of the drive and shuts the door. In no time, she's out the back door and on her way to the Airstream—ignoring the hungry nickers coming from the barn.

The Airstream door is unlocked like always, and Kate sticks her head inside. "Em?" Silence. *Please, just be sleeping.* Kate steps in. Takes four steps through the living room/kitchen/dining room area and wraps her fingers around the bedroom doorknob. "Emma Lee!" She knocks and waits. Takes a deep breath, then twists the knob and opens the door. The double bed is made. Kate glances alongside the bed, checks the shower. Tragedy has cautioned her to expect the worst, but grit forces her to rule it out.

Walking back toward the house, the slight possibility that Em could be sleeping in her old bed in her old room has not been ruled out. Kate hurries. Again, ignoring the hungry horses nickering in the barn.

The doorjamb swells every winter and especially in this wet spring. After two failed attempts to open the door, Kate turns the knob and rams it hard with her shoulder. It gives with a pop. Kate looks around the room that held so much promise. Wallpaper that once was white, now withered and peeling—making the room smell like old books. Em's blue ribbons. Shelves of Breyer horses. Pencil sketches of mountains vistas and riders on the trail. So much of her still here. That familiar motherly panic begins to form—sickening her. She pushes the worry aside. Horses have to be fed.

In the barn, Kate approaches the haystack. Dipping in the front pocket with two bandaged fingers, she pulls a knife and saws at the orange twine on a bale of alfalfa. It pops open like an accordion. Two heavy flakes fall into her arms.

"I already fed." Em lifts the saddle off a black horse tied at the feed manger. Dried sweat coats his short back, leaving a salty white crust.

"Where the hell have you been?" Kate fights to stay calm.

"Went to meet Dad," Em mumbles.

Kate drops the hay. Walks to Em and wants so badly to slap some sense into her child, even beat it into her if it would help. Lost—she struggles to ask. The words will not come. She stares at Em and chews her lower lip. After two deep breaths: "You see him?"

Em turns away and walks the horse to his stall.

Kate follows, asking soft, slow, and steady, "Emma Lee—did—you—see him?"

"I waited there. He said—"

"Where? You waited where?"

Em unbuckles the horse's halter and turns him loose in his stall. He drops and rolls in fresh pine shavings, then jumps up and shakes like a wet dog.

"Em, please tell me where you went?"

"You know."

Kate shakes her head as every nerve in her body fires. "Where?" She has to hear it. Assumptions are too risky.

"Hunt camp." Em's voice cracks as she begins to cry. "I'm sorry, Mom."

"Goddamn it." Kate sits against the feed manger, tasting the shit that just hit the fan.

"He didn't even show up, okay." Em shuts the stall door and sits next to Kate. "I had to. I didn't know what else to do."

Kate wishes Em would laugh, fess up that she's just messing around. One of those bad jokes that you don't realize isn't funny until you tell it out loud. And she's sorry, she won't do it again. Life can go on the way it should. Kate knows too well the suffering to come. How could such a strong woman, built of solid bone, thick skin, nerve, and grit, suddenly want to trade places with that fly feasting on a pile of shit.

Hooves splash and slap through wet gravel as Joe's paint colt trots into the barn. Without his bridle, he tears at the haystack. His saddle hangs sideways. Left stirrup missing. Dried blood crusted on his white legs.

"Oh God." Em rushes over. Runs her hands down the colt's hind legs. "Mom! I can't find where he's bleeding." Looking under his belly for an injury. "There's nothing. No cuts." Em stands and looks at her mom for help. "God, Mom, where's Joe? What if something happened to him?"

"Cowboy justice," Kate whispers as she halters the colt and ties him to the feed manger.

"We gotta find him!"

"I'll call the sheriff—they can send help. If Joe's hurt, there's nothing you can do." Kate holds her hand out, waiting for her little girl to take it. "We pay taxes. Let them bastards do their job." Em's doe eyes look desperate as she takes Kate's hand. "You go get in your old bed and give that baby some rest."

"Mom. I'm so scared."

"I know, sweetie. Don't borrow trouble, we'll worry when we know we got somethin' to worry about. Okay?" She squeezes Em's hand.

"Okay."

"Em . . . you can*not* tell anyone you talked to your father. Understand?"

Em nods and rubs her eyes.

SIX

A framed eight-by-ten of happy little Em on Daddy's shoulders. An autographed poster of George Strait grins down from the ceiling as Em falls into her antique bed. Iron springs and Em bounce and groan in unison. Kate pulls Em's boots off just like she has for so many years after a long weekend of junior rodeos. "Want a pair of my sweats?"

"No, I'm fine."

"I'll get your quilt." Kate reaches it off a shelf in the closet and covers Em.

In the fetal position, Em closes her eyes as Kate brushes the hair from her face.

"Get some rest." Kate moves to the faded denim curtains and unties the sashes. The heavy material falls together like hands in prayer and darkens the room. Life looks better in the dark.

"I'll call the sheriff." Kate leaves the door ajar and tries to go quietly, but the creaking wood floor won't allow it. In under a minute, Em is up. Pulling her boots on. Behind the curtain, she unlatches the window and slides it open. The screen pops out as easily as it always has and falls onto the ground.

Kate pulls Deputy Lipinski's card from her back pocket and grabs the phone from the charger. She presses the green call button. The dial tone as intrusive and obnoxious as the thought of Joe cheating on Em with Savannah. Kate hangs up and tosses the card on the counter. "Rotten bastard."

From the junk drawer, Kate brings out a worn address book and flips it open to the letter *C.* Skimming her bandaged fingers down past Joyce Cabett—a best friend through high school last seen or heard from freshman year at San Francisco State. Down past Ike Cagliari, a welder Will never paid for building their pipe roping arena. Stops at Sally Cahill—holds her dirty nail under the name. Sal was the best neighbor a person could have had until she allowed her daughter to babysit two-year-old Em while Kate attended her grandfather's funeral in San Francisco. Sally was the first to accuse Will of inappropriately touching her daughter. No one believed it, including Kate. They never spoke again, and Sal moved to Idaho the next year.

Patrick Callahan's number is there. Faded but there. Kate has always been the kind of woman who is more comfortable doing favors for others, never able to accept them for herself. She needs help and doesn't have single friend left. Patrick is the only option. She dials her brother and waits. His cheerful voice instantly warms her heart as it instructs her to please leave a message and he will call back as soon as he can. *"Don't forget to have a great day."*

"Pat . . . Hi. I wasn't sure this was still your number. Um, it's Kate, remember me? I, uhh . . ." She pauses. Squeezes her brow with her hand. "You said if I ever needed anything to call you." Her voice fighting the lump bloating deep in her throat. "So, I guess . . . that's why I'm callin'." She hangs up quick. Doubts he'll call back, but stares at the phone anyway, willing it to ring.

A cast-iron teakettle simmers on the stove. Through the kitchen window, Kate watches a bay mare nurse her buckskin foal. She can't help but wonder what kind of mother Em could be now with all that has happened. Imagines her grandchild will ride and rope off the well-bred buckskin. How can she protect Em now? Protect her grandchild? Boiling water steams from the kettle, but Kate ignores it, trying to find a way to deal with Em and her father. How did it get to this? An hour passes before Kate realizes she's done nothing but dwell on the past. On Will. This is stupid. Kate occupies her anxiety by scrubbing the refrigerator inside and out.

Carrying a meat loaf sandwich made just the way Em likes it, with pepper jack and barbeque sauce, Kate shuffles down the hall to Em's room. She pushes the door open with her hip and sets lunch on the dresser before noticing she's alone. "Em?" She looks around. "Em?"

Em trots a high-headed sorrel uphill, picking her way through a brushy deer trail—a twenty-minute shortcut to

Devil's Nose. Riding bareback, she grabs a fistful of the mare's mane, chokes up on her reins, and kicks the mare into a full-throttle run. The horse struggles to gain elevation, front legs digging, hind legs pushing harder and harder. All Em can think of is Joe. He has to be okay. Dread energizes, forcing her to kick and kick until they top the incline. A few strides farther, then down a gully and up the other side. Her heavy breathing rivals the mare's until they become one rhythmic force. A fire road offers five miles of open track. The mare drops her head and runs as fast as she can. Hooves moving so quick and smooth, it's as if she's flying.

Kate runs into the kitchen, holding Deputy Paul Lipinski's card. Reaches for the phone as it rings and draws back a moment before snagging up the receiver. "Hello?" Hoping she doesn't sound panicked. "Patrick . . . oh, thank God." Her shoulders drop as a shred of relief washes over her. "How soon can you get here?" She waits. Nods. "Okay. I can't talk now, but call me when you get out of the city. I'll explain the whole damn mess." She hangs up. Dials Deputy Lipinski and waits. Biting her thumbnail. "Um, this is Kate Dunnigan. Joe's horse came back without him and had blood all over his legs but not a scratch on him. I think Joe could be hurt and Emma Lee took off lookin' for him, up to Devil's Nose." Kate waits for Lipinski to digest all the information. She agrees when he puts her on hold. She cradles the receiver on her shoulder and takes a glass from the dish drainer. Fills it with cold water from the tap and drinks. *Keep it together*. The glass half empty, she sets it down and takes consecutive long breaths. In deep—through the nose. Out through the mouth until Lipinski is back. "A helicopter?"

A distant whump, whump, whump. A hidden chopper haunts a cloudless sky as Em pushes through another narrow deer trail. Weaving through the shade of thick pines and cedars, her exhausted eyes want to close as they drift along the treetops. A chill shakes her focus back to the forest floor. Crisp pine needles crump and crunch under horse's hooves.

Ahead, the trail widens—pines and cedars thin. A high-pitched yip, then several clear and present yelps, stop Em and her horse in their tracks. Her eyes dart in every direction. Waiting. Listening as movement catches her peripheral vision. Vultures, fwap, fwap, fwap, lifting their heavy wings, exploding from somewhere on her right. Tapping the mare's sides with her spurs, Em reins to the right and guides the horse between boulders. Two coyotes tug at a piece of meat, then examine Em with amber eyes before reluctantly creeping away. Her heart kicking. Her head thumping in her ears as she presses the mare forward. Suddenly, Huck runs out from behind a split juniper, spooking Em and the mare. "Huck!" The dog sucks back for a moment. "Huck, come here, buddy." He darts and disappears into the shadowy forest underbrush. "Huckster!" Em kicks the horse toward the thick manzanita, but the brush is impenetrable. "Shit." The mare spins as Em lifts the reins and rides back to the trail.

Sunlight heats mountain misery, pines, and cedars,

causing the forest to smell like a sixty-five-dollar candle. Light spills in sections across the trail and backlights a leg. "Joe!" Em jumps down and runs to it, but stops the minute a boot with a stirrup over it comes into focus. "Joe?" It feels unreal. Her legs are heavy, hard to move, like wading through mud. She wants to leave but wants Joe more. Turn around. Go home. Back to the way things were. Slowly, she steps forward to Joe's mangled and muddy corpse. "Joe!" Rolling him onto his back, she can never unsee the warped skull, the abstract face like a macabre Picasso. A debris-filled socket that once held the hazel eye that could impress her so effortlessly. Shaking, gasping, she steps back, rubs her eyes—wipes them hard. Harder. On her knees, she whispers, "Keep your eyes shut . . . Keep your eyes shut, don't look."

SEVEN

A bald and burly man steps softly out of Em's room, trying to quietly get the door to latch, but he quits after the third attempt. He pulls off heavy black-rimmed glasses with a used syringe in his hand. "I gave her a mild sedative." His gentle voice as caring as his touch against Kate's back as he walks her down the hall.

"Patrick, I told you, she's pregnant."

"It's much less detrimental than the trauma she just experienced."

"Sorry." Kate forces a decent conversation with the brother she hasn't seen in nearly nine years. "I can't believe you retired, thought you loved fixing hearts."

"I retired based on the idea that Bev and I would travel." A sarcastic laugh spurts from somewhere deep inside him. "Listen, you remember Maureen Yamaguchi?"

Kate thinks. "The gal you swore was not your girlfriend?"

"Yes. And for the record, she was more than just a girlfriend. I loved her for a long time. Another story for another time. She was the director of the psychiatric department at Berkeley. She runs a private clinic now. Why don't I call her—see what she suggests?"

"I don't know. There's some things—"

"Kate, she's going to need professional help. You can't expect someone to cope with this type of trauma on their own. If it's the money, please . . . don't worry; I'll take care of it."

"No way. I'm not puttin' this on you."

"Still as stubborn as always. I'm not offering because I feel obligated. I'm insisting because I'm selfish. It'll make me feel good to help." He flops onto a chair at the kitchen table and packs the used syringe into a red plastic box. "You and Em are all I have left. Well, besides Mom. Beverly moved out, somewhat—her things are still there, but I don't think she'll return for them."

"What, when?" Kate slides into the chair at the head of the table, sorry that so much time has passed. Sorry that she allowed her husband to come between them. Sorry that she couldn't tell Patrick she was sorry.

"Four months ago. She went to Paris for a conference and realized she was a lesbian. She is *not* a lesbian."

"You should of called."

"I expected her to realize her error and return. And, I didn't want her angry because I shared her sexual experiments with everyone. Now, I would sincerely enjoy sharing that information with anyone who would care to listen."

"I care." Avoiding holidays, birthdays, Dad's funeral, Patrick's wedding, slowly turned into total dissociation. Giving a shit is for amateurs, but Kate can't help herself. She stands. Walks over to Pat and hugs him long and hard. "I'm sorry."

"Timing is everything. Right now, I need you as much as you need me. And the thought of someone addressing me as 'Uncle Pat' sounds terrific."

"Ought to be somethin' good comes outta this hell, Uncle Pat."

Uncle Pat grins. "I'll call Maureen."

"Be sure and tell her about Bev's lesbianism."

With a hardy laugh, he nods. "She knows."

Clouds churn and swell in a murky morning sky above apple blossoms twitching in the gray drizzle. Steam spouts from a herd of cattle like a candescent fountain. Wetness darkens the log barn and gathers—dripping from the eaves. In their stalls, horses tear at their alfalfa breakfast while Joe's colt waits impatiently for his. Em holds a flake of hay, considers starvation as a form of retaliation against the ignorant beast for killing Joe. "You want this? Huh? You stupid piece of shit." Throwing the hay in his face, Em watches the hungry colt shake tiny dried leaves from his head and eat unoffended.

Like a tombstone, Joe's saddle leans against the feed manger. Em lies on his bedroll and cradles her belly. Crawling under the canvas and wool blankets, Joe's scent is strong—a potpourri of toast, leather, and cow shit. Salty tears saturate her smile as she remembers the first time with Joe under these same blankets—in this very bedroll. How scared she was, but how badly she'd wanted him. As if her body were possessed by an entity that fed off him and never left. That night, Joe had confessed that he loved her and asked if she would please, please, please marry him. She knew she would before he'd asked.

Em looks at her wedding band, the crud and scratches dishonoring it. Flipping the covers aside, she sits up and spits on the ring—polishing it with the tail of her denim shirt. As she holds the ring up to the light, she catches a glimpse of the aluminum fly rod tube back above the tack room door. In an instant, she's up, but time feels misplaced as she works the tube down with a manure rake. Hands shaking and weak, unwilling to cooperate, she unscrews the cap from the tube, like in a dream, where the world is warped and simple tasks become fragmented and damn near impossible. The cap drops in a prolonged moment. Rolls hesitantly across the dirt floor. She tips the case until the three-pieced rod creeps out. Sickening nausea spirals through her.

On the kitchen table, the Calaveras Yellow Pages advertise six cemeteries. Sunset and Murphy's take up an entire page. Kate circles the number for Sunset.

"Mom!" Em explodes through the back door, waking Uncle Pat on the sofa sleeper. "Mom!"

Kate slaps the phone book shut.

"Did you put this away?" Em holds the fly rod out with both hands.

"Why?"

"'Cause Joe took it with him! It wasn't with his stuff when the colt came back. I checked! I specifically checked!"

Em's arms bounce. "How'd it get back here?" Her eyes jump around the room. "Who put it back above the tack room?" Out of breath, her heart racing, anxious for a reasonable answer.

EIGHT

The fly rod and tube decorate the kitchen table like a vulgar centerpiece as Deputy Lipinski sits, filling out his report. "Who knew where the fishing pole belongs?"

"Rod." Em crosses her arms and leans against the doorway.

"Rod who?" Lipinski asks as he writes.

"It's a fishing *rod*. A pole goes in the ground." Em smirks. Lipinski looks up without lifting his head.

"What about Roper?" Kate offers. "You need to talk to that boy, he was threatin' Joe, I could hear him all the way over here." Everyone stares at the rod, analyzing the possibility of Roper being a killer.

"I can't picture him doing it." Em cracks her knuckles. "He woulda hired someone, he's got money. And I've never seen him crazy mad like that, and we been best friends since forever."

"Why bother with the rod?" Uncle Pat wonders out loud.

Em suddenly stunned, her mouth drops and she looks like she's just lost her innocence. Her eyes move to Kate as Lipinski observes her.

"What?" Uncle Pat asks.

Kate deflects. "I'm sure this is all just a—"

"My dad," Em says. "He could of . . . He loved that rod. And I told him what Roper said, and . . ."

Kate grins and runs her fingers across her forehead. Down her temple. "I don't think—"

"What's his name?" Lipinski presses his pen on his pad.

"Will—William Dunnigan." Em immediately wishes she hadn't spoken. She pictures her dad, his enormous smile, the way he has always defended her, regardless of right or wrong. He would *never* point a finger at her, never suggest her as a murder suspect. The air turns thick, and breathing becomes a task. "I need to find Huck." Em scrambles out the door.

"Who's Huck? I have to complete her statement." Lipinski looks back and forth between Kate and Uncle Pat.

"Huck's Joe's dog, and you're wastin' your time anyway. Her dad ain't been around for . . . gosh"—Kate shrugs—"gotta be fifteen, sixteen years."

"Perhaps he contacted her. It is possible. Or, Em could have found him. Google, Facebook, there are multiple ways." Uncle Pat's authoritative conclusion forces Kate's unease to surface.

"He was a *rotten, no-good son of a bitch* and would *never* come back. Last I heard, he was on the run for sellin' fake Navajo rugs, went to Brazil or somethin'. Maybe even back to Australia."

"Why would your daughter consider him a suspect?" Lipinski asks.

"Goddamn! She's pregnant, her husband's accused of

raping a girl—now he's dead. She finds him all tore up and her baby ain't got a father. There's a real good chance she ain't thinkin' clearly." Kate finally takes a breath. Lipinski pets his mustache and looks to Uncle Pat.

"Em may be so desperate to make sense of current events that she's focusing on finding empathy for Joe by crafting him into the victim role. And the fact that she must carry a deep-rooted resentment for her father's abandonment. I think Kate has a valid point." Patrick offers.

Lipinski slaps his notebook closed. "We don't have enough evidence to support further investigation. Mr. Quick's death appears to be accidental, and therefore the charges that were filed against him will be dismissed."

"An autopsy could reveal evidence, right?" Uncle Pat asks.

"That's the coroner's decision." Lipinski grasps the doorknob.

"I believe family has the right to request one. Unless Calaveras County has jurisdiction over California law." Uncle Pat seems to know his rights. "Especially if we pay for it."

Kate slams her palms on the table. "That poor boy has no family but us—let him rest in peace!"

Hugging her knees, Em sits on Joe's bedroll in the barn. Her cell phone ready and waiting in her hand. Ready and waiting to reveal Dad's guilt or innocence. Either will surely devastate their rekindled relationship.

"Hi, sweetie." Kate sits next to her. "How you doin'?"

"This is crazy, right?"

"We passed crazy days ago." Kate wraps an arm around Em and squeezes.

"If I call Dad and accuse him, he'll take off again, I'll never see him."

"I wish you wouldn't worry about your dad. He ain't comin' back and you know that."

"Why would you say that?"

Kate stares at Em like she's a stranger. Improv, insults, and a pocketknife were tools Kate kept ready at all times. "Let's talk to Roper. See how he acts."

Em buries her head between her knees and offers Kate her cell. "Call him."

"No way. I want to look him in the eye. I've known that boy since he was five, and I'll know if he's been up to no good."

"There's a roping in Moke Hill tonight. He'll be there."

"How about you go take a nice, warm bath. That always makes you feel better."

Em hugs her mom and kisses her cheek.

"Uncle Pat has a friend he wants you to talk to. She's a big-time expert, comin' all the way from the Bay Area to help you out. Should be here around three. Maybe I can talk to her when you're done." Kate's crossed eyes and silly smile force a grin out of Em.

NINE

From the kitchen window, Kate watches Em and Maureen walk the path through the orchard and disappear behind the oaks at the pond. The urge to know what Em is sharing forces Kate to concoct reasons to walk down—certain to listen as long as possible before interrupting. *Take them cookies? Too obvious. Ask Maureen to stay for dinner? No. Stop*, Kate thinks. *Leave them alone. Give Em the chance to heal.*

"Trauma is an emotional response to a terrible event such as an accident, a violent act, physically abuse, sexual assault, or even a natural disaster. Immediately following the event, a person is likely to experience shock and, very likely, denial." Maureen Yamaguchi and Em sit on a log overlooking the pond. "It's the mind's way of protecting us."

"You think I'm crazy?" Em reaches down and plucks a red flower.

"Not at all, but I do believe professional help is necessary. Would you be willing to commit to treatment?"

"Couldn't hurt, I guess." Em hands Maureen the flower. "Indian paintbrush."

"Beautiful. Did Native Americans paint with these?"

"They used them to poison their enemies." Em turns. "Mom?"

"Hi. Sorry to interrupt. I'm starting dinner—can you stay, Maureen?" Kate sets her palms on her lower back and rocks onto her heels.

"No, thank you for asking. I have to get back to the clinic."

"How 'bout a steak to-go plate? Homemade potato salad."

"I'm a vegetarian, but I do appreciate the thought. I'll speak to Pat and be on my way." Maureen stands, daintily pinching the Indian paintbrush between her thumb and index finger.

As sunlight fades, floodlights pop on in the Mokelumne Hill Arena. Dozens of riders lope in the same direction to warm up their horses—swinging ropes in a cloud of dust. "Get signed up, guys! We're starting in ten minutes," a woman's voice announces over a loudspeaker. Em lets the plastic door on the blue outhouse slam behind her as she steps out. Up ahead, Savannah Rivera rides a beefy red roan and Em makes a beeline for her.

"Hey, Savannah!"

Savannah keeps riding at a walk and Em follows, her anger mounting. "Savannah!" The girl finally stops the horse just behind the roping box. "Oh, hey, Em, didn't see you." Savannah sips from a strawberry-kiwi wine cooler. "What are you up to?"

"What am I up to? Seriously?" Em locks her thumbs in her belt loops, fighting the urge to rip Savannah down off that horse and kick the shit out of her.

"I'm super sorry about Joe."

Em studies Savannah and crosses her arms. "Why you sorry?"

Savannah rolls her eyes and raises her brow. "Ughhh, 'cause—it's, like, super sad?"

"Why the hell would you be sad? Or sorry, after what he did to you?"

"Forget it." Savannah rides away sucking down a wine cooler.

"You're sorry 'cause you're lying, huh? I know you!" Everyone within earshot turns to watch. "You're a lying little bitch!"

Roper trots up and stops his horse next to Em. "Knock it off, Em."

"She's lying, Rope. Supposed to be pregnant and she's drinking? Give me a break."

"Let's go." Kate snatches Em's arm. "Making a scene is not going to help." She pulls Em back toward the truck. "I talked to Roper. He didn't do anything. It was just an accident, okay?"

"But, Mom, Savannah's lying!"

"Doesn't matter—it's over. Understand? Done." Kate puts her arm around Em as the walk.

"This is not right, Mom. I mean, does she even realize?"

"Em! Listen here, damn it." Kate steps in front of her daughter. "Look at me." Em crosses her arms, still pissed, but eventually obeys. "I want you to understand something— believing a thing *never* makes it true."

TEN

At 3:20 a.m., clouds cover the bottom of a waning half-moon. Mr. and Mrs. Rivera sleep in their California king bed, in their upstairs master suite, in their five-thousand-square-foot custom Colonial. Fuck them and the well-bred, overpriced, ill-broke horses they rode in on.

A shadow spills down the mahogany staircase, along the family-photo-lined hall. A lanky cowboy silhouette approaches a picture of twelve-year-old Roper with braces atop a white horse. The shadow stops in front of an airbrushed portrait of Mr. and Mrs. Rivera, then moves silently past a snapshot of seven-year-old Roper holding his baby sister Savannah's hand. Past Roper's high school graduation. Slowly darkening a recent shot of Roper and Savannah frolicking in the Maui surf, Savannah's bikini top unable to keep up with the surf and her blossoming bosom. The hall dead-ends at a white door. A gloved hand reaches out. Twists the brass knob.

Above a purple comforter, Savannah sleeps on her side like an unholy cherub. Her plump lips spread, exposing an overbite suitable for breathing. Flaunting a leg designed for Broadway. Worn black boots shuffle across thick pink carpet as gloved fingers tighten their grip on a jagged hunk of granite. The moment Savannah is within reach, the killer lifts the rock and whips it down. Up and down and up and down again. Smack, smack, smack, pounding the girl's brunette head. She doesn't move, doesn't make a sound, doesn't seem to mind being killed. A long, satisfying breath accompanies an appreciative moment. Then the second series of smacks. Deep into the girl's abdomen. The killer's cowboy hat rears and bucks with each strike. Then, like a caring mother, the gloved hand drags the purple comforter over the girl and tucks her in. A bloody glove brushes bloody hair from her bloody face. The killer slams the door on the way out.

ELEVEN

Kate slams a cast-iron skillet onto the stove as Uncle Pat drifts in with hints of Old Spice trailing him.

"Jeez, you smell like Dad." Kate layers the skillet with thick bacon.

"You act like him." He smirks, pouring coffee into a red tin cup. Bacon sizzles and pops in the pan. "She's going to be fine."

Kate shakes her head. "What'd Maureen think after talkin' to her?"

"She can't disclose information to me or anyone else."

"Thought you two are close?"

"We are, but patient privileges don't allow her to share information. She could lose her license."

"She can't tell you anything? At all?"

"Katie, it's complicated."

"No shit." She shoots Uncle Pat a look meant to remind him that she's not an uneducated bumpkin.

After long sips of coffee followed by an uncomfortable silence, Uncle Pat breaks. "She said that Em has been traumatized and that most patients suppress memories when something that drastic happens. It's the mind's way of defending itself during extremely difficult situations. She suspects that, in time, Em will accept the reality of what happened and relinquish her blame and/or guilt. We agree that weekly visits are essential to recovery."

"You're a doctor. You have that same patient privilege thing?" Kate flips the dripping bacon with a fork. "Do you?" Kate looks at him.

"I would *never* share information about my patients. It would be unethical. Why?"

Hot grease pops onto Kate's hand as she unnecessarily flips the bacon—eyes watering. "Are you crying?" he asks.

"It's this goddamn smoke."

"Katie, we don't need doctor-patient privileges. I'm always on your side. No matter what." Uncle Pat rubs her shoulder. "It's okay to cry; being tough all the time isn't a virtue."

"Remember when Will left?" Her faded brown eyes beg for help.

"Yes."

"He was always up to no good, you know. I showed up one night, up at his hunting camp."

Two Calaveras County Sheriff's vehicles roll down the driveway and stop at the house.

"Good Lord, now what?" Kate stomps outside as Officer Hernandez and Officer Ladd follow Lipinski to the porch.

"Hello, Ms. Dunnigan. Is Emma Lee home?" Lipinski asks.

"She's sleeping. Why?"

"Savannah Rivera was attacked early this morning."

"Attacked? What do you mean, attacked?"

"That's privileged information at this point. A detective would like to ask Emma Lee a few questions. I have to bring her in."

"But she's been right here all night, and she would never—"

"Could you get her please, ma'am?"

"Is Savannah okay?"

"I can't share that information."

"Holy hell." Kate's heart begins to flap in her chest, like a bird trying to escape an awful fate. She staggers to the screen door and grips the handle but can't bring herself to open it as smoke from burning bacon goes unnoticed.

Lipinski drives away followed by a sedan with Emma Lee in the back seat. Watching from the front porch, Kate turns to Uncle Pat. "When's it gonna stop?" That familiar sick feeling of helplessness boils up inside her. The feeling she thought she had learned to conquer years ago. A woodpecker knocks hard against the eaves on the side of the house, like an intrusive jackhammer. Kate hurls a piece of firewood at him. The bird squawks and flies into a nearby tree. "Sons a bitches . . . always somethin'. *Always*."

"Kate, is Will capable of this?"

"Of course." Kate's voice thickening. "If he was still alive."

TWELVE

A heavy steel door shuts with a clang. In the tight questioning room, mint-colored cinder blocks radiate a frothy green hue, accentuating Detective Ed Rocha's alien-like features. Round, dark eyes. A compact, thin-lipped mouth below a flat nose. An abnormally large bald head carried around on a delicate neck and diminutive body. The windowless room narrowly accommodates a small table and three metal folding chairs. With his elbows on the table, Rocha steeples his fingers under his chin. "We have witnesses that claim you were harassing Savannah at a roping competition last night." His voice surprisingly deep and smelling of coffee and cigarettes. He slides Em an eight-by-ten close-up of Savannah's mutilated face. Em glances at the evidence that resembles roadkill. Meat and muscle, flesh and hair, tendons and tissue.

"Doesn't look like her." She pushes the photo away, closes her eyes, and lifts her brow. Squeezing unrecognizable Savanah out of her mind. Rocha studies Em as she rubs her eyes with her sleeves. "Keep your eyes shut, don't look. I have to go to the bathroom." She says, then stands, clinging to the edge of the table with both hands.

"You just went." Rocha pushes the picture back to her. It's too much, and she can't stop it—she covers her mouth, but the vomit escapes.

"Don't look," She utters and wobbles. Her chin catches the edge of the table just before she hits the floor.

"They took her to Mark Twain Hospital." Kate closes her beat-up flip phone and inhales that new-car smell of Uncle Pat's BMW before locating the button to roll the window down. Thick grass carpets her foothills as they wind down the two-lane bordering the ranch. "Should have plenty a feed this year."

"Christ, after what you just told me, I'd say that's the least of your worries." Uncle Pat fists the steering wheel, then attempts to pass a hay truck. "Fuck! You should know, I feel very uncomfortable with this." Head-on, a black Cadillac forces him back behind the hay truck. "Tell her the truth. You asked for my help, and I think the hospital is the perfect opportunity." He passes and veers in front of the hay truck. Looks into his side mirror and accepts the driver's middle finger waving out the window.

I know that guy, Kate is about to say as she squints and looks out the rear window, but an army-green peacoat in the back seat distracts her. "Is that Dad's old wool coat?"

"Yes. You can't buy them anymore."

Something passes through Kate before she realizes it's a twinge of happiness at the thought of Patrick wearing Dad's old coat. Glad at the possibility he wasn't as injured by Dad's heartless management.

They ride five miles before Patrick speaks. "If you doubt my authority, consider Freud. He believed that lancing old wounds and dealing with that pain is the only way to transcend our past and overcome our neuroses. That's *exactly* what this is."

A poster of a fully formed fetus sucking its thumb, a red plastic needle disposal box, and a corner chair piled with Em's clothes decorate the hospital room. White tape covers the stitches in Em's chin, and an IV pumps fluid into her vein as she stares at the poster. Lysol and fresh ivory enamel infuse the cold room as the door opens and Kate peeks in. "Hi, hon."

"Mom. Hi, Uncle Pat." Em's voice is throaty and tired.

Kate hugs her. "How ya feelin'?"

"Hungry, actually."

"Good. That's a good sign. What did the doctor say?" Uncle Pat inspects her stitches.

"They're running tests. They took a bunch a blood, and now my arm really, really hurts. So does my head. And my chin is numb." She smacks her chin with the back of her fingers.

"I'm going to get you a sandwich and speak to your doctor, alright?" Uncle Pat eyes Kate.

"Okay. Thanks, Uncle Pat." Em smiles. As Uncle Pat goes, he shoots Kate one last insistent glare.

"Aw, sweetie." Kate rubs Em's arm. "I love you so much."

"Love you too, Mom."

"Listen, I have to know something. It's important, okay?"

Em waits.

Kate takes a deep breath. "You said you talked to your dad. That he was gonna meet you?"

"Yeah?"

Not the answer Kate wants. Not even close. She takes Em's hands and squeezes them. *Best not to consider this any longer. Do it!* "Your dad is dead." Ripped off like a full-body Band-Aid. "There ain't no way you talked to him."

"Not funny, Mom."

"No, it's not. Now, no more bullshit. He's dead and you know it 'cause you were there."

Em pulls her hands away and takes time to consider the possibilities. "I just talked to him." She drops her legs off the bed. "What are you doing?"

"Trying to help you get a grip on reality." That was harsh. Probably too much.

"Trying keep us apart? You jealous? Is that it?" Em wipes her eye.

"I'm just trying to help. I'm sorry to have to make you remember, but—"

"You're seriously fucked up. You're the one needs a psychiatrist!" Em rubs both eyes.

"Em, come on now. You were there when it happened."

"When what happened?"

"I killed him. And buried him. You just don't want to remember . . . hunting camp." Kate watches Em's conclusion build.

"I thought it was Dad. I thought maybe he was doin' this—but I totally get it now." Panic. Buzzing. Em swats at her left ear and squints, then drags her fingers across her eyes.

"Please don't rub your eyes. You know what happened, don't let him ruin you."

"You're a bitter old bitch who's terrified of being alone." Em yanks her IV out, and blood splatters the linoleum. "You lost Dad, and I'm all that's left."

"Em, stop! Get back in bed."

Em opens and shuts her eyes. The room is hazy and obscure, like looking underwater. "Do you have my phone? You take it?" She searches her clothes piled on the chair.

"I'm gonna get Uncle Pat." Kate rushes out.

Em finds her phone, then pulls her jeans on under her gown. "Keep your eyes shut. Don't look," she whispers twice as she wiggles the sweatshirt on over the gown, then slips on UGGS. While feeling her way out of the room, she dials Dad.

Through swinging *Staff Only* double doors, Em stumbles down the corridor. "Dad? Thank God, Mom's at it again. Sayin' you're dead!" Em pulls open the stairwell door and exits. "I know, that's exactly what I said." Her voice and steps echo all four floors. "She killed Joe and did her best to kill little Savannah. She thinks she's protecting me, and she'd do *anything* to keep that stupid ranch." Em sits on a cold aluminum step. "Yeah . . . okay, I call him right now. I'll meet you there tomorrow . . . I'm sorry too. I love you." She hangs up and digs Rocha's card from her sweatshirt.

THIRTEEN

In his office, Detective Rocha sits behind cigarette smoke and a chaotic desk bound on both sides by gray metal filing cabinets. The soft buzz of an air filter struggles to keep up while Rocha tokes under a *No Smoking* sign. With the phone pinched between his ear and shoulder, he writes on a pink pad in capital letters—*KATHERINE DUNNIGAN*. "Uh-huh, age?" He writes *51*. "Approximate height and weight?" *5'4". 130 lbs. Mark Twain Hospital.* "You need to come in, Emma Lee, finish your statement." Rocha tears the note from the pad. "Hello? Hello?"

"Hello. Can I help you?" A uniformed dispatcher requiring little effort to impersonate Mrs. Potato Head plants herself in a snug Naugahyde chair and smiles at Uncle Pat. It screeches under the load as she swaps her Diet Dr Pepper for a bag of microwave popcorn. The front office of the Calaveras County Sheriff's Department represents the 1970s inferior design. A faded ficus tree clings to dark wood paneling as Uncle Pat brushes past.

"I'm Kate Dunnigan. I need to talk to someone about

the attacks on Savannah Rivera and Joe Quick. I think my daughter might have—"

Rocha slaps the pink note on the dispatcher's desk and walks away. "I called Lipinski, he's at the hospital locating the daughter. I want an APB on the mother."

"Ed?" The dispatcher says with sweet sarcasm.

"*What?*" Rocha's annoyance is blatant.

"This lady would like to speak with you about Savannah Rivera."

Rocha turns back.

The dispatcher reads the note, looks at Kate, then back at the note. She balls up the pink piece of paper and tosses it at Rocha. "This *is* Kate Dunnigan, *Detective.*"

He inspects Kate and offers a routine smile to the dispatcher. "Wonderful. Follow me, Ms. Dunnigan." At the end of the corridor, Rocha points an upturned palm above a set of orange plastic chairs. "Have a seat, I'll be right with you." Kate and Uncle Pat obey as Rocha steps into his office. A consistent and hushed pounding escapes from behind the steel lockup door. A small one-way window rattles with each bang. Someone wants out. Staring at the scuffed parquet, Kate chews her lower lip, unable to come up with a better option.

"There is no other way to go about this, Kate," Uncle Pat reassures her and sets his hand on her shoulder. "You're doing the right thing."

Lipinski escorts Em in through a back door, her hands cuffed in front of her. Kate rushes over and cradles Em's face in her hands. "Are you okay?"

Without hesitation, Em shoves Kate into the opposite wall. "Why isn't she cuffed? She's slaughtering people, and you frigin' idiots are *arresting me*?" Nothing makes sense. She wants Joe. Wants to go home, but like in a bad dream, for some crazy reason, it's impossible.

"We're just holding you," Rocha explains, emerging from his office. The banging coming from behind the cell door stops as Lipinski unlocks it. "Get back and sit down *now*, Ramona."

"Can I braid your hair, pleeeeeease?" Ramona begs as Lipinski forces Em through the door.

"Hands to yourself, Ramona," Lipinski warns before slamming the door.

The jingle of keys locking the steel dead bolt punch Kate in the gut. Years of turbulence release like a cloud burst. Light-headed, she bends over, bracing her hands against her knees. "Let her go." She takes inhales and stands upright. "Let her go. She's right, I did it! I killed Joe. And that nasty little bitch too." Kate grabs Uncle Pat, presses up close, and whispers, "Get her outta here, she can't take this, not with that baby. You promised. *You* promised." Rocha gathers Kate's wrists behind her and sets a cuff. "I'll tell ya everything." Kate spins around and faces Rocha, offering her both hands for cuffing. "Full confession. But first, you let her go home. She's exhausted. You got me, you don't need her. She's innocent. It's me, that's what I came to tell you." It comes out so easy that Kate momentarily convinces herself.

Uncle Pat removes his glasses and scrubs his brow. Rocha

crosses his arms and widens his stance as Lipinski watches and waits.

"A mother's and child's health is in your hands, Detective. I cannot conceive of an unsympathetic jury if something were to go wrong."

Kate leans into Rocha's face, eye to eye, tears streaming. "I ain't sayin' a word 'til you release her."

From behind the cell door, the pounding begins again. "Get her out of here," Rocha orders.

Kate closes her eyes as Rocha cuffs her.

FOURTEEN

"Thank you, Maureen. Your help is immeasurable. I don't know what she's capable of." A dying cell phone beeps as Uncle Pat struggles to find the outlet in Kate's dark kitchen. "I can have her to your facility Monday morning if you have a room available?" After listening to Maureen explain ideal treatment, Uncle Pat shakes his head. "What if she doesn't want to go? I can't force her." He smooths what's left of his hair.

In the questioning room, Kate looks up at a blinking red light on the camera peering down at her from the corner. Rocha licks his front teeth, back and forth, and waits for more. "When I overheard Roper tell Em what Joe had done to Savannah, I just snapped. I couldn't sit back and watch my daughter suffer through a trial. She'd *have* to side with him no matter what, and that would mean a lawyer, and a lawyer means money they didn't have. Then I'd have to put up the ranch to defend him. And there ain't no way, come hell or high water, I'm losin' the ranch." *What a cliché*, Kate thinks and crosses her arms. "What do you really need to know?"

"Why Savannah?"

"Finish cleanin' up the mess Joe left. Em didn't need any more triggers."

"Triggers?"

"That's the wrong word. You know, *reminders . . .* is what I meant. I'm really tired, gotta be after midnight. I'm done."

Spread out across the sofa sleeper, Uncle Pat snores until a bang against the screen door jolts him awake. Staring into blackness, he sits up. Waits. Listens. The hum of the refrigerator and the soft bong of wind chimes lull him back to sleep. In no time, there it is again—a clear and present bang against the screen door, causing him to shoot up.

From the window, he can see the top half of the door under the porch light. No one is there. The porch creaks. He stumbles over his shoes, then feels for his glasses on the coffee table but only finds his cell phone. The glow from the cell enables him to locate his glasses and put them on. With a shaking finger, he dials *9*, then *1*, and waits. Another bang forces him back to the window. Peeking through the side of the curtain. Nothing. "Who is it?" Nothing. "Okay, well, I called the police!" His voice cracks as he grabs the heavy poker leaning near the woodstove. "They'll be here any minute." Two bangs cause him to raise and ready the poker. "Who's there, *damn it?*" He looks out the window. Bang. The screen door bounces twice. Trembling, Uncle Pat swings open the front door to find Huck wagging his tail. "Oh, good God." He leans the poker next to the door and pats his thumping chest as he opens the screen for Huck. "You practically gave me a heart attack, mister."

Early the next morning, Huck follows Uncle Pat and a plate of fried eggs, with bacon and toast, down the hall to Em's room. "You already had yours," he whispers to Huck as he knocks on Em's door.

Huck barges in and curls up next to Em as she wakes. "Huck!" She hugs and kisses and rubs his ears as he moans with pleasure. "Hi, buddy."

"He arrived late last night."

"Oh my gosh, Huckleberry, I missed you. Where have you been—huh?" She sits up.

"I made breakfast." He hands her the plate.

"Thanks." She stabs the yokes with her fork, and they bleed under the bacon and onto the buttered toast. "Mmm, I don't know . . . I feel kinda queasy." Em hands the plate back to him.

"Maybe later, then." Uncle Pat opens the curtains, allowing the rising sun to light the room. "I'll make you a cup of tea. And crackers. That should help with nausea."

Em snuggles with Huck. "You don't have to take care a me, Uncle Pat, I'm a big girl."

"I know, but I want to, so . . . Look, I'd like you to come home with me. Maureen has offered to let you stay at her clinic for a few days or whatever you, uh, it's in Half Moon Bay. You can rest and focus on yourself. They have beautiful rooms overlooking the ocean. Wonderful food. It'll be kind of like a vacation. And, when you're ready . . . you can stay with me, or you can have the pool house, whichever you like."

"Sounds great." Em nods.

"Really?"

"Yeah. Soon as I see Dad, we'll go. He's waiting for me up at camp."

"Call him. Have him come here."

"I would, but he's already up there—no cell service."

"I'd love to see your father, mind if I tag along?"

Em hesitates. "I don't wanna talk about Mom, at all. Okay?"

"Fair enough. I'll pack some food." Halfway out the door, he stops. "Em, I hope you can comprehend . . . I, uh. I want you to know I love you and I'm going to do everything possible to help. Okay?"

"Okay." She doesn't doubt him and smiles. The anticipation of seeing Dad sort of soothes the pain of losing Joe. "I'll saddle a horse for you. Do you even know how to ride?"

"Not at all."

"I'll get you a hat and some boots. Pretty sure Mom still has some of Dad's stuff hidden in her closet."

Clutching his cell to his ear, Uncle Pat paces the front porch and struggles to keeps his panicked voice to a whisper. "She agreed to go to the clinic but wants to see her father first." The wind chimes bang and bong, and Uncle Pat stops them with his hand. "She talks to him on the damn phone— thinks he is going to meet her up there, and I agreed to go. What the hell could I do?" Grasping the porch post, he takes a seat on the steps. "Oh, I can certainly prove it to her."

Maureen's voice comes through the phone, loud and clear. "*How?*"

"I am not at liberty to say . . . but if I were able to show her something that may trigger her memory? Should I?"

"Absolutely!"

FIFTEEN

A black cowboy hat tilts on Uncle Pat's head as he grips the saddle horn and follows Em. Blackberry bushes coat the sides of the shaded trail, forcing Em to pluck a few and pop them in her mouth as they ride by. "Like blackberries?" Em asks.

"No, I don't care for the seeds, they stick in my teeth." Uncle Pat stops his horse and climbs off, groaning. "Ohhhhh, my everything hurts. I may walk for a while." He digs the heels of his black boots into the red clay, then stretches his fingers in the direction of his toes.

With another handful of berries in her mouth, Em twists back toward Uncle Pat. "We'll be there in twenty minutes. Dad'll have a fire and hopefully a skillet of trout. He always starts cooking as soon as the sun gets two fingers above Squaw Ridge. We'd eat and watch the sunset." Em laughs. "He'd give me a cup of blackberry juice and—" She stops and stares at the purple stains on her fingers. A queasy feeling takes hold of her. Her mouth begins to water, and for some reason, she suddenly wants to cry.

"He was a good dad, huh?" Uncle Pat stretches his arms above his head.

"Yeah." Em spits the blackberries from her mouth.

"Why would he leave you for all those years?"

"Ask him." Em rides away.

Veronica Ames—public defender—Calaveras County. A fidgety young woman who seems to go to great lengths to avoid eye contact. Currently obsessed with picking lint balls off her white sweater. "I'm asking you to help me help you. Okay, Ms. Duncan?" She waits a long, uncomfortable while for an answer.

"Dunnigan. Not Duncan. And, I don't need a lawyer." *Especially one that can't even get my name right.* Uncomfortable in her extra-large jumpsuit, Kate nervously pushes her sweaty palms down her orange jumpsuit thighs.

"Are you officially refusing legal counsel? You understand I'm a public defender. You don't have to pay me."

"Get what you pay for," Kate mumbles.

"Excuse me?"

"I did it. End of story. I don't want to go to trial." *I'm not going to trial. No way.*

"It's my responsibility to make sure you're aware of the consequences, regardless of how you plea, you have rights. And there is a possibility of sanity issues."

Hunting camp is perched on a parcel of meadow between Squaw Ridge and Lost Lake. A deep, dark hidden lake that surfaces at timberline. In the meadow, one massive juniper reaches out across a log-lined camp. Its roots like gnarled fingers, desperately searching for something.

"Wow, this is beautiful." Uncle Pat dismounts.

Em trots past the juniper and toward the lake. "Dad!

Uncle Pat unstraps his dad's wool peacoat from behind his saddle and puts it on, exposing a folding shovel as Em rides back.

"He's not here." Concern smothers Em. "God, what the heck. He said he'd be here." She checks her phone for a signal, lifting it in every direction.

The sun sinks below Squaw Ridge, sending a wave of deep violet into an ocean of orange and blue. "I'm almost sixty, and this is the finest sunset I have ever seen," Uncle Pat confesses through the last bite of a chunky-peanut-butter-and-jelly sandwich. "I can see why your father loved this place."

Em zips her coat and stacks rocks into a fire ring. *Dad hasn't even been here.* "Where is he? Something's wrong."

With shovel in hand, Uncle Pat walks stiff-legged to the giant juniper, stopping at the large triangular rock under it, and kneels.

Em watches him struggle to roll the saddle-size hunk of granite. With a mighty groan, he lifts and flips it. "What are you doing?"

"Trying to figure out why your mother would lie to you."

"Because she's insane, and she could never deal with Dad dumping her. Made me and that bullshit ranch her life."

"Well, she insisted that if I didn't believe her story about your father, that I should dig under this rock." He stabs the shovel into the fresh dirt. Outlining the removed rock.

"You think she's full of it too, don't ya?" Em scoops pine needles and sets them in the rock fire ring.

"She does have a morbid obsession with that ranch and an idealistic lifestyle." He digs.

"I used to feel sorry for her. So did everyone else, and she *loved* it. Anytime anyone was around, all she'd talk about is how Dad left her and how heartbroken and miserable she was. Just became a pathetic victim after a while. It's why she doesn't have any friends." Em tosses pine cones into the ring. "What'd she say's under there?"

"The truth."

Em gathers twigs. "You're being weird."

"I know, but I have to do this. Maureen thinks I should show you the truth. It's somewhat like rebooting your memory." He shovels harder and faster.

"What truth?" Em places twigs on pine cones.

"Can you remember the last time you were here? With your father?" Sweat rolls from under the black hat.

Staring into the purple sunset, Em recalls Dad. He's kneeling over a cast-iron skillet of sizzling trout and scraping the browning skins with a spatula. Dad letting her reel in those fish with his fly rod. The way the rod jumped and pulled in her hands. "*Keep the tip up,*" he'd constantly remind her. Swimming in the lake, because they had caught their limit by noon. Picking wildflowers to bring back to Mom. Filling the old coffee can with blackberries. "Yeah, I remember. I remember everything."

"Do you remember your mother arriving that evening?"

"She never came up here. It was *always* only me and Dad." Em tosses wood into the fire ring.

"Your mom said she rode up here to surprise you." Uncle Pat digs efficiently for a man who has probably never handled a shovel.

Resisting the urge to argue, Em strikes a wooden match and watches it burn out. Squinting, she kneels and lights another. The flame burns her fingers, and she drops the match onto the pine needles.

"You know what else she told me?"

"I don't care! You promised you wouldn't talk about her!" Leaning back on her knees, Em watches a tiny flame develop, then struggle to live.

Digging in rhythmic tempo, Uncle Pat raises his voice with unusual firmness. "She said he had gotten you drunk. He gave you blackberry juice mixed with sloe gin." Dirt piling and rising under the juniper like a polluted tide.

"Stop it. Just stop!" Em stares into the flames licking skyward and rubs her eyes. Flaming explosions jolt her brain, and a vivid picture of her father handing her a red tin cup flashes like lightning. She squeezes her eyes shut tight and wipes hard, then opens them wide, trying to see through the blur. Swaying, she goes from her knees to sitting with legs stretched in front of her.

Uncle Pat slams the shovel into the dirt again and again, but Em fixates through the foggy haze on Uncle Pat's hat—moving back and forth and back and forth. Suddenly, the storm in her head subsides and the fragmented visions come into focus. Her young voice whispers, *"He gave me blackberry juice."* Em lies back, pressing her palms deep into her eyes, then sees and hears the girl as if she were right there next to her.

"Dad filled the cup with blackberry juice from his jar, 'member? Sittin' by the fire, and it looked like the flames were in his jar when he drank, and I laughed. 'Member? I laughed so hard that I had to go to the bathroom. Dad followed me to that big juniper tree, and I told him I could do it myself. Said I was twelve and didn't need no help. But then, when I got all done—I couldn't stand up—got real dizzy and fell over. 'Member? Then . . . I kinda sorta woke up and Dad was on top a me. His hat was moving—up and down, and up and down, and I couldn't move, and I couldn't breathe. His face looked funny at first like he was tryin' to make me laugh. But then the stabbing hurt inside made me cry. I wanted to cry loud but couldn't 'cause he was squishing me. Then . . . the noise. 'Member? The loud CRACK noise? Like when Dad spilt firewood. Then he was squishing me even more. Then a worse CRACKING noise, and Mom was there! She had a rock in her hands, and she looked crazy and really, really mad. She held the rock up, way up, over her head, and she smashed it into Dad's head. She hit him again and blood got in my eyes. Lots and lots a blood got in my eyes. 'Member? It felt weird . . . sticky, and all warm, and I couldn't see nothin'. Mom grabbed my arm and jerked me up, and dragged me outta there. Away from Dad. And she was yelling, "KEEP YOUR EYES SHUT! DON'T LOOK!"

"Keep your eyes shut! Don't look." Em wipes her eyes and stands.

"Em, you have to see this, you have to understand what happened. Your mother was trying to protect you." The sound of the shovel piercing the earth turns to the sound of rock cracking skull—again and again, as Uncle Pat hits something solid. He drops to his knees and digs with his hands. "Look! Jesus Christ, she wasn't lying, Em. Your dad *is* dead." He leans into the grave and lifts a dirty skull. "I'm so sorry, Em, but you have to see the tru—"

"Don't look!" Em slams a rock into the side of Uncle Pat's head, and the black Stetson flies across the grave as he collapses. His broken glasses fall alongside Will's warped skull. CRACK! Blood splatters the dirty skull and glasses.

SIXTEEN

Leaning against the wall in the questioning room, Kate's orange jumpsuit clashes with the minty-green cinder blocks. The door buzzes, and Miss Ames comes in with an armful of files. "Sorry to keep you waiting. I just received a phone call. Please, sit down." Kate straightens as Miss Ames takes a seat on the cold metal chair. "The good news is that Savannah Rivera is going to survive and she's talking. A lot." Miss Ames avoids looking at Kate. "They can't charge you with her murder if she isn't dead. The other news is that she confessed to lying about Joe." Miss Ames slips in a moment of eye contact, then opens a cardboard accordion file and pulls one out. "She was never pregnant. And it appears there was no sexual relationship whatsoever with Mr. Quick. She made the entire story up— we don't know why yet. They're still getting her statement. Her father's attorney is making it difficult."

Kate sits. "Difficult?" She doesn't know whether to laugh or cry. She waits for something else. Anything to salvage what's left of this hell. Staring vacantly at the hands on her knees. Her hands. Gnarled and scarred, but strong. She grunts and shakes her head. "Difficult. Difficult? Difficult would be a fucking relief." Leaning against the chair, she lets her head fall back under the florescent lights. Refusing to blink until the light burns her eyes. She feels nothing. Disconnected from her emotions like a hand severed at the wrist. She wanted to see Emma Lee happy and consider herself a good mom. Impossible now. Perhaps this was God's vindictive vengeance for killing Will. For condemning poor Joe before he even had the chance to defend himself. For passing judgment. For thinking she knew anything at all.

Miss Ames touches Kate's shoulder. "I'm going to make an appointment with the state psychologist. Temporary insanity is a good defense."

"Uncle Pat said I can stay as long as I want, and the obstetricians are probably way better in San Francisco." Em's cell cradled between her ear and shoulder as she smiles at the dented black Stetson resting comfortably on the passenger seat. Black boots on the floorboard. Huck curled up on the back seat. "Yeah, he said I can use his credit cards, whatever I need, and I still have the money Joe gave me too." Em nods as her father's Australian accent haunts her.

"Sounds like you're doing just great, angel. Told you everything would be peachy. I'll come for a visit—we can decide what to do about your mum." Uncle Pat's BMW crosses the Golden Gate Bridge.

PART TWO

SEVENTEEN

S tanding naked with her arms above her head, Kate Dunnigan craves the orange jumpsuit she despised less than a half hour ago. Black ink stains each fingertip as she stares into the florescent light, attempting to distract herself from the little woman lifting and inspecting beneath her sagging breast for contraband. Blue latex gloves protect Detention Officer Garcia's fingers as they glide along Kate's skin like icicles.

"Okeydokey, please turn around and touch your toes," Officer Garcia says, gnawing on minty Nicorette gum with the crevassed lips of a heavy smoker.

Kate looks into Garcia's eyes for a speck of sympathy.

Garcia groans, "It's procedure, you know. You'd be shocked at what we find up in there."

Tears roll down Kate's face as she begs, "Please."

"Ma'am, I don't wanna look at your anus or your vagina any more than you want me to, but we both gotta do it, so let's not turn it into a cavity probe."

With bare feet, Kate turns in short increments, feeling the bite of cold cement. She slides her hands down her stubbled shins, stopping just above her ankles. The world turns upside down. For a moment, the pain tugging at her lower back distracts her. But the consequences of confessing to a crime she did not commit disrupts her focus. A crime only a monster could carry out. A monster that she created not through birth but through an overabundance of love encouraged by a protective instinct. The same protective instinct that creates reasonable doubt when it comes to her daughter. Did Em kill Joe or was it an accident? She might have attacked Savannah, but who could blame her, she wasn't thinking straight after that lying bitch accused Joe of rape. Taking comfort in vindicating Em, Kate would gladly suffer the rest of her life.

Prison would be a fair trade for Em and her unborn child's happiness. A momentary peace washes over Kate until she realizes that today is Em's birthday. Instead of celebrating with her pregnant daughter, she is being processed into the Calaveras County Detention Center on first-degree murder and attempted murder charges. Breathing becomes a difficult task. A crushing pain in her chest, as if the hand of God is tightening his grip on her heart and laughing. In that instant, Kate craves death, wants it now more than ever. A banging inside her hanging head reminds her to breathe. Living takes courage. More courage than Kate can muster.

"I been working here twenty-two years, and let me tell you, I will not miss body searches when I retire," Garcia shares as Kate's thoughts twist away from the now and back to good times with Em. When they were happy. Memories of chocolate-chip waffles. The way Em would surprise her every Mother's Day with waffles and a card filled with coupons good for one hug, one kiss, and a foot massage. She would give anything to have that love back.

"Cough please."

Kate coughs and can't help but fear the future. Premonitions of her and Em in the same prison. Her grandchild being raised by a stranger or, worse, Kate's mother. The thought sends her heart sinking. She was surprised at how quick and clear her mother's voice plays in her head. *No one has the right to complain about life because no one has to endure it.* These were the words her mother offered when Kate needed her most. Now, the advice seemed absolutely appropriate.

"All done, Ms. Dunnigan. That wasn't so bad, was it?" Garcia asks as if she were speaking to a child for whom she just yanked off a Band-Aid. Kate seizes her *Property of Calaveras County Jail* towel from the stainless-steel bench and hides her flabby self behind it.

Em pulls an oversized towel from the heated rack as Huck watches in the doorway wagging his tail. Steam and lemongrass body wash trail her from Uncle Pat's marble shower. Catching sight of herself in the mirror, Em wipes away the foggy blur. With hair the color of wet sand and a farmer's tan, she examines her naked profile. Accentuating the arrival of the baby bump on her lanky body by forcing her stomach out. Arching her back as she rubs her bulging belly. Seagulls cry in panicked voices from outside the open window of the Nob Hill Victorian.

"Oh, thanks . . . I don't really care, a girl or boy, as longs as he's healthy." Em laughs, then continues the conversation. "We haven't decided on a name, but I—"

"Hello?" A voice interrupts the fantasy. Footsteps fall heavy in the hall and hurry toward the bedroom. Huck hides under the bed while Em swaddles herself in the towel, then runs to the bedroom door and locks it. Flipping off the light, she hopes the intruder will be convinced no one is home and just go away. Darkness sends panic scratching up her spine, then forces her to wilt against the door.

"Hello?" A hard knock. "Patrick! I know you're in there. I heard you guys laughing, and your car is in the driveway. I don't care who you're fucking, open the damn door. We need to talk." Her words seep through the door like noxious fumes.

Em could ignore her. Wait her out. Simply not open the door, ever. Eventually, she'd have to leave.

"I want my suitcases."

Suitcases?

"Damn it, Patrick, open the door, I don't have time for this shit!" The woman bangs her fists against the door, then stomps away. While Em's heart hammers, she attempts to process the possibilities of who this woman is, but fear glitches her reasoning. Footsteps returning. Now, the knob is wiggling. *Shit!* The knob pops. Em looks at the bed, considering the option of squeezing under it, when the door bangs open. Em pushes hard against the wall and holds her breath. A middle-aged woman gives Em a glance as she stomps past. Her chunky gold necklace, earrings, and stacked bracelets chime with jeweled flip-flops, seeming to say, *I'm on my way to a wine tasting but I have yoga class first, so fuck off.*

"Where's Patrick?" She disappears into the walk-in closet, and Em sucks a deep breath. From the closet, a soft light flushes the room, followed by the woman's perfume so spicy you could taste it.

"Are you Aunt Beverly?" Em tightens her towel and looks back at the photo framed with seashells on the nightstand. Uncle Pat's baby face, which could never hide his kindness, is pushed against Beverly's porcelain cheek. The adorable smiles of true love.

Rolling the biggest Louis Vuitton ever made, the woman comes out of the closet, ignores Em, and hoists the suitcase onto the bed.

"I'm Emma Lee. Uncle Pat's my—uncle."

"Huh?" She inspects Em, then unzips the suitcase.

"Uncle Pat's sister, Kate. That's my mom. You're my aunt."

"Oh, okay." With one hand on her hip, the other rubbing her neck, Beverly stares at the empty suitcase as if contemplating the key to life. "We're getting a divorce." She looks at Em for a moment and grins. "It's nice to meet you, finally." Beverly scoops an entire drawer of white cotton underpants and white cotton T-shirts and drops the garments into the suitcase.

Em laughs. "You scared the crap outta me."

"Sorry."

"It's okay." Em holds her belly.

"Where's Pat?" Beverly rifles through the drawer in the nightstand.

"Camping. We rode up to camp on Squaw and—"

"He *rode*? A horse?" Bev asks, attempting to conceal a tiny pink vibrator behind a jumbo bottle of Tums.

"He did *really* good. Had a blast fishing and decided to stay awhile." Em takes a seat next to the suitcase. "Where you goin'?" Huck pokes his head out from under the bed.

"That's not like Pat. But good, good for him. I'll call him." Beverly buries her toy from the nightstand in the corner of the suitcase under the T-shirts.

"Phones don't work up there. Have you been talkin' to my mom?"

"I've never met your mom." She gathers jeans from the dresser drawer. "Did Pat say when he'd be back?"

"Nope."

"Shit. He has to sign the divorce papers, and I'm leaving for Paris in two days." She drops the jeans into the suitcase followed by a few sweaters and a pillow from the bed. After zipping the suitcase, she spreads her hands across the top of the bag like she's going to resurrect it. Suddenly possessed by an idea, she lifts her finger along with her entire face. "Hey! Can I leave them with you, the papers, if you're going to be here? Do you mind? He just has to sign and mail them."

"Sure. You never met my mom? Really?"

At first, the six-by-nine cell appears cold—with stainless-steel bunks, sink, and toilet. Its heavy gray bars and gray cinder-block walls. But once inside, the forced-air heat is more suffocating than a hug from someone you hate. Kate shuffles along the cement floor avoiding her cellmate. The meth mouth, with wiry red hair and graying roots, watches Kate from the bottom bunk.

"Hello," Kate says, then nods and smiles respectfully, but Meth Mouth does not respond. Just purses her thin lips and eyes Kate with an intimidating glare. Kate looks away. Focusing on the toilet sitting out in the open—threatening to put her next bowel movement on display.

Is it too much to hope for a bit of sympathy from her new roommate? Hope for the sisterhood that shared suffering and ugly uniforms could bring, the way it did back at St. Mary's Catholic School? Kate wonders if she'd even bother to fight back if Meth Mouth attacked. Fighting was never a skill Kate acquired. The first time she got beat up was the very first day of kindergarten. The boy sitting next to little Katherine wanted the green crayon she was using, and tried to take it without her consent. Kate held tight to the crayon with both hands as he pulled and pulled until it broke into pieces. Kate called him a son of a bitch, and the next thing she knew, he had one of her pigtails and was pulling so hard she fell out of the chair.

At the sink, Kate combs her long graying locks with her fingers and notices excessive amounts of hair falling out. At this rate, her thick braid will soon be a pathetic pigtail.

"I killed my son," Inmate 2051, as is stamped on her jumpsuit, confesses and sits up. She crosses her ankles and clasps her hands on her lap. If only she had wings, she would resemble a statue of a convicted cherub looking down at a headstone. "What'd you do?"

"Nothin'." Kate presses the top of the faucet and cups cool, chlorinated water into her swollen red eyes. Her stomach churning and grinding like gears.

"Nothin'? Haaa, sure. Guess you ain't learned God's Word yet, but it's real. The truth'll set you free. You'll see." Her disobedient jaw kicks from side to side. "Where you from? Nowhere?" Meth Mouth laughs, then coughs like a heavy smoker.

Kate splashes water on her face. Lets it drip down her neck and chest.

"I live in Wilseyville. You know, where those crazy fucks Leonard Lake and Charles Ng killed a bunch a people. Guess, technically speaking, I'm from here 'til I go to trial, which my piece-a-shit public defender says will be at least a year. Already been here six fucking months."

Kate can't think of a safe response, so she offers a sympathetic grin and shakes her head as she climbs the ladder at the foot of the bunk. The bunk is solid, screwed into the wall, and Kate collapses on her back, then pulls the covers over her head.

"I'm Tanya Fisher. You hear about me? What I did?" Tanya's feet slap the floor as she walks to the toilet.

"No," Kate answers without lowering the blanket from her face.

"No? Been like all over the news and shit."

Kate hasn't prayed or asked God for a damn thing since her first year of college, but she's running out of options and considering it now. Closing her eyes. Focusing on how to begin. She brings her hands together, presses her steepled fingers into her forehead, and silently pleads, *Please, please help her.*

"You ain't suppose to be under the covers during the day," Tanya says as an unrestrained rush of piss echoes across the cell followed by a fart. Kate wishes she were already dead as she imagines trying to take care of business in front of her new cellmate. "For reals, girl, being under the covers during the day is an infraction. Wanna go downstairs and watch *Real Housewives*?"

Kate lowers the blanket, wondering what would cause a woman to kill her own son.

Tanya doesn't flush. "Gotta conserve water, you know, the drought and all, but if it's brown, flush it down." She rinses her hands, then dries them under the armpits of her jumpsuit. She walks over to the bunk and squeezes the rail on Kate's bed. Leans in way too close. Pepperoni on her breath. Kate faces her and can't help but notice the round rosy scar marring her top lip like a glob of candle wax. "How come you ain't heard a me? You don't read newspapers or nothin'? Watch the news?"

"I've been sick of bad news for a long while. Plus, I really don't have the time." *Ignore the nasty scar. Look at her eyes. Her squinty little eyes.*

"Ha, ha, ha!" Tanya crows. "You'll have plenty of time now. I suggest Bible study. We got a group meets every day. You wanna come?"

"Maybe."

"I tell ya, bein' right with the Lord makes all the difference. I ain't afraid a nothin' no more—just tell it like it is, you know?" Tanya shakes her head. "I'll tell you what I did to my Joshie. I put him down, like a dog. A rabid dog. He was tweakin' *so* bad, and come up after me one night. Went to beatin' on me, sayin' he was sorry, he didn't mean to hurt nobody. Remember that girl they found in the bark teepee at the West Point school?"

Kate thinks and then recalls that someone had slashed an *X* across a sixteen-year-old's entire face. Most of the locals assumed it was someone from the res, since that was standard procedure for an unfaithful woman. "I remember. Kids found her before school. Can't remember if she lived."

"Yeah, she lived, but he 'bout killed her. Told me awful things he did to her. I tried to help him way before that happened, but—he was gone. Long gone."

Kate sits up.

"Wasn't my boy no more, you know. Devil took him. So, I called the sheriff, told them what he did." Tanya hesitates, her eyes start to fill. "Cocksuckers didn't believe me, said they ain't got no proof. My word against his, you know." Tanya blinks away the tears and licks her scarred lip. "I might be a lot a things, but I ain't no liar—why the fuck would I lie about that shit . . . my own son. I loved that boy, you know. Sometimes"—Tanya shakes her head and squeezes her eyes shut—"you just gotta take care a your own shit." Tanya inhales a long breath and faces Kate. "So, when he come back—I took care of it. If I gotta be in here, so he ain't out there—fair trade."

The urge to respond with personal insight is overwhelming, but no adequate words come to mind. Enduring the uncomfortable silence is all you can do when a woman you just met confesses that she murdered her own son. Kate reaches over and reassuringly squeezes Tanya's shoulder. "He give you that scar on your lip?" Kate asks with an unconvincing smile.

"Naw." Tanya holds her fingers over the disfigurement as if she'd forgotten it was there. Suddenly, a smile fills her face. "Short crack pipes are a bitch. But, seriously, what the fuck did you do?"

For a moment, Kate craves the intimacy that sharing secrets offers. A kinship with this woman, this mother, who, like her, has sacrificed herself and will wallow in shit the rest of her life. "I lied."

"'Bout what?"

"Murdering my son-in-law. And an attempted murder."

"Whacha mean? You did it? Or you didn't?"

Kate rolls onto her side and faces the wall. "Didn't."

"Confess to a killin' you didn't do—that's batshit crazy."

EIGHTEEN

A doorbell chimes in Uncle Pat and Aunt Beverly's entry-level living room. It echoes up into the second-level gothic-inspired dining room where creamy walls accentuate a carved dark-wood fireplace. A matching mantel clock ticks obnoxiously while Huck snores. Velvety deep-purple drapes frame a massive picture window, offering a spectacular view of the Golden Gate Bridge at dusk. Em lights the last of four candles centered on a long table surrounded by ten diamond-tucked leather chairs. The table looks incomplete set for only two. The doorbell dings again.

"Dad!" In an instant, Em is across the dining room, Huck trailing her down the stairs and through the unlit living room. Another ding-dong speeds her up. "I'm coming!" Down the teakwood entry in her socks, sliding to a stop. Huck behind her—she turns on the light and flings open the door. Out of breath. "Hi, Da—"

"Hello." Maureen smiles.

Em looks past Maureen's skeletal frame, past her pearl-colored pixie cut, expecting to see Dad hiding in the background waiting to jump out and surprise her.

"How are you, Emma Lee?"

"Fine." Disappointment and Maureen's coffee breath manifest on Em's face.

"Patrick said he was bringing you to see me today. I've been calling him for two days, and he has yet to return my calls." Maureen clasps her hands at her waist. "That's not like him. In fact, it is quite odd since he was extremely adamant about bringing you in."

"Oh yeah, I totally forgot. We rode up to Squaw Ridge and he decided to stay. Wanted to camp and fish, he really likes it up there." Em rubs her temple.

Maureen raises her brow and studies Em with a smile. "That's interesting." She takes a sharp breath. "To be completely honest, it concerns me, Emma Lee. I think we should talk?" Her face twists out a grin.

"Sure. Tomorrow. Okay? My dad's coming for dinner tonight."

She hesitates. "Emma Lee, I think we should—"

"See you tomorrow." Em starts to shut the door.

"Tomorrow morning, then? Eight o'clock?" Maureen digs in her tote and pulls out her card. "I'll come here, that will be easier than you driving through the city." She writes on the card. "This is my cell number. Call me if you need anything, anything at all." She hands Em the card.

"Alright." Em shoves the card into her jean pocket, mangling it on the way down. "Maureen."

Maureen stop and turns.

"You're a doctor, I have been having awful headaches. I

didn't take anything 'cause I wasn't sure it'd be okay for the baby."

"Headaches are common with hormonal changes. You can take Tylenol, and sometimes a cold cloth helps. Have you seen an obstetrician?"

"No, I need one."

"I can help you with that tomorrow."

"Thanks. See ya later." Em shuts the door and turns the dead bolt.

In her Prius, Maureen googles the phone number for the Calaveras County Sheriff's Department, and dials.

"This is Doctor Maureen Yamaguchi, I'd like to speak with a detective please." She listens to the dispatcher. "I'm concerned about a colleague of mine; his sister and niece are involved in an investigation in your jurisdiction." She turns the key and rolls the window down. "Perhaps we save time. I am the director at Coastside Clinic, a private psychiatric unit in Half Moon Bay, and I insist that you get me to a detective immediately, not after you take a note, and *not* in a few days when someone gets around to calling me back. Lives may be at stake."

Slurping from a mug of cold coffee, Detective Rocha rolls his chair away from his desk, and glares at Tanya. Her handcuffs jangle like bracelets as she leans on Rocha's desk. Detention Officer Garcia steps from the doorway and into the office. "Hands on your lap please." Tanya obeys, and Garcia steps back, constantly watching.

"Did she talk?" Rocha, asks Tanya.

Tanya nods. "Says she lied, and I believe her. That woman didn't do nothin'. Question is why?"

Rocha studies Tanya and runs his hand over his bald head. "This jail's full of innocent women."

"I did what you asked. I'm tellin' you what she said. I want my tweezers back."

Debbie, the heavy-duty dispatcher, doesn't attempt to press past Garcia, and stops outside the doorway. "There's a"—she looks at the note in her hand—"Maureen Yamaguchi on the line. Says she's some psychiatrist at some clinic, and"—she uses air quotes—"insists on talking to a detective immediately."

"About?" Rocha asks.

"Something about Kate Dunnigan and her daughter." Debbie hands Rocha the note.

"Put her through. Thank you, Tanya, your cooperation will be duly noted, and we'll see about the tweezers."

"We'll *see*?" Tanya slaps her hands on her thighs. "That ain't the deal. I want my *goddamn* tweezers! You see these chin hairs?" Tanya leans toward Rocha and rubs her chin with the back of her fingers. "Got a goatee growin' here." Tanya stands. "This is utter bullshit." She shakes her head as Garcia grabs her arm and pulls her out the door. "If I can't have the tweezers, I want the baptism! You promised."

In a hallway of white cinder blocks, just beyond the rec room, comes the aftermath of burnt popcorn and a chorus of cheers and encouragement for the hair-pulling and scratching taking place. Kate squeezes a pay-phone receiver.

FUCK U carved on the outside and a penis on the underside. A computerized operator asks for a name. "Kate." She waits and pushes her hand against her chest. The collect call goes through and the line clicks twice. Straight to voice mail again. "Hello, you've reached Patrick Callahan, please leave—" The computerized operator interrupts. "I'm sorry, the party you are trying to reach—" She hangs up. *Why aren't you answering?* Her chest tightens. *Where are you?* A heaviness grows—makes breathing painful.

"Let's go, ladies!" Garcia breaks up the trouble in the rec room. "Back to your cells, prep for lights out. Everyone! Let's go!"

Kate grabs the receiver. Her hand shaking as she dials. Sweating and waiting, pressing herself against the phone. She follows the instructions, now routine, and presses the number one. A computer voice asks who is calling. "Mom." The line clicks twice and rings four times before Kate hears Em's, "Hello?"

The computer kicks in: "You have a collect call from an inmate at the Calaveras County Jail."

Kate's prerecorded voice: "Mom."

Then: "Press one to accept the charges."

"Go to hell," Em says before the line clicks.

Kate keeps the phone pressed to her ear after the computer apologizes. Pressed to her ear after the computer disconnects the call. Worry sucking at her bones, sucking down at the marrow. Bathed in an icy sweat, her arms begin to tingle and go numb. She drops the receiver as all the pain and suffering in the world lingers in the everlasting moment.

"Let's go, Dunnigan." Garcia stands behind Kate. "Return to your room now, please."

A massive wave of pain slams Kate's chest—intense and sharp, seizing movement.

"Hey, back to your room." Garcia hangs up the dangling receiver.

Kate clenches her jaw and wobbles back and forth before her body sags and she drops to her knees.

"Dunnigan?"

"Ow." Kate groans, then presses her right arm across her breast and struggles to stand.

Garcia draws the radio from her hip. "This is Garcia, possible ten-fifteen in women's unit."

A brief buzzing, then silence as darkness hits.

NINETEEN

The dining room goes dark as Em blows out the last cinnamon candle. Pounding her palm against her forehead, she walks past Dad's clean plate at the head of the table and slaps it across the room. It crashes onto the sable rug, spooking Huck out of the room. Anger turns to worry as Em bangs her forehead against the massive picture window. The twinkling San Francisco skyline doesn't distract from fixating on the dad she wants now more than anything. Dad from the snapshot that she kept hidden from Mom all those years. Hidden in her sock, her back pocket, or her bra once she needed one. Dad looked into the camera with an openmouthed smile, a thick mop of dirty-blond hair and those icy-blue eyes.

Running up the stairs, into the master bedroom, Em ignores Huck curled on the bed and digs through her purse for Tylenol but only finds ibuprofen. She opens her wallet. From behind her driver's license, she slides out a faded and folded photo. It reminds her how good love feels. In the photo, Em is too big to be sitting on Dad's broad shoulders, his meaty hands around her ankles. The memory of the moment before the snapshot was taken plays in her head. Dad pretending to be a bucking brumby and throwing her off his shoulders. She tucks the photo into her back pocket. "Okay, okay, I'm coming." Determined to find him, she hustles into her manure-stained white Converse and a jean jacket.

Uncle Pat's BMW revs to life in the cool night. Leather seats and remnants of Old Spice chill Em to the core. Wishing Uncle Pat were here to help and not camping up on Squaw Ridge causes the back of her head to tingle. Goose bumps and the image of a bloody rock falling into a campfire flickers in her mind. The seat-belt warning chimes her back to now as Patsy Cline sings, "I Fall to Pieces," and Em joins in. Headlights cut through fog and the swanky Nob Hill neighborhood. Coasting fast down steep California Street, past colorful Victorian apartments with wedding-cake façades, all the way down into the bawdiness of Polk Gulch below.

Waiting to turn left onto Polk Street, a screaming siren startles Em. The light turns green, and Em speeds through the intersection, looking in the rearview. A black-and-white SFPD sedan tails her. She takes the first right. Parked cars line the busy street, but Em finds an open space and quickly pulls over. Slamming the front tire into the curb in front of a *Designated Bus Stop Only* sign. Sirens steal attention away from a group of college girls looking to escape their adolescence with micro-miniskirts and padded push-up bras. The police car, followed by an ambulance, passes. Life goes back to unusual in Polk Village.

A teenage girl in fake fur comes off the bus stop bench, toward the BMW. Bending over, she looks in the passenger window. Her short black hair falls across her innocent face and cocoa-colored lips. "You good?"

The passenger window lowers. "'Scuse me?" Em leans toward the girl.

"You alright?"

"Yeah. Just, kinda lost."

"Aren't we all?" The girl looking at her black nails smirks. "Where you need to be?"

"I don't know." Em shakes her head. "I'm looking for my dad. I got this picture . . ." Em reaches in her back pocket, pulls out the photo, and offers it.

The girl reaches through the window. Takes the photo and a close look. "No way."

"What?"

"Yeah . . . yeah, this is the dude." She taps her nail against the photo. "He bought me a drink at the Holy Grail." Her face is filled with abundant disbelief.

"No way."

"Swear to God. Just like, I don't know, maybe, two hours ago."

"I knew it," Em assures herself of the special unexplainable connection between her and her dad with a low fist pump. "What's the Holy Grail?"

"A bar, few blocks from funkytown. I got nothin' goin', drop twenty and I'll show you." The girl hands Em the photo.

"Would you? I'm not from here." Em wedges the photo into the speedometer where she can see it.

"Yeah, yeah, I got ya." The girl opens the door, and the reek of pot follows her into the car. "Your dad's cool, take a left up here. I'm Courtney. Got a smoke?"

"No, sorry. I'm Emma Lee." She pulls the BMW away from the curb and stomps the brakes, sending Courtney into the dash but missing a burly man on a bike dressed like Dorothy from *The Wizard of Oz*. The white poodle in his basket tips forward and almost falls out. The gender bender stops, comforts the dog, and turns around.

"Ignoramus!" His ruby slippers peddle away defiantly slow.

Slapping the dash, Courtney cracks up as Em squeezes the steering wheel and braces. Every muscle tenses. "Oh my God." Em looks at Courtney, who is pulling her seat belt on and still laughing.

"You're a horrible driver."

"I could have killed him." The thought makes her nauseous. "I can't believe all these cars. All these people." Em looks in every possible direction before slowly pulling out.

"Why you looking for your dad? Can't you just, like, call him?"

"He's not answering. I haven't seen him since I was little, and we have this, I don't know what you call it—like a connection. We just know when something's wrong. How was he when you saw him? How'd he seem?"

"Fine. I mean, I don't know the dude—seemed cool,

though. Holy Grail's up here on the right. Parking sucks, so keep going. Don't worry, just keep going."

Imagining seeing her dad causes Em to bristle, then shiver. A thrill exceeding anticipation blossoms as she passes the Holy Grail. Its black canvas-covered entry offers patrons a choice of two stained-glass doors in which to enter. A sign above each door identifies *Saints* from *Sinners*.

In the blackness, Kate is at peace, in a better place at a better time. A time when being in love with Will made her feel like the entire world could crumble around her and she would be just fine. It was the kind of love that consumes you. Makes you so happy you burst out laughing for no reason at all and the thought of losing them makes you nauseous. A love that wakes you in the middle of the night just to stare at his bare shoulders. And that's when you realize the phrase *madly in love* is a valid cliché.

Kate feels Will's warm body against hers. Skin to skin. His heart beating unusually loud. The fuzzy hair on his chest tickling and warming her nipples, sending an intense wave of hot passion somewhere deep inside. His face against hers, working his way to her neck. Breathing heavy and hot. Inhaling each other. Cigarettes and whiskey linger on him as he rears up and looks into her eyes. A bitter scent suddenly overwhelms, and Kate turns her head away. His heartbeat constant in her ears. Holding her breath, fighting to remain in the moment, her body tenses. But the biting stench threatens to pull her away as her eyelids flutter under a bright light. A smiling woman with thick pink lips looks down at her. Another breath and the ammonia vapors under her nose trigger a sharp inhalation reflex—her eyes water—expelling the remnants of thought. "I loved you!" Tears roll down her temples and disappear into her hair.

"There we go." A man's voice pulls Kate's attention to a ponytailed fellow on her right. "Ms. Dunnigan? Wake up," he instructs, shaking her knee.

Kate closes her eyes, wanting so badly to return and stay forever in the happy place only a moment away. But the siren, the movement of sterile whiteness surrounding her, a constant beep, and another blast of ammonia gas force her eyes open.

"Come on now." Pink Lips works the tube, like a magic wand, under Kate's nose.

"Okay!" The word is an effort as Kate attempts to cover her face, but her wrists are cuffed to a gurney. An IV punctures a vein bulging and blue on top of her hand. Clues are beginning to unravel in her head.

"You're on your way to the hospital, Ms. Dunnigan." Pink Lips solves the mystery.

Mr. Ponytail rolls stray hairs behind his ears and moves in. "Can you tell me your name?" he asks with a familiar caring that reminds Kate of Patrick, the brother, who isn't answering his damn phone. Think positive: *Maybe, just maybe, he lost his phone. Bullshit.* She would have heard from him somehow. Something's wrong. Bad wrong. She can feel it.

"Whaaat?" Her dry mouth causes her tongue to feel thick—so thick, she tries to swallow, but can't.

"Try to relax, okay. We're almost there." Pink Lips tucks the tube of ammonia into a red plastic bag, zips the top, then stuffs that into a red container strapped inside a white cabinet. The ambulance slows for a left turn as a deputy leans out from the passenger seat and eyes Kate.

In an exam room, Kate closes her eyes as a doctor with invisible braces that aren't invisible smiles too much, slurps air too often, and moves his lips as if someone were reading them. "According to the EKG"—he slurps—"I feel confident that you did not"—slurp—"experience a heart attack."

Kate opens her eyes.

He smiles even bigger, then slurps again. "That's the good news." Still smiling, he manages to complete a sentence in one breath. "The bad news is, I suspect you experienced a severe panic attack." Getting a complete sentence out seems to exasperate him, and he gulps an extra-long breath.

"Panic attack?" Kate doubts it.

"Yes. A severe one." He softens his slurp. "I administered benzodiazepine to stop the attack."

The effects of the drug on Kate's brain fuels an odd bliss at the knowledge of having had a panic attack.

"You're under an exorbitant amount of stress." He says it as if she's unaware of the fact.

An alarm from the other side of the room goes off, and Doc slides the neighboring curtain open. In the bed, an ancient woman stares at a blank wall in front of her with gray hollow eyes that died long ago. Doc lifts her bony arm, the wrinkled flesh hanging like it may fall off at any moment, and checks her pulse while pressing his stethoscope on her chest. A nurse arrives as Doc shuts off the alarm and looks at his watch.

"TOD. Eleven fifty-nine?" the nurse asks.

"Close enough." Doc steps away and pulls the curtain closed behind him.

The wretchedness of this old woman's insignificant death feels foreboding. Kate sees herself lying there. Dying alone. There is no such thing as a good life when you choose the wrong man. All the dread of a pathetic death—suddenly gone—washed away with an abundant dose of Klonopin.

"Some patients have conquered these episodes"—this time, his slurp is uninhibited, probably from the excitement of a dead patient—"with hypnosis."

"You mean like hypnotized?"

"Yes, I can recommend someone."

The answer comes like a light bulb being switched on. Maybe it's the drugs fueling her thoughts, but with the idea comes a preposterous hope. "I have someone," she blurts. "Maureen . . ." She can't remember Maureen's last name. Her words are slow and slurred. "Maureen . . . she's, uhhh, uhhh, a psychologist, near San Francisco somewhere. I need her. Please, call her and tell her I'm Patrick Callahan's sister and it's an emergency."

"Are you a patient of hers?"

Kate wants to lie but can only nod and close her eyes.

TWENTY

A thick fog coats the five blocks they'd driven past the Holy Grail. Courtney instructs Em to turn left and pull down an alley. A *Dead End* sign warns Em as she pulls down the narrow road. "This seems too far to walk back to—" Courtney presses the barrel of a Saturday Night Special into Em's ribs. "Hey!"

"Pull the ride to the side, bitch." She pokes Em's side with a gun. A thumping heartbeat hurts Em's head as she swipes her eyes with the back of her hand and stops the car.

"Ray Ray was right. This motherfucker pay for itself first time you pull it. Now get the fuck out."

"Please don't—"

"Don't! Don't! Don't 'spect no fucking sympathy from me. Driving a Beamer and shit!" She smacks Em upside the head. "Now get yo' ass out an' get to moseying, *cowgirl.*"

Pain in her head detonates, and Em closes her eyes, whispering, "Keep your eyes shut, don't look."

"What? Get the *fuck* out now, or I'm shootin' you in the fucking leg, I swear to God!" Courtney reaches across Em, keeping the gun pressed against her, and unbuckles Em's seat belt. She opens the door. "Out!"

The cool night and fog surround Em as Courtney shoves her from the car, then quickly closes the door and locks it. Em grabs the handle and pulls. Like a rat, Courtney crawls from the passenger seat into the driver's and slams the car into reverse. The handle jerks from Em's fingers, sending a tingle up her arm. Speakers thump a heavy bass as the blur of BMW headlights disappear.

Fear triggers flight, and Em turns and hurries up the alley. Trying to remember the route out of here, back to the place with lights and traffic and trees trimmed to nubs. Wanting her dad now more than her next breath, she begins to snivel like a child. Tears and fog and dark hinder her pace as she rubs her eyes. The reek of old beer and urine float from a dumpster and into the mist. A soft, "Hey, girl," sends Em back, between a dumpster and a tagged cement wall. That itch in the back of her head begins. Covering her eyes, she crouches. "Keep your eyes shut, don't look. Keep your eyes shut, don't look. Keep your eyes shut."

In the process of falling apart behind a dumpster, Em squats, hugs her knees. Buries her head in her arms. Eyes squeezed shut so tightly they ache. Fear crawling up through her like a mass of parasites. "Dad," she begs. "Dad." The ringing in her ears drowns distant honking and barking somewhere beyond the alley. Boot steps and jangling spurs coming closer mingle with the ringing. She raises her head, peeks out from behind the dumpster and scans the fog for Dad. With a brazen Aussie accent, she hears him: *"Angel? Come away from the rubbish."* That comforting drawl brings her to her feet. She hears him but can't yet see him.

"Dad?"

"Who else 'id be muckin' about in the middle a the night?"

"Dad!" Em squeals, her eyes adapting to the blur and the fog. "You're here." With open arms, she rushes from the dumpster—forward to Dad. "I knew it, I knew you'd come." The pale-blue building across the alley listing a bit as she stands waiting to regain her balance.

"I'd a been to supper, but your mum was after me, she conked me head a good one."

A man toting a shopping cart filled with worn treasures stops. Pulls a push broom from the side of his cart and prepares to defend himself against the girl walking toward him with arms outstretched like a petite Frankenstein.

"Hey, girl," the man warns her. "Don't need no trouble, you hear?"

"Can we go home?" Em sees Dad exactly as he was in her photo. His dirty-blond hair just as thick, his taut tan skin still accentuating his blue eyes and brilliant smile. He hasn't aged in over a decade. "I just wanna go home."

"Sure, angel. But we have to be careful, your mum's after us, and she's got the cops after us now too."

Cops? Why would the cops be after me? After Dad? What the hell did we do? Mom must be so mad that she's lying to the police. Poor Dad. I can see why he left.

The man hustles his cart away from Em the best his poor old bent leg will allow, but she reaches for him.

"I missed you so much."

"Get back!" The old man shoves the push broom into

Em's belly, knocking her backward. An empty wine bottle underfoot sends her ass over end, smacking the back of her head on wet asphalt. While down, Dad disappears. "Dad!" The alley spins just before Em's eyes roll back in her head. Arms spread wide, palms up, and feet crossed like she's nailed to an urban crucifix. Stale wine and urine burrowing into her hair.

"Hey, girl . . . Hey now . . . You alright?" The man crouches, keeping a safe distance. She doesn't move even after the man nudges her with his broom. "Awww, damn. I—I—didn't mean to—" The man lifts Em's arm and checks her pulse. "Come on now, you just, you fine. Talkin' that crazy-ass nonsense like you high on smack, what I suppose to do?"

Em's face tenses and twists, as if the world is sitting on her.

"You ain't dead! Come on now."

She rolls her head.

"Alright. There you go."

Her eyes crack open with heavy lids, and she touches the back of her head. "Where's my dad?" A tender spot on the back of her head causes Em to check her hand for blood.

"You—you—you bleedin'?" the man asks.

"I don't think so. What happened?" Em sits up.

"Hell, I don't know, I didn't see nothin'. But you sho' did crack yo' noggin. Lemme see." He reaches into his overcoat, finds his cell phone, and shines the light on the back of Em's head. "You gonna have one good ole goose egg, but I reckon you live. Might oughta go to the hospital."

"No. No way. My mom could—did you see her?"

"No. Weren't nobody here, but you was talkin' like there was," the man says softly, like he's delivering bad news.

"She hit me with a rock, didn't she?"

"Bes' you don't hang 'round here. Call somebody to come get you."

"I don't have my phone. A girl. That girl, she took it, she stole—oh God . . . my money."

"You wanna call the police?"

"Did you see a man? With a cowboy hat?"

"Ain't no cowboys 'round here. You hittin' the pipe?"

"I gotta get back to Uncle Pat's."

"Uncle Pat. Okay. Good. Where's 'at?"

"Up, way up, umm . . . California Street."

"California?" His voice gains several octaves. "Yo Uncle live up on California?"

"Yeah, I'm stayin' there."

"Call a cab, take you right there."

"I don't have any money."

"Nothin'?"

"No! Everything was in my purse. In the car. The girl, I can't remember her name, she took the car."

"You can't walk that far with yo' messed-up head. And the bus cost two fifty." The man scratches his head. "Can't do my bankin' 'til mornin'."

"What am I gonna do?" Em remembers Maureen's card and pulls it from her pocket, then shoves it back down. "I can walk. Just tell me how to go." Em slides her feet under her, and, hands on the ground, she gets to her knees.

"You get yo'self kill't or maybe worse." He takes Em's arm and helps her to her feet.

"Come with me? There's so many extra rooms. You can take a shower."

"A shower?" The man's face drops like a shot. "I need a shower? Aw, man . . . I stink? For reals?"

"No. No, I just thought . . ."

"Damn. I hate people be stinkin' all the time." He shakes his head and fits his broom back into its place on the side of his cart. "Damn shame." He turns his cart around and heads out of the alley. Em watches him disappear in the fog. "Come on, girl." She moves like an injured slug.

Hope springs eternal, and Em refuses to consider the massive throbbing throughout her skull to be anything more than a headache. Concentrating on getting back to Uncle Pat's, back into the king-size pillow top and snuggling under that fur comforter with Huck. She follows the limping man and his cart out of the dead end.

TWENTY-ONE

Climbing the ladder to her bunk, Kate hopes she doesn't wake Tanya and crawls across the bed as stealthily as a cat across pillows. Slow, deliberate— silent. The metal frame squeaks when she rolls onto her back and slides her legs under the thin blanket. Exhausted, Kate melts. The cold, hard mattress feels good on her back as she pulls the blanket up to her chin and anticipates Maureen's response. The doctor had promised he would get in touch with Maureen first thing tomorrow, which was technically today since it was after midnight. Maureen had only promised to help Em, but that was before things went from bad to worse to criminally insane. If Maureen shows—Kate promises herself— *tell the truth*. All of it from the ugly beginning to the bitter end.

"Good thing you didn't die." Tanya coughs and clears the phlegm from her throat.

"Why?" Dying would be a lot easier.

"Word is Rocha ain't got shit. Not one bit of evidence besides your confession that proves you did that girl or your son-in-law. Means DA ain't got enough to arraign you tomorrow."

Kate drops her head over the side and looks down at Tanya. "A *confession* isn't enough?"

"*Hell* no." Tanya sits up. "'Specially if you ain't got no record."

"I don't. But, how do you know all this?"

"I made friends with the Lord, and I have a lot of brothers and sisters now. Amen." She makes the sign of the cross. "They have to release you or charge you. Even your sorry-ass public defender can get you outta here."

"If they release me, I can just go home?"

"Yep."

Home. The thought excites Kate. She drops her head on the flat pillow and stares up into the darkness. Momentary hope is attacked by thoughts of the unknown waiting at home. Klonopin battles for dominance, suffocating give-a-shit into submission.

Closing in on two a.m., the dark streets are finally uncluttered of traffic, transvestites, and the ghosts of the mentally unstable. Em and the old man pushing his cart make their way through the intersection of Post and Larkin.

"I have to pee." The sudden urge is so intense, it takes a determined effort to not wet her pants. She crosses her legs like a little girl.

"There's a bar up the block." The old man stops and turns back to her. "Don't sit on the commode," he yells as Em trots by him and a closed coffeehouse. She hurries by a secondhand store window where a naked and headless mannequin poses with her hands on her hips, past a record shop called Vintage Vinyl, then past an oily-smelling Jose's Auto Repair on the corner. Across the street, a sign advertising the *Gangway* protrudes from the side of a brown four-story brick building. Four fire escapes zigzag like rusted lightning bolts. Code compliance at its best. Wedged under the three floors is the façade of a ship's bow. Rainbow flags line a plank leading into the dingy bar.

In the Gangway, a few remaining men spin their heads toward Em as she blasts through the door. "Where's the bathroom?" Urgency on her face and in her tone.

The tattooed bartender looks at Em with his one good eye but refuses to respond. An elderly man sitting at the end of the bar dramatically points his ringed index finger in the direction of the restroom. "You shit or puke on that goddamn floor, your cleanin' it up." The bartender slams a can of Budweiser on the bar. "Sick of this shit."

Fighting to control her bladder, Em charges into the bright-blue bathroom covered in graffiti. She can't unzip fast enough, and tugs her jeans down. Squats just above the pink toilet. The welcome relief of emptying her bladder, and the scent of urine marinating in her hair, prevents Em from being disgusted by the filthy latrine. She wipes, then notices blood on the toilet paper. In the toilet, below a brown ring, a bowl of bright red. Blood. Bright-red blood. In her underwear. More blood. Smeared. It's her. *Oh God, my baby.* She rolls toilet paper around and around her hand, over and over, until she has a thick wad, then slips it off and folds it before tucking it between her legs. Carefully, she pulls up her pants and zips them. Leaving the top button undone so as not to put any pressure on the baby.

Her heart racing, she spins the water faucet on and bangs the empty soap dispenser. A mirror reveals matted hair, eyes swollen and red as she splashes cold water across her face. *Am I losing my baby? I need help. I need a doctor. Maureen.* Em pulls the card from her pocket and runs out of the bathroom, to the pissed-off bartender. "Can I please use your phone. It's an emergency?"

The bartender grins. "Of course"—he pauses—"not."

"You're not very nice." Em holds her stomach with both hands as she leaves.

Below the bow of the ship, she searches for the old man and his cart. Nothing. No one. She wants to call out his name, then remembers she doesn't know it.

"Hey, girl." Comes from the old man exiting a rusted white Volkswagen bus. "Wanda gonna give us a ride if she can use your oven." The old man holds the van door open, and Em looks inside. His shopping cart occupying most of the space.

"I— Can I just use your phone?" Em clutches her stomach and leans against the door.

"I'd let you, but I ain't got no minutes left on it. Sorry, girlie."

"How far to California Street?"

"Fifteen minutes if you don't gotta piss again."

Pain like knives slashing Em's insides force her to consider getting into this van with two strangers. Unable to create a better option, she climbs in behind the cart and lands on the back seat. The old man gently slides the door shut like he's returning a sword to its sheath.

"Please hurry, I need to call—" Pain doubles her over.

The Volkswagen engine whines, then rattles the back seat as it labors away from the curb leaving a trail of sound that dwindles into silence as strangers ride the first few blocks. Em inhales the musty coated air and lets go a nasty moan. The woman, Wanda, pushes a tape into the eight-track. Creedence Clearwater drowns the pitiful moans coming from the back seat. The cart bangs Em's knees as Wanda downshifts before climbing California Street.

"It's on the left." Em watches out the front window as a hypnotic string of shells swing from the rearview mirror. The pain dulls as the shells and the two heads upfront sway with Creedence's "Bad Moon Rising." The top of the hill is in sight. Em points. "That's it! Right there." The van slows.

Two SFPD units are parked across Uncle Pat's driveway, and two uniformed officers stand on the stairs talking to Maureen. "Don't stop!" Em slaps the handle on the cart. "Keep going, keep going." *Why are cops at Uncle Pat's? Why is Maureen talking to them? What the hell?*

Wanda winds the engine one block past Uncle Pat's house and pulls over next to a flowering cherry tree. "Out!" Wanda demands.

"Come on, Wanda, don't be like that."

"Not you—her. Out, now! I cannot chance associating with a criminal." Wanda slaps her visor down and jacks a switchblade. She flicks it open like she could carve your insides out before you had a chance to scream.

"Please take me to the hospital."

"No can do. Can't chance it. Nope. Sorry. Out."

Em grabs the door handle, jerks it with both hands, and ducks out of the van. Her arms wrapped around her waist as the van pulls away. Pain stabbing her below the belly button, and now it's getting worse. She can't take it. Slowly, she sits on the cold curb beside a grassy patch. Unrelenting hurt triggers the need for Mom—the need to go home to her old squeaky bed. Mom always rubbed her back with warm calloused hands when she didn't feel good. A vague memory or maybe a dream comes to mind. Em on her antique iron bed screaming. The pain so bad she wanted to die. Her insides splitting her in two. She lies on her side—curls into the fetal position on the cool grass. Cries in pathetic gasps like a baby bird that has fallen from its nest.

A silver Prius passes without a sound. Brake lights brighten, then white reverse lights as the car backs and stops. Maureen rushes out. "Emma Lee?"

Em looks like death and smells worse.

"What in the world?" Maureen sits on the curb and puts her arm around Em.

"Why are the police at Uncle Pat's? I didn't steal his car, a girl did."

"They just want to talk to you. We need to find Patrick, can you—"

"My head hurts so bad. And the pain in my gut." Em sobs and touches the back of her head. "And I'm bleeding."

"Where?"

"You know, down there . . . I'm not supposed to be bleeding, right?"

"You require medical attention." Maureen stands and helps Em up. Blood stains the curb.

"I don't want to go to the hospital, please, please don't make me." Em grips Maureen's arms. "Please. You said I could trust you."

"The clinic has an obstetrician on call." Maureen opens the passenger door, and Em climbs in.

TWENTY-TWO

At ten a.m., Garcia escorts Kate from her cell to a small questioning room and opens the door. Detective Rocha waits, sitting at a table with two coffees and a smile. Handcuffed, Kate takes the chair across from him.

"Coffee?" Rocha asks as he slides the cup to Kate.

"Thank you." Her cuffs clang as she sips. The satisfying dark roast and the thought of going home lifts her spirits.

"Call me when you're done." Garcia shuts the door behind her.

"Feeling better?"

Kate nods and sips.

"My sister has panic attacks, I know how debilitating they can be."

Debilitating? Kate hadn't considered future episodes—of panic attacks becoming a common occurrence. The awful possibilities burrowing in her mind as she presses against the chair and lets her head fall back.

"I'm not trying to upset you, Ms. Dunnigan, but I *am* going to share what I know about this case. Before I ask any questions, I want you to consider *only* the facts. Will you do that for me?"

Kate brings her head down and nods.

"For the record, could you please verbalize your responses."

"Yes." It dawns on Kate that they must be recording her. "Do I need a lawyer?"

"That's up to you, Ms. Dunnigan. Do you want a lawyer? I'm sharing our evidence with you, but if you feel you need a lawyer, I'd be happy to allow it. May take a few days, but—"

"No, it's fine. Go ahead." She sips her coffee.

"Now"—Rocha stands and flips opens the folder on the table, but doesn't look at it—"I spoke with a Maureen Yamaguchi yesterday evening. She informed me that your brother, Patrick Callahan, had an appointment to meet with her Monday morning to admit your daughter, Emma Lee Quick, to a mental health facility in Half Moon Bay. Correct so far?"

Kate nods again. "Yes."

"When they never arrived, Miss Yamaguchi began calling Mr. Callahan and received no response. Monday evening, she went to Mr. Callahan's residence and found your daughter there." Rocha grips the back of his chair, and leans on it. He looks down, shaking his head and grinning as if completely amused by the story.

"Em was at Pat's?" Kate sets her coffee down and leans in.

"Yes. But"—Rocha pauses for effect—"no Patrick Callahan. Emma Lee claims he's camping. I contacted

SFPD, they tried to pick her up."

"Where? Where's he camping? Did she say?" Filling the space with questions knowing it doesn't make sense. *Why would Em be at Pat's house without him?* An inkling of dread sprouts in her mind and blossoms in her chest.

Rocha looks at his notes. "Squaw Ridge."

"Oh fuck." Her heart sinks as she stands, knocking over her coffee.

Rocha lifts the chair and slams it back down. "What, Kate? Want to confess again?" Rocha pushes his face way too close to Kate's. "Maybe tell the truth this time?"

Kate steps away from the coffee running off the table and puddling on the floor. With the help of her newly prescribed Lexapro, fear and panic no longer cloud her judgment. She looks Rocha in the eye. "I want the truth too. I honestly don't know what the hell that is right now."

Rocha sits and takes a deep, calming breath. "What *do* you know?"

Kate crosses her arms, looks at the spilt coffee, and racks her brain. Too many thoughts race for dominance: *Em might be guilty, she probably is, but why throw her to the lions until we know for sure. Truth is not an option until we know it for sure. Believing a thing does not make it true. Em will go to prison. She can't have her baby in prison. Patrick!* We have a winner. The thought of him needing her help surpasses all. The overwhelming urge to get out of this jail now, right now, and get to Squaw Ridge is all that matters. Kate presses her lips. "I know you're gonna have to turn me loose pretty soon. And the sooner you do, the sooner I can get to Squaw

Ridge and find my brother." They stare at each other, considering the next move. Rocha grins and nods. A knock on the door breaks the silence. Rocha leans over and opens it from his chair. Garcia pops a Nicorette from its package, and tosses it in her mouth.

"Sorry to interrupt, but Debbie insisted I tell you that the psychologist is on the line. Says she's got"—Garcia stops short and slows down—"the, uhhh, suspect you want to question."

Rocha stands and gathers his folder. "Release her," he orders as he walks out.

"What psychologist? Are you talking about Maureen? Does she have Em?"

Rocha stops, looks back like he'd like to punch her in the face.

"I just want to know if my daughter's alright." Rocha is gone before she can get the words out.

"Back to your cell, I'll bring your clothes. Should be out of here by noon." Garcia takes Kate by the arm.

Rain splatters Maureen's windshield as the silent Prius climbs California Street. "This is Detective Rocha." His voices in stereo on the car speakers.

"Hello, Detective, this is Maureen Yamaguchi, we spoke yesterday." She sips her chai soy latte.

"What can I do for you?"

"I am calling to inform you that Emma Lee Quick has committed herself to the Coastside Clinic under my care."

"She's a suspect in an attempted murder. I need to question her."

"Surely you are aware that psychiatric patients cannot be questioned unless all parties agree."

"Why wouldn't we agree?"

"Right now, Emma Lee is . . . very fragile. Also, she has experienced a few health issues with her pregnancy. I am certain you can appreciate that."

"I would think you'd want to do everything possible to find Mr. Callahan."

"I do. Very much so. I spoke with Emma Lee this morning, and she insists he is currently camping. I would assume you have sent law enforcement to the Squaw Ridge area?" Maureen turns into Uncle Pat's driveway.

"Procedure requires me to wait forty-eight hours to process a missing person. I'm certain you can appreciate that."

"Patrick Callahan is not camping! He could be injured or lost, or—" Maureen slaps the steering wheel.

"If you want us to find Mr. Callahan, I need to speak with Emma Lee. I'm not wasting department time investigating something because you suggested it! That's not how things work, Miss Yamaguchi." His voice rattles the dashboard speakers.

Maureen turns the volume down. "I'd like to request visitation with Kate Callahan. She requested my services last night."

"She's being released."

"When?"

"I can't discuss it, I'm sure you can appreciate that."

TWENTY-THREE

In the process of being released, Kate signs her fifth form without reading it. Garcia slides a cowhide purse across the counter, and a ziplock bag inventoried mostly with spare change, a dead cell phone, a tube of ChapStick, and a cowhide wallet. "How do I get home?"

"You can use the pay phone outside to call someone." Garcia checks items off her list, and sets Kate's value-size bottle of ibuprofen and her prescription of Lexapro on the counter. "Here's a taxi company." She writes the number on a Post-it and hands it to Kate.

Kate dumps the contents of the ziplock into her purse, but a forgotten silver Celtic knot ring escapes, tinging as it twirls across the floor. In an instant, Kate has the ring, cradling it in her hand as if it were so fragile it might die. Christmas day ten—maybe more—years ago, Em gave it to her, and explained that the knot represented love that had no beginning and no end, just like theirs. Overflowing with emotion, Kate told Em how Grandfather Callahan wore the same knot around his neck until the day he died. He was just seventeen and Ireland couldn't compare to America. His mother gently placed the necklace around his neck, then slapped his face with tears in her eyes. In her best imitation of Grandfather Callahan's garbled brogue, Kate would replay the way he swore that the necklace warded off sickness and setbacks that might interfere with a stable life.

"Well, that's it. You're officially released." Garcia shuffles the papers into a stack and taps them against the counter.

After years in her purse, the ring still refuses to slide over Kate's arthritic knuckle. She slips it on her pinky, grabs her pills, and hurries out the door.

A blustery wind rattles the old oaks, as Kate inhales the damp air and descends the brick steps of the Calaveras County Detention Facility. *Feels like a storm. We need the rain.* The hum of a distant lawn mower and being outside, in the cool, brings a sense of purpose to the day. *Get to Patrick.* Nearing the pay phone, Kate notices Rocha pulling long and hard on a cigarette. He lifts his jaw and blows a cloud into the designated outdoor smoking area. A low helicopter drums overhead and lands somewhere behind the facility.

Kate avoids Rocha's gaze as he approaches. She straightens her back and digs a quarter from her purse. Instinct and experience force her to hate him. *He's just doing his job*, she tries to convince herself.

Rocha leans against the rail at the top of the steps smoking. The rich blend of tobacco drifts past Kate and ignites a craving for an old habit. She wants to ask him for one. Smoking was a way to think, to get through the day, moment by moment, after she buried Will. It was only for a brief time and only when she was alone in the barn. The day Em mentioned Kate smelled like smoke, she quit.

"What now?" Rocha asks.

"Wait here 'til my cab comes." Kate refuses to look at him and searches her purse for the Post-it with the number to the cab company.

"After that?"

"Find my brother and my daughter."

Rocha nods and takes another drag. "Looks like we want the same thing—but I know where your daughter is."

She finally looks at him. "Where?"

"Can't discuss an open investigation with a known suspect."

"Is she okay?" Kate moves toward Rocha.

"I'm not sure."

"Any word on Pat?"

"Is it possible he's camping on Squaw Ridge?" Rocha steps closer.

"Can I have a cigarette?"

Rocha digs inside his jacket, then hands her the soft pack of Pall Mall. Kate pulls a smoke and waits for Rocha to strike a match and cups it until the cigarette flames. Kate sucks hard and fills her lungs. Lets the heavy burn linger in her chest, then exhales into the cool air like a freight train. "I don't know why they would have gone up there. Makes absolutely no sense." The nicotine headrush is a pleasing calm. "Something's wrong. *We* need to go see." She leans hard on the *we*, then instantly regrets it. The good in her wants to tell Rocha about Will. Tell him what she did up on

Squaw Ridge and why she did it, but just the thought of confessing brings up the same nausea that confessing to Father O'Reilly used to. The suffocating smell of stale perfume and body odor in the confessional booth made it feel like a used coffin. Looking up at rays of light penetrating the clouds, Kate shades her eyes and smokes.

Rocha dials his cell, presses it against his ear. "Sam, you fueled up?" Rocha looks at Kate and listens to someone on his phone. "Okay, good enough. Get her warm." He hangs up and slides the phone back into its holder on his hip. "Wind is bad near the ridge. Chopper can get us about two to three miles from the camp. You okay to walk the rest?"

"A helicopter?"

"Yeah, and time is money, so decide."

Kate hits the cigarette hard, then releases a smoke-filled sigh along with her inhibition. "You got a shovel?"

Rocha furrows his brow, gets on his radio. "Lipinski."

The radio squeals. "This is Lipinsk, go ahead."

"Grab a shovel."

"A shovel?"

"Yes."

"Why?"

"Because I said so."

Following Rocha a short distance around the back of the jail, it surprises Kate when she realizes that the detective had predicted her full cooperation, and for the first time, there's a tinge of respect.

A small section of asphalt dots a grassy field just starting to sprout green. The blades on the helicopter are loud, and

Rocha instructs Kate to keep her head down by yelling and pressing his hand on the back of her head. The black-and-gold chopper looks brand new and somehow fake, Kate thinks. She's never ridden in a helicopter. As she climbs into the rear jump seat, she notices a ridiculous amount of gauges and knobs and toggle switches that fill the instrument panel. Two digital touch screens look more like hi-tech video games than a matter of life or death should they go down.

Rocha buckles Kate's crisscrossing seat belt and hands her a set of headphones connected with a curly cable to the padded wall behind her. The minute Kate slides the headphones on, the world gets quiet, until a voice instructs Sam, the pilot, of his destination and a lot of other mumbo jumbo that Kate didn't bother to try and make sense of. Without warning, the chopper wiggles, then lifts its rear end like a dragonfly—hoovering a moment before lifting and floating east toward Squaw Ridge.

"I have something for you." Maureen pokes her head in the open door and leads Huck to Em's queen-size bed. His nails click against the linoleum floor as he runs to her. "Huck!" The room is warm and as upscale as a Hyatt suite without a view. Behind the curtains are windowless walls. Windows invite opportunity to the deranged.

"Hey, Huckster." Em rolls on her side, her groggy voice creaks. "Come here. Thanks, Maureen." The simple pleasure of unconditional love.

"How are you feeling?" Maureen asks.

"Good." Falling into her pillow, Em smiles as Huck

jumps on the bed and flips on his back. "Just really tired."

"I spoke to Dr. White, she said you are nearing the end of your first trimester."

"What's that?"

"The fetus is approximately three months old and the chances of miscarriage drop significantly."

"That's a relief."

"But she explained the importance of bed rest. And you do understand the possible repercussions, correct?"

"For sure, that won't be a problem." With nails chewed to the quick, Em scrubs Huck's chest, sending his hind leg bouncing out of control. "Can I get my phone back?"

"They aren't allowed here. I'm sorry. But we can arrange a phone call if there is someone you feel you must speak with."

"I don't want my dad to worry." Em forces up the sleeve on her complimentary oversized sweatshirt and tugs at the alarm band strapped around her wrist. "Can you cut this thing off? It's driving me crazy."

"No, I'm sorry."

"Why?" Em sounds childish, complete with the overaccentuated sad face.

"Because there is an alarm chip in there that will alert staff if you leave your room unsupervised. It's for your own protection. If you need anything, just press the intercom, someone is always available."

Em raises a single brow. "Does my mom know I'm here?"

Setting her tote on the desk, Maureen retrieves Em's file. "I have not spoken to your mother." She shuts the door.

"There are a few things I'd like to ask you. Would that be alright?"

"Sure." Em sits against the padded gray headboard.

"Great." Maureen rolls the desk chair next to the bed and takes a seat. "Do you remember when I came to the ranch and we spoke?" She opens Em's file and clicks a silver pen.

"Why wouldn't I remember?"

"I must ask." She smiles sympathetically. "Do you remember last night when I drove you here?"

"Of course."

"You told me that your mom hit you on the head. Do you remember that?"

"Yeah. Got the proof right here." Em almost touches the tender knot on the back of her head.

Maureen makes a few notes, then leans in toward Em. "What would you think if I told you your mother was incarcerated last night?"

"I don't know." She stares at Huck, searching for an answer. "Maybe she had someone do it." It was the first thing that came to mind.

"You think she could have arranged it while being detained? They monitor calls."

Crossing her arms, Em grins and slightly shakes her head. Knowing it doesn't make perfect sense but knowing it just the same.

"How would she have known where you were?"

"How did she kill Joe?" Em raises her voice. "She's way smarter than you think."

"I just want to know if it makes sense to you that your

mother could be in two places at once?"

"No, Maureen, it does not make sense." Her tone seasoned with irritation. "None of this makes sense."

"Can you tell me why your mother would want to hurt you?"

"Because she's completely insane. And she knows that I know she killed Joe."

"So, you do not believe Joe's death was an accident?"

"No way! Was Savannah being beat to shit in her sleep an accident?" Huck cowers.

"I was not aware that she was attacked in her sleep. How do you know that?" Maureen sounds so soft and sweet.

"Her brother, Roper, is my best friend. He told me." Em is breathing hard.

"I am sorry to have upset you, that is not my intent. These next few questions are a way for me to get to know you better. There is no right or wrong answer. Okay with you?"

Em cocks her head. Waits, then takes a deep breath and crosses her arms. *Mom must have gotten to Maureen and sweet-talked her. What kind of psychologist psychiatrist whatever the hell she is would be so easily fooled?* "Fine." *I'll play along.*

"What would you say was the best day of your life?"

Seriously? "I don't know, I've had lots of 'em. Maybe, if I had to pick, probably when my dad took me to Australia and I got to meet his family. My family. Cousins, Granny and Grampy."

"That sounds fantastic. How old were you?"

"Fourteen."

Maureen refers to her notes, turns a page, and reads. "You were twelve when your father left, correct?"

"Yeah." Her brow and lips tighten. She uncrosses her arms.

Maureen writes. "What part of Australia?"

Em hesitates. "A small station in South Queensland."

"That must have been a wonderful experience for a young girl."

Duh. "That's why I picked it."

"Good, great, okay. Now, what would you say was your worst day?"

Don't react. Em's eyes fill to spite herself. "The day I found Joe. My husband. Dead."

"I'm sorry, that was an awful day."

"Still is."

"I'm sorry. Can you think of an awful day when you were younger?"

Tears fall down Em's face as she rubs Huck's ear. "The day my dad left. I remember Mom crying, I was so scared I was never gonna see him again."

Maureen's eyes on Em. "Can you share that day with me?"

Swiping at her tears, Em looks at Maureen, then away. "I remember I was really sick. Throwin' up. Purple. Purple all over the place."

Tears flood Em's face as Maureen takes notes. "My mom told me Dad had to go back to Australia for a while."

"Did she say why?"

"I think they had a fight and he left. But I think she said he had to help take care of his family's station. It's fuzzy. Like when you try so hard to remember a dream, but no matter what, you can't. These little pieces pop up, but nothin' fits together or makes any sense."

"Did he come back?" Maureen writes, but her eyes are still locked on Em.

"He sent me letters before he actually came back. Little notes and stuff." Em wipes her nose.

"Do you remember how long he'd been gone when you got the first letter?"

"Hmmm." Em lifts her eyes and doesn't answer for a long while. "Maybe, like, a couple months."

"How were you feeling back then?"

"I don't know, that was a long time ago. I missed him. I got sick because of it."

"Sick?"

"Yeah, I was throwin' up a lot. I barfed on the school bus, all over some kids, it was so embarrassing."

"Did you see a doctor?"

"No. Mom said I was worrying myself sick. Put me on homeschool. Got me some medicine."

Maureen leans in and focuses on Em. "Em, have you ever been pregnant before now?"

"No!" Em dries her tears with the sheet.

"You understand that honesty is of the utmost importance right now?"

"You think I'm lying?"

"I do not think you are lying. I just want you to

understand that you can trust me. I am only here because I want to help you." She closes her file and clicks her pen. "I will see you tomorrow, unless you need anything?"

"No. Thanks for bringin' Huck." His head on Em's knee and his eyes closed.

"Buzz Manny when he needs to go out." Maureen slides Em's file into her tote and pulls out a new drawing pad and a pack of crayons. "This is for you." She sets them on the nightstand. "In case you get bored, which I'm sure you will. It may seem childish, but drawing is a good way to recall little details. I would like you to draw yourself when you were on homeschool. Things you did. Anything that comes to mind. Do not overthink it."

"Why?" *She thinks I'm a damn child.*

Maureen's smile is unconvincing. "It's just a tool that can help determine the root of the problem. Some patients—"

"The problem is my mother."

"Em, your treatment will only benefit you if you cooperate and—"

"Treatment? What do you mean, treatment?" Treatment is what you do to someone with cancer. She wants to like Maureen, wants to trust her, but something about the cold authority in her words *treatment* and *cooperate* reminds Em of her mother. "You think I'm sick, not thinkin' straight, like mental? You been talkin' to my mom, I knew it. She try and tell you my dad's dead? Cause that's a sick lie!"

"Getting upset is the last thing you should be doing right now. Especially with the baby." Maureen shoulders her tote. "I know you are a good person, Em. Pat told me so, and I believe him. That is why I'm here trying my best to help you." With a reassuring smile, Maureen puts a hand on Em's shoulder. "And you are going to be a great mom once you are thinking straight again."

"What exactly do you think's wrong with me?" Em fully expects to hear nothing.

"You appear paranoid." She reaches for the door. A red light blinks from a device the size of a walkie-talkie hanging from her belt loop.

"Are you *recording this*?" Em slams her hands alongside her legs.

"No. What makes you think that?"

"That thing. Hanging from your belt."

"That is a personal alarm. In case of an attack."

"And I'm paranoid?"

Maureen presses her ID card against the lock, and the door clicks open. "I've not yet spoken with your mother, but I am going to see her. We will talk tomorrow." The door shuts behind her.

With a deep breath, Em looks down at her belly. *Appear paranoid?* What the hell does that mean? She rubs her hand across her belly and considers leaving, going back to Uncle Pat's, but how to get there? How to get anywhere? And the baby, he won't take it, Maureen said so. Complete bed rest, the lady doctor said. And the baby, Joe's son, is the only thing left. A living tribute of their love. His name will be Joseph Theodore, like his father. The father who saved Em when he promised to love and cherish her all the days of his life in a ceremony at the top of Caesars Palace. They were on top of the world. A dozen friends watching while they danced, fitting together so perfectly, like pieces of a puzzle that when attached become one.

Good times with Joe run through her mind like a favorite movie. Roping, fishing, showering together. How they always knew what the other was thinking. Out of the blue, Joe would ask about something random that Em had been thinking. Once, while driving to the circuit finals rodeo in Great Falls, Montana, Em thought how nice it would be if she and Joe could afford to get a room instead of sleeping in the horse trailer again. Within three seconds of the thought entering her mind, Joe suggested they get a room with a hot tub. His ability to read her mind was a turn-on for both of them—a special connection that confirmed their love was far beyond average. But, for Em, it was the first time in years that she'd quit missing her dad.

TWENTY-FOUR

Kate leads Rocha and Lipinski toward Squaw Ridge from the east, grateful to have her feet on solid ground. Once in the air, the helicopter ride was smooth and reminded her of the way her mother's Cadillac seemed to float. The landing was the worst. The little aircraft was at the mercy of the wind, and Kate did not like it one bit when the thing teetered and bobbed as if it were afraid to touch down. Funny how a person can think they want to die, and the moment it becomes clear that they might, good old survival kicks in without consent. It must have energized her step as she keeps ahead of Rocha and well ahead of Lipinski.

"He gave her blackberry juice with somethin' in it. Some concoction he'd been makin' for years. After Em got done throwin' up, I asked her what she remembered from the night before. *A real bad dream*, she said." Kate stops at Tragedy Creek as it swells its bank with melting Sierra snow—turbulent as her memories. She steps in. An aggressive wind splashes fresh pine and icy water over Kate's boots as she zigzags from rock to rock, followed closely by

Rocha. Deputy Lipinski burdened with a backpack and a short shovel.

"Said she remembered me and her dad fighting. Figured she was too damn drunk or it was some drug Will put in the juice—either way, she didn't remember. That's when I decided, why not let her believe he left us? Why let it ruin her?" Kate says, keeping far enough ahead of Rocha, it's as if he isn't there at all and Kate is simply confessing to the wind. Letting it carry her words away up into the trees and mountains to do with as they see fit.

"If Em couldn't remember her father raping her—" All the jumpable rocks have disappeared. Kate stops. "And she didn't recall me bashing his head in—why the hell would I want to explain it to her?" She steps off the rock and into rushing knee-deep water that seems to attack her equilibrium. Forcing her to step back. A strange, disjointed feeling soaks through her as she watches her feet contort under the unstoppable flow. Wind roars off the ridge, meeting Kate head-on, as she climbs out of the creek, wishing that all the ugliness of long-buried secrets could be washed away with the current.

"That's going to be difficult to prove, especially if Emma Lee doesn't remember." Rocha crawls out of the creek.

Using the shovel as a fulcrum, Lipinski hops for a boulder to his left, but the wet rock offers little traction, and he plunks in up to his waist. "Shit!"

Rocha turns. "Cold?"

"Freezing." Lipinski gasps.

"That's the top a Squaw." Kate points above the wall of

trees to the ridgeline less than a half mile away. "Other side's camp."

"Didn't his family question his disappearance?" Rocha follows Kate through a forest of cedars, junipers, and pines.

"When he left Australia, he never talked to any of 'em again. Far as I know."

"What about friends? No one?"

"Told everyone we knew that I'd caught him campin' with some girl. They never even questioned it and never came back around. Didn't even call to see how I was doin', and some of 'em were our good friends. Least I thought they were."

The empty camp is filled with sunshine, spring grass, and lupine—and not nearly as hideous as Kate remembered. She wasn't sure if it was a justified hunch, or plain old hope, but she fully expected to find Patrick sitting against the old giant juniper lost, scared, hungry, and waiting for someone to find him. He was smart, and Kate knew he would know to stay put. "Pat!" Kate yells, then cups her hands around the sides of her mouth and yells again. "Patrick!"

Lipinski feels the ashes in the campfire and announces, "They're cold. Definitely cold." Kate's hope begins its descent. Without a word, Kate hurries past Lipinski kneeling at the fire ring, past Rocha studying tracks, and stops at the triangular rock under the giant juniper. The dirt surrounding the rock should be packed solid, covered with new grass. Instead, it's soft and loose, which means recently disturbed. All the Klonopin and antidepressants in the world won't stop the swelling panic as she kneels and—adrenaline fueling her—lifts the flat granite and flips it over.

"Jesus, Kate! Is this it? This where you buried him?" Rocha helps Kate to her feet.

"Yes." She steps back. "But the ground . . ."

"Give me the shovel." Rocha holds his hand out until Lipinski hands over the shovel.

"That ground isn't right." The urge to scratch her nails into the earth is almost unbearable. Like diving into a roiling ocean to save a drowning child. She squeezes her fists.

Rocha carefully plows the shovel along the grave so as not to disrupt any evidence. A tree squirrel protests the intrusion with a constant high-pitched chirp as Rocha works the shovel and Kate paces, refusing the memories that keep intruding. Memories of Will lying there on his belly. Grabbing the heart-shaped rock and being aware in that horrific moment of how perfectly it fit her hand. How good it felt the first time she landed it. The sound his skull made when it cracked, then caved, with the second blow. She shakes it off and thinks of Patrick. His lovable round face. His crooked nose that she convinced him was definitely not crooked the day he'd asked. It was just the way he was looking at it in the mirror, she swore. But above all, it was that damn smile. A smile so real and honest, it persuaded anyone in its path. "Maybe we should look for tracks, if Patrick was up here, maybe he got lost tryin' to find his way back. Maybe we should get search and—"

"Hold up!" Lipinski reaches down, brushes the dirt with his fingers until he reveals the seam of what was once a white sock. He digs around the sock, then gently pulls it up. The sock sprouts with a foot in it, and Lipinski lets go. "Shit!"

"No. Oh God, no." Kate covers her mouth and turns away. Something constricts her. Squeezing, then flattening her. She's suddenly so cold she can't move. Breathing is damn near impossible, and it's as if she's the one buried in the heavy soil.

"Call it in," Rocha instructs Lipinski. "And tape it off."

Refusing to look, "Maybe it ain't Patrick," Kate mutters, knowing it is. But *believing something doesn't make it true.* Isn't that what she preached to Em?

"Radio's dead. Got wet in the creek. Want me to call it in on the chopper radio?" Lipinski asks.

Rocha looks up. "Kate, you can go back and wait with the pilot." Like an anthropologist, he scoops little loads of dirt in the shovel.

"No." Kate turns around and watches Rocha. "We have to be sure. Can't assume anything. Stranger things have happened, right?" Possibility bleeds into fact. Em attacked Savannah, killed Joe, and now Patrick. "It's my fault. All of it." The words spill without tears this time. "I *let* this happen. Just tryin' to protect her—and the baby—keep her out of jail. What the *hell* was I thinking?"

From the shallow grave, Rocha unearths a hand. Fingers slightly curled and rigid.

"He wasn't dead, he was reaching!" Lipinski seems shocked.

"Lipinski! Keep your thoughts to yourself." Rocha glares at him with a look that says, *Say another word and I'll smack you in the mouth with this shovel.*

"He wasn't dead?" Kate can hardly get the words out. "She buried him—and he wasn't dead?" The need to sit is overwhelming, but instead, Kate drops to her knees.

"We do *not* know that." Rocha stops shoveling soil as Kate scratches and digs. "Kate, stop!"

Kate ignores him and digs. Her hands cupped and removing earth as if her life depends on it. "Kate, please stop."

"Cuff her," Lipinski chimes as Kate feels something soft. Something green.

"Aw, Patrick." Kate stops as she recognizes Patrick's wool coat. She grabs his wrist and pulls like she can still save him. "Patrick!" She stands, spreads her feet for leverage, and pulls with all her strength. Rocha takes Kate's arm and tries to stop her, but sheer determination is a powerful thing. Patrick's stiff and bloated body floats to the surface like an old sea captain, the water distorting his face. The left side of his head demolished. Dried blood and dirt blacken his lips and splatter his cheek. Kate gasps and lets him go. For a long while, they just stand there letting it all sink in.

"I'm sorry." Pain infecting her, but not tears. Maybe it's the antidepressant, maybe a person only has so many tears, and once they're gone, they're gone. It feels like a double shot of anger with a guilt chaser. Anger feels better. It grows stronger and hotter by the second until it burns in her chest. To be angry at someone other than herself for a change feels kind of good. Anger turns to rage. Em was fathered by a monster. A monster that Kate took responsibility for, and now that responsibility is clear.

"She's rabid," Kate says with the same disdain Tanya had for her son. "Completely rabid." Kate steps away from what remains of Patrick and looks at Rocha with clenched fists. "Where is she?"

TWENTY-FIVE

Crayon sketches of horses running and bucking litter the floor. With the aqua-blue crayon, Em colors in Huck's one blue eye. Her attempt at the dog's portrait—expressionism at its best. "You're way cuter than this." She flips the drawing pad to a fresh page and trades the blue crayon for black. "Me." She ponders Maureen's instructions. "When I was on homeschool. Homeschool." Nothing comes to mind. Closing her eyes, she pictures her old room. On her bed, struggling with algebra. Mom explaining how it was more important to balance a checkbook, and how grass equaled money, and if the cattle gained a pound a day, how much would they be worth by fall? Common-sense math. Why waste time on that algebra nobody uses anyway, she'd say. A big red dictionary on the bed. Thin, musty pages, tinged orange around the edges, filled with more words than a person could use in a lifetime. *S*, the letter *S* comes to mind. With the black crayon, she writes *S* on the paper. Her mind's eye in tune with her finger sliding down the soft dictionary page—past familiar words. *Spark, sparrow, sparse.* She turns the fragile page. *Spasm.*

Unconscious that her hand writes a crooked *P* on the page. The memory plays—close up on her finger sliding down *Sp* words. *Spasm, spat, spavin.* Her finger stops. There it was at the very bottom of the page. Em opens her eyes.

"Spawn?" She knows the word. Remembers looking it up in the red dictionary. Remembers it scared her and for some reason still does. She can feel her heart beating harder and louder and tries to dismiss it, but it won't go away. She swallows the sick feeling rising in her throat.

SPAWN . . . SPAWN. SPAWN? She writes the word over and over again, in a rainbow of colors. Filling sheet after sheet of paper until the bed and floor are covered with pages advertising *SPAWN.* With Huck at her feet, Em gathers the papers and balls them up. "Spawn." She tosses the paper balls into the trash and smashes them down. Starring at the trash, she smacks her forehead with her palm, and holds it there. "Spawn." Thoughts return to the red dictionary and her old bed. *"What the heck?"* The frustration is too much. She flops onto the bed and covers her face with a pillow, then lets go a scream. Loud and long. The sound of her scream stops her cold, and she pulls her face out of the pillow. Feels the deep, thick sound of her scream and the strange release it brings.

This time, she shoves her face deeper into the pillow and screams with everything she's got until it triggers a flash as quick as a blink, but there it is—her screaming, that same deep scream in her old room, in her old bed. She comes up for a quick breath, then pushes her face as hard as she can into the pillow. Closes her eyes and screams. Deeper, longer, louder, until her vocal cords ache. A twinge of panic and pain. A horrible aching burst in her center, then deep down in her bowels. *"Push that spawn out,"* she hears mom yelling over her screaming. With a red face, she drops the pillow and gasps for air. The pain suddenly gone. "Oh my God." Em sucks air in and out as fast as she can. The premonition strikes hard—*Oh my God, Mom wants my baby.*

Mare and foal race across the pasture as Rocha pulls the white Calaveras County Cherokee down the road to the ranch. "How many acres do you have?"

Kate checks the fence from the passenger seat. "Twenty-five hundred." Unbuckling her seat belt.

"You should be able to make bail, then."

Kate faces Rocha.

"Soon as your husband's remains are identified, you'll be arrested. A decent lawyer, maybe even Veronica, should be able to get you bail with no priors." For the first time, he looks at Kate with what seems to be a sincere smile and parks in front of the house. Hank doesn't get off the porch. Doesn't get off his bed. His weak bark seems to take too much effort and doesn't last long.

"What about Patrick? What'll they do with him? I mean, they still have Joe. Don't even know if they done the autopsy yet." Kate runs her fingers up her temples. "Patrick would want a service. He was very Catholic."

"Things move slow around here. We aren't equipped like the bigger counties. Have to get the coroner from Sacramento, so it could take a while."

Kate opens the door. "Thanks for the ride and the helicopter." Sounds more like a question than a statement. He still feels too much like the enemy to truly appreciate his help.

"Sure. And stick around, okay? You can't leave the county."

"I'll cancel that trip to the Caribbean." Kate gets out, looks at her house, then leans into the Jeep. "Want some coffee?"

"Love to, but I'm late. My son has a ball game in San Andreas tonight."

"Oh." Kate grunts thinking of Rocha as a dad. "Will you call me if there's any news?"

He nods with a hint of reluctance. Kate shuts the door and watches him back up the driveway, turn, and leave.

The house somehow looks different as Kate steps onto the porch. It will never be home again. She stares out at the pasture, her place of contentment, where, for a moment in time, she had everything she ever wanted and everyone. Before reaching for the hidden key hanging from the porch eaves, Kate turns the doorknob and the front door opens. The cripple cat climbs out of the wood stack, insisting with a constant raaar, raaar, raaar, that she fill his bowl. "Go catch a mouse, you lazy bastard." She unscrews the lid to a gallon jar and pours cat food into a metal bowl. His winter coats drifts and floats away as Kate strokes his back.

Inside the front door, she tosses her purse, grabs a plaid jacket off the coatrack, and puts it on as she hurries to check the horses in the barn.

A cold quietness turns the barn into an unfamiliar place.

Apocalyptic and damn near intolerable without nickers or movement. Every stall door open. Horses gone. Kate stands, staring and wondering what it would be like if she gathered a few things. Just up and leave. Go somewhere far away like the Caribbean. Hawaii—maybe Mexico, it's closer. Start a new life without cattle. Without horses. No responsibilities. It all sounded so perfect, but it would mean no grandchild. Leave that innocent child with Em, or in foster care? Or worse, Kate's own mother—*never*.

Kate buttons her wool coat and shoves her hands deep into her pockets as she cuts through the apple orchard toward the pasture. Swirling clouds of violet haze at sunset cause her to stop and watch for a moment. Horses have been turned out with the cattle. Good old Roper. He's always been like family. After a quick head count, an out-of-place boulder at the bottom of the tree line catches Kate's attention. She doesn't remember a boulder there. *There's no boulder there*. And she focuses her eyes at the thing through a thin veil of darkness. No way she wants to walk down there, but it has to be done. She opens the gate and as she gets closer confirms that it *is* a cow. Probably that red Angus heifer, and odds are she's calving.

Hank's determined barking drifts from the house, and Kate looks toward the house. A horn toots and Kate slogs back up the hill to the house. Halfway there, she spots Maureen getting out of her silver Prius. Her practical heels and cashmere fringed wrap make her look like she's flapping her wings instead of trying to keep her balance on the way to the house.

"I'm down here," Kate yells, slowly making her way through the orchard on exhausted legs.

Maureen waves as she tiptoes toward Kate. "Hello."

After a minute, the women meet in the middle of the apple orchard. "Hey." Kate catches her breath.

"Have you heard from Pat?"

"Walk with me," Kate says as Maureen follows her to the downed heifer.

Daylight fades as Kate peels off her coat and hands it to Maureen. The red heifer moaning, trying hard to rid herself of the breech calf. Her shaking legs straight and ridged as two-by-fours.

"Em told Rocha Patrick was campin' on Squaw. I knew that wasn't right, minute I heard it. No way he'd be campin'. 'Specially with all that's goin' on."

Under the heifer's tail, Kate slowly slides one hand deep inside and pushes the calf as hard as she can. Forcing him or her back into the uterus. Using all her strength to reposition the head toward the birth canal. Maureen's face twists as she steps back.

"Patrick knew Will was buried up there. Doesn't make sense, why would he go up there?" Growling like a weight lifter, Kate shoves with all her might and turns that calf around inside its mother.

"He called me," Maureen confesses softly. "He asked me if proving to Em that her father was dead was a good idea. I suggested it was." She tightens her arms around Kate's coat, hugging it as reality sinks in.

"Oh." Kate wants to scream at Maureen. Tell her how

her shitty advice got Pat killed. But she holds the calf forward with one hand and grasps a leg with the other. A contraction tightens the heifer's entire body and her eye rolls back. "Well, there ain't no easy way to say it— Pat's dead." With guilt and grief strengthening her grip, Kate lifts the calf's hock upward, then rotates it. "Jesus!" Her sweaty face straining and red in the cool evening.

Maureen kneels next to the heifer's head and begins to cry. "I knew something was wrong. But I—"

"Got it! Give me a hand!" The soft, wet hoof of a front foot peeks out from the heifer, and Kate resets her grip. "I need you to grab a leg with both hands and pull as hard as you can!"

Maureen stands—stutter steps, then sidesteps around the heifer. "What, what should I— Where do I set your coat?"

"Doesn't matter—just pull while she's having a contraction. And now would be good!"

Maureen sets the coat on the ground and her cashmere shawl on top of it. Kneeling next to Kate, Maureen takes a deep breath and flutters her fingers before wrapping them around the mucus-covered leg.

"One, two, three, *puuulll!*" Kate and Maureen strain and pull as the heifer bellows and pushes. After a minute, the two are spent and the heifer has quit pushing. "Shit, I gotta go get the pullers." Kate shakes her head. "I think there's a pair in Joe's truck. I told him that bull was too damn big. This calf's gonna kill her."

"Should we call a veterinarian?"

"Nothin' he could do we ain't already doin,' besides

charge me." Kate stands. "I'll be back as quick as I can. Don't let her kick you." Kate wipes her hands on her jeans and tries to hurry to the gate, feeling like each step may be her last.

Fifteen minutes later, Kate parks Joe's truck at the gate and jumps out with a pair of calf pullers. Exhausted, she stumbles toward the heifer as Maureen yells and waves her arms. "Hurry, hurry! It came out all by itself, but I am afraid it's dead."

Kate can't hurry anymore. Her legs are done, but the heifer is standing. Maureen's mascara is a mess. She's crying and not holding back one bit. A newborn bull calf lies outstretched on his side. Limp and glassy eyed. "Shit." Kate feels the calf's chest just behind his front leg. "He ain't dead yet." She grabs a pine needle off the ground and pushes it up the calf's nostril. Maureen bows her head, clasps her hands at her chin, and closes her eyes. The calf won't respond. Kate drops the pine needle. Squeezes his wet muzzle with one hand while covering one nostril with the other. A long, full breath from her to him via the open nostril. Once. Twice. Three times, and the calf's rib cage rises.

"There we go. Come on, baby." Kate waits. Watches for a moment before giving a fourth breath. Maureen kneels next to her. Mama cow licks her baby's back, and he takes a breath. All on his own, he takes a breath. They wait for what seems like forever until the little guy takes a second breath, bawls, and opens his eyes.

"You did it, Kate! My God, you did it. That was amazing." Maureen sobs.

Kate collapses backward onto the ground. "Probably all your praying." She wants to laugh but hasn't the energy.

TWENTY-SIX

E m gets out of bed and studies the monitor clamped around her wrist. Tapping her fingers against the device. Quick rhythmic snaps. Snapping. Pacing. Snapping. "We gotta get outta here. Think." Huck watches her pace. With what little strength she has, Em pulls and twists the alarm on her wrist. Searching the room. Thinking. *Cut it off.* But, with what? The mirrorless bathroom. She looks in the shower. Opens the cabinet under the sink. Empty, of course. She holds the monitor under the faucet and turns the hot water on. Steam rises and burns as she grits her teeth. Closes her eyes. Thinks of Mom killing Joe. Beating Savannah and ending up with her baby, her son, while she rots in this room. "Bitch, rotten, no-good bitch." Beads of sweat and steam form on Em's forehead. "I'll kill her." She tugs on the band again and again, her wrist a pretty pink, then bites on it until her central incisors ache. Determined, she leans her head to the side and digs in with her canine. Chewing and tearing and hardly leaving a mark. "What the hell?"

Opening the top dresser drawer, she lets it glide gently

back into place. Think. She pulls it open and watches it slide shut. Again and again and again. She slides the windowless curtains open. Slams the band against the wall, trying to smash it. The pain shoots from her wrist up her arm. "Damn it!" Huck cowers on the bed as Em falls next to him. He jumps down, then stares at the door. A grin grows on Em. "I love you!" She bangs the buzzer next to the door.

A girlish voice comes through the intercom. "Yes?"

"Hi. Um, my dog, Huck, he needs to go out. Maureen said to call when I need to take him out."

"Well . . . Manny is on break, so I don't know . . . . Can you, like, wait for—"

"Oh God! No! He's squatting on the floor. I think he has diarrhea. Maureen fed him canned food and I told her— *Ahhh*, hurry before he poops all over the place!" Huck drops his head like a punished pup.

"Okay, okay, hold on. I'll send someone."

Em pushes the desk chair next to the door and runs to the bathroom. The porcelain lid from the toilet tank is heavier than she imagined but desperation creates willpower and willpower has conquered many obstacles. As she steps up onto the chair, the door buzzes. Em raises the lid overhead and the door clicks open. She tightens her grip.

"Hello, miss?" Manny has one foot in the door, but Em waits. Not yet. Patience. *One more step, and now!* Em cracks the lid down on the top of his head. Manny, a middle-aged man built like a tank in green scrubs, drops and then crashes on his butt against the doorjamb. He's surrounded by porcelain rubble. A burst of adrenaline floods Em's veins as she jumps off the chair and snags the cell phone in his shirt pocket. She swallows against a painfully dry throat and lifts the lanyard with Manny's ID from around his neck. In that moment, she is aware of how easily this just went down. *Luck?* she wonders. *Skill?* Either way, the cliché rings true— *like taking candy from a baby.* "Come on, Huck," Em demands, but Huck refuses to emerge. "Huck!" Sluggishly, Manny brings his hand to his head. Em vaults over him and out the door without her dog.

Down the hallway, Em presses Manny's ID card against a locked door. It clicks open, and Em quietly enters an obese man's room. She holds the door until it closes silently. The man sleeps propped up, occupying the majority of an extra-wide hospital bed. The flesh and flab on his chins quiver as he snores through an oxygen mask in rhythm with his sleep apnea machine. His huge wrists are wrapped in gauze and white tape. Em removes an extra pillow and blanket from a shelf in the open closet, then slides them and herself under the big bed without a sound. Rolling up in the blanket makes Em feel safe. Her head finds the pillow. Soft. Comforting. *This will work for the night.* They'll look everywhere but here. A smug satisfaction and feeling Joe snuggling up from behind calms her. *"I love you."* Impressed with her newfound skills as the massive man slumbers overhead.

Kate opens the door and steps into a chilly living room followed by old Hank and Maureen. "Sorry it's so cold in here. I'll get a fire goin'."

"Do not worry about me. I have not been cold since I turned fifty-four."

"Menopause?"

"Yes. I am always hot and not the good kind."

Kate grins. "More to look forward to, I suppose." She layers the woodstove with wadded-up newspaper, an extra-long pine cone full of pitch, and some kindling. With the whoosh of a match, she sets it ablaze.

"Make yourself at home."

Maureen takes a seat at the kitchen table.

"I want to apologize for the awful way I told you about Pat."

"There is no proper way."

"The whole thing still feels so unreal," Kate confesses.

"I can't imagine never seeing him again. He was the best person I've ever known."

"I know. I think of all the years I wasted being too ashamed to call him. I should have known Pat wouldn't hold a grudge." The fire takes off, and Kate moves her purse to the kitchen table. Takes a deep breath and digs the antidepressants out. The next dose isn't due for an hour, but why wait. Without water, she downs two pills instead of one as Maureen watches.

"He told me he could show Emma Lee something that would prove her father was dead. I agreed that it *might* be a good idea. He didn't tell me he was taking her to his grave." Maureen closes her eyes as more tears come. She tightens her wrap and bites her upper lip.

"She buried him on top of her father. How's that for deranged?"

"Are you absolutely certain that Emma Lee did it?"

"There's not a doubt in my mind—I wish there were." Kate sits next to Maureen.

"I'll have her moved to one of our advanced security rooms in the morning."

"I think you should let Rocha have her."

"I cannot help her if she is incarcerated."

"She's beyond help. And she sure can't tell you what happened, 'cause she doesn't remember. I don't know if it was the booze or she somehow blocked it out. She calls her *dad*. Her *dead* dad! Tells me she talks to him. I should of got her help when she showed me the letters."

"Letters from her father?"

"Yeah."

"Emma Lee said they started a few months after he left?"

"That's right."

"I know you're struggling. Losing Pat this way is devastating. I loved him too. But, please don't think Emma Lee is beyond help. She is paranoid and delusional, so I need to understand what triggered the delusions. Typically, it is a defense mechanism against a traumatic experience."

"Her father was raping her. I don't know how long— when it began. I caught him and bashed his damn head in." Kate is surprised at how saying the words, for the second time today, came a little easier and with less guilt. Giving Maureen the truth brings a slight sense of satisfaction, something she hadn't felt sharing the news with Rocha.

Maureen leans toward Kate. "What do you mean *exactly?*"

"I can't explain the way I felt when I saw my husband on my daughter. *His* daughter. It was animalistic. Instinct. I had to save her. The rock was there and—" Her tone suddenly becomes defensive. "*What should I have done?* Ask him to stop?" Kate unwinds her braid and runs her hands through her hair.

Maureen stares into silent space, folds her fist under her chin, a modern imitation of *The Thinker*. "My goodness." She pulls Em's file and a pen from her tote. "Kate, I must be blunt."

"Be my guest."

"Did Em have a child?"

A grin attempts to hide Kate's phobia of the spawn. Her spine straightens. She hadn't thought of him in years, except in dreams. *Time for a drink*. Whiskey should poison some of the pain.

"Kate? She has a significant episiotomy scar."

The unopened bottle of Pendleton Whiskey has been waiting in the cabinet above the refrigerator for a moment just like this. Kate ignores Maureen as she pulls the chair next to the refrigerator, steps up, and reaches the bottle down. "I delivered him. The spawn." Kate's face twists with the word. "Easier than that heifer." She grunts as she steps down off the chair. "Went to the library ahead a time and read all about it just in case somethin' went sideways." She fingers two coffee cups from the dish drainer and sets them on the table.

"Kate. Mixing alcohol with prescription pills is never a good idea." Maureen's mouth is half open and she stops taking.

Kate ignores her and sets a cup in front of Maureen and pours them both a double. "She was only in labor a few hours. And once he started comin', he came fast." She takes a drink of whiskey and sits.

"It was a boy?"

Kate downs her shot in two gulps. Savors the burn, then release a long, hot breath. "Yep."

"He was healthy?"

"Seemed to be. Want some pie?"

"What did you do with him, Kate?" A stern expression comes over Maureen as Kate pours herself another.

"Took him to church. They used to leave the doors unlocked at night. I called the priest from a pay phone, told him the baby was on his pulpit."

"What did they do with him?"

"I have no idea." Kate takes a swig of her whiskey, wishing it would hurry up and work. Guilt was rearing its ugly head.

Maureen writes fast. Filling half of a page and flipping back and forth and writing. "You homeschooled Em, and kept the pregnancy a secret?"

"Only the last few months."

"No one saw her while she was pregnant?"

"You see where we live. If someone came over, she hid in her room. I told everyone she went to visit her dad in Australia. Her friend Roper was the only one who ever really doubted me, but he gave up soon as I told him I needed help cleaning stalls."

"Has Em ever been to Australia?"

"No." Kate confesses shaking her head. "Maureen, I need to see her."

"I don't recommend it. Delusional and extremely paranoid patients do not need triggers. She believes you are a threat to her and her baby, and that you killed Joe." Maureen closes her file. "In situations like these, I try—"

"Situations like these! You've dealt with shit like this before?" Kate says a bit too loudly, her irritation unmistakable. "I need you to give it to me straight. What's gonna happen to her? And my grandchild?"

"Eventually, she will be charged with murder and possibly attempted murder. There will likely be a trial, even if she pleads guilty, because odds are good that the prosecutor will seek the death penalty."

Kate looks up at a translucent spiderweb clinging to the corner of the ceiling. The death penalty hadn't entered her mind. Staring at the silky strands woven as intricately as a dreamcatcher, the tiny spider hangs by a thread.

"I promise I will do my best to keep her in a facility where she can get the help she needs. I will do whatever it takes. I made a big mistake and owe it to Pat not to give up on her." Maureen gently squeezes Kate's arm. "One day at a time for now."

Kate stares. "She would have been a great mom. Should of got her help years ago. Most the time, she seemed good. I thought, why force her to remember, to go through all that hell again?"

"Kate?" Maureen waits for Kate's full attention. "I think the best way to help Em is to work with both of you. You've been through just as much trauma as she has, and I'd like you to come to the clinic. You could stay at Pat's, or if that makes you uncomfortable, I can arrange a room."

Kate doesn't answer for a long while, filling the time and the silence sipping whiskey like it's hot coffee. "Do crazy people ever realize they're crazy?"

"Crazy is an exaggerated generalization. People get sick. No different than if they had cancer. But, to answer your question, the vast majority of seriously ill patients do not realize they're ill."

"What about insanity—I mean, she *is* insane. Not guilty by reason of insanity?"

"In my experience, insanity pleas are very tricky. I have testified in two cases, and in my opinion, the criminal who I diagnosed to be insane at the time of his crime went to prison, and the defendant that I diagnosed as intensely narcissistic, but not criminally insane, went to an institution." Her cell phone buzzes.

"God." Kate cracks her knuckles. "Sounds like a good lawyer makes all the difference."

"Sometimes."

Kate swallows the remaining whiskey down. "I don't have much money. Could sell the cows. Probably wouldn't be enough. Don't know what the ranch is worth with the second mortgage I took out last year."

Maureen squints to see the number on her cell. "It's the clinic, excuse me, but I have to take this. Hello?" She pauses. Looks at her phone. "Hello?"

"Here." Kate grabs the cordless phone and hands it to

Maureen. "The service up here is awful."

Maureen dials the clinic. "Patty, this is Maureen." She listens. The volume on the phone is set high, and Kate can hear most of Patty's panicked account of Em's escape.

"How's Manny?" Maureen asks.

"They're taking him to hospital. I think he's okay. Maybe a concussion." Her voice cracks. "Ma'am, the police are here. They want to know if she's dangerous?"

"Yes." Maureen turns away from Kate. "Follow procedure."

"Yes, ma'am. I have to go now, an officer needs me." She hangs up.

"She's rabid, isn't she?" Kate tangles her fingers. "Completely rabid."

"I'd like you to pack a bag and come with me. Just to be safe."

Kate takes a moment to digest what she thinks Maureen is implying. The pills and alcohol burying all give-a-shit.

"Kate, it was my impression that Emma Lee is fixating on you as the source of all her trouble. She may attempt to come after you."

"I can't leave. I have animals to take care of."

"Can you call someone? I'm certain they will find her very soon."

"I can't leave. Detective Rocha said so."

"It isn't safe here. I'm certain he will agree."

Kate nods, staring at the spider on the ceiling.

TWENTY-SEVEN

A monitor beeps, and the sound of breathing, shallow and ragged, wakes Em. Each breath the obese man takes sounds as if this may be his last. It feels like morning, but Em can't be sure. Her sleep was one of those intense slumbers that creates confusion sometimes after only fifteen minutes. That and the fact there are no windows. Inching her way out from under the bed, Em freezes when the bed creaks. She waits. Then, rolls twice before getting to her hands and knees. Nearing the door, she stands and looks back at the pathetic man. The glow from machinery reveals his empty blue eyes fastened on her. She steps back. The hint of a smile forms on the obese man's cracked lips, and Em takes a tight step toward him. He holds out his right hand with the sorrowful look of a wounded animal. The gauze and white tape around his wrist stained where blood leaked and dried sometime in the night. The beep of the heart monitor speeds up as the man reaches his upturned hand out to her for what seems like an ounce of humanity.

Em takes a cautious step toward the suffering man and drops her petite hand into his fat paw. Softly, he glides his thumb back and forth, across the top of her hand, and a smile lifts his stubbled face. Without taking his eyes off her, his left hand finds the call button hanging from a cord above his bed. By the time Em realizes the man is calling for help, he tightens his grip. She pulls, jerks twice, but somewhere under all that fat is enough muscle to end her. The dread of being caged kicks in. She grabs the man's sweaty index finger with her free hand, peels it away. Bends it back until she feels and hears the lowest joint pop. He can't help but release his grip and howls while his head lolls from side to side. His left hand grabs Em's hair but snags only enough to dip her back for a moment before she can get to the door.

She presses Manny's key card against the lock. It doesn't click. She tries again. Nothing. She bangs the key card over and over. "Shit." It's probably been deactivated. She should have thought of that. The lock clicks, and a lanky woman rushes through the door to the man's side. Her long black hair swinging behind her. Before the door closes, Em spins full circle through it, out into the narrow corridor.

The bright-yellow walls are like industrial sunshine. A fire alarm grabs Em's attention, and she pulls the little red lever. Within seconds, lights are flashing. An alarm screeches like a hard-core carnival ride. Em follows the corridor, taking a hard left at the intersection. An exit sign hangs above a metal door at the end of the corridor. She races to it and lunges against the bar with the heels of her hands. The door pops. Fresh air and blinding sunlight hit her like an awakening. The fire alarm fades as Em walks down the tree-lined street kneading her aching temples.

Dark eyes like open graves taint Kate's face in the morning light. She shoves two happy pills into her mouth, then washes them down with coffee. A suitcase waits by the door. Rocha told her not to leave, but images of pregnant and penniless Em, scared and wandering the dank, unfamiliar streets, played in Kate's head all night. The notion of the girl attacking a random stranger drove Kate to pack. She has to be found. Has to be stopped. No way can Kate bear the responsibility of another death. She opens the door, rolls her suitcase onto the porch as the house phone rings. Kate rushes to it. "Hello?" No one answers. "Hello?" Through the phone, Kate hears a horn honk. "Em, is that you?" A seagull cries in the background. "Where are you? I'll come get you. It'll be okay."

"I'll come to you. I knew you weren't in jail." Em sounded strange. Threatening.

"What? You're coming here?" Kate tries to ignore her racing heart. "Emma Lee?"

Seagulls scream, fighting over a dead starfish. Incoming waves wash against mounds of rotting kelp that liter the crescent-shaped beach. Em hurls Manny's phone into the ocean, then follows a surfer in a hooded wet suit to the parking lot above the beach. Vehicles carrying surfboards inside and out come and go. From a distance, Em watches a surfer set his board in the back of his truck and reach behind the front tire to retrieve his key. When he catches her watching, she skims the sour off her face and bends over to tie a shoelace that doesn't exist. Stolen by someone at the clinic. Probably staff. Probably that bastard Manny. It lessens the guilt of busting his head. Believing a thing can make it true to spite what mom says.

A maroon minivan parks, and two girls study the surf from the inside. Attempting to blend in, Em leans against a damp rock, crosses her arms, and watches the waves through a light mist. The slate-blue water swells and rises. Surfers covered in black like lanky seals lie prone and paddle for position. The swell builds, then peaks, and suddenly a man is standing, racing down the face of an overhead wave. The wave closes on top of him, and he disappears into the churning white wash.

The girls from the minivan unload their boards and pull on wetsuits. "Isn't it a school day?" an old man asks as he walks his Labradoodle toward the beach.

"Hi, Mr. Porter." The girls zip up the back of each other's wet suits. "We're going to class," one says, "at some point." They giggle and the driver looks around, then opens the gas tank door and hides the key inside. The girls watch the waves and never notice Em as they pass. Irrelevant or invisible? Doesn't matter. Em watches the girls bounce down the path to the beach. In unison as they step into the water, dive onto their boards, and paddle out into the lineup. The moment is now. Em opens the gas tank and removes the key.

The gas gauge rests a hair above *E*, and Em hopes she'll make it across the Bay Bridge. A solid afternoon sun has burned away the fog as the minivan climbs the bridge in the slow lane. The bay twinkles like a million Fourth of July sparklers and reminds Em of Fourth of July with Dad at the rodeos. Him helping her hold a hissing, crackling sparkler in each hand. Twirling them in circles, leaving flaming streaks in the night.

"Use the left two lanes to merge onto I-880 North," instructs the woman's voice coming from the pink iPhone included with the minivan. After merging off the bridge, Em takes the second exit and pulls into an Arco gas station.

On the back seat, under the pile of what was probably the surfer girls' school clothes, Em scores two backpacks. Digging inside the first pack, she tosses an American history book on the floor, followed by psychology 101 and a blue binder. She inspects the contents of an overfull makeup bag before tossing it. A small zippered pocket inside hides seventeen dollars and change. "Score." Em stuffs the cash into the cup holder, then searches the second pack. No cash, only a Bank of the West ATM card with the name *Simone A. Wise.*

Em changes from her clinic-issued sweat suit into a pair of cutoff Levis and a Roxy flannel shirt she found. She replaces her laceless Nikes and decides that after she kills Kate, she will go to Australia. Live in the outback, on a big station, with her son, her dad, and all the relatives. She grabs the phone and lies across the back seat with her feet out the window.

"Hi, Daddy."

"Em, is 'at you?"

"Yes." Tears fall, and before she knows it, she's sobbing. "I miss you so much."

"I miss you too, angel."

"I really need your help with Mom. She's trying to get my baby and we have to stop her."

"No worries. Let's have a chat with your Mum tonight, shall we?"

"Talking isn't going to help."

"I wasn't planning on talking. Actions speak louder than words. Haven't you heard?"

"I'll meet you in the barn at midnight."

"You are on the fastest route. You should reach your destination by—" Em mutes the woman's voice coming through the cell phone.

TWENTY-EIGHT

"I'm fine." Kate keeps the phone pressed to her ear and her fingers pressed to her temple. Last night's whiskey taking vengeance this morning. At least it got her through the night. That and thoughts of suicide. *No one has the right to complain about life because no one has to endure it,* is written on a Post-it stuck to the floor. Written in Kate's own cursive, she doesn't remember writing it but knows she did. The whiskey-Klonopin cocktail had reincarnated Kate's mother's philosophical torment. Words to live by, she decided, and stuck it on the refrigerator. "Hey, if I tell you something in private, you have to keep it a secret, right?" She steps out of the screen door and onto the porch. "That doctor-patient thing, like Pat had?" She leans against the rail and looks at pitiful old Hank.

"Of course, everything you share is confidential. Unless I feel someone is in danger. Then, legally, I have to report it," Maureen says after a long pause. "Is someone in danger, Kate?"

Kate sits on the porch step. "I don't know." Hank limps over. "I know it's wrong, believe me, but I don't want her to go to prison, they'll beat her." She pets Hank and wipes his gunky eyes. "She goes to prison, we both know she'll lose the baby."

"I don't want her in prison either. But public safety must be a priority."

"Yeah." A wasp buzzes Kate. Then another. "I must be out of my mind for thinking I could still save her." Kate stands and notices a wasp's nest hanging from an eve. The papery sculpture like a delicate work of art.

"You love Emma Lee. Wanting to help her and especially an innocent child is completely understandable. But, Kate?"

Kate watches the wasps float in and out of their hanging home. "Yeah?"

"I do believe you should be in therapy."

Kate walks back inside and heads for the kitchen. "I got funerals to plan."

"Of course. Would you be willing to commit to daily sessions over the phone?"

"Okay." Kate reaches under the kitchen sink and brings up an extra-tall can of wasp killer.

"Can we speak tomorrow at seven p.m.?"

"Sure."

"But you can call me anytime, you have my private number."

"Thanks, Maureen. Take care." Kate hangs up the phone and immediately regrets not telling Maureen that Em called. Not telling her about the threat feels like lying. Em's menacing voice that sounded nothing like the beautiful and kind child she knew. That voice—*I'll come to you*—sends shivers scratching from the inside out. Would she really come? Could she really hurt her own mother? Kate can't picture it as she pries the safety cap off the can of wasp spray. But sitting here waiting to find out if Em was serious seems like volunteering to be the assistant for an amateur ax thrower.

On the front porch, Kate shakes the can of wasp killer. Aims the nozzle at the silvery-gray nest and sprays until the foaming stream of poison floods their lovely home. Kate saturates the nest, and it falls. Quickly, she trades the spray for a broom and pounds the remaining survivors. She stares at the dead and dying, and an idea forms. She looks at the empty can of wasp killer. Then rushes back inside to the kitchen. Under the sink is a second can of wasp killer, and Kate brings it up, onto the counter. She dials Maureen's private number.

"Kate?"

"Hey, if Em turns herself in to you, could you keep her safe—in an institution or hospital or something besides prison?"

After a pause that lasts long enough to wrench Kate's heart a few times: "Possibly."

Kate's sigh is obvious. "Okay. Good. Good."

"Em probably is not going to walk into the clinic and commit herself."

"You never know." Kate hangs up the phone and tosses the wasp spray in the air and catches it. Momentary hopefulness is better than Klonopin and whiskey anytime.

In the barn, Kate shakes the dust off a pair of old leather-and-chain horse hobbles. With pliers, she threads a piece of baling wire through the chain links to shorten the distance between each hobble. Then twists the wire tight and tests the buckle strength with a few tugs.

Joe's bedrolls lay open next to the feed manger where Em had left it not long ago. With attention to detail, Kate straightens the wool blankets until they are perfect. Next, she pulls up the canvas that covers the top and bottom like a bag and sets the leather hobbles inside before rolling the entire thing up.

The bedroll is heavy and awkward, and Kate stops twice to rest before getting it to the aluminum stock trailer. As soon as she opens the tack room door, the smell of manure and citronella fly spray remind her of better days. Days when she and Em would haul horses up and down the state to high school rodeos. Kate sat in the stands and cheered like a maniac as her daughter outran the other girls in the barrel racing. Beat most the boys in the team roping. And was the National High School Rodeo state champion three years straight in the girls' breakaway roping. Em was amazing—had been through more hell as a child and came back beautiful inside and out. But, now . . . dear God. Regret rots the memorable smiles. *Keep busy,* Kate thinks. *Keep fighting. Keep focused.*

Hoof picks, shoeing tools, saddles and saddle pads, medication, combs, brushes, fly spray, Kate throws all of it out of the tack compartment. All onto the ground except the half case of water coated with arena dust. Fighting like mad to force the bedroll through the narrow trailer door, Kate grunts and shoves it in. On her hands and knees, she catches her breath and unrolls the bedroll. She takes a moment to lie back and consider her own sanity. How much suffering should be endured before maintaining sanity becomes a losing battle?

After a few a "practice runs"—this was the phrase Em had always used when she could not align the gooseneck hitch of the livestock trailer with the ball in the bed of the truck—Kate hooks the truck and trailer together, then pulls it as close as she can to the house. Only a few steps from the back door.

After a long, hot shower, Kate stares at her tuna-sandwich dinner unable to eat or remember the last time she had. Lack of sleep, excess chores, and Klonopin force her to nod off at the table. Never has she gone so long without sleep, and she's got to be sharp, got to have a clear head. She shakes herself awake and moves the .38 revolver, the can of wasp spray, and a handful of zip ties off the kitchen counter and onto the coffee table. Muscles in her lower back refuse to relax as she stretches out on the couch and yawns. Sleep comes quick, before worry can interrupt.

Eons of rushing water allowed Coyote Creek to eroded a train-size tunnel through the limestone hillside. Dripping with heavy moss and ivory-colored stalactites, the quarter-mile-long tunnel is like venturing into the belly of a whale. But today, it's an oasis and a perfect place for Em to hide out until dark. The cool water and smell of warm, wet limestone and granite wash away the stench of the last few days. Her legs float in the clear stream as she lies against a boulder perfectly smoothed and shaped for reclining. Voices echo from somewhere deep downstream. Kids laughing, splashing, and screaming, and Em can't wait to meet her child. She caresses the baby in her bloating belly and imagines their future in Australia. Teaching baby Joe to swim and fish with Dad—*no, Grandpa*. Riding horses, gathering cattle, and maybe even a few wild brumbies in the outback. Camping and hunting. Em feels him kick in agreement. "I love you."

"I love you too," a sarcastic voice spouts and laughter spills from behind her. She turns. Two dudes in the shadows sitting on a limestone ledge, watching. "Come here and feel my love." One of them releases a raspy stoner's laugh, and the strong, tangy smell of pot floats in the air.

Another voice offers, "Want a hit?"

Em stands, rubbing her eyes while walking over. "Got a light?"

"Yeah, yeah." The boy seems nervous and hands Em a cheap lighter.

"Thanks." Em walks away.

"Are you leaving?"

Em slides the lighter into her front pocket of her cutoffs and walks away.

"Dude, that chick's stealing your lighter." Echoes as Em follows the stream, grabbing a small unattended ice chest on her way out of the tunnel. It's a thirty-minute climb up the path and back to the minivan.

After an hour's worth of psychology 101, Em's head is pounding. She closes her eyes and drifts into slumber until the sun finally sets. After consuming the can of coke and two egg salad sandwiches from the stolen ice chest, Em drives toward home listening to the Justin Bieber CD stuck in the player. It's dark by the time she pulls the van under an old oak alongside the road that borders the west end of the ranch. From there to the house is the shortest walk, just over a quarter of a mile, and she knows it well. She'll wait here until the darkest part of dark.

Night has a chill to it, and Em changes back into her baggy clinic sweat suit. At 11:45, she slips the stolen lighter and cell into her bra and climbs out of the van. After working her way through the barbwire fence, she digs out the cell phone and calls Dad.

"Dad, I'm here."

"Me too."

TWENTY-NINE

Kate wakes, unsure if the scream she just heard was real or a dream. Her hell forgotten for just a moment. She rubs her eyes when reality hits like an avalanche. The house is dark. She jumps up—looks at the clock: 11:59 as Hank barks from the porch. The revolver waits on the coffee table. Slowly, Kate picks it up, walks to the porch light switch, and turns it on. Careful to not disturb the curtains, Kate gets low and peeks out the window. So many trees offering cover, and she can't be sure if it's Em or just shadows. *This is insane, it'll never work.* She should call Rocha right now. He might help. He'll understand that Em should be in an institution and not prison. Surely, he'll understand. She turns the kitchen light on. The cordless phone sits on the kitchen table where Kate left it after talking to Maureen. She brings the phone with her while searching the counter for Rocha's card. It's not there. *The bedroom.*

In the bedroom, Kate flips on the light. Her purse hangs behind the door and she grabs it, dumps the contents onto the bed. Nope. No card. *Pants.* The clothes Kate was wearing when she came home are piled in the corner. She digs in the pockets, and there in the right front is Rocha's card. "Hellafuckenluia." Kate turns the phone on and reads the card. When she presses the numbers, they don't make that familiar beeping sound. She looks at the handset and presses the power button over and over as hard as she can, but it's dead. "No." *Fuck.* Why hadn't she remembered to put it back on the charger? Something that damn simple. If she can't get simple things right, how on earth is she going to help Em?

Kate slams the dead phone into the base, a red light confirms charging. She should have called Rocha the minute Em called. *It's obvious I need help.* She watches the light knowing it will be at least thirty minutes before the current will power the phone enough to make a call. The red light suddenly dies as does every light in the house. In the blackness, Kate feels along the wall until she finds the switch. She flips it. Nothing. Kate stops. Trying to reason through the situation. *Power goes out all the time up here.* The wind blows, a tree falls and takes down a line. Doesn't mean Em's here or that she somehow cut the power. Then facts emerge. It's not windy. A downed power line is an unrealistic excuse and nothing other than Em. That sick-dropping sensation in her gut is becoming way too familiar. Kate knows the way to her room.

The porch is dark, but Em knows the hatchet is always buried in the same stump next to the stacked firewood. Without missing a stride, she jerks the hatchet from the stump, ignores Hank, and stops at the front door. *"Go on,"* Dad whispers.

Em's hand in her bra. Searching. "I lost the lighter. Shit."

"Watch your mouth or I'll wash it out. Now, let's get on with it, shall we?" Slowly, Em opens the front door without a sound and walks in.

Like a cunning assassin, she slides along the walls scanning the living room for Mom. Then the kitchen. Silence is eerie until she feels a comforting warmth and the hint of woodsmoke from the stove. *"Use the coals."* Em opens the door of the big woodstove and slaps the hatchet down into a glowing log. Carefully, she brings the hatchet out and drops the flaming log into an old fruit box filled with sappy pine cones, newspaper, and kindling. *"Attagirl."* A flame jumps from the box, working its way up the wall. Up to the rodeo pictures, trophies, and buckles. Em's eyes fill with flames.

With a tight grip on the hatchet, she walks the hall looking for Mom. Peeks into the bathroom and behind the shower curtain. Then, moves into Mom's room. From the doorway, she sees her in bed, sleeping on her side. Like a mouse, Em takes slow, tiny steps on her toes until she's there. Standing right behind her sleeping mother. She lifts the hatchet as high as she can, gripping it tight with both hands, and slams it down. "Bitch!" Em shouts and buries the hatchet a second time. *It's too soft.* Something's wrong. Stop. Feathers swirl around the room like a slow-moving blizzard.

Bam! A flash fills the room like lightning, and a burning pain shoots up Em's leg. She screams and goes down hard. The pain in her leg won't let go, and Em twists and grips her shin. It's wet. "Dad! Daddy," Em cries, "my leg."

Kate crawls out from under the opposite side of the bed. Em sees her mom and squeezes the hatchet. "You shot me, you crazy witch!" Em stands.

"I'm trying to save you!"

"I'll kill you!"

"Get her, Em."

Em drags her leg toward Kate. Readies the hatchet, but Kate attacks first. From six feet away, Kate sprays a long, foamy stream of wasp spray. It coats Em's forehead and quickly drains down into her eyes. The screams stab at Kate's ears, piercing her resolve as Em drops the hatchet and claws her eyes. Writhing. Kate takes the hatchet and throws it in the closet. "Give me your hands. Hold your hands out and I'll help you," Kate yells.

"Please, Mom," Em cries, "please help me." Em holds her hands out in front of her. "I'm sorry."

"If you move a muscle, I'm going to shoot you again. Understand?"

"Mommy . . ." Em sobs like an inconsolable child.

Kate zip-ties Em's wrists together—the chemicals in the spray burning her nose and eyes. Em gives in. Doesn't move as Kate grabs the hobbles off the dresser and buckles one of the leather straps around Em's bloody ankle. "I'm warning you, if you move a muscle—" Em kicks like a mule into Kate's solar plexus. The air leaves her lungs as she crashes backward, shattering a long mirror.

Smoke crawls into the bedroom and chokes Em. Coughing and crying, she scrubs her eyes and face with the bedspread, then heaves. Kate requires oxygen and cannot move. On the bed, Em is freeing her ankle of the hobbles, then throws them as hard as she can.

"I can't see!" Em limps, feeling her way with tied wrists, nearing the open the door. Kate is able to catch a bit of breath and reaches for the gun lying on the floor.

"Emma Lee, stop! The house is on fire!" Smoke engulfs the room followed by a glowing light. "Shut the door!" Flames snap at Em as Kate jumps up, shoves her aside, and slams the door. Their coughing drowns the sounds of the crackling fire.

"Finish her!"

"I can't," Em cries as Kate steps up onto the bed and slides the window open. She punches out the screen, then lies the comforter across the sill. "Come here. Come on, let's go."

"Dad! Help me!" Spit and tears mix with desperation. "Help me!"

"Dad's waiting for you outside." Kate sounds so reassuring.

"You're lying, Liar!"

"If you don't get up and get out this window, you and your baby are going to die. Understand?" Kate goes to Em and attempts to lift her. It's impossible. "Goddamn it, Em, I'm going out this window, and if you want to kill me, I'll be outside. Come and get me." Kate steps onto the bed and lifts a leg onto the sill. She looks back at Em and waits.

"You've really mucked it up this time."

"I can't see!"

"I have to go."

"Wait! I'm coming with you. I can't see." Em's eyes are red and swelling shut as she stumbles to the bed. Crawls on top of the sheets and feathers. Feathers floating and sticking in a trail of blood as she drags her leg toward the window.

"Almost there. Stand up." Kate waits until Em pulls herself up, then she drops over and out.

"Just lean forward and slide down. I'm here. I'll catch you." Kate uses the comforter to cradle Em until her weight pulls the blanket through the window. In one quick motion, Kate is under Em and on the ground. Without hesitation, she wraps her arms under Em's shoulders and drags her to the nearby stock trailer.

The tack compartment door is open and the bedroll waiting. With all her might, Kate lifts Em just enough to roll her upper body through the tack compartment door, then flips her hips and legs over and inside like a sack of grain. The moment all of Em is clear, Kate slams the door and latches it with the locking lever. Like a pissed-off filly, Em kicks the trailer with her one good leg. "Let me out!"

"There's water in there. Open a bottle and pour it in your eyes." Hank watches, slowly wagging his tail. Kate opens the back-seat door and Hank looks to her for assistance. "Come on, Hank!" She lifts his hindquarters and slides him in.

Flames stab through the roof as Kate pulls the truck away from the house. Rolls the window down and smoke drifts in. Looking ahead, but unable to resist looking behind—the extra-large side mirror plays a scene from an absurdist memoir. Flames torch the old pine that stood like a sentinel—watching over the house since before Kate was born. A torrent of red sparks rush the dark like a wretched aurora. Crackling and popping follow Kate as she drives along the cold asphalt trail. Trading everything she thought she ever wanted for Em and an unborn child.

Without the benefit of heavy stock, the trailer bounces and bangs as Kate crosses the cattle guard, then pulls out along the two-lane. Passing the parked minivan. By the time she reaches Sandy Gulch, she imagines most of her home and belongings are gone when a fire truck with lights flashing and siren blaring pass.

At the Calaveras County line, Kate's cell phone grabs a signal and dings. She pulls over. Sees the missed calls from Maureen and dials her.

"Hello? This is Maureen Yamaguchi."

"I've got her."

"Who?"

"Em."

"What? How?" Her voice rises several octaves.

"Can you meet me, so I can follow you to the clinic?"

"Kate, call the police. Right now."

"You promised to help. I've blinded her. And shot her in the leg. God knows about the baby. This is where you shit or get off the goddamn pot, Maureen. Decide!" After a long silence, it seems Maureen has hung up. Probably calling the police. "Hello?"

"Where are you?" Maureen finally asks.

"Copperopolis. Meet me on the west side of the bridge.

187

Bring the police if you want. Your call. I can't do no more."

"How will I find you?"

"I'm pulling a thirty-foot stock trailer." Kate hangs up.

THIRTY

On a patch of dirt before the bridge, Kate watches headlights whiz by while the trailer shakes every now and then. Dread comes no matter which way Kate plays out the future in her head. Odds are good Maureen will bring the police. If she doesn't, maybe Kate could share a room with Em at the loony bin. Only a crazy person would have blinded their own daughter with wasp spray, shot her in the leg, trapped her in a stock trailer, and hauled her down the road like an animal on its way to slaughter. Kate's ludicrous intervention, at best, will allow her to turn Em out in a nuthouse so she can spend the rest of her life finger painting with Jell-O. Twinkling lights on the Bay Bridge are hypnotic, and Kate closes her eyes. Considers driving north. Get to Alaska where she and Em and her grandchild could live in— A hard knock on the driver's window kills the fantasy, and Kate jumps. A highway patrol officer signals for Kate to roll the window down. *This is how it ends.* Kate hesitates, and after a deep, deep breath, accepts her fate. She fights the sticky handle, uses two hands to roll the window down.

"Everything okay?" The pinch-faced patrolwoman asks.

"Yes. Fine, thanks. How are you?" *Oh God, shut the hell up. Keep cool,* she tells herself.

"I'm well." The officer lifts her dark-blue cap away from her eyes. "Ma'am, you can't park here."

"Oh gosh, sorry. Okay, sure. No problem. Sorry." Before Kate can start the ignition, Em bangs against the aluminum and rocks the trailer.

The officer steps back and studies the trailer. "What do you have in there?"

"Um, just an old crippled horse. She wants out." Em's cries are hushed by the roar of traffic.

"Wow."

"She's mean. And crazy. Needs to be put down, really. I just can't do it, so I'm meeting my friend here. She's going to take her. Keep her until time makes a burden of years. You know . . ."

"Oh, boy do I. I remember taking our old Lab to be put to sleep. It was devastating."

"Devastating is right."

"You have a nice night, ma'am. Best of luck with the old horse. I know it's hard."

"Thank you, you too. Is it okay to wait here just a bit longer?" Kate asks as the officer walks away.

"Fifteen minutes."

"Thank you."

The officer disappears behind the trailer and pulls her patrol car into the slow lane. Kate breaths again. Hides her mouth with her hands. Swallows the scream kicking inside her. *Focus on your breath*, the ponytailed doctor had said. *Focus.* A sickening wail escapes the trailer, fills the truck as Kate waits. And waits for Maureen.

The demon mother backs Em into a dark corner. Cold metal walls bend and wrap around her as she pushes against them. The demon mother gurgles with each breath, long and loud, and frothy. Charred flesh emanates and slithers up Em's nose and she heaves.

"I don't need eyes to see you!" Em screams. Fangs and claws grow—quickly becoming more demon than mother. Eyes glowing red, bulging like a snake filled with hate.

"Give me the spawn," she screeches. *"Give me the spawn!"* Spit shoots from her fangs. Stinging, then burning, Em's skin like acid. Burning holes into her arms and face.

"No!" Em thrashes, wiping at her skin. Screaming. Melting herself further into the corner. Banging her head. "No!"

"Give him here."

"No! Dad!" Em swats and slaps at the demon. "Dad!" Fighting and kicking for her life. For the life of her child. The trailer banging. Rocking.

"Angel, shhh . . . Quiet down now." Dad's soothing tone calms her. *"It's okay, she's gone."*

The silver Prius coasts past the trailer, next to the truck, and stops. Kate steps out as Maureen rolls the passenger window down and holds out a manila folder with shaky fingers. "Here are the directions to the facility and a false court order." Kate takes them. "I've attached the phone number of a family attorney who can file for guardianship and submit my evaluation for the courts. He is expecting your call," she instructs efficiently. "Is Em restrained?"

"Yeah."

"Get to the clinic. Ring the bell and tell Patty you have a court-ordered guardianship and to admit Em to the secured treatment area in restraints. Make *certain* that she calls Dr. White and myself immediately. Understand?"

"What's this court order?"

"A counterfeit I printed. It will speed up the process and get Em the medical attention she needs without taking her to a hospital. If anyone questions it, *you* printed it off the internet. Patty hasn't seen enough of them to recognize a fraud. Em will be admitted before anyone discovers the infringement."

Kate stretches her hand out to Maureen. "Thank you."

"Okay." Maureen gives Kate's hand an awkward squeeze.

In less than an hour, Kate brings the rig to a stop in front of the sliding glass doors at the Coastside Clinic and parks in the fire lane. The place looks nothing like the madhouse she had imagined. Beige and plain as a bankrupt car dealership converted to a place of worship. Without hesitation, Kate grabs the counterfeit court order and hurries past the potted palm to the sliding glass doors. They don't open. Kate waits. Presses against the glass and looks inside to see a well-lit but empty curved reception desk. She knocks hard and waits. The irony of being unable to get *into* a mental institution strikes her funny bone. She turns back toward the trailer. It all feels so unreal. Like she's living someone else's life. *The bell. Ring the bell,* Maureen had said. A button, like a doorbell on a model home, to the right of the door. Kate presses it. Then presses it harder.

"May I help you?" a voice like an angel sings from somewhere above.

"Yes! Hi. I have a court order to admit my daughter Emma Lee Quick. She was here, but—" The door buzzes, unlocks with a click, and slides open.

"Please wait at the front desk."

Curled up like a snake in the corner, Em sleeps with her arms wrapped around her belly until the rattle of the trailer door shakes her. Kate opens the door and moves aside as Manny, with his two black eyes, slides Em by her arms toward the door. She's too exhausted to resist or care why men in matching green scrubs snatch her legs, then strap them together. They maneuver her through the narrow door with the precision of pilfering pirates and lay her on a gurney.

As they strap her down, Kate looks away. Streetlamps burn holes through pearlescent fog. The dividing yellow line disappears into obscurity. Night is suddenly silent, and for the first time in a long time, Kate feels the unexpected cold and shivers. She stops. Stands—savoring the moment. Anything to prevent searing the barbaric memory of delivering her captive child into her mind.

PART THREE

THIRTY-ONE

Warmth trickles, then streams from the top of Em's head, tingling her spine to the depths of her being. Almost orgasmic, she shivers, breathes, her whereabouts muddled. The situation diluted. Echoes of water surround and soothe. Splashing. Splattering water. Movement somewhere above. Then a hand on her head—rubbing. Two hands massaging her scalp. The tingling roams her body accompanied by a blast of peppermint that stimulates. A groan escapes her uncooperative mouth.

"Feel good?" The owner of the rubbing hands asks.

Em opens her eyes to cloudy light, wondering if this is one of those dreams where you're aware you're dreaming.

"I used to love it when my mom washed my hair." The voice is soft and feminine.

Water begins from somewhere above, and Em releases a sigh as her head lolls. "Aw caa," Em mutters. "Uhh caan . . ." It's as if someone has tied her tongue to her jaw. No matter how hard she tries, she can't force the movement necessary to produce the right sound.

"You're okay, Emma Lee. Just relax." The hand works a

cloth up and down her bare back. Pleasure drops the tension in her shoulders. "Almost done." A cool spray of water zigzags. All fight-or-flight response turned off.

"Aw caaan eee." *S*'s are impossible.

"All done. Can you stand up for me?" the woman asks. "You're okay. Your eyes are still healing, but your leg has improved unbelievably well. You're one lucky girl."

"Huh?" Em's breaths quicken as panic swells.

"You're okay. You're at Coastside Clinic having a bath. You've been here a little over a week. Don't worry if you can't remember. That's okay. Let's get you dressed so you can see the doctor." Em stands from a seated position, and a warm towel immediately hugs her. She grabs the towel and wraps it—feeling her belly. Bigger than before. "I preg—" She doesn't try to finish the word. "Mom?" Nothing makes sense. *Mom.*

The autopsy report concluded that Joseph Michael Quick's death was accidental, and Kate was relieved that the forty-eight-hundred-dollar autopsy bill would be paid for by the county. A momentary respite from worry was terminated soon as she thought about Joe's memorial. It wasn't just the cost, it was the scornful looks she knew would come with blame that she would never dispute.

An inexpensive coffin and a flat grave marker put her Visa over its limit. A gray wool skirt and black silk blouse from the thrift store were far from fashionable but benefitted the suffering Kate felt she deserved. She traded the uncomfortable high heels for a pair of dress boots from Em's trailer. Since the Airstream hadn't been affected by the fire, Kate spent the last week attempting to sleep on the pullout sofa. It was like trying to sleep in an aluminum sarcophagus, so mostly she read outside on a lounge chair. After dressing for the funeral, she saw a cheap countryfied version of her mother in the mirror. A bullet to the brain would be much less painful. She considered stopping by the Trading Post for a bottle of booze, but Joe deserves better. He deserves respect.

The Gold Digger Saloon holds Joe's memorial and a sea of cowboy hats. But not one of those hats belongs to any of Joe's family members. The only time Kate had asked Joe about his family, he looked down. Crossed his arms and explained that he never knew his father. His mother's second husband was abusive so he left home at fifteen and never associated with them again. It was obvious by the way Joe's nostrils flared when he spoke about it that the subject needn't be discussed again.

The patio is filled to capacity. Mostly with men gathered around the rising smoke of a massive barbecue. Dozens of beef tri-tips sizzle as a fat man in an apron flips the head-size hunks of meat with a long metal hook. Kate avoids the familiar faces that would see her for what she really is—single mother of a maniac. Friends with sympathetic smiles that seem to scream, *I'm smiling but I'd prefer to scratch your eyes out.* All except one woman, sitting cross-legged at the end of a picnic table nursing a Coke and smiling at Kate. The woman waves Kate over. *Shit, do I know her? She does look familiar. I have no idea.* "Hello." Kate offers her hand as she stands in front of the woman. Her hazel eyes are impressive and familiar as she shakes Kate's hand. "How are you?"

"I've had better days. Guess I'll get through this one too." Kate smiles. "You look familiar. I'm sorry my memory is so bad."

"No, no. I'm just—I knew Joe. Thought I should pay my respects. I hadn't seen him in years." She sips her coke.

"That's sweet. I'm Kate Dunnigan. I'm—*was* Joe's mother-in-law."

"Nice to meet you." She nods and Kate can't shake the feeling that she knows this woman. "I'm Jessica."

Odd. You don't have a last name? Kate tries to not be suspicious, maybe it's just a generational thing. "How'd you know Joe?"

She grins, and hesitates. Her eyes never leaving Kate, as if she's editing her words. "School. We went to school together." Jessica nods and stands—lanky in her sleeveless black dress. "I'm sorry for your loss." Her dirty-blonde hair flaps along the tops of her bony shoulders as she walks away. *Strange. Very strange.*

Inside, retellings of Joe's grace and courage while fighting rank bulls to save riders go on and on. Potato, macaroni, and Jell-O salads are spread buffet style along the bar. Corn bread, garlic bread, cakes, and a variety of fruit pies decorate a corner table below a Coors poster with Joe and his signature move—his hand slapping the center of a big black bull's head, forcing the beast's eyes on him and not the cowboy on the ground.

Jake, one of Joe's employers and owner of Wild West Rodeo Company, hollers from behind the bar, "Drinks on me! Here's to Joe!" and downs a shot. Kate can't help but smile and take the shot Jake hands her. The burn stings before warming enough that she almost wants another. Roper puts an arm around her.

"Hey, Miss Kate." He smiles that toothy smile that reminds her of when he and Em had lost their front teeth. Roper's teeth grew as fast and as big as a colt's. "I don't know what the hell's going on, but I know you did *not* hurt Savannah." He looks up at the embossed tin ceiling as tears fill his eyes.

Kate rubs his back.

"Was it Em?"

Kate pulls her eyes away from Roper and nods. He covers his mouth with his hand.

"She's sick, Rope. She's in a facility in the Bay Area getting' help." Kate lifts her glass to Jake, and he accommodates. The percussion of the bottle striking the glass, the glug, glug, glug of the whiskey working its way to the top of the glass, allow Kate and Roper a moment of acceptance.

Roper wraps his arms around Kate and sobs with his head on her shoulder. "If Savannah didn't lie—"

"Don't blame her." The whiskey starts to work as Roper moves to the stool next to Kate. "I'd love to blame Will. He was such a piece a shit. But I chose him. I chose to marry a monster. This whole thing"—Kate twirls her index finger and looks around the room—"this entire disaster is on me."

The background chatter seems to fade as Roper leans into Kate. "You were more like a mom to me than my own mother. You were always, *always* there, you know, when I was afraid of who I really was. Love you for that. So, here I am. Right here, right now, for you."

"Appreciate if you'd check on the animals. I'm gonna stay in San Francisco to be close to Em and—"

"Done. Anything, just call me." Roper wipes his tears with his palm.

The room feels tight, but the upright angle of the bed is perfect. "How long have I been here?" Em asks Maureen.

"Eight days." Maureen shines a light into Em's eyes. "The pupils are reacting. That is a very good sign."

"What happened to my eyes?" She turns her head toward the sound of Maureen flipping paper.

"Does the light bother you? I can close the drapes." Maureen smells like cigar tobacco.

"No. It's fine. I wanna know what's going on." Em moves her leg and feels a sharp pain turn to a bone-deep throbbing. "Why does my leg hurt? Is it broken? Was I in a wreck?"

"You were not in an accident. Let me assure you that you are being very well cared for and that you are in a safe place. No one here is going to harm you in any way. Do you understand?"

"No." The confusion sets in and memories are blurrier than her eyes, but the grief of missing Joe remains. She wants to cry but doesn't know why.

"Do you remember me bringing you to the Coastside Clinic?" Before Em can answer, a woman's rant interrupts from outside the open door. Chanting—

"Medications don't work. This place is hell. I hate it here! Medications don't work. This place is hell. I hate it here." On and on until Maureen soft steps to the door and closes it. The rant is muffled but not muted.

"Do you remember being here before today?" Maureen asks as the pleather on her chair squeaks.

"Sort of." Em remembers it more like a dream, hazy and in fragmented pieces. "Huck? Where's my dog?"

"He's being well cared for by my assistant, Patty, and her ten-year-old daughter."

Annoyed, Em feels like a child who wants her favorite toy back. "He's my dog."

"Yes. They're only watching him while you heal. Now, can you tell me about when you first arrived at the clinic?"

Propped up by the raised bed and two pillows, Em adjusts herself. "You brought me here and Dr. White examined me. Did an ultrasound on the baby. Then—" Em pauses and clasps her hands on her lap. "I remember my mom. She was—wasn't really . . . She wasn't really like my mom, she wanted to kill my baby. Maybe it was a dream? I know my mom would never hurt me, or anyone."

"Uh-huh. And do you remember going home?"

"I remember"—Em thinks—"driving . . . a van."

"Where did you get the van?"

Em thinks, then shakes her head. "I—I don't know."

"Where did you drive the van?"

Em thinks a long, long while. "Coyote Creek! I went to the cave and—" She struggles to recall, but the memory stops there. "In the water in the dark cave. And—" She shrugs. "I don't know. I can't remember. Why can't I remember? What's wrong with me? I can't . . ." Panic scratches up the back of Em's head. "What the hell is happening?"

"It's okay. We'll work together to fill in the blank spaces. If I feed you information, the memory will always feel false. What is important at this time is that you are making tremendous progress."

"Where's my mom?"

Under a foot of ash and heavy soot, Kate yanks on the corner of a blackened picture frame. The charred glass won't budge, and a sick tug-o-war erupts, freeing the reek of an incinerated life.

"Goddamn it!" It's as if the cremated remains of her home refuse to release the treasured possession. Kate grabs a shovel resting against a nearby oak and digs up the blistered eight-by-ten of fifteen-year-old Em receiving her All-Around Cowgirl buckle at the National High School Rodeo Finals in New Mexico. The picture had hung in the hall with a dozen others that proved Em had once been happy. Had once buried secrets so deep that she was able to accomplish what most would consider an above-average life.

After evaluating what is left of the image, something severs inside Kate. That familiar urge to drown herself in guilt and regret is losing its grip. She drops the photo onto a wall of rubble when the insurance adjuster arrives. Kate steps out of the muck and greets her with a wave. The greasy-faced girl makes her way to Kate and lacks any resemblance of a personality. The girl steps away from Hank as he sniffs her black Crocs.

"You afraid of dogs?"

"No," the girl answers, uncapping the lens on her camera. Her expressionless face reveals nothing.

"How come they sent you to take more pictures?"

The adjuster lifts her flabby arm and camera toward her eye. "Your policy does not cover intentional loss." The camera snapping at the ruins.

"What's intentional loss?"

"Arson."

"But it wasn't intentional. I didn't do *this*." Kate's irritation growing fast.

"Your daughter is listed on your declarations page." She lowers the camera, looks over Kate's shoulder. "The loss may not arise from a spouse, a child, or any family member."

"So, after paying you for over twenty years, I'm not covered?" Kate smiles in disbelief at the girl.

"A claims agent will contact you." Sweat fills the folds of her plus-size neck.

"You sorry sons a bitches. Get the hell outta here." Kate grabs the shovel as the girl looks at her but doesn't speak. "If I don't have insurance, then you're trespassin'."

"I have to photograph all existing structures."

"Get! Now!"

The girl toddles up the drive and crowds into her fuel-efficient car. Old Hank follows Kate around to where the back porch once stood. All proof of a well-tended rose garden is gone, but an uninjured statue of the Virgin Mary waits with lifted hands. After she killed Will, Kate couldn't bear the two-foot statue's judgmental stare and shoved it deep into the thorny bushes. Without a second thought, Kate kicks the statue over on the way to the truck. Mary's head breaks off.

With a hefty grunt, Kate lifts Hank into the truck and shuts the door. Instantly, he hangs his head and tongue out the window and seems to smile as Kate climbs in. All at once, the engine, air-conditioning, and radio blast. As if on cue, Gloria Gaynor rattles the speakers, claiming she will survive. "I will survive hey, hey!" Kate kills the radio, says, "Jesus Christ," and leaves the ranch.

By the time her cell phone has a decent signal, three voice mails wait. The first, from Detective Rocha confirming he understood Kate's unique circumstances and would request she be allowed to leave the county for an extended period. He also hinted at the prospect of prosecuting her on the grounds of aiding and abetting. Obstruction of justice wasn't off the table either. The second message is from an attorney named Conner Malloy who claims he represents Patrick Callahan's estate and could she contact him at her earliest convenience. The third message causes Kate to pull off to the side of the road.

"Kate, it's Maureen. I have excellent news. Em is lucid and would like to see you. I'm not certain it will last. Her memory is limited, I suggest you do not delay. Also, I've scheduled an appointment for you on Monday at two fifteen."

Kate couldn't return Maureen's call fast enough. Of course, it went to voice mail. "Hi! It's Kate. I see you called yesterday, but I just got your message. I'll be there in about two hours. It's one now. Thanks—nice to get some good news for a change."

"Help him. Help him. Help him." Em's fingers gently trace the tiny bumps on the plastered white wall in front of her. She stares through bandaged eyes and cocks her head as if to listen to an imaginary friend inside the wall. Shared secrets are indistinct and repetitive as Kate watches the video-recorded scene on a monitor in Maureen's office.

"What the hell's she sayin'?" Kate asks.

"She was catatonic. The rhetoric is called logorrhea. She will go on mumbling for hours without moving away from the wall."

"But her leg, where I shot her. She's standing on it. Doesn't it hurt?"

"While in this state, she does not feel pain."

Kate leans into the monitor, still wanting to make sense of the jumbled words. Only "help him, help him, help him, rim, dim, whim, gym" is audible.

"When was this?"

"Five days ago." Maureen presses another thumbnail at the bottom of the screen and jumps ahead to a new scene. "But as medication and intensive therapy are applied, we began to see improvement." Maureen presses play, and pudgy fingers with hairy knuckles carefully remove Em's bandages from her eyes. The scabby and swollen burns cause Kate to twist in her chair.

Em doesn't move, doesn't say a word, as the camera focuses on her closed eyes. "Open your eyes, Emma Lee," a man's voice instructs.

"That is Dr. Barker," Maureen says.

"Emma Lee, please *open your eyes*!" he demands.

Suddenly, Em rubs her eyes as if she's just woken up but doesn't open them. "Keep your eyes shut, don't look, book, crook, hook."

Kate turns away. "What's the point, Maureen?"

"You should understand that there will consistently be progress and setbacks. Don't be discouraged because Em was only lucid for a short while."

"Discouraged?" Kate considers the word. "Give me a break."

"Keep your eyes shut, don't look," Em's voice whispers.

"Em, open your eyes!" Maureen's voice snaps, and Kate looks back at the monitor. Em opens her eyes. The camera zooms into her blue eyes hidden behind gray clouds.

"Is she blind?" Kate asks.

"She can see light, and that is very encouraging. Dr. Barker believes it is possible that she may eventually regain her sight. Also, her leg has maintained most of its integrity."

"How's the baby?"

Maureen closes the screen. "Dr. White did an ultrasound and a few other tests, and they are amazingly healthy—both of them."

Kate takes a minute. Takes it in. "Both of them? You mean *twins*?"

"Yes." Maureen allows a seldom-seen grin to crack her face.

Both of them. The words echo and blend all that is right and wrong with the world. Traffic crawls into the city, and Kate is glad. Heavy traffic offers Kate time to digest the fact that Em is having twins. Doubling the opportunity for failure. At an intersection, Kate rolls her window down. Fog and an undeniable scent of urine permeate the air and scour pessimism from her mind. Homeless fill the streets, sidewalks, and underpasses. Kate wonders how she'd fare on the streets at night. Pissing in doorways. The light turns green, and vehicles lunge like cattle through an open gate. At the next red light, a slender mom with a jogging stroller strides past Kate. Fantasies of pushing the babies through Golden Gate Park, kissing twenty baby toes, four chubby toddler arms reaching up for her after a skinned knee, two baby-bird mouths open wide and waiting to be fed. Redemption twice as nice.

THIRTY-TWO

Monday morning shakes Kate awake with a 4.3 magnitude earthquake. In the realm between conscious and not, Kate is lost. The blue walls feel cold and metallic, mysterious. When she sits up in bed, the familiar squeak is absent and immediately spurs a hesitation to rise. Barking dogs keep rhythm with car alarms. Old Hank at her feet. This is Patrick's house, his guest room. Then, she remembers that ignoring earthquakes was part of her San Francisco childhood.

Two aftershocks hit before Kate can dress and get Hank off the bed and outside. A siren overrides the car alarms now squawking up and down the block. An ambulance slows. The driver looks at Kate as if to say: *Do you need an ambulance?* While Hank craps on the shiny onyx stones smothering life out of the yard.

"Hey!" A man in a short robe waves from the sidewalk and the ambulance stops next door. His three-story house of glass reflects the spinning red lights. *Wonder if they knew Patrick? Were they friends? If they knew Patrick, they were friends.* He had that way of connecting with people no matter their social status or ethnicity. He was the guy that everyone instantly liked because he made them feel important. And even if it'd been years, people remembered him. *Does he know Patrick is dead?* She should tell him, but now is not the time. Now, she hopes the incident requiring an ambulance isn't life threatening and retreats to the kitchen with Hank.

Marble floors and counters are spotless and accentuates the click-clack of Hank's nails as he walks with a hitch in his hip to the water bowl. Kate still hasn't conquered the Keurig Pro one-cup coffee maker next to the sink. Instead, she empties the grounds from a single serving pod into a mug and adds boiling water from a teakettle.

At eight o'clock, Kate dials the number left by Connor Malloy, attorney at law. Normal business hours are ten a.m. to five p.m. says a lyrical voice that has had plenty of sleep. Must be nice to have such soft working hours. Kate leaves a message. Considers calling Rocha. She knows she should but decides he can wait. Why ruin the day so early on? Coffee grounds settle to the bottom of the mug, and Kate sips just as the doorbell rings.

Through the peephole, she sees the back of an old woman's head. Her hair coiffed in loose white curls. Black slacks and tweed blazer. Kate can almost smell the Chanel seeping through the door and see the constant smirk on her mother's face even before she turns and rings the bell five more times. Her entire face sags now and wrinkles have flourished. No longer resembling the coldhearted, judgmental bitch, just a feeble old woman with a four-legged cane.

"Katherine! That ridiculous pickup truck of yours is tainting the front of your brother's house. The entire neighborhood for that matter. Regardless, I know you're in there. I have a key."

Kate opens the door. "Then why didn't you use it?"

"I've misplaced it." Kate's mother does not walk like an eighty-year-old woman with a cane. Her stride is that of a thoroughbred as she moves past Kate and into the kitchen.

"What do you want, Shannon?" Kate asks.

"Coffee. Then the details of my son's death if you don't mind."

"You won't like either one."

"I don't expect to." Shannon crosses her arms and leans against the counter.

Kate sighs. Knows accommodating her mother will be easier and less time consuming than not. "I can't work that contraption." Kate points at the stainless-steel Keurig coffee maker.

The smirk comes with a slight snicker as Shannon manhandles a pod into the Keurig and slams the handle down. She rams the brew button with her apricot-polished thumbnail, then pulls one mug from the cupboard. In less than a minute, she's back in position against the counter with her arms crossed. "You look old, Katherine," Shannon releases with an unearned Irish brogue.

"So do you." They grin.

Atop a tripod, a tiny red light on a video camera blinks like a warning. In the corner of her office, Maureen presses the record button and the light turns green.

"I have the right. Prissy told me. I have rights." Em crosses her slippered feet and tucks them under her chair. She scratches at a bit of remaining scab on the outer corner of her eye.

"Yes"—Maureen sits and rolls her chair closer to her desk— "you do. I gave you a Patient Rights handbook. Remember?"

"I have the right to telephone access and unopened mail, writing material, and stamps." Em looks at the wall to her left.

"Of course. Is there someone—"

"I want to call my dad."

Maureen can't hide the disappointment on her face and looks away from the camera. "Emma Lee, your father is . . ." She hesitates as Em begins to rock back and forth. "What's his number? I'll dial it for you." Maureen lifts the receiver from her desk phone.

"Two-oh-nine. Seven-three-six. Two-one-nine-one." Em scratches at the top of her hand.

Maureen waits for a connection. "It's ringing." Em reaches for the phone. "I'd like to speak to your father. I'll put him on speakerphone." Maureen presses a button and a loud ring vibrates the speaker.

After a second ring, Em wipes her eyes with her thumb. "He won't like that."

"Hello? Jumping Frog Motel." A raspy voice waits on the line. Maureen leans forward onto her desk and steeples her fingers. "Hello? Jumping Frog Motel, this is Amy."

Em rubs her eyes and shakes her heads. "Wrong number. You dialed the wrong number!" She stands, her body rigid, fists pressing into her thighs. Staring at a blur that must be Maureen.

"I'm sorry, Emma Lee. Do you want to dial it?" Maureen offers Em the receiver.

"Can't see the numbers, stupid." Em swipes at the phone in Maureen's hand but misses. "Twenty-seven pages of detailed rights."

"Emma Lee, please sit down.

"Right to social activity, recreation, and exercise. Right to education. Right to practice freedom of religion. I want to see a priest."

"If you sit down, we can talk about it."

Em sits, rubs her eyes. "When my dad finds out about this—"

"Em, your conscious mind is not in control of how you are thinking or behaving. Your mother killed your father while he was raping you. You are repressing these memories. Blocking them because they are unacceptable to you." Maureen stands and slaps her hand on her desk, clearly frustrated. "We must find the strength to accept the truth and what we have done!" She stares at Em until tears tumble onto her desk. "We must attempt an undoing of our unconscious behavior by asking for forgiveness."

At exactly ten a.m., the phone rings and saves Kate from more of Shannon's damning testimony over Pat's death.

"Hello?" Kate walks out of the kitchen and down the hall with her cell to her ear.

"Hi. Ms. Dunnigan?"

"Yes."

"This is Brian Cormac. I'm Mr. Malloy's assistant. I'm calling to set up an appointment to go over Patrick Callahan's estate."

"Oh. Okay."

"Mr. Malloy has appointments this morning"—there's a long pause—"but I see here he has an appointment with Mrs. Beverly Callahan and Ms. Shannon Callahan at eleven thirty. It would work well to include you in the reading if you're available."

"Yeah. Sure, I'm available."

"Great. Eleven thirty. Do you know where we're located?"

"I'm sure Shannon Callahan does. Thanks." Kate returns to the kitchen to find Shannon pretending to be searching for something in the fridge, since it put her within earshot of the conversation. "Hungry?"

"This food is rancid. You need to clean the refrigerator, Kathrine. Who were you talking to?"

"Patrick's attorney. Well, the assistant."

"Why?" Shannon shuts the stainless-steel door, her full attention on Kate.

"Because we have an appointment at eleven thirty."

"I've an appointment." Shannon's brogue building with her irritation. "You've nothing to do with it."

"I've been invited by Mr. Malloy. You wanna ride over?"

"I have a driver."

"Well, then, I'll ride with you."

"Grand." Shannon glares at Kate's old dog lying on the cool tile. "Do you have something decent to wear?"

Beverly Callahan's biker boots thump across the polished marble floor. She places herself on the edge of a leather chair in Malloy and Associates' lobby. Her leather pants groan against the chair as she crosses her legs. "Hello, Shannon, how are you?"

"Thought you were in Paris?" Shannon never takes her eyes off the *People* magazine in her hands.

"I was until Conner contacted me and informed me of Pat's death. You could have called me out of respect for your son. I was his wife."

"You could have stayed committed to your marriage out of respect for yourself, not to mention Patrick." Her eyes still on the page. The brogue growing with each word. "Respect. Jesus, Mary, and Joseph, as if you know the meaning of the word. Degenerate."

Kate tenses, unaccustomed to someone else being the subject of her mother's condemnation, and brushes nothing off her pant leg. Beverly makes eye contact. "I'm Kate. Pat's sister." Kate stands—pressing her sweaty palms into the side of her thighs.

"Nice to meet you, Kate." Beverly stands, and professionally holds out her hand. Kate takes it, but quickly releases it. Recalling the pain that Beverly caused Pat.

"Mr. Malloy is ready for you." The receptionist with a well-trimmed beard steps out from behind a tall desk and opens the door for the women.

Alarms sound as heavy doors swing open. Manny and an assistant, who appears barely old enough to drive or big enough to see over the steering wheel, drag Em into a dark room. The relief from the bright lights and the hint of rubbing alcohol encourages her to put up a good fight. A scream smothered in dread escapes her as she jerks and twists and pulls to free herself from the demon claws. Maureen flips on a small light that hangs above a bed—a white cotton sheet and wide leather straps tucked neatly and ready for Em to resist. Manny and the kid lift Em onto the bed, but the kid loses his grip and Em breaks free. Maureen locks the door.

"Emma Lee, take a deep breath." Maureen steps toward her. "Calm yourself and focus on breathing." Manny moves behind Em, and the kid is ready. But, before anyone can get a grip on her, Em lunges at the blurry devil near the door. Her nails dig deep, tearing into flesh. Maureen screams and folds herself into a ball on the floor as Manny and the kid snatch Em's arms. They toss her like a rag doll onto the bed. Her head bounces and hair sticks to her sweaty face to spite the frantic head shaking.

Maureen is up and cinching a chest strap over the deranged patient while Manny cuffs Em's right arm. He shoves the kid aside while he works on the left arm. Em's flip-flops take flight as she thrashes her unbound legs. The kid attempts to wrestle and pin Em's legs, but one quick jerk and a kick sends him flying into the wall.

Manny moves in with the precision of a ninja nurse. Kneeling, he keeps his head down and reaches up to catch an ankle, then launches himself. All 265 pounds of Manny lying on her legs, and Em is done. Maureen straps both ankles while Em howls like a sick coyote.

"You okay, Miss Maureen?" Manny asks.

Maureen touches her cheek and looks at the blood on her

fingers. "She's getting worse. She should be getting better, but she's not. Something is missing." She sighs and pulls a handful of tissues from a box on the counter. Two for her, the rest for new kid's bloody nose. "I'll call Dr. White before we sedate her again. I want an MRI ASAP." She presses the tissues against her bleeding cheek.

From behind his desk, Conner Malloy hands Shannon a box of tissue. "I'm sorry for your loss, Ms. Callahan, but these are Patrick's wishes. I wrote them. It is *not* a mistake. May I finish reading the entire testament?" Conner Malloy waits for Shannon's permission to continue.

"No." Shannon pulls a tissue and dabs a tear from her eye. "Send a complete copy to my attorney at Brown and Vickers."

"Of course." Conner Malloy leans back in his ergonomic chair and runs his fingers through thick gravel-colored hair. "Should I do the same for you, Mrs. Callahan?" He looks at Beverly, who hasn't said a word. Hasn't reacted whatsoever to the news that Patrick Callahan's entire estate was left to Katherine Callahan Dunnigan and Emma Lee Dunnigan Quick.

"I'm gonna get some water." Kate stands and goes for the door.

"There's water in the fridge. Here." Conner Malloy goes to a refrigerator disguised as a cabinet and hands Kate a bottle of water.

"Thanks." Kate gulps and guzzles. "Let me get this straight. I get Pat's house, his savings, his car. And, Beverly gets nothing? I don't understand?"

"There was a prenuptial agreement. The house was purchased solely by Mr. Callahan. When Mrs. Callahan left the home, Mr. Callahan indicated he wished to revise his estate. There are stocks, bonds, investments, and incidentals such as jewelry and four syndicated racehorses that will be transferred to you." Conner Malloy flips the pages of Patrick's last will and testament. "Mr. Callahan also arranged for the activation of a trust in which Emma Lee Dunnigan Quick is the sole beneficiary."

Shannon snatches up her cane. Props herself up from her chair, and walks out. Beverly recrosses her legs in the opposite direction. "I'll arrange to get my things from the house as soon as possible." Beverly looks at Kate.

"You don't have to do that."

"Yes. I do." Beverly grins. "I'll see you soon, Kate. Thank you, Conner." Beverly walks out.

Kate steps up to Conner Malloy's desk. "I need a family attorney. Can you help me get the best lawyer possible? One who knows all about guardianship? My daughter is in serious trouble."

"What kind of trouble?"

THIRTY-THREE

A heartbeat flutters. Filling the room with the echo of life underwater. "The risk of *not* medicating her far outweighs the risk of antipsychotics affecting the fetuses." Dr. White plows the handheld ultrasound through a glob of gel on Em's belly until she finds the second heartbeat. "I'm concerned that the bpms are slightly higher than normal." She adjusts the monitor as Em squirms against her restraints. "Also, please note, I'd like to track and increase mom's caloric intake. These little guys are underweight."

"I'll start her on two milligrams of risperidone and supplements three times a day." Maureen writes on Em's chart without looking up.

"Where's my mom?" Em sounds like a little girl. "I want my mom."

"Okay, Emma Lee. I'll contact your mother and have her come for a visit if you rest and remain calm. Can you do that for me please?"

After two hours of fighting traffic, Kate checks in with the receptionist at the Coastside Clinic. "I'll let her know you're here." The young woman dials the desk phone as Kate finds a seat, but before she can choose a magazine, Maureen arrives with her scratched face.

"Hello, Kate."

"What the hell happened to you?"

"A mishap with one of my patients. Emma Lee is lucid and asking for you. I think this is a good time to see her." Kate follows Maureen onto the elevator. "Try not to stress her in any way. Allow Emma Lee to direct the conversation, and if she does not want to talk, please do not attempt to force her."

"Okay." Kate pulls a half-eaten roll of generic antacids from her jean's pocket. "When you say lucid—you mean she knows what's going on? Knows what she did?" Kate pops four remaining antacids into her mouth and stuffs the wrapper back into her jeans.

"No. She has yet to recall certain events. But there may be a very good reason why. We can discuss it after you see Emma Lee." Maureen presses the second-floor button and the door closes.

Em's room no longer has the hotel-suite vibe. A simple ten-by-twelve room with walls covered in baby blue and nothing other than a twin memory-foam mattress on a wood base, since metal springs allow for creative thinking.

Maureen taps Em's door and pokes her head in. "Emma Lee? Someone is here to see you."

Em wakes and slowly sits up as Kate waits at the doorway.

"It's Mom, can I come in?"

"Mom?" Em holds one of her sedated arms out since the

other is strapped down, and Kate rushes over. All sins redacted by maternal love. Kate cradles Em's head and rocks her slightly. "I love you, Mom."

"I love you, sweetie."

"Maureen said Dad—"

Kate wipes the tears running down Em's face and looks at Maureen for permission and gets an approving nod.

"Your dad was a very damaged person." Kate holds Em's face in her hands and looks into her cloudy eyes. So much to say, but where to start? "I love you is all that matters. I always have and I always will."

"I love you too," Em whispers and drops her head on Kate's shoulder. "Why can't I remember?" Kate strokes Em's hair and looks at Maureen for guidance.

Maureen steps closer. "I'd like to conduct intense psycho-dynamic therapy. In most circumstances, I would conduct this therapy involving only the patient, but in this case, I'd like to include you, Kate."

"When?"

"Emma Lee seems to do well in the morning. Say, nine a.m. tomorrow?"

"Of course. Does that fit your schedule, sweetie?" Kate's sarcastic grin as familiar and comforting as old sweats.

Em shares a laugh that seems like it hasn't been heard in years. "Wait, what day is tomorrow?"

"Tuesday," Maureen and Kate answer.

"I can't, I have to work." Em looks serious. Kate looks at Maureen. For an awkward moment, no one breathes. "Just kidding."

"Jeez." Kate breathes a sigh of relief, but Maureen fails to find humor in the situation.

"Wonder what everyone at work thinks?" Em asks.

"Who cares. Don't worry about that." Kate squeezes Em's hand and notices the bruises left on her wrist from the restraints. Growls bellow from Em's belly.

"Whoa." Em smiles. "Guess it's time to feed these boys."

"Good!" Maureen perks up. "I'll bring your dinner. Would you like to eat, Kate?"

"If you have enough. I'm starving."

"We have more than enough." Maureen shuts the door behind her as she leaves, and Em leans back against her pillow.

"They're really growin'," Kate says as she rubs Em's belly.

"Dr. White says they're underweight. I have to eat more."

"How's the food here? I can bring you whatever you want. A Whopper with extra cheese?" Kate grins, knowing that that was Em's favorite while they were on the rodeo trail together.

Em closes her eyes. "The food here is fine."

"Tired?"

"I think it's the medication. Probably why I can't remember anything."

After a poached salmon dinner with roasted carrots, jasmine rice, and conversation that included reliving the calving incident with Maureen, Kate kisses Em good night and makes her way to Maureen's office packing an extra helping of hope. She takes a seat on an overstuffed couch. "Are you familiar with the term *delirium*?" Maureen asks from behind her desk.

"I've heard of it, don't really know what it is, though."

"Delirium has waxing and waning psychotic symptoms. A delirious person may be acutely psychotic for part of the day, then perfectly clear the rest. Such as in Emma Lee's case."

Kate crosses her legs and clasps her hands around her knee.

"Knowing Emma Lee's situation and history, I focused solely on her illness being psychological. Regrettably, I overlooked several telltale symptoms. Delirium is caused by a physical illness, but it creates dramatic mental symptoms. There are a variety of causes, with brain tumors being the most common. And the most logical." Maureen seems down. No longer her usual perky and positive-everything-will-work-out self.

Kate uncrosses her legs and leans on her knees, wishing Maureen would get to the point and stop fiddling with the pen in her hand.

"I ran several tests today, including an MRI on Emma Lee's brain. The results revealed a tumor pressing on the temporal lobe."

"A tumor? You got to be *kidding* me." She leans forward and drops her head on her knees, knowing the news should devastate her. It doesn't. Maybe the antidepressants are doing their job. Maybe there's just so much shit a person can take before they quit and go numb. Like some of those ill-broke tough horses that would throw themselves down and close their eyes, shutting the entire world out. Kate wondered where those misfit horses went in their minds, and she was grateful to be numb. Wished she could throw herself down right here and now. Just close her eyes and make the world go away.

"I realize this sounds detrimental, but I suspect we are dealing with a meningiomas tumor. They are common and grow dramatically in pregnant women due to changing hormone levels. If you consider the possibility of correcting Em's psychotic behavior with the removal of the tumor, she stands a very good chance of recovery or, at the very least, responding well to therapy and medication."

Kate sits up. "They can do surgery? With her being pregnant and all?"

"I've contacted a specialist. A highly regarded neurologist. Any surgery done under anesthesia during pregnancy creates a risk to the fetus. But being well into her second trimester lessens that risk."

"Poor Em. Maybe she ain't crazy after all, but this—all this—is completely fucking crazy." Then, after taking a breath, it hits her. *Maybe it's not all my fault.*

"We cannot assume that the tumor is the absolute cause of Emma Lee's psychotic behavior. It is only a possibility at this point, but it is a very *good* possibility." Maureen takes a breath and straightens her back. "I cannot tell you how sorry I am for my incompetence, Kate. I am going to put a team together. I have contacted two other psychiatrists and—"

Kate walks over to Maureen and bends over. Planting a long, hard, uncomfortable hug on her. "Without you, Em would be dead or in prison. You've given us a chance at some sort of life."

Kate releases her and sees tears filling Maureen's eyes. Tears of guilt that Kate is all too familiar with. "Let's get some coffee—or whatever four-worded specialty drink you like."

"I really shouldn't. If anyone were to see us, it would be a blatant boundary violation, of which, in this case, I have committed too many to count already."

"Pat has this awful coffee machine, you probably know how to work it. It makes all those fancy drinks, but—"

"I can't. I appreciate the offer, but I have hours of paperwork to complete."

"I don't have any friends left, Maureen." It should be a painful confession, but it isn't. "No one to talk to at all. Should I just find a bar? Is that what lonely people do?"

"I don't recommend it." Maureen stands and gathers a stack of files. "Go home and get a good night's sleep. You'll feel better in the morning. I promise."

"Good night."

Kate's hood is up on her truck as Maureen crosses the small parking lot and unlocks her Prius with her key fab. "Maureen!" Kate rushes after her, catching up just as she opens her door. "My truck won't start."

Maureen looks over at the incongruous heap. "Would you like me to call a tow truck?"

"Can you just give me a ride home? Please?"

The silence of the Prius and low-volume talk radio allow Kate to force casual conversation on Maureen. "I forgot how cold summer is here."

"Yes."

Kate looks out the window toward the lights of the Golden Gate. "It really is beautiful. As a kid, I never noticed." Kate smiles at Maureen as she slows for traffic. "You grow up here?"

"Massachusetts, until I was eighteen. Moved here to go to school."

"That when you met Pat?"

"Yes."

"He was a lot a fun. 'Til he married the Wicked Witch of the West." Kate smirks.

"Yes." Maureen nods.

Kate undoes her loose side braid and brings all the stray hair back around. "Pat got his driver's license the day he turned sixteen. Drove us everywhere. My dad hated to drive and always picked on my mother whenever she drove. So, Pat was the family chauffeur. Dad would doze off after about ten minutes in the passenger seat. Every time he did, Pat would slam the brakes and scream as if we were about to die. Dad would yell and smack him upside the head. Pat always swore there was a squirrel, or a cat, or some critter in the road, but kept his fingers crossed." Kate laughs as she braids her hair.

"That sounds like something he would do." After a minute, Maureen glances at Kate. "When we were at school, we were always broke. Pat went around the nicer neighborhoods collecting food for the homeless. In a few hours, he'd have boxes of food. I don't think we bought groceries for an entire semester. I know it's awful, but . . ."

Maureen confesses with a smile.

"Partners in crime." Kate smiles.

"Years ago, we were reminiscing about it and decided to donate five thousand dollars each to a shelter in the Mission District."

"He always had to make things right. Always went out of his way to help anyone who needed it."

Maureen guns the engine. It whines, climbing the curves up Nob Hill. "He saved my life."

"How's that?" Kate asks.

"Oh, it was a long time ago and not something— I'd rather not."

Kate watches Maureen's index finger tap the gear shift. "Is that why you're helping us?"

Maureen bites her upper lip as she pulls into Pat's driveway. "I hadn't analyzed it, but perhaps, partially."

"Well, I'm grateful." Kate squeezes Maureen's arm, but Maureen looks straight ahead. "I met with Pat's attorney today. I'd really like to tell you what happened. I still can't believe it myself. Can you come in for twenty minutes?"

"Kate, I really can't."

In the kitchen, Pat's wine collection is vast, and Kate pops the cork on a bottle of pinot noir. Scents of fermented rose and plumb escape as she lets the wine trickle into a glass, then fills another.

"I certainly do not mean to be offensive, but do you realize that that is a five-hundred-dollar bottle of pinot?" Maureen asks.

"Better be damn good, then." She hands a glass to Maureen and offers a toast. "To friendship."

Maureen drinks. "Oh, this is exceptional." She swirls the wine in her glass.

"Pretty dang tasty." Kate clicks her tongue as she grabs the bottle and follows Maureen into the living room.

"Did you know Pat and Beverly had a prenuptial agreement?"

"Yes. I suggested it."

"Oh." Kate's impressed. "Did you know Pat left everything to me and Em?"

"He mentioned that he was considering it."

"Well, he did more than consider it."

"Good. That will allow you to hire a qualified family attorney and assist with your living arrangements."

"Yeah. Maybe a way around this mess."

"You have handled the situation better than most." Maureen takes a sip and watches the legs slide down the glass.

"Is that your professional opinion?"

"Yes."

Kate laughs. "God, Maureen."

"What?"

"You're so . . . therapeutic."

"Perhaps." Maureen sips her wine. "I don't intend to be cold."

"You're not cold. Exactly the opposite." The wine warms Kate. "We all have our own shit piles—I suspect you're no exception."

Maureen nods her head and takes another sip. "Perhaps

I haven't buried my *pile* as well as I thought I had."

"Shit piles shrink a lot faster with two people diggin' at 'em."

"Pat was that person for me. You very much remind me of him. You have his tenacity—his mannerisms. You attempt to conceal your kindness with cynicism."

"You loved him," Kate blurts the instant she realizes.

"I did. But there are some things that are more important than love." Maureen lets go of a tear.

"Like what?"

Maureen sets her glass down. "Thank you for the wine and the company, I will see you in the morning. nine a.m. Don't forget to allow for traffic."

Kate walks Maureen to the door. "How about dinner tomorrow night. I'd love to have someone to cook for."

"I don't eat meat."

"I'll barbecue broccoli. Cauliflower? Whatever you like?"

Maureen laughs. She has a good laugh, not too loud, not too soft. "It's difficult for me to make plans—I never know how my day will go or when it will end.

"Okay. See you in the morning."

"What will you do about your pickup truck?"

"I'll figure it out. I got money now, I can take a cab."

Maureen tightens her face, then her shawl "There isn't anything wrong with your pickup truck, is there?"

Kate smiles and confesses with a slight head shake.

"You are quite intriguing, Katherine. Good night."

"Good night." Kate forces another hug on Maureen before she can refuse.

THIRTY-FOUR

Kate had never noticed the beauty of the stained-glass window above the reception desk at the Coastside Clinic. This morning, the sunshine is brighter and illuminates the glass like a beacon as she waits to check in. She sips a dark roast from the Coffee Bean down the street where the taxi dropped her off and realizes how grateful she is for the tinge of hope she now has. When your head is being squeezed in a vise, the slightest release of pressure is appreciated.

"Hello, Ms. Dunnigan."

Kate turns to see Detective Rocha rise from his seat in the waiting area. *Shit.*

"You haven't returned my calls."

"I was going to call you today. Right after my visit here." Kate forces a smile.

"Forensics concluded their testing on your husband. We have the coroner's report and I have to arrest you."

"Now? Here?"

"Yes, I'm sorry. Do you have a lawyer you can call?"

Maureen strolls into the waiting room. Sees the panic on Kate. "What is going on?"

"Maureen, this is Detective Ray Rocha. He's arresting me." She wants to run back outside, back into the fresh air and sunshine. Back to where moments ago the day was still good.

"Nice to put a face to the name," Rocha says, inspecting Maureen.

"Yes." Maureen doesn't smile either. "You are aware of her situation, correct? Emma Lee is in treatment and has made tremendous progress."

"Good." Rocha hands Maureen an envelope. "According to California State Law, your patient's stay here is almost over. Officers will bring her into custody by the end of the week."

"This Friday?" Kate panics.

Maureen opens the envelope and skims the three-page document. "I'll call Connor Malloy, tell him what has happened. He'll refer you to a competent defense lawyer."

"Would you like to step outside, Ms. Dunnigan? We have to proceed with the arrest."

"What about Em?" Kate asks Maureen. "How will I know what the doctor says?"

"You can make phone calls." Rocha takes Kate's arm and assists her to the door.

"Hank," Kate says to Maureen. "He's at the house."

"I'll take care of it."

"You need my key."

"I have one," Maureen says as Rocha escorts Kate outside. Doors slide closed behind them.

The back seat of Rocha's unmarked sedan smells like cigarettes and Lysol.

"I know a good attorney in San Andreas. Probably cost a lot less than one from San Francisco."

"Probably not a smart move to trust the advice of someone who wants me in jail."

"I don't *want* you in jail. This is protocol. That's all."

"My daughter has a brain tumor. It could be what made her—act out."

"Never heard of a tumor forcing someone to kill people. Might be difficult to prove, even with a San Francisco attorney."

"She's sick. She needs treatment, not prison."

"So do over half the inmates. Unfortunately, it's hard to prove insanity and get sent to a state hospital. There's just no room."

"But she's already in a facility. A good one, where they can take care of her. Why force her into prison *or* a state hospital?"

"Because that's how our system works. If not, every criminal with money would run to a psychiatric unit and act crazy in order to avoid prosecution."

"Put psychiatric units in prisons. Separate the mentally ill from the rest, so they can get help."

Rocha thinks. "Look, everything comes down to money. State and federal prisons are bad business. But, I'll vote for you if you run for governor. Newsom's a real asshat."

After a two-thousand-calorie breakfast of French toast, eggs, and bacon, a muscular nurse's aide escorts Em to Maureen's office.

"Hello, hello." A short man in his sixties springs off the couch and holds his hand out to Em.

"I'm Dr. Sanchez." He smiles and takes Em's hand. "Very glad to meet you."

"Nice meeting you." She tries not to panic but wonders who he is and why he's here.

"Dr. Sanchez is a neurologist. Have a seat," Maureen says, and Em lowers herself gently onto the couch. "Do you remember when you went in the MRI machine and we scanned images of your brain?"

"Yeah. That was yesterday."

"Well, Dr. Sanchez is who interpreted the results for us." Maureen's voice slows and softens as she sits on the edge of her desk. Em rubs her palms down her thighs and blinks, still trying to clear the blur from her eyes and not panic.

"That is correct," Dr. Sanchez says like someone just won a prize. "And, the results of your MRI revealed an abnormal growth of tissue."

Em turns to Maureen for an explanation. "Like cancer?"

"No. Not necessarily. The tumor doesn't appear to be malignant, but we cannot confirm that until removing it." Dr. Sanchez sits on the sofa opposite Em and crosses his short legs. "I've spoken with your OB, Dr."—he flips through his file—"White. She feels that surgery, while not without risk, validates removal of the growth. She agrees that we move forward with the procedure, as do I."

"Em, we all agree that surgery is the best option. Quite possibly, the tumor could be a cause of some of your mental issues."

"You mean—I might not be crazy?"

"You are not crazy. Your mind is sick, and removing the tumor might allow a certain degree of recovery."

"How soon can we do it?" asks Em.

From the prison pay phone, Kate tries to ignore the girl waiting next in line for the phone and listens. "This Friday. UCSF at seven a.m. Dr. Sanchez labeled it life threatening and it becomes a priority surgery. She will be transported from the clinic to the hospital via ambulance. There is no way they can legally prevent her from obtaining medical treatment, especially in this situation." Maureen finally takes a breath. "She can be in recovery for at least five days, maybe more. It depends if there are complications."

"Complications?" Kate switches the receiver from one ear to the other when Garcia points to her watch and holds up two fingers. Behind Kate, the impatient two-hundred-pound girl with pink and purple hair is still eyeing her. Still recrossing her arms every few seconds and cocking her head as she huffs loudly. Kate recognizes the girl as the head Hmong Tanya had warned her about. Kate ran into her old cellmate, Tanya, the minute she entered the hall to the commons. One hell of a shiner closed Tanya's left eye. "Who dotted your eye?" Kate had asked.

"Mee Chow Fun jumped me in the bathrooms. Fucking Hmong growers are taking over. They outnumber the Mexicans grows, now. I'll catch her." She explained the girl's name was Mee and she got busted for forcing her mother and grandmother to work her illegal pot farm in West Point.

"I only have a minute to talk," Kate tells Maureen. "Will you be there during the surgery, I mean, if anything goes wrong?"

"Yes. I will be there. And I will be there when she wakes."

"Hug her for me, please, Maureen. Hug her tight and don't rush to let go." Kate's voice catches.

Maureen hesitates. "Okay. I'll do it."

"Thank you."

"Have you seen your attorney?"

"I talked to his secretary yesterday. Supposed to be here before my arraignment."

"Does he feel the judge will set bail?"

"Said the odds were fifty-fifty in a county this small. I asked Rocha, and he said murders don't usually get bail unless it's special circumstances. Too many repercussions for the judge if something goes wrong. I might be in here awhile." Kate chews at a hangnail on her thumb.

"Em is in extremely qualified hands, Kate. I've also brought in a second therapist."

"Why?" She knows why, but doesn't know what else to say. She's too caught up in the fact that Maureen called Em—Em. Not Emma Lee.

"I want someone to assist with future diagnosis and treatment. Just to confirm my—"

"Times up." Garcia stands next to Kate.

"How's Hank?"

"He's fine. The girl next door comes over—"

"I have to go."

"Wait, Kate! Your mother called, Patrick's funeral will

be—" Garcia hangs up the phone.

Mee steps forward uncomfortably close to Kate. "About fucking time *mob pim*."

Kate looks at the girl and shakes her head.

"Oh, don't even mad-dog me, old bitch!"

"Make your call," Garcia says.

Kate ignores the girl and walks to the rec room where someone has left a book cart. "We allowed to get a book?" Kate asks Monkey, a lanky Hmong girl she sat with at dinner who is now lying sideways across a chair watching *Jeopardy!* Shouting the questions to the answers before the contestants.

"Yeppers, that's why they're here. I just finished *Shutter Island*. It's sooo good. You should check it out if you like twisted, crazy shit."

"Ha! Not really." Kate slides out a copy of *Lonesome Dove*. "I read this one years ago. It's really—" From out of nowhere, Mee smacks the book out of Kate's hand. Monkey jumps over the back of the chair and picks it up. Hands it to Kate. Mee slaps the book down again.

"Don't like Westerns?" Kate says as anger and fear clash inside her.

"Don't do Miss D like that," Monkey says.

"She rude. No bitch gonna be disrespecting me. Old lady got to be schooled." Mee lifts her fleshy arm and points toward the bathrooms where there is no camera and no guards. "Bring it."

"Bring what?" Kate picks the book up off the ground.

"She wants to fight you in the bathroom, Miss D." Monkey says.

"Fight me?"

Mee shoves Kate and again points to the bathroom. "Now!"

"I'm too old for this kinda—" With both hands, Kate swings the book like a bat into Mee's fat face. As the girl grabs her nose, Kate fills her fist with pink and purple hair and drags all two hundred pounds to the ground. Something snaps in Kate. Rage encouraged by a survival instinct, and before she knows it, Kate is straddling the girl, pummeling her face over and over like a cage fighter. Mee attempts to throw punches, but as soon as she removes her protective arms from her face, Kate is there, beating her like a drum and enjoying the hell out of it.

"Miss D. Miss D. Stop! Garcia's coming, stop," Monkey says, then exits as Garcia enters. The guard punches the alarm on her belt, and sirens wail, waking Kate from the hypnotic explosion of fury that comes with the release of pent-up anger. Almost like stepping off a horse, Kate dismounts the beaten girl.

Garcia and her backup lock arms with Kate. Mee rolls over and up. Clumps of pink and purple hair decorate Mee's orange jumpsuit and the floor. With a high-pitched squeal, Mee sucker punches Kate in the face. The tingling turns to pain in an instant, and Kate's nose feels like it has been smeared across her entire face. Her eyes water as she kicks in Mee's general direction, but it doesn't connect. Three more guards appear and take Mee down. Her arm severely bent behind her back while someone slaps cuffs around her full wrists.

Kate struggles to catch her breath through the blood gushing from her nose and smiles like a winning prizefighter. "I'm not takin' shit from you or anyone else!" In one simple move, a guard bangs a cold cuff around Kate's wrist. The spring-loaded arm closes quick as if this guy has had a lot of practice. He jerks Kate's free hand into the adjoining cuff and assists Garcia in walking her to the isolation unit.

The heavy door closes behind her like a jaw snapping shut. Alone in a dim seven-by-nine concrete cell, Kate sits on a moldy mat in the corner. Hugs her knees. The odor of mildew, wet cement, and her own foul scent seep through her blood-clogged nose. No food. No bedding. Wearing only the extra-large granny panties and a stained sports bra that were assigned to her when she arrived. The crime was worth the punishment, Kate decides, as she runs her tongue along the cuts her teeth left on the inside of her lips. Beating that girl felt good—like shedding a second skin that constantly caused an irritation.

In this moment, this right now, replaying the fight over and over in her head, the satisfaction is undeniable and eases the pain in her back, her swollen and busted-up knuckles that won't bend, and the throbbing that comes with a broken nose. Blood trickles into Kate's mouth, and she grabs her nose. A flash of lightning flips in her brain like a child turning a light on and off, again and again as fast as they can. The explosion of pain causes Kate to heave up the meatloaf she had for dinner and clots of blood the color of old ketchup.

With each heartbeat, she gulps a breath and then curls into the corner on the mat. Her swollen eyes shut easily. Tiny pins prick at her cheeks as her laughter reverberates off the cold walls. "Miss D." Kate likes the way it sounds and the respect it implies. "Don't mess with Miss D, that ole bitch be *crazy,*" she mutters. "Crazy," she screams. "Craaaaaazy!" To be pushing fifty and lying here in used underwear wishing she had fought this hard so many times before.

All the whys and what-ifs come rushing back at once. The weight is like water holding her down, drowning her in memories. Then, as if Pat were reaching down and pulling her from the depths of remorse, she hears him. *"You have to lance old wounds and deal with that pain. It's the only way to transcend the past and overcome it."*

She revives it all. As far back as her memories will go. Banging her cold metal leg braces against her crib. A sock monkey just out of reach. The fear and panic of drowning when, at the age of six, Dad reached down to hug her but instead lifted her over his head and flung her backward into the pool in order to teach her to swim. It was the first of many betrayals. All through the night attempting to pinpoint the exact moment her life went wrong. Moaning Cavern continues to writhe through her mind like a parasite. Back when she went from being Katherine to becoming Katie. Over and over again, the memory punctures her intent to move forward. She decides to deal with it—*lance* the recollection wide open. Determined to escape this prison, she dives headfirst down the rabbit hole.

PART FOUR

THIRTY-FIVE

November 1983

Mist seeped through fog as Katherine pulled her Saab off the winding two lane. She ran to the edge of the bluff and looked out over an ocean of raw wilderness. Rolling hills like massive green swells brought to a halt and frozen in time. Rusted autumn leaves swirled as an intrusive wind held her back, suggesting she shouldn't jump. The stench of a rotting deer carcass made her nauseous, last night's indulgence of Grey Goose more likely the culprit.

She hardly felt it come up, but when it did, it spewed. Crashed over the red cliff and garnished the granite below. Bile blew back. Caught in the tangles of her over-permed hair as she shivered and gasped for her next breath. All alone on the side of the road. Not a single car had passed. How long would it be before someone came along? Stopped? Noticed she was gone?

She stepped forward, allowed her toes to cross the precipice. The next little step was the hardest. She imagined the fall. One, maybe two, hard slaps against the rock below. Savoring the momentary sting. Bleeding out. The futile last-minute will to survive, then the acceptance of that peaceful deep, dark sleep. Pain had chewed her up and swallowed. A burning in her throat forced a cough, then a sick laugh that was anything but funny. *Miserable little rich bitch. Such a cliché. A pathetic, overweight cliché.* Jumping would put an end to the constant haunting of the attack and, worse, disbelieving parents. It was the rape that resulted in an abortion nine months ago that kept the bleeding wound from healing. Kept her from leaving her dorm and not showering for up to two weeks.

Eye contact with mirrors was avoided, as was contact with her few remaining friends. Mother called it a phase, but Father put his foot down when he noticed Katherine's weight gain. The psychiatrist probably thought he was enlightening her when he explained how the trauma of sexual abuse often manifests through a preoccupation with food, and that gaining weight was a subconscious desire to become less noticeable. "*Duh.*" Katherine had glanced up at Dr. Sullivan for the first time in four sessions, then quickly averted her eyes.

"I've had it!" Father, better known as Judge Callahan, slammed his fist on the dining room table as the family shared Sunday dinner. "I'm not paying for school if you're not going to attend."

"Okay." Katherine continued to plop mashed potatoes onto her plate, then drowned them in gravy.

"I spoke to Phil at the *Chronicle*. He's got an assignment for you."

"Gee-whiz, that's great." Patrick, Katherine's older brother, looked at her—hopeful—waiting for conformation.

"I'm not qualified," Katherine said around a mouthful.

The veins on Judge Callahan's neck bulged as he set his fork down and wiped his mouth with a black cloth napkin. "If you don't take this job"—he set his hands along with the napkin on his lap—"there is a position for you at Grandpa Callahan's import business. I'm certain you're qualified to answer the telephone."

The assignment was to cover the eradication of wild cattle from the Moaning Cavern Ranch. Most of the twelve thousand acres were being subdivided, but a small section contained a massive cavern that moaned when it rained. Moaning Cavern would be open to the public by spring and making a profit by summer. The remaining herd of feral cattle, which had escaped capture year after year, had to be removed.

Editor Phil at the *San Francisco Chronicle* told Katherine that he was offering her the story due to her previous dressage experience and on the recommendation of her journalism professor at San Francisco State. Katherine knew better. There was little doubt that he owed the judge a favor.

She had never heard of Calaveras County or Moaning Cavern Ranch. Had no idea where it was located and tried not to panic or turn around when, after an hour out of San Francisco, she realized she'd forgotten the map. The gas station attendant in Jackson clicked his tongue, shook his head, and explained she'd gone the long way around. He drew her a map on a blue paper towel.

Katherine probably would have jumped if it weren't for an overheating RV that pulled up and parked behind her. She lost her nerve when the older couple got out to inspect their steaming engine and waved. Katherine stepped back from the edge and hurried to her car. She drove fast as she could, tires screaming through the curves, until Sheep Ranch, where the road was blocked by an impenetrable flock of unsheared sheep. With one road through town—Sheep Ranch Road—barbed wire on either side prevented going around. There wasn't another human in sight as Katherine honked. Sheep didn't give a shit when she punched the horn and held it down for nearly a minute. She got out of the car. Shushed them to one side of the road. But could not get back in the car before the hostile flock surrounded her again. Their bleats more like laughter. It took twenty minutes to push through the mob, and the acrid smell rode with her the rest of the trip.

The road forked just outside of Sheep Ranch, and Katherine cursed the map. Talked to herself as she wandered the back roads. "This here's hillbilly country, and we ain't got no use for gol dern street signs or fully paved roads. Fuck dividing lines, them's for city folk. How else logging trucks gonna legally run you off the fucking road?" She was lost long before she crumpled the blue paper towel map and tossed it out.

Back and forth and back and forth, the road curved so

sharply and so often it made her sick. Took almost half an hour to go eight miles. She would have turned around, went home, and explained the sincere attempt she'd made, but hadn't a clue how to get back.

Metal signs shot full of holes were strung along rusted barbed-wire fencing: *No Hunting. No Trespassing.* Katherine noticed the way the wire wrapped around trees and disappeared into their flesh but ignored the warning and pulled into a rutted drive. She stopped at a dilapidated barn where an old man worked on a tractor that looked like it wouldn't run even if he worked on it for the rest of his life. He smelled like gasoline and wore two oily ball caps. He laughed when Katherine told him she was looking for Moaning Cavern Ranch. Said she couldn't get there from here. Called her *girlie*, then drew a map in the red dirt with his grimy finger and said, "Shoulda stayed *right* at the fork."

Sheep Ranch Road dumped her out in the quaint town of Murphy's. The sun was down, and it was too dark to find Moaning Cavern. Judge Callahan's American Express bought dinner, a room with a hot shower, and a fresh start in the morning.

***

Rain had moved east, and the sun warmed the world as Katherine drove under a log entrance that read *Moaning Cavern Ranch*. A covey of quail panicked and scattered along the gravel drive. Dust trailed her as she passed a traditional ranch-style home with a *For Sale* sign. The road descended, and at the bottom sat a corrugated metal barn. Her instructions were to meet a William Dunnigan at the barn, but that was yesterday. The Saab's obnoxious brakes squeaked like a sigh of relief when Katherine pulled up and parked.

A man with caramel-colored muscles on a five-foot frame watched from inside the barn as Katherine approached. Green high-heeled boots covered his skinny legs up to his knees. He walked toward her and removed his weathered hat, revealing tufts of hair that resembled popcorn. "You dat lady gone write a story 'bout me?" His smile was extraordinarily large.

Katherine explained that the story would focus on the process of removing the wild cattle from the ranch but didn't mention that the odds were better than good that the story would never be published. Dego Sonje just smiled and nodded. Constantly nodded, and looked down more often than not, as he spoke about anything and everything.

The rhythm of his words were hypnotic. A real Creole, "dey French be dey only kind is real Creole." Katherine petted his palomino as he rambled about guiding President Reagan and his wife on a pack trip through the Grand Canyon, years before he was "dat president." He'd been in "tree films," one with John Wayne and two he couldn't remember because he still "ain't see'd 'em." The only time he was quiet and unsmiling was when he struggled to address an envelope he had filled with cash to Reverend Jimmy Swaggart. Dego insisted the minister needed the money "so real bad," and it made him feel happy down in his bones to donate half his pay since he didn't need it anyway. Already had a good horse and a custom-built saddle.

Dego's tale of being raised in a three-story whorehouse in the French Quarter was much more entertaining than the list of Pulitzer Prize winners Katherine had been reading all summer. He claimed he didn't know his "mama or papa."

"No matta, dey all my mama, and dey all loved me. You cain't never have too much love." For the first time in nine months, Katherine smiled. She envied this man who smelled like horse manure sprinkled with peppermint.

They waited almost two hours for the boss, Will Dunnigan, to arrive. Dego shared the story of meeting Will while they gathered cattle in a Louisiana swamp. Said Will was the best cowboy he'd ever seen as he filled the right side of his mouth with soft tobacco leaves until his cheek puffed to near capacity. He spit a long stream of brown juice and saddled his palomino. Katherine was about to ask him how many wild cattle he thought were on this ranch when he looked up at her and said, "Twenty-tree."

"Twenty-three what?" she asked.

"Cattle," he said, like it was the punch line to a joke and she should laugh. There was a long silence. "I been affected, I tink on my daddy's side because his mama told me in a dream. I know tings. Sometimes." He cinched his saddle. "Is just . . . comes into my head. Not always. Only sometime." It was over a full minute before Katherine realized her mouth was open.

Dego brought a short sorrel mare from her stall and tied her next to the tack room. "Dis Will's horse, but I tink is okay for you."

Katherine brushed the horse's back as Will rode up on a big gray. He didn't say a word. Just inspected the girl and rubbed his stubbled jaw with the back of his hand. He looked more like a surfer than a cowboy, with spikes of shaggy blond hair that dangled under a sweat-stained ball cap. Dego asked Will, "Is okay Miss Katrine use dis horse," in a way that sounded more like a suggestion than a question.

Will stepped off his horse without taking his eyes off Katherine.

"Katie? I'm Will. Looks like I'll be your babysitter for the next few days," he said in a raspy Australian accent. *Arrogant prick*—Katherine caught the words before they escaped. She remembered how Dr. Sullivan had explained that arrogance was a sign of low self-esteem. Then considered explaining that she'd ridden with some of the top dressage trainers in the world, that she was *not* a helpless princess. Instead, she offered her hand and a slight grin.

"I'm Katherine Callahan. Could you help me saddle this horse?" His rough hand smothered hers, and he squeezed too hard for too long. She pulled twice before he let go. He tied the gray next to the mare. A tranquilizer gun tucked in a small leather scabbard strapped to the side of Will's saddle.

"Christ, you ain't old enough to be a writer. You still in high school?"

"I attend San Francisco State."

"Now watch carefully." He looked to make sure she was watching while his words took too much time. "I'll only show ya this once." He began saddling the mare.

"What's her name?" Katherine asked.

"You never name things you might have to eat." His dark eyes reminded her of Rorschach tests.

A pack of five or six dogs ran ahead as Will rode next to Katherine and warned her about the dangers of dealing with wild cattle. His slow, menacing tone like an Australian Vincent Price.

"They're an evil lot to muster. Most renegade cattle ain't never seen a human, and they're ready for a fight if they can't run. Split your horse's belly open with a horn, then when your mount goes down, they'll come back for ya. Don't ever try to outrun 'um. Get up a tree."

He looked at her as if he was waiting for an answer. Finally, she nodded.

"This ain't no holiday, lady, it's dangerous work." He described in horrific detail the way he'd lost one of his best colts when a wild old cow had stuck her horn between the colt's ribs and punctured his lung. Imitated, over and over again, the choking gasps the colt made during the half hour it took for him to die. When Katherine did not react, he unsnapped the top of his denim shirt, showed her the waxy pink scar that ran half the length of his collarbone. Said it happened when he was gathering scrub bulls in the outback.

"A bull chased me into the muck of a billabong and me horse fell. Stirred up a nest of crocks." Besides the compound fracture of his collarbone, he swore one of the buggers took a chunk of flesh out of his ass. He didn't share that scar, just trotted ahead and ordered Katherine to stay back and stay quiet.

The trail was flanked by lichen-covered granite, squatty bull pines, and oaks older than the Constitution. Dego trotted up from behind on his fancy palomino and pointed out a bald eagle for Katherine to shoot. She lifted the Pentax hanging from her neck and unfastened the lens cap. Dego kept her mare still while she zoomed in on the majestic bird.

"Beautiful." Katherine captured a dozen photos before the eagle flew off. She turned the camera on Dego. Grabbed a few headshots, then zoomed in on the chicken leg hanging from his saddle skirt. She was about to ask why but was interrupted by barking. Dego spun his horse and loped off. Katherine kicked and followed.

A narrow path wound down and disappeared into a manzanita-covered canyon. Will looked back and signaled to Katherine with his hand to wait while he followed the dogs into the canyon. Dego removed the rope from his saddle horn, then uncoiled it and built a loop. He swung it, never moving his squinted eyes away from the canyon below. Katherine straightened in her saddle and cradled the camera. Within minutes, the dogs took their barking to the next level, and Crocodile Dundee was chasing a cow and her calf through the brush. Katherine focused her camera. The excitement sent a flood of adrenaline and caused a heart-pounding high.

The instant the cow and her calf emerged from the lower trail, Will threw his rope around her horns. Wrapped the remainder of rope around his saddle horn. The slack tightened and spun the cow at Will. Dego pitched his rope under her hind legs, scooped them up, and dallyed his rope around his saddle horn. They backed their horses in opposite directions until the irate cow was taut and couldn't move. She bellowed and swung her head at the barking dogs. Thick slobber flew in all directions like a malfunctioning sprinkler. Her calf started back down the narrow trail, but a red-and-white border collie stopped him. Katherine watched in awe and missed the photo opportunity while Will tied the cow by her horns to a substantial oak. Dego released her hind legs. The cow pulled back and fought hard against the tree to no avail.

At noon, they watered the horses and ate dried apricots along a creek shaded by oaks and bordered by blackberries.

"Like apricots, Katie?" Will asked.

"I've never eaten them dried. They're good." Katherine had worked up an appetite. She popped the chewy fruit in her mouth and hoped they were an odd appetizer before the main course. When no solid sustenance was presented, she finished the pouch of apricots, then several handfuls of blackberries.

"Careful, Miss Katrin', all dat fruit gone turn you inside out."

Will laughed until he spotted fresh cattle tracks. Instantly, they were off across a field of golden grass. The dogs raced up a ridge to the south and disappeared. Will and Dego loped up the ridge while Katherine pulled on her reins and dodged squirrel holes. The camera banged against the saddle as the irritated mare jigged from being left behind. Will and Dego disappeared over the top of the ridge, and by the time Katherine arrived, there was no sign of them. Only miles and miles of rolling wilderness. She stopped and searched in every direction. Looked for tracks, but who was she kidding. She had no tracking skills. A pang of dread shot through her, then grew into a gurgle. Suddenly, her bowels began to churn and panic kicked inside her.

She rode hard to the bottom of the canyon and found a thicket of tall manzanita. A large opening offered privacy. She dismounted, ran backward, and unbuttoned her jeans just in time. The mare spooked and tried to pull away. "Whoa!" She held tight to the leather reins as the horse snorted and pricked her ears. A low, guttural vibration came from somewhere other than Katherine's stomach. The mare reared. Jerked the reins loose. In an instant, the horse spun and was gone. Hooves hammered the hard clay—publicizing Katherine's runaway horse.

With her jeans at her knees, Katherine pulled off a boot. Fell on her ass, then removed a sock to replace much-needed toilet paper. As she turned to bury the sock at the bottom of the bushes, a twig snapped. She froze. The silence was eerie. Deep in the shadow of brush was breathing. Abnormally loud, raspy breathing. Then a low grumble and the glint of an eye. A huge, bulging eye the size of a tennis ball. It blinked, and Katherine ran for her life. For the first time ever, she ran hard and she ran far, every so often exchanging the hand that held the boot.

Gasping at the top of the ridge, Katherine stopped. Scanned the area for the monster before sitting and inspecting the cuts and scrapes on the bottom of her foot.

She slipped her sockless foot back into the boot, and heat swamped her. As if it were August and not November, the air was thick. Felt like being trapped in the center of a freshly baked muffin. Sun scorched the top of her head, caused it to throb. She wished she had water. Wished she hadn't eaten the goddamn apricots. The fucking blackberries. Wished she weren't so fat.

Across a wide valley, waves of heat rolled and floated. After walking for what seemed like hours but, in reality, was only one, Katherine missed Frisco and the gloomy cold. In the distance, a rusted windmill came into view. Then a water tank sparked ambition and forced Katherine to increase her lame stride.

An amplified buzz zapped her like an electrical current when she found the mare nibbling sparse blades of grass behind the water tank. A wooden trough completed the oasis. Katherine splashed her sweaty face. Scooped water into her mouth. It worked like an elixir. She recognized her luck when she gathered the reins that the mare had dragged but not broken. A faint echo of barking pricked Katherine's ears, along with the mare's, and she climbed back into the saddle.

A short black bull was tied from his stubby horns to an oak. He didn't move a muscle when Katherine rode by. She decided to let the mare choose the way, knowing her sense of direction was better. The dogs stopped barking when Katherine approached another black bull tied to a tree. She snapped a few pictures. Was refocusing her lens when Will's filthy face filled the shot.

"You missed all the fun. Where you been?" he asked, smiling and sweating.

"Something's in the bushes over the ridge," she told him.

"A cow?" He climbed off his horse, opened his saddlebag.

"It was bigger than any cow I've ever seen. Had an eye as big as a tennis ball. And it *growled.*"

"You play tennis, don't you?"

"What the hell difference does that make?"

Dego rode up, and Will's eyes puckered as he grinned. "Kate here thinks she seen a critter with an eye big as a baseball."

"Tennis ball," she said.

"You any good at it?" Will asked.

"At what?"

"Tennis?"

"No. I suck."

"Da steer, he 'ave only one big eye?" Dego's smile left his face. He wiped his forehead with the back of his sleeve.

"Yes."

"Cyclops."

"What the hell is it?" she asked, and Will suddenly paid attention.

"Ghost steer. Old fella work here tell me 'bout 'im. Twenty year ago when he was a calf, dey catch 'im. Castrate 'im. But next year, dey no can catch 'im. Dey chase 'im and he run off a cliff. Onto da rocks. 'Is skull, it break in half. He is dead . . . But, when dey come back, he is only gone. A ghost. No one will catch a ghost."

"Aww, bullshit." Will pulled a can of peaches from his

saddlebag, popped the top, and offered it to Katherine. She shook her head no and held her stomach. "Mate, you got your visions and reality jumbled up again."

"He is real." Dego looked at Katherine, then at Will. "Believe."

"Bet half your pay?" A mischievous smile filled Will's face.

Dego watched Will drink the syrup from the can, then slurp out a peach before he agreed. "Where did you see 'im?" Dego asked Katherine.

"I can show you. He was hiding in some bushes."

The sun was sinking fast. It lit the gold leaves like hanging candles—casting a soft glow as they crossed the ridge toward the brush where she hoped to prove Will wrong. Coyotes yipped close by and bristled the hairs on the back of her neck, along with two of the dogs.

"Coyotes can't hurt you if you don't pet dem," Dego said, scanning the ground for tracks.

They dropped off the ridge and into the canyon. The landscape was familiar, but every set of bushes looked the same. Katherine could not pinpoint her encounter until Will stopped his horse and looked down.

"Someone was walking, there's tracks." Will lifted Katherine's boot, then looked up at her, the light diluting his eyes. "What the hell, Katie?"

"Felt like walking. And stop calling me Katie, that's not my name."

"Felt like walking? Without your horse, and only one boot? Huh."

"You should give her a name."

"Hung up on names, ain't ya?"

"People and pets have names. You should respect that, Wilbur." She trotted away. "Think I was over here."

Before she could find the exact spot, Dego jumped from his horse and knelt. "Look." He drew a circle in the dirt the size of a salad plate. They looked down. The circle encompassed the hoofprint of one massive bovine. Will scanned the entire area as Dego pulled some feathers and another chicken leg from his saddlebag. He began to tap the items around the print.

Darkness was closing in, and the loss of light made it difficult to study the ground for more tracks. Will interrupted Dego's chanting. "Hey! We should stick Katie in the Slammer?" That familiar tinge of panic flushed through her without consent when she realized she was at the mercy of two rough men whom she knew nothing about. Will looked at her, tilted his head, and grinned. The instinct of fight or flight forced Katherine to turn her horse and ride toward the barn. She was suffocating. Her heart thumped and echoed in her ears as Will and Dego followed.

"She might like it," Will said plenty loud so Katherine was sure to hear.

"If you tink is okay." Dego sounded concerned.

She stopped her horse. Turned and faced Will, trying to hide her fear. "What's the Slammer?"

"You'll see." Will loped off.

They rode west toward the ranch headquarters. Daylight sunk into an ocean of deep violet and turned the sky into a raging fire. It was dark by the time they reached the barn, and Katherine convinced herself she was being paranoid. The Slammer was nothing to beg scared of. Dego promised.

***

For the first time in a long time, Katherine slept and dreamed without waking in a panic. An entire night without the heaviness of sleeping pills and/or a solid buzz. Doves contributed to the morning with joyous coos, but it was the lack of a hangover headache plus the aroma of coffee that brought an unfamiliar enthusiasm. Then, bacon. The smoky scent lifted her out of bed like a rising swell.

Will broke eggs into a sizzling skillet and yelled out the window, "Dego get your ass in here and eat. How'd you want your eggs, Katie?"

"I don't care." Will could not ruin the best morning since she couldn't remember when. At the table, she swatted away crumbs that looked like mouse droppings. Breathing somehow felt better—easier.

"Here ya go." Will set a plate in front of her. Three pieces of fried bacon and two eggs still in the shell. He ate standing up—like no one was watching. "How old are you?" he asked through a mouth full of runny yolks.

"Old enough to deserve some goddamn respect." She took her eggs to the hot skillet and broke them.

"Respect is something you earn, Katie."

"Whatever, Wilbur." She rolled her eyes and scrambled her eggs.

"Wilbur?" He laughed. "Me mum used to call me that.

When she was *really* pissed." He shoved an entire strip of bacon into his mouth. "You pissed, Katie?"

"I want to know about the Slammer." She crossed her arms.

By six a.m., Will had the horses saddled and the Slammer loaded with two ice chests full of food, a pile of extra ropes, hay bales, three sacks of grain, and fifty pounds of dog food. Dego cranked the engine at least eight times before the Slammer finally roared to life with a belch of burnt oil. It looked more like something you'd see rumbling across an African savannah. A green military truck used in World War II to haul weapons, it had been retrofitted with several strategically placed winches to force uncooperative cattle into a large cage in the back. Katherine studied, then petted, the lifeless coyote stretched and strapped across the truck's grill. Repulsed by her admiration.

Fighting the gears and the heavy clutch, Katherine banged the Slammer up a long and rutted dirt road as Will, Dego, and the pack of dogs followed. In less than a mile, the dogs stopped, lifted their noses, and sniffed the air. An ash-colored Catahoula, named Mr. Robichaux, made his move. The pack and Dego followed.

"Wait at the top of Yayali Peak. 'Bout two more miles, there'll be a big ole cave at the top—don't go in. Yayali will eat you alive," Will said.

"Yayali?" Katherine grinned.

"Yayali is a Mi-Wuk monster that eats the children who go into his cave." Will turned and kicked his horse.

"Guess I'll be safe, then. Since I'm not a child. Asshole," Katherine said to no one.

Yayali Peak offered a spectacular view as Katherine stopped the Slammer and stepped out. Treetops blanketed the foothills as far as she could see. With a fresh roll of film, she snapped away. Walked along the road and saw the mouth of Yayali's cave. Quietly, she stepped toward it. Got as close as she could without being inside. Knelt and focused on the darkness. The click of the shutter seemed loud, then echoed. A dank coolness flowed from the cave, and with it came the scent of wet dog. Katherine could not resist the temptation and yelled, "Hello!"

"*Bonswa*!"

Kate spun. "Dego!" He rode toward the Slammer, pulling a cow at the end of his rope like an unwilling dance partner. Will arrived doing the same. Horseback and in sync, they pulled the captured cattle toward the Slammer.

"Let the ramp down, Katie!" Will yelled, and Katherine moved. She unlatched both sides, and the ramp fell hard and fast. The dogs barked and snapped at the heels of the wild cattle as Katherine photographed the entire event. Exhausted cattle waited at the bottom of the ramp while Dego placed a steel cable attached to a winch around their horns and released his rope. "Katie! The lever's behind you."

Katherine saw a knob that resembled a small gear shift. "This?" She pointed to the thing.

"Yep."

"Okay, Miss Katrine." Dego raised his hand high for

Katherine to pull the lever. When she did, the motor whined and wound the cable. In no time, the unwilling animal was dragged into the Slammer. Will dismounted his horse and followed the critter in. He grabbed a coiled rope that hung from the top rail and secured the cow. They repeated the entire process until the Slammer was full.

The crew had delivered seven head of wild cattle to the corrals when Will decided the horses had had enough. Dego loaded his palomino and Mr. Robichaux into the Slammer and headed for the cabin in Tobacco Canyon. Katherine was untying the mare, who she decided to name Cyndi, after Cyndi Lauper, when she noticed the intense look that Will and one of the dogs had. They stared toward the top of a ridge about one hundred yards up. Will spun into his saddlebag and dug out a pair of binoculars. Pointed them to the top of the ridge. Katherine positioned her camera and slowly scanned the same direction. A red-and-white-speckled steer with huge horns looked down at them.

"Holy shit," Will mumbled and adjusted his binoculars. "He's fucking watching us."

Katherine zoomed in until the creature filled her view. The steer's face looked like a clay sculpture that had started to melt, fell sideways, then hid under a horribly scarred hide to cover the messy mistake. His nose veered impossibly to the right. The left eye followed and bulged from the center of his skull while a hollow and withered right eye socket sat below his right ear. Massive horns were bent like twisted tree trunks—burdening him constantly. He was the Elephant

Man of cattle, ostracized and alone.

"Stay here. I'll try and slip around him." Will rode away fast while Kate replaced her film and shot the monster watching her. Will emerged like a toy soldier riding up the far end of the ridge. Building his loop bigger and bigger as he closed in on Cyclops. The reality of what she was watching sunk in, and she focused the lens with shaky fingers. Her comprehension of cattle was nil, but she understood that this behemoth was something phenomenal that astonished and delighted her.

Cyclops must have sensed danger and stepped off the steep ravine before Will got within rope-throwing distance. Like a runaway semi, Cyclops crashed and plowed through the brush, leaving a swatch for Will to follow. Straight down, Will's horse sat and slid exactly like *The Man From Snowy River*, Katherine thought as she rode toward the action.

Manzanita cracked below and announced the bovine's whereabouts. The tips of his massive horns peeked over the brush, thwarting any attempt to hide. Will pushed his horse through the river of slapping and stinging branches until they disappeared under the foliage.

"He's about fifty feet to your right," Katherine yelled. The beast was as tall as Will's horse. The brush quickly turned into a tangled, impassable wall.

"*Where'd he go?*"

"I don't see him."

Cyclops had vanished into the thick growth. Will's cussing echoed through the canyon, and Katherine hoped it was due to the frustration of donating his pay to Dego and ultimately Jimmy Swaggart.

Tobacco cabin sat at the back of Tobacco Meadow. It was as basic and weathered as a one-room cabin could be. A twenty-by-twenty wood box. Just before dark, Will lit a lantern and hung it above a small kitchen table surrounded by four mismatched chairs. The white light swung, revealed, then shadowed, a woodstove, two sets of bunk beds that looked like they would not survive a heavy wind, and a small rust-stained sink topped by a shelf with a broken hand mirror.

"Dunny's out back," Will informed Katherine, then corrected himself: "You know—the crapper, shit shack. What'd you call it?"

"Bathroom," she said.

"That's dumb. There ain't no bath, and it's more like a closet than a room." He ripped a green wool blanket from the top bunk and tossed it to her. "Take it out, an' give 'er a good shake."

The smell of sour milk and mothballs engulfed her. "Outhouse, then!" She walked out.

"It's definitely *not* a house," Will shouted from inside. She wondered if he had been the head of the debate team back in Australia. A distant rumble interrupted her attempt at a sarcastic comeback. A beam of light cut through the dark and lit the meadow. Dogs barked. Dego gunned the Slammer and bounced the heavy truck across the rutted road to the cabin. Katherine could not wait to tell him that they'd seen Cyclops. That Will had tried to catch him, but the monster had outsmarted him. As Dego jumped out of the driver's seat and shut the door, Will walked up behind Kate. "Keep quiet about the big steer," he said, then placed his hand on her shoulder and gave it a gentle massage.

She turned around, faced him, and said, "No fucking way."

Dego smiled as he hurried toward them carrying an ice chest. Before she could confirm the reality of Cyclops, he chuckled, and said, "Ahhh, look like you seen da ghost." He set the ice chest down, slapped his knee, and broke into a from-the-gut laughing fit. "Gone be a good payday for me."

"You voodoo son of bitch." Will shook his head and lugged the ice chest into the cabin.

A thick rib eye bled into the bread and beans on Katherine's tin plate. Her appetite had returned with a vengeance as she sliced juicy chunks of meat one after the other and listened to Will give Dego a play-by-play account of the Cyclops encounter.

"I'll get that bastard if it's the last thing I do, mate." He quit eating, leaned forward, and eyed Dego. "There's a fella in Los Angeles owns carnivals and has them sideshow attractions, you know? Makes the big fella worth a pretty penny."

Dego looked at Katherine, rubbed his nose with the palm of his hand. After a long while, he shook his head. "Nope."

"Nope? What the hell's that mean?" Will asked.

"You cannot sell a ghost." Dego mopped his beans with his bread.

265

"Bullshit. Enough voodoo, you fuck-wit! Understand, mate? I reckon I'm the boss, and I say we ain't doin' nothin' 'til we catch the bugger." Will's face turned red.

"Okay, boss." Dego smiled and chewed.

***

Morning fog hid the sun while scrub oaks huddled at the bottom of Tobacco Canyon and housed a small herd of deer. They broke from their cover as Katherine, Will, and Dego approached—hooves slapping hard red clay. They'd searched and searched for Cyclops since sunrise three hours ago. More grounds-filled coffee consumed Katherine's mind as she yawned and stretched in her saddle. Dego stopped his horse. "*Laissez les bon temps rouler!*" Dego sang.

There he stood, one hundred yards above, looking down on them like a mythical creature. In an instant, the dogs spread out and up the canyon wall. Will rode at an angle to head the steer off while Dego went in the opposite direction. Katherine wasn't sure where to go or what to do. Straight ahead seemed the best photo opportunity and the safest.

The steer waited. Taunting them. Dogs came barking from every direction and the battle began. Mr. Robichaux locked down in front of Cyclops. Tried to distract and slow the steer until Will and Dego could catch up. Cyclops played along. Slowly, he lowered his head, tipped his horns, until Mr. Robichaux made a move. The dog lunged and nipped at Cyclops's nose, but the big beast was surprisingly quick. His mighty horn caught Mr. Robichaux. Flung him so hard and fast that the dog barely whimpered before disappearing into the forest. Katherine reined Cyndi behind a giant oak and readied her camera.

Cyclops ran down a steep deer trail. Deeper into the canyon with Will and Dego gaining at a breakneck speed. The remaining dogs snarled and snapped at Cyclops's nose, but never intimidated or slowed him. Katherine kicked Cyndi into a fast lope and followed.

The canyon widened. Will was gaining and the dogs backed off. He slipped his coiled rope from his saddle and in one quick motion built an extra-large loop. Dego hung back—his rope ready in his hand. The hulking creature, who'd previously enjoyed a leisurely life, was tiring fast. Riding hard alongside the steer's left hip, Will took one last swing before pitching his loop. The moment he threw, the wise brute skidded to a stop, avoiding capture by at least four feet. Cyclops turned and faced Will with that horribly disfigured snout. Faced him with that single bulging eye. Will's horse spooked, then stumbled and like a tag team, Dego rode in. The second before he threw his rope, Cyclops charged him. Katherine screamed as the steer swung his massive horn under Dego's horse's belly, lifted him off all four feet, and flung him effortlessly against an oak. "Dego!"

Will's horse refused to move into the cloud of dust that hid Cyclops and the carnage. Without hesitation, Will dismounted and ran to Dego. Katherine jumped from her saddle and followed fast. As the dust settled, Cyclops was halfway back up the canyon—dogs tailing at a respectful distance. He stopped, looked back, and probably would have laughed if he could.

Dego was on his hands and knees gasping for air—pale for a dark man. Will knelt beside him. The downed horse thrashed against the oak, kicking up chunks of bark, before finding his feet.

"Dego! You okay?" Katherine squatted in front of him. He looked up with that beautiful smile, and slowly said, "You get my photo?"

She aimed her camera at his dirt-encrusted smile and took a close-up. With little effort, Cyclops could have killed Dego and his horse. Lifting her lens, Katherine searched for the bovine beast in the coagulating fog.

Holding his ribs, Dego limped to his horse. Bloody cuts and scrapes scattered the palomino's white legs. Will inspected his underbelly, but the expected gaping wound did not exist. He felt for swelling or a painful reaction, but there was none. They looked at each other, knowing the lack of damages was not due to luck.

"We'll get that crooked-faced cunt come hell or high water," Will said, mounting his horse. "Let's go if we're goin'." He left them behind. Followed the huge tracks up the canyon and into the fog. Dego led his horse a few steps before noticing the wet on his saddlebag. He unbuckled the medicine bag, looked inside, and found the shattered bottle of Rompun.

"I gone find Mr. Robichaux, den get mo' tranquilize out de barn," he told Katherine, then cringed as he pulled himself into the saddle. Sweat left tracks on his cheeks.

"Dego, are you sure you're okay?"

"Fine as frog's hair, Miss Katrine." He squeezed his ribs.

"Sure hope Mr. Robichaux be fine too." Then he trotted into the forest to help his dog.

Katherine caught Will at the top of the canyon and suggested they take a break. Told him that Dego went to look for his dog and get more Rompun from the barn.

"Fuck me dead! We finally know Cyclops is headed west! Dogs are on him, and that bloody derro mucks off about his mutt?" He looked at Katherine like he expected her to agree. She did not. "We'll take a break once the old fella's in the Slammer. Okay?" He didn't wait for her consent—just rode west along the ridge.

A high noon sun burned off the fog. Will and four dogs stood in a slow creek surrounded by mossy oaks. When Katherine caught up, Will turned toward her and pressed his index finger against his lips, the universal sign to be quiet. She stopped Cyndi just before the creek. Realized Will was studying the jungle of bushes opposite the creek. A mass of poison oak bordered the creek as far as she could see. Dogs panted in the water. The entire scene looked like a Charlie Russell painting come to life. The soft rush of water spilling over stone and the chirp of cheerful birds brought contentment to the portrait.

Will pointed out the abnormally large tracks that disappeared into the thickest section of poison oak. For ten minutes, she watched Will stare at the bush. He never blinked. Finally, he said, "At's one smart son of a bitch. He'll lay up, get a good night's rest in there. Fuck wad!" He rode up the creek, and it hit Katherine that *this* was the story. The

269

real story. Will's crusade to capture Cyclops had a Moby Dick feel. For the first time in a long time, she was itching to sit down and write the story she wanted to write. Fuck the *Chronicle* and fuck Judge Callahan.

After an hour and a half, Will had picked his way through thickets of manzanita and chamise, down a twenty-five-foot ravine, and surveyed the entire perimeter of poison oak. Strategically, he tied each of the dogs to a tree that bordered the massive patch. If Cyclops emerged, the barking dog would work as an alarm. It was his dedication, not his expertise, that Katherine began to admire when she decided to record everything and take detailed notes.

Horses were tied to trees along the creek while Will and Katherine sat on a downed log. It was the first conversation they'd had that did not include sarcasm, insults, or instructions.

Will had come to the States when he was seventeen to ride rodeo broncs and was fairly successful until a double compound fracture to his riding arm had ended his career. He hadn't graduated or attended college, but he had been taking care of himself since he'd run away at the age of thirteen. Got a job exercising racehorses on the track in Melbourne. After two years, he'd become too husky to ride the lanky thoroughbreds. Found work mustering and breaking brumbies in the northern territory. With a six-hundred-dollar paycheck and a new bronc saddle, he'd begun his rodeo career in Australia. Beginner's luck, he called seven straight wins. He wore the last buckle he won at

San Francisco's Cow Palace in 1980.

"I was there that year—showing hunter jumpers!" It felt like more than a coincident to Katherine.

"I knew you'd ridden before." Will squeezed her knee, and she jumped. "Fancy warmblood gals don't notice cowboys."

A dog barked close by and ended the chitchat. They ran—didn't bother with the horses. A black-and-tan kelpie was the culprit. He had pissed off a rattlesnake, and neither were backing down. The coiled snake was as thick as a hissing radiator hose.

"They like to shade up in the bushes." Will stepped toward the pup. "Down!" he yelled, and the animal dropped his ears, and body, and didn't bark again. "He's a beaut," Will said as he approached the snake.

"What the hell are you doing?" she asked, but Will didn't answer. He picked up a stick. Then, in an instant, he had the stick pressed against the back of the rattler's head. In one fluid motion, he snatched the snake's tail, swung it over his head, and flung the angry serpent back into the bushes. "Holy shit." She shivered as the willies crept up and down her spine.

On the way back to the horses, Will noticed new tracks. Cyclops had escaped without a sound. Will stomped and kicked and screamed like a wild stallion. Beat a boulder with his hat. Walked out and stood in the middle of the creek—boots and all. With both hands, he reached down and cupped water onto his face and scrubbed it. Did his hair next. Then stepped out of the creek, slapped his hat on his head. "I need to heal. I 'spect you could use some too."

Katherine didn't respond.

"Don't talk. Just follow."

They rode up the creek about four miles in silence until Will dismounted. "Let's go if we're goin'." He finally smiled. They unsaddled and entered a forest of limestone outcroppings that sprung from the ground in angled slats. Weaved their way up and over and around and down a limestone maze. Topped a knoll. Below sat a building the size of a two-car garage. Will pulled his pocketknife as they approached and then whittled the window lock until it popped.

"What is this place?" Katherine asked.

"This is where I heal. It'll do ya good." He crawled through the window, and she followed, unconcerned that they were breaking and entering. Inside, a soon-to-be gift shop waited for tourists. Two walls of bare shelves. Empty glass cabinets. Stacks of boxes. Chrome clothes racks held a variety of Moaning Cavern T-shirts.

"This is where you come to heal? Need a shopping fix, and this is the only game in town?"

Will ignored her and unlocked a sliding glass door with his knife. "Let's go if we're goin'." He grabbed a backpack off the floor and started down the dark wooden stairs. Spurs jingled as she followed. In less than a minute, the temperature dropped and the air was comfortably cool and smelled like wet cement. After a sharp left, they were walled in on both sides by rock. Will pulled two flashlights out of the pack and handed her one. "Watch your noggin."

The steps narrowed and the stone walls tightened as they sank deeper and deeper into the earth. They crossed a platform and stepped onto a spiral staircase surrounded by a heavy wire mesh that should prevent patrons from falling to their death. A single spotlight revealed small sections of inconceivable limestone formations. Ivory-colored demons. Gathered souls frozen as they screamed and reached out for salvation. Spindles and spires like polished bone. A stillness filled the ocean of emptiness. Herds of ice-colored jellyfish—their long, stringy tentacles waiting to capture prey. Down they wound for what seemed like an eternity. Fear manifested but did not stop her. She counted the steps. Fifty. Seventy-five. Two hundred. No longer part of the known world, she felt alive as their footfalls echoed the dark abyss.

"Almost there. How ya doin'?" Will had lost his sharp tone.

"I'm okay." The stairway ended at three hundred fifty-six, and Will took her hand. Lead her onto solid ground. She scanned the massive chamber with her light.

"What is this place?"

"Give me your torch and don't move," Will whispered. "Trust me."

She passed him her flashlight. He turned it off, then turned his off. Blackness swarmed them. Unable to detect even a shadow or her hand in front of her face.

"Are your eyes closed?"

She closed them. "Yes."

Something clicked. "Open them."

Light anointed her. The cavern was enormous. Looking up was dizzying. You could fit the Statue of Liberty in the place. Shellacked clouds of million-year-old calcium carbonate, marble, and limestone shaped the sparkling underground realm.

"This is the Moaning Cavern?" she asked.

"Yep. Next month, the place'll be filled with tourists and school kids. You're gettin' the VIP tour. Look here, Katie." Will took her hand and led her to a crystal-clear pool. Water fell from stalactites that hung like huge melting icicles. It was perfection. Without warning, he was naked and in the water. "This is healing, Katie."

"We call it skinny-dipping here." She turned and pretended to admire a massive limestone bubble the size of a VW bug. It reminded her of Chewbacca from *Star Wars*. She had her camera, but no flash, and was down to the last roll of film. Will suggested she take his picture. She ignored him and explored. Ran her hand along the smooth, cool stone wishing she could stay forever.

"You old enough to drink, Katie?"

"I don't drink," she lied.

"You gotta be over eighteen, but ya look like fifteen or sixteen." He said it as if it were a compliment. His wet feet slapped closer and closer—she prayed he was dressed.

His jeans were unbuttoned and he was shirtless. He wore the pink scar on his chest like a hallmark and leaned into her. "Your turn." So close, his breath stroked her neck.

"That's okay." No way she was getting naked in front of him.

"Don't be bashful." His hands felt big and strong and good as he squeezed her shoulders. "Use this opportunity to heal. I'll give you some privacy." With a wink, he slid down a rock and disappeared.

"Where you going?"

"Boneyard. There's a hole up top where critters fall in. Never know what ya might find." The acoustics were spectacular.

Katherine walked to the pool. Ran her hand across the turquoise water. The sound washed from side to side, then slowly faded. She pulled off her boots and rolled up her pants. The water wasn't cool but wasn't exactly warm either. It was simply soothing liquid that felt inviting. She caught a glimpse of her dirt-streaked reflection. The girl in the water shook her frizzy head at Katherine—saying, *Stop being such an uptight bitch and get your sorry ass in the water. Drown your sorrows, stupid girl.* Out of habit, Katherine looked away from herself.

"Will?"

A faint "Yeah?" came from somewhere far off.

"Just checking." She abandoned her clothes and walked in. The soft bottom felt like silk between her toes. The water sucked her in. Silently—thoughtlessly—she floated like an embryo. No yesterday. No tomorrow. Only here and now as she held her breath and sank with open eyes. Blue held her like an embrace. She didn't feel fat or ugly or angry as she bathed in the tranquility. When she surfaced, breathing felt new. Her lungs expanded. Each breath infused with an inexplicable enthusiasm. Maybe it was the water. Maybe the natural instinct of a body in fluid that triggered rebirth. Either way, Will was right, she had never felt better. Never so wide awake.

"Katherine?"

"Hang on." She swam to the shallow side and sat. Reached for her denim shirt and dried the top half of herself. Skipped the bra and buttoned her shirt. Pulling jeans on over wet skin was war. She had them to her hips when Will popped his head out of a crevice about fifty feet above.

"Was I right?"

"How'd you get up there?"

"There's tunnels and cracks all over the place. You can wiggle your way just 'bout anywhere. Look what I found." He held out a small skull.

"Oh my God."

"Yeah. Probably a Mi-Wuk kid muckin' about and fell down the hole. Didn't die right off and tried to find a way out. Tragic, aye?" He sucked back into the crevice, and she shoved her bra and panties in her boot. A woman watched her from the water. Wet curls ringed her fresh face as she grinned at herself. For the first time in nearly a year, Katherine didn't look away.

"You're beautiful, Katie. You know that?" Will set the skull on a ledge and walked over. "I mean it. I think you're lovely."

"Okay." The spiciness of his sweat touched her. When he lifted her hand, she did not resist. He looked at her hands. Stroked her fingers. An odd weakness felt good—made her warm. An inexplicable impulse bloomed, and for no good reason, she leaned toward him. His hard lips, chapped by the sun, kissed her. Kissed her neck. Shivers splashed up inside her as his sturdy hand found its way under her shirt. She wondered if he could feel her heart pounding under his hand. The urge was undeniable. She had left the rape hundreds of miles away, but it was there now—with her always. Will might drown the guilt, the unwelcome sense of danger, and set her free. Panic began to conquer passion. Will guided her hand to the throbbing hardness between his legs. She jerked back like she had touched fire.

"Stop!" She felt all her breath leave her body. Without hesitation, he stopped. Pulled his shaggy hair away from his face. Tears burst and she shook her head. "I'm sorry" She was more confused than sorry.

Fury overrode fear, and she buried her head in her hands and bawled like an inconsolable child. Will rubbed her back as if he understood. When that didn't quiet her, he lifted her onto his lap and cradled her. She felt as light as a Communion wafer as he rocked her in his arms and waited patiently while she purged her demons. Fear was a stone she carried in her chest, and Will was chiseling it into something beautiful.

"You a virgin, Katie?" he whispered in her ear and kissed it.

"Yes." It felt like the truth. Rape did *not* count. No way she was going to let her first encounter with a boy ruin her chance with a man. She forced a hurried kiss to his cheek, then unbuttoned her shirt. His lips touched her nipple and warmed it with his hot breath. He rolled his tongue around and sucked on it. The urge was back in full force and kicking the shit out of anxiety as she stepped out of her jeans and into the pool.

Will shed his jeans, then stood watching her with the beginnings of an erection. "You certain, Katie?"

"I won't stop you. I promise."

His erection improved and he dove in. Wrapped himself behind her. Then reached around and worked a magical finger that set her left thigh quivering uncontrollably. She wondered if that was it—the orgasm everyone talked about—until he stepped in front of her and slid himself inside. Her heart and hips lifted without consideration and thumped against him. They floated in perfect rhythm with each stroke. Tingles swam up her legs, through her soul, and emerged in her head. They drifted into the shallows, sending waves in and out until it came from somewhere deep. The intensity grew as he moved faster, harder, on top of her. His monstrous shadow contorted against the stone wall as he consumed her.

"At a girl. There you go." He licked her earlobe. "Heal."

The rush of pure euphoria hit like an explosion from the inside out. Containing herself was not an option once every muscle in their bodies stiffened. Moans filled the cavern, and when they were through, Will said, "Now you know why it's called Moaning Cavern." Katherine's laughter echoed as she clung to Will like a barnacle.

***

Campfire smoke drifted under a canopy of oaks as the smell of sex and boiled coffee persuaded Katherine into the morning. She poked her head out from under Will's bedroll. Cyndi munched at a flake of hay, and Will was long gone. She sat up—her hair felt like a nest and she was glad to be alone.

The metal coffeepot balanced on a rock between a few remaining coals. Katherine used her shirttail like a pot holder and poured herself a cup. Grounds floated, then settled to the bottom as she sipped. Steam swirled. She inhaled. A damn good time to pick up her pen and fill some pages.

After a dozen pages, Katherine noticed the Slammer parked above camp and wondered how she had not heard Dego arrive. She walked over. Mr. Robichaux was curled on a blanket in the passenger seat. She petted and told him he would be okay. He licked her dirty hand and looked up at her as if to say, *You'll be okay too.*

It had to be close to noon when Katherine rode Cyndi by the poison oak patch. Three miles north, she found Will and Dego tracking Cyclops. The steer had headed due north, then circled back to the south as if he were intentionally attempting to mislead them. Even the dogs seemed unsure of his route—weaving back and forth—sniffing the ground and air for a solid scent.

"That fat bastard's gotta be gettin' tired," Will said, and Dego agreed. Will's frustration or obsession forced him to ride well ahead. Dego slowed his horse and rode next to Katherine. He dug into his jacket pocket, pulled out a handful of peanuts, and offered them to her.

"Thanks." She held out her hand and he filled it.

"Mr. Will possessed by dis ghost. No good. Brought

yo'self over here, Miss Katrin." Dego stopped his horse and waited for her to do the same. He leaned in and lowered his voice. "I gone tell you." He looked down, sighed, and shook his head. "Will . . . He gots himself a real bad sickness. Real bad. You don't want none of it." He handed her a second helping of peanuts, then rode away before she could comprehend.

She was down to cracking the last nut when the dogs went wild. They strained up an embankment to her left and bayed like a pack of hounds on a fox. Dego stopped his horse, pulled the bottle of tranquilizer from his saddlebag, and handed it to Will. Dego spurred his horse into a full gallop while Will filled two tranquilizer darts. Slid one dart into the gun and set the other in his saddlebag. Katherine's pulse raced as they rode.

The dogs had gathered a wild cow and her calf. Had them cornered against a wall of boulders. Dego swung his rope.

"Les get 'em, boss."

Will lowered the gun. "No."

The dogs were relentless with their barking. They never hear him. Cyclops came at Will like a freight train with that one giant eye like a light. His horse spun before the steer could impale his flank. They all stumbled sideways. Cyclops stubbed his toe and went down on his heavy chest as a grin swept across Will's face. Katherine pointed her camera, didn't look through it, just snapped in Cyclops's general direction. Dego and the dogs distracted Cyclops long enough for Will to take careful aim and fire. The dart sunk deep into Cyclops's shoulder and caused him to spin like a bucking bull. He snorted twice before attempting to outrun them. They chased him out of the trees and through a seemingly endless field as the steer gained speed, then suddenly veered west. After about five minutes, he was no longer just running away. He seemed to be headed somewhere in particular.

"Shot 'im again, boss," Dego yelled.

"Too much'll kill him."

Cyclops loped over a section of rolling hills and up a brushy ravine.

"Keep on him, Dego!" Will stopped his horse and reloaded the tranquilizer gun as Cyclops, Dego, and the dogs disappeared like a parade over the hill.

At the top of the hill, Katherine waited, doing her best to stay out of the way. In less than a minute, Will passed, kicking hard with each stride. He passed Dego. Passed the dogs. Gaining on Cyclops. Will hardly aimed. Held the gun at arm's length and took a long shot. The second dart hit the steer in the ass, and worry hit Dego's face.

Another five minutes passed before the tranquilizer slowed Cyclops. They kept their distance but matched his slowing stride. Farther and farther west they went until Cyclops found what he was looking for. A rusted section of wire fence that snapped with little effort when Cyclops lowered his head and forced his way through. The breaking wires, like guitar strings being tuned by an amateur, shook a long length of fence line.

At last, Cyclops had nowhere left to go. Sixty-to-seventy-foot bluffs stretched north and south for at least a mile, with only the waters of the mighty Stanislaus River below. Cyclops stopped at the edge of the bluff covered in sweat and foaming at the mouth. He raised his heavy head, then, for a brief moment, scrutinized them with that single bulging eye as he defiantly backed off the cliff.

"Will!" Katherine doubted her own eyes and looked to Will for confirmation. He only stared in disbelief. Her lungs felt like lead. Desperately, she gulped air as quick as she could. *He's fooled us again*, she hoped. The ledge had an escape route the old steer knew was below him. Dego rode dangerously close and leaned out and over the edge. He looked at them and shook his head. Katherine refused to believe it. "*No!*" She dismounted and neared the edge. The ground seemed to tilt and knocked her off-balance. She dropped to her hands and knees and crawled to the edge. Deepwater splashed and banged against the red bluffs below, drowning the possibility of a beach. Cyclops drifted downstream like an abandoned rowboat. There was no ledge. No escape route. No way out. She couldn't look away and waited for him to move. "Swim!" A sudden affinity for this animal surged through her. Guilt stung as she fought back tears and swallowed hard.

Dinner at Tobacco cabin was void of conversation. Sometimes silence is the appropriate choice. While Will washed the dishes, Katherine went outside and wrote in her journal. Frogs and crickets sang under a low-hanging moon in a black sky. Melancholy surrounded her, and after a few pages, she decided she had all the story she needed or could handle. Tomorrow the cabin would be quiet, a peaceful place to compile notes and start a rough draft of the Cyclops story.

Will came out, plucked a coiled rope off the fence post, and swung it. "Ever rope?" he asked.

"Never needed to." He sat beside her. Made her feel warm when he put his arm around her. "Are you sick?"

"Don't reckon so." He took his arm back. "Why?"

"Dego said you have a sickness. That I should stay away from you."

Will's face hardened—turned red. "He's a fuck-wit. You know that." He put his arm back. "I want you to come with me when I leave here next week. Got a job gathering cattle off Santa Rosa Island. You'll love it there. And it'd make a fantastic story. California State Parks stole the island from Vail & Vickers Cattle Company, and now—"

"I can't."

"Why?"

"I doubt the paper will ever publish this story. The editor only hired me because he owed my father a favor."

"Fuck them. Write the story anyhow. It'll be grand."

"I am." He had a clean citrusy smell.

"You pissed? Katherine." The way he said her name reminded her of Father O'Reilly. She cringed.

"What would I have to be pissed about?"

"Dego say anything else?" He stood and swung his rope.

"What difference does it make? He's a fuck-wit, right?" An overwhelming feeling of dread forced her toward the cabin. Will spun his rope and caught both her feet as she walked. He pulled the slack out of the rope and stopped her. From behind, he wrapped himself around her.

"You ain't leavin'. I'll tie you to a tree if I have to." He threw her over his shoulder like a sack of grain and carried her away from the cabin. Set her down next to a gnarled oak. She leaned against it as he kissed her. Resisting was an option until he put his lips behind her earlobe and stoked the fire.

"Come on, I'll teach you to rope." He took her hand, and after her roping lesson, they did things that send Catholic girls straight to hell.

***

Last night, Katherine learned she loved being cuddled while she slept. Writing helped her realize she liked herself when she was with Will and Dego. She mattered when she was with them. During breakfast, Will convinced her to spend one more day gathering and then promised Dego would drive her back to the corrals this evening. She could either spend the night in the main house or head back to the city. Her choice.

"I'll split me paycheck with ya if ya stay," Will offered.

"You bet Dego your pay. And he won fair and square," Katherine said.

"He owes me three million. We just keep bettin', makes work a bit more tolerable," Will said, and Dego nodded.

"We bet on ever't'ing, even de bird we gone see next." Dego cleared his plate. "I tink I take Miss Katrine back now. Be best for her."

The veins in Will's neck budged and his jaw tightened. He grinned. "What's waitin' at home, Katie?"

"Just . . . stuff." She sounded like a child.

The morning gather had been a success. Six head of cattle tied and ready for the Slammer. Dego had a steer roped around the horns, and Will handed Katherine his rope. She swung and swung and missed the steer's heels four times before he accidentally stepped into the open loop on the ground.

"Lift your rope!" Will hooped when she raised the tail of the rope as high as she could. "Dally, dally!" Awkwardly, she wound the end of the rope around her saddle horn and Will roared, "At's my girl!"

"I did it! Oh my God!" She laughed. A hearty, unprotected laugh. One that made her think she'd never been this happy.

"You done fine, Miss Katrin. Real fine." Dego pulled the tired steer to an oak, then rode around the tree until the rope wound the trunk twice. The steer didn't reject when Dego dismounted and tied the end of his rope—securing the animal until the Slammer arrived.

Their happiness was tangible as they ate tri-tip sandwiches back at the corrals, and they seemed genuinely impressed at Katherine's ability to swallow and then belch the alphabet. Will was a gifted yodeler, but Dego won the contest of useless skills when he stood atop the rail fence, somersaulted to the ground, then walked on his hands. Katherine was amazed; she imagined the disgusted look her mother would have given. The way her red upper lip would have curled if she were here. Father would laugh and say, "Fantastic, absolutely fantastic," and consider him no better than a well-trained pet. What would her life have been surrounded by real people like Dego and Will?

After lunch, Katherine was assigned the duty of driving the Slammer and left Cyndi behind. The diesel engine idled violently while she used the outhouse before the long, bumpy ride. From inside the outhouse, she heard Dego. His harsh tone grabbed her attention.

"You tell 'er dey truth, or I do!" Dego sounded mad.

"No worries, mate. I'll tell her. Calm down," Will answered in a high tone that felt all wrong. She listened and was zipping her pants while she rushed out to investigate. They rode away.

Only three head of fat cattle fit into the Slammer, so they left two tied. Although it had eaten on Katherine most of the day, there hadn't been an appropriate time to mention the conversation she'd overheard. Will asked her to drive the loaded Slammer back to the corrals and wait. He and Dego would go and see if Cyclops had washed up along the river. She thought it was morbid until Will explained how bacteria in the animal's gut turns to methane gas, causing them to "bloat and float." And that his skull would be worth at least a couple hundred, maybe more.

Cattle bawled continuously—fought the confines of the Slammer every now and then while Katherine waited, and waited, at the corrals. The first hour, she propped her feet out the window and napped on the Slammer's seat with Mr. Robichaux. She stretched. Walked around the corals.

Considered attempting to unload the cattle herself, but untying them was too complicated and dangerous. She waited.

After two hours, worry caused her head to ache. A dead and dismembered tree lay behind the barn, and a thick patch of grass invited her to sit down and write. She brought her bag out of the Slammer and wrote.

The sun had nearly dropped by the time Will arrived leading Dego's sweaty horse. A sick feeling took hold before she could ask. He yelled in a slow, deliberate manner. "Go to the cavern. Find the phone at the gift shop. Call 911. Tell them Dego fell in the river and I cannot find him. Hurry."

Katherine ran for her car as chills blew up her spine like an icy gust of wind and scratched the back of her neck and head. She drove fast, struggling with a scenario of what could have happened. The Saab slid to a stop on the gravel in front of the gift shop. She took the stairs two at a time. Will had flipped the latches back to a locked position when they'd left. "Fuck!" she yelled. Banged and screamed for help, but knew no one was there. The stillness was eerie, and time slowed as she searched for a rock, then remembered the tire iron in her trunk.

The window broke on the second swing. She batted away the sharp edges and climbed in. Time toyed with her as moments became endless. She felt Dego's life slipping away, but not the cuts and slivers of glass in the back of her thigh. She searched behind the counter and along the wall for a phone line. Panic was taking over fast—*slow down. Focus!*

Fuck! Think! It had to be here. Somewhere. And it was. Hanging just inside the hall behind the counter.

The 911 operator answered after a half dozen rings, and Katherine told her what she knew. Desperate for Dego to be okay, she prayed. On her knees, she closed her eyes and bargained with the Lord. "Please dear God, let him be okay. I promise to attend mass and go to confession from now on." She gripped her fingers. "Vengeance is mine saith the Lord, please forgive me and my evil thoughts about Allen. I swear I'll resist wrath and . . . lust." Her throat so dry it felt like swallowing broken glass. A four-wheeler skidded up outside, and Katherine ran out. It was Will.

"Did you call?"

"Yes."

"Let's keep looking." Will moved forward as Katherine climbed on behind him.

They charged along the ridge, then up a butte. Careening down steeps with little regard for safety, Will leaned into the throttle. Branches slapped and stung. Katherine stayed tucked in tight behind him until they hit the trail that ran above the twisted Stanislaus. Water roared as they searched and searched but saw no sign of Dego.

It was impossible for the ambulance to reach them. A Calaveras County Search and Rescue helicopter hovered back and forth until it was too dark. Will and Katherine held to hope well into the frigid night. She clung to him on the back of the four-wheeler until he stopped, turned off the engine and swung himself around to face her. "Dego thought Cyclops might a washed into one of the caves along the river. I didn't see him, but he could be in there. I shouldn't have let him go. He just slipped and set sail like a twig someone tossed in the current." Blackness masked his grief.

"*Tell her or I will*," played over and over in Katherine's mind as they rode the four-wheeler back to the corrals. The authentic look of concern on Dego's face when he said Will had a bad sickness. She tried to shut it off. The timing was horrible. She knew she was being immature and selfish, but the thoughts were menacing in the silence. She needed to know Will's sickness. Had the right to know.

The corrals were dark and lonely with shadows everywhere. No one from the Calaveras County Sheriff's Department had arrived yet. Cattle were still banging in the Slammer when Will killed the four-wheeler and rolled to a stop in front of the corrals.

"He told me," she said. "Dego told me about your sickness." She wrapped her arms around herself. Breath steaming with each word.

Will looked at her. Furrowed his brow.

"You should have told me." She slid off the four-wheeler and Will grabbed her arm.

"I don't have a sickness."

"I know about AIDS! I'm from San Francisco, you know!" She jerked her arm away. Gravel crunched beneath her boots, loud and obnoxious as she headed for the main house. Will stepped in front of her. He looked old.

"I ain't got AIDS or any fuckin' sickness! Swear to God." She stepped around him and walked faster. He followed. "Katherine, please stop." Tears filled his eyes. "I can't lose me best mate *and* me best girl. Christ." His voice cracked and shook something loose inside her. The world was such an unjust eternal damnation filled with senseless suffering. She stopped. Reached for him, but he had already buried himself in her chest. The shared sobs shook and warmed them.

Metal gates and latches clanged as Will and Katherine unloaded cattle from the Slammer and answered the sheriff's questions. He finished his report just after ten and left. The sky was moonless and crickets were silent. Soon as the horses were unsaddled and fed, Will brought a bottle of blackberry wine from the tack room. They sat, shed a few more tears, and eventually drank the entire bottle.

The main house was cold as they slept on the floor of an empty living room. In a drunken stupor, Will snored behind Katherine. A *For Sale* sign stood outside the window like a billboard. Sometime in the night, Katherine woke spinning in the haze of blackberry wine. She stumbled down the tilted hall for the bathroom. Through the darkness, she heard him whisper, "Miss Katrin?" She froze. Waited for the voice in her head to return while she straddled the territory between reality and make-believe. "Miss Katrin?" The whisper was clear and had Dego's twang. She staggered toward the sound. A silhouette stood at the end of the dark hall. Her heart and head raced while she pushed against the walls—working her way toward him.

"Dego?"

His eyes glinted and he smiled as Katherine held her arms out. She hugged him—he was cold. Icy cold. "Miss Katrin, you gone get yo-self in terrible trouble you stay 'round Will. He tried killin' me today. Shoot me wit' dat dart gun when I's crawlin' 'round them slick rocks at de river. You get yo-self shed a him quick." He whispered so fast she couldn't keep up. "He done got himself lock up in Baton Rouge for messin' wit' a little girl. 'Er daddy try an' kill Will wit' his pocketknife. Dat how he get dat scar on he's chest. Ain't no crock, Miss—"

"Katie?" Will's footsteps fell fast down the hall as Dego began to float—his mouth open as if in a muted scream. A ringing in her ears grew louder and louder as time crawled around on all fours. A tingling, then suddenly Katherine felt heavy. Something tugged her from below. The moment before the world went black, Katherine knew Dego was not floating. She was falling.

***

Katherine woke naked with Will holding a cold cloth against her forehead. Mr. Robichaux snored next to the fireplace. There was a big blank spot in her memory, and the harder she tried to recall last night's events, the more her head hurt.

"Last night"—she pressed her temples—"what the hell happened?"

"You were bloody pissed."

"Pissed?" She attempted to sit up, but a severe pressure and the real possibility of her head imploding forced her to retreat. "What was I pissed about?"

"Translation—shit-faced. Found ya passed out in the hallway."

Nausea gripped her gullet, and she swallowed hard. Took several deep breaths. Closed her eyes and tried to soothe the turbulence. Set her mind back to last night. That's when the image of Dego streaked across her mind like a strange comet. "Did you see him?" she asked without opening her eyes.

"Who?" He tossed a log into the fireplace.

"Dego. He was here." Sparks fluttered up the chimney as the fire cracked.

"Naw. That was blackberry wine and wishful thinking." He brushed aside a lock of hair from her face and presented two pills and a canteen of water.

"I'm well acquainted with wine, and I've never blacked out after one bottle." She swallowed the pills and washed them down.

"You said you didn't drink." He raised his brow.

"I lied."

"Me too. The wine's kind of a blackberry concoction with a kicker. Make it meself."

"This is all just . . ." She shook her head, and the pain pulsed from side to side. "It's too much. I'm really . . . God, I feel like shit."

"Go back to sleep. I left you some coffee and biscuits on the stove." He kissed her forehead. "I'll retrieve the cattle we left tied and be back by noon."

"I need to go."

"You can write your story in peace and quiet."

"What about Dego?"

"Search and rescue are out. Nothin' more we can do."

Katherine sat up. "It's cold." She slid back under the wool blankets in the bedroll.

"Stay put. The fire 'll get goin' and I'll be back in no time." He headed for the door.

"Will?" He stopped—looked back at her. "You ever been to Baton Rouge, Louisiana?"

"Nope," he answered and left as if it weren't an odd question.

When she woke up, it was well past noon. The fire had turned to ash and she felt much better. Clothes were scattered across the floor near the front door. It took a moment to realize they were hers. Last night was still obscure. She pondered Dego. Had he seen her naked? It had to be a dream. A vivid mindfuck caused by Will's blackberry wine.

Fall was giving way to winter, but the chill felt good as Katherine walked to the barn. She found her journal inside the tack room but didn't remember leaving it there. She wondered if Will had read it. Couldn't help but go back to Dego's appearance last night. If he were alive, wouldn't he take his horse? She searched each stall. Cyndi was the only horse in the barn.

The sound of the Slammer startled her. Diesel fumes seeped into the barn as Will backed the truck up to the corrals and left it to idle while he unloaded the last two captured cattle. She gathered her courage and marched out to meet him.

"Why the hell isn't Dego's horse here? 'Cause he was here, that's why! And he—"

"Whoa, Katie." He held out his dirty palms. "I recon his horse wandered off because I didn't tie him properly. Just jumped on the four-wheeler an' took off. Settle down." He squeezed her shoulders. "They found Dego."

She considered all of it for a long while. "Where?"

"Near the dam."

It was like being punched in the heart. "I hoped somehow . . ."

"I know. Me too." He pulled her in, and they clung to each other. Will let go first. Told her he would pay whatever it cost to get Dego's body back to Louisiana and bury him properly.

"Think you could lend a hand for an hour or so? I caught a calf not a mile from here, and his mama ain't goin' far."

"Don't think I'd be much help."

"Always underestimating yourself." Will seemed serious, and for a moment, Katherine felt proud that he wanted her help.

They saddled Cyndi, and Katherine mounted. Will slid the bit into his horse's mouth as Katherine noticed movement on the hill west of the barn. She squinted hard into the sun and pointed. "Oh my God, Will, look."

He turned his head and aimed his sight with hers. "No fucking way." They stared in silent disbelief at Cyclops watching them. "You bastard." Will mounted. "Come on, Katie."

They came at Cyclops from opposite directions. The steer refused to run. Stood his ground atop the treeless hill, as the riders approached vigilantly. Will swung his rope from the front as Katherine came up from behind. The enormous beast had lost so much weight, his ribs showed through. His speckled hide looked loose against his spine and pointed hip bones. The huge head that sprang so proudly now hung low, and his giant eye seemed to be looking somewhere far away.

"What's wrong with him?" Katherine yelled.

"Just pay attention. He's waitin' 'til he can get a good shot at us!" Will threw his rope. It sailed perfectly and dropped around Cyclops's massive horns. "You're done, ya useless cunt!" Will dallied his rope around his saddle horn. Cyclops didn't move. "Rope his heels, Katherine."

Her hands shook as she unstrapped the rope from her saddle and slowly built a loop. The rope felt stiff and heavy and difficult to swing.

"Take your time and bring it around his hind legs. Now!" She threw, and the rope missed the steer's legs. "Come on, Katherine. Gather your rope and try again. You can do it." She rebuilt her loop and missed again. Twice more, she missed, until the loop fell in front of Cyclops's hind legs and Will dragged the beast forward, forcing him to step into the trap. "Lift your rope, Katherine! Lift it up." She did and had Cyclops's hind legs trapped inside her loop. "Now dally! Dally!"

Awkwardly, she wrapped the rope around her saddle horn two, then three, times, and froze. Breathing like she had just run a marathon. Cyclops never fought.

"Now hold tight. I'm gonna take him down." Will backed his horse until their ropes came tight and they had stretched old Cyclops as far as he could go. Slowly, he crashed to earth with the thud of an ancient redwood.

Will stared at the pitiful animal lying there. Not a speck of fight left in him. They waited. Every muscle in Katherine's body tense on the rope.

"He ain't even tryin'. He's givin' up." Will shook his head. "Keep your rope tight." He released his rope and shook it loose. Cautiously, he dismounted. Cyclops closed his eye as Will approached. In one swift motion, Will pulled the rope from around Cyclops's horns.

"Let him go, Katherine." He wiped the crust and flies from Cyclops's eye. Scratched between his horns and locked eyes with him for a while.

In that long moment, Katherine saw more compassion than she thought existed in the world. She laughed and cried until all doubt set sail on a teardrop. Something in the fabric of her life tore free when she released her rope and Will pulled it away from Cyclops's hind legs. She had just received the key to eternal bliss and became privy to the exact moment she fell in love.

"Bugger off now." He swatted old Cyclops on the ass. Slowly, the pitiful brute lifted his heavy horns and head, then struggled to his feet. Tears streaked her face as she stepped off Cyndi and slipped her hand into Will's. He traded her hand for an arm around her shoulder. They watched Cyclops disappear over the hill.

"You're good help. You lookin' for work, *Katherine?*" He leaned hard on the name.

She looked up at him and smiled. "I like it better when you call me Katie."

"Could use your help gathering the mob off Santa Rosa Island, Katie. But we'd need to leave tomorrow."

"Let's go if we're goin'." The words would forever haunt her.

THIRTY-SIX

The release of a lock. The clang of a door opening wakes Kate from the cement floor like an alarm. The joy of loving Will replaced with the reality of regret and a rapid heartbeat. The last few hours seemed like a week, and Kate feels the pain of her busted nose. A throb in her spine shoots to her head as an unfamiliar guard enters. "Let's go if we're going?" a stout young woman asks.

"What?"

"Time for your meds. Then breakfast. Maybe a massage?" Grinning as if impressed by her own sarcasm, she tosses Kate a folded orange jumpsuit.

"I've never had a massage—I mean, a professional one. I'm gonna do that." Kate slips on the jumpsuit still sore as hell, but somehow feeling better, stronger, less guilty about all that has gone wrong in her life. With Em's life. Maybe Freud was right. Reliving the past could have freed some long-festering pressure. She shoves the thought aside.

"Turn around." The woman cuffs Kate's hands behind her back and clamps down on her arm.

"You work out?" Kate asks, flexing her bicep and trying

hard to ignore the guard's extra-strong grip as they walk to the pill line.

A dozen women wait to be administered opioids, injected for diabetes, and creamed with hormones. Kate gets in line and waits patiently for her morning dose of Klonopin and hopes for the approval of a double dose of ibuprofen. If not, she knows Tanya can get her what she needs.

Blood has been drawn, urine samples collected, and at least a dozen forms filled out, all before ten o'clock. Em sits on Maureen's plush couch while fighting images of her skull being hammered and cracked open—exposing her darkest thoughts. Jamal Jindahl, a silver-haired psychiatrist who smells like thieves oil, introduces himself as Em yawns. "Maureen tells me that you like horses."

"Uh-huh."

"My granddaughter loves them also. She is always requesting to go to Golden Gate Park to see the horses. She wants so badly to ride, but she is only five, and her mother will not allow it."

"I won my first buckle when I was four."

"You're kidding me." He looks to Maureen for confirmation.

"Yes, Em is quite an accomplished horsewoman."

"That's incredible." Dr. Jindal seems genuinely impressed. "Well, I look forward to assisting Maureen and speaking with you more when you are recovered from your surgery. How are you feeling about tomorrow?"

"Good, I guess. Ready to get my head straightened out."

Em's vision of Dr. Jindal comes into focus. "Wish I didn't have to wait until tomorrow."

"That's a very good attitude." Dr. Jindal writes in his file.

Maureen's face lights up like a proud parent. "I will be there throughout the entire procedure."

"You will?" Em looks at Maureen.

"Dr. White will also be there monitoring the fetuses."

"If I die"—Em scratches at a clump of oatmeal on her sweatpants—"will the babies be okay?"

"Em, Dr. Sanchez is one of the best neurologists in the country. His surgeries have been very successful."

"I know, but if something goes wrong—I mean, it could go wrong—who will take care of my boys? Mom's in jail. What'll happen to them?" The thought of the boys leading an unfortunate life quickly fouls Em's mood. "Oh God. Maybe you should just strap me down in a straightjacket 'til I go into labor." Em drops her head in her hands.

"Em." Maureen sounds disappointed. "Your sons are going to be fine. As will you. And if by the slightest of odds anything does go wrong, I will personally take responsibility for maintaining their care." Maureen waits while Dr. Jindal watches her.

Em rubs her eyes.

"Perhaps you will feel better after lunch," Maureen suggests.

Em nods.

"It was nice to meet you, Emma Lee, and I look forward to speaking with you again soon."

The Tramadol Tanya slipped Kate earlier, mixed with Klonopin, causes Kate to nod off in the visitation room until her San Francisco attorney finally arrives. "Ms. Dunnigan. Sorry I'm late." Steven Kline holds his hand out and Kate shakes it.

"Nice to meet you." Kate stands, a pretty powdery blue broadening under her swollen eyes.

"Your arraignment is in an hour, so I'll get to the point." Steven pushes his heavy-rimmed glasses up his aggressive nose. "I have good news. The prosecutor is charging you with voluntary manslaughter based on the forensic evidence and your confession and not first-degree murder."

"Voluntary manslaughter doesn't sound very good."

"Voluntary manslaughter is the unlawful killing of a human being without malice during a sudden quarrel or in the heat of passion. Heat of passion varies depending on the situation, but generally refers to an irresistible emotion that a reasonable person would experience under the same facts and circumstances. I've had a fair amount of success with these cases. And with what you told me, we focus on proving Mr. Dunnigan was abusing your daughter."

Kate sits and sighs. "And just how do we do that?"

"Did you ever file a report? Tell *anyone* about the abuse?"

"No."

Steven writes on a yellow legal tablet. "Would your daughter be willing to testify?"

"Not an option."

"Any other victims who would testify?"

"Not that I'm aware of. But—"

Steven stops writing, looks up, and waits, then says, "We have to prove sexual abuse or at the very least introduce the valid possibility of it."

Kate focuses on dust dancing on a sunbeam coming through a high window. "There was—or is, I guess—a child."

Steven straightens in his chair and waits.

Kate chews her ragged thumbnail, then spits it out fast. "Em had a son with her father. Soon as he was born, I dropped him off at Saint Joseph's."

Steven clicks his pen twice. "I need the date you dropped him off."

"Maybe I just plead guilty—tell 'em it was self-defense— whatever happens, happens."

"After reviewing the evidence, I suggest we request postponing the arraignment. Put off entering a plea until Monday. You're looking at a year, maybe two, before we go to trial. Right now, today"—he taps the table with his index finger—"the judge won't set bail, but if there's evidence that the state is not aware of, such as sexual abuse . . ." He smiles, crosses his arms, and leans back in his chair. "If we get DNA evidence—you're out of here on bail."

"Really?"

"I'm being paid to advise you. I recommend we retain a local lawyer to assist in the case and locate this child *immediately*. If we can obtain DNA, the judge has to consider bail. Hell, when we hit them with incest and back it up with DNA proof—add on some self-defense, dropping the damn charges will be the least they can do. Can you endure a few more days in here?"

Kate lets her swollen and bruised eyelids drop. "He'd be 'bout fifteen, I guess."

THIRTY-SEVEN

riday morning, Kate is allowed back into the general population to clean bathrooms. As she mops around a toilet, all she can think of is Em and her surgery. Brain surgery—even the words are repulsive. Garcia walks across the freshly mopped floor—her rubber soles barking like the ravens that constantly followed Kate around the ranch. Giving her the creeps. "Ed Manetti scheduled an attorney consultation with you today at one."

"Oh. Okay. Thanks." Kate pulls on rubber gloves.

Garcia stays and watches. Resting her hands on her heavy leather belt until finally sharing what's on her mind. "Between you and me, he's not a very good attorney. Blankenship is better. You should hire him—your life could depend on it." She says it like she has a stake in the outcome.

"I'm not even sure what he wants." Kate sprays disinfectant on the toilet, then lifts the seat and sprays some more.

"He said he was representing you."

"My lawyer must a hired him."

"Okay." She sighs and looks around the bathroom, then back at Kate. "You didn't hear this from me, but FYI, he's a convicted felon." Garcia turns. Walks away taking her barking raven steps with her.

A felon? Could be just what I need.

A fetal monitor beeps a prenatal percussion accompanied by two quick backbeats and a thumping underwater bass as Em falls under sedation.

"This is Emma Lee Quick. She has a left posterior temporal tumor. Does everyone agree?" His voice is muffled, and Em laughs as an evil Ronald McDonald lookalike nods an exaggerated agreement.

"*Yep, yep.*" The cross-eyed clown claps, then hands Em a Happy Meal. Suddenly, a Skilsaw, screeching like a lunatic, penetrates a cash register. Em wants to run, but she's paralyzed as smoke and money and meat gush from the machine. Ronald tosses the saw aside. *"Take the tumor— leave the brains."* He sounds like Goofy. *"Take the tumor— leave the brains."*

"Emma Lee? Emma Lee?" The new voice is firm. Professional. Insistent. "Can you open your eyes?"

Em savors the calm darkness now that the crazed clown has disappeared.

"Open your eyes, Emma Lee." Something metal clangs. "Oh my gosh."

"I did the same thing last week."

"This tray should not be here."

Em lingers in the tranquility of sedation.

"Emma Lee, you have to wake up. Open your eyes for me, dear," he commands.

Light seeps in as Em cracks her eyes. The brightness stings. She clinches her eyes and turns her head but can't escape the pain in her throat, like swallowing razor blades. "Ma thro . . ." She murmurs. The fetal monitor banging away.

"Emma Lee, you're in recovery. Your surgery went well."

"Maa thro."

"I know your throat hurts. It's from the tube, dear. It will get better. I performed your surgery and you did wonderful."

"Mmm . . ." Em sucks in a deep breath.

"The surgery did not affect your fetuses whatsoever."

Em smiles.

"Can you call Dr. Yamaguchi, let her know that Emma Lee is awake."

"Of course," a soft voice replies.

A green door buzzes. Garcia opens it and allows Kate to pass through. Her leg chains rattle in an attempt to convince her she's suddenly a dangerous criminal as she drags her feet to a seat at the table. Ed Manetti stands as Kate sits. Her hands instinctively want to rest on the table, but the chain around her waist keeps her cuffed hands from roaming. Garcia steps inside the door before it clicks shut and the buzzing stops.

"I'm Edward Manetti." His silver hair couldn't be cropped any closer to his head, and the stubble on his face could be considered chic but feels more like laziness. His gray-blue eyes keep her guessing.

"Hi, Edward. I'm Kate, but suppose you know that—and a whole lot more." She resists the urge to chant, *"Edd-ie*

Man-etti, Edd-ie Man-etti." It has a nice ring to it.

"Attorney Steven Kline contacted me." He's tall even when he's sitting and kicks a foot under the table. His imitation leather loafers are split along the side. That's when doubt enters Kate's mind. A successful or even competent lawyer could afford a decent pair of shoes. "Mr. Kline explained your situation, and I've read your files and the charges against you. You should know, locating missing persons is not something I usually do, but in this case—"

"He's not missing."

"The procedure is the same." He spins a few papers and slides them in front of Kate. "I'll need your signature before we proceed." He sets the stem of a pen next to the papers, and Kate catches a whiff of him, like cedar on a hot summer day.

Kate sighs. Looks at the ink-filled tube minus its sturdy body and wonders how someone would kill a lawyer with a real pen. Nailing the carotid artery with precision would take expert skill and damn good luck. But why? Why would anyone want to kill someone who's trying to help them? "What's this gonna cost?"

"I bill by the hour and typically require a retainer. I understand your situation is unique." Mr. Manetti leans back in his chair. "Finding the boy could take a while. Mr. Kline suggested a flat rate, and I agreed."

Kate stands, leans over the table, and lifts the guts of the pen. "Sure. How much?"

He looks her in the eye. "Eight thousand plus expenses."

Kate raises her brow, chews on the number. Digests it.

Suddenly aware of why a person would want to stab their lawyer with a pen. With cuffed hands, she tosses the pen to Curtis. "No, thanks." The reaction was a natural reflex. A learned habit from years of buying and selling horses that made trading half the fun. Besides her daughter, it was one of the few useful things Will had left her. Kate looks at Garcia, a feeling of doubt quickly turns to regret. *Should have just signed the damn contracts. Pay whatever the son of a bitch wants to charge no matter how ridiculous and get the hell out of here. This is no time to dicker. Christ.*

"Excuse me?"

"That's too much. So, no, thanks." Too late to back down now. Kate indicates to Garcia that she's ready to go with a twist of her thumb.

"Ma'am, locating people is not simple. It can be extremely time consuming. I have to neglect my other clients in order to focus on your case." Mr. Manetti stands. Pressing his fingers into the table while a half smile curdles his lip. Kate and Garcia watch him. "I don't think you comprehend the situation you're in. You don't have time to waste shopping for attorneys. Unless you like it in here?" His pronounced Adam's apple bobs as he swallows.

"The baby was dropped off. You have all the pertinent information. Calaveras County is small, records ain't hard to find. And people love to talk. If you can't find that kid in a few days, you ain't tryin'. I'll give you three thousand if you find him by Monday. *Before* I'm arraigned."

Mr. Manetti sucks his teeth while his face turns red. His fake grin widens as he shakes his head. "Ma'am. I did not come here to negotiate a deal with you. Eight thousand dollars to locate someone is a very standard and reasonable rate. I assure you."

"Not in Calaveras. It'd take most folks three or four months to make eight thousand bucks." Kate waits. Garcia smiles, clearly enjoying the negotiating. "Three thousand— take it or leave it." Kate looks deadpan at the man. "And *only* if you find him by Monday."

"Ma'am . . ." He massages the bridge of his nose. Clearly frustrated.

Garcia raises her brow at Mr. Manetti. Clasps her hands in front of her crouch and stands wide legged. Silence lingers while they wait for Mr. Manetti's response. Sweat beads his brow while he fumbles with his papers, then laces his fingers. "Christ. I can probably give you a discount."

"And I can probably give you three thousand dollars."

He glares at Kate. "I'll give you a fifty-percent discount. Best I can do." He scratches on the contracts with his stab-proof pen. Crossing out numbers and initialing paragraphs. Barely legible. Garcia stops her smile by pressing her lips together while looking at the floor. Without a word, Manetti slides Kate the contracts along with the pen.

"Get a hold of pastor Ken Berry. He was at Saint Joseph's church back then. Maybe still is, I don't know." Kate leans and reaches the pen. Manetti watches as she struggles to sign them. "You wanna write that down? Pastor Ken Berry. Bet he knows right where that baby went."

"He did," Manetti says, straight-faced.

"What?" Kate signs the last page and Manetti gathers them.

"I spoke to him this morning." He looks up at Kate—a

half smile creases his face as satisfaction radiates off him. He looks good. Really good, Kate thinks.

"Huh." Kate sits. "What'd he say?"

"Kid was adopted. Lives in Rail Road Flat."

"Holy shit." *That baby. That spawn is living in Rail Road?* "You seen him?"

"No. I'll contact the parents today, explain the situation and see if they'll agree to DNA without a court order."

"Holy shit." Kate shuts her eyes. Takes a deep breath through her nose. "Son of a bitch." Kate opens her eyes and sits up smiling. "You're good, Ed-die Man-etti."

"So are you. Definitely the first to ever get a discount."

"Got a soft spot for hostile women, huh?" Kate smiles.

"Perceptive ones. Have a nice day, Ms. Dunnigan." Eddie pats her shoulder on the way out the door.

A hand lightly touches Em's shoulder. "Em? It's Maureen."

"Hey." Em turns her head toward Maureen but doesn't bother to open her useless eyes—happy to hear something other than the continuous whomp, whomp, whomp of the fetal monitor. "Feels like I got a pillow wrapped around my head." Em tries to touch her head, but her right hand is cuffed to the bed.

"How are you feeling?"

"Like I just had brain surgery." Em reaches for Maureen's hand. Finds it and holds it tight. "When will we know if I'm crazy?"

"When you've recovered, we can begin analyzing that. Dr. Sanchez removed a sizable tumor. He will go over all the details of your recovery with you later. Just know that you and your twins are healthy."

"The nurse said it was the size of a lemon."

"You know what they say about life giving you lemons?"

"You make lemonade?" Em opens her eyes just so she can roll them.

"Oh my gosh, that was absolutely awful of me. I am so sorry." Maureen shakes her head as Em lets out a weak laugh, then yawns. "You should sleep, it is getting late."

"Stay," Em mumbles. "Please?"

"Okay." Maureen drags a chair next to Em's bed. "I'll be right here."

"Tell me about Uncle Pat."

Maureen clears her throat and sits. "I do not think that's a good idea. I understand—"

"Please. I just want to know him."

"He was the best person I have ever known." Monitors fill the long silence. Em finds Maureen's hand and places it on her belly as one of the babies kicks. "Oh my!" Maureen gasps. "Pat would have loved this. He wanted children so badly." Maureen presses on Em's belly. "We met at Stanford and . . ." Em can hear the caution in Maureen as she takes a long breath. "We fell in love. For me, it was love at first sight. I had never had a real boyfriend before. We had so much in common, both wanting to practice medicine and help people." Her tone suddenly honeyed. "I couldn't manage the graphic sight of the operating theater. My ears would start ringing. I would break out in a cold sweat and faint. After the third time, Pat suggested I see a psychiatrist. He even set up an appointment for me, but I refused. Thought I needed to medicate." Maureen grunts, then waits, maybe for a reaction from Em, but gets none. "I began drinking and . . ." Maureen takes her hand off Em's belly and her voice turns somber. "I am not exaggerating when I say Patrick saved my life. If it were not for him, I would likely be in prison—or dead." Em waits quietly, hoping for more. "There is not a day that goes by that I do not try to make amends. You want to hear about your uncle, and I went completely off track."

"I like the sound of your voice."

"Hello?" A nurse opens the door. "Hi. Time to check vitals. How are you feeling, Miss Quick?"

"I will see you later." Maureen pats Em's hand.

"Hugs." Em holds her arm out.

"Um. Yes. Okay." Maureen steps to the far side of the bed and avoids Em's IV. She carefully hovers and puts her hands on Em's shoulders. Gives them an awkward squeeze while Em wraps her free arm around Maureen and demonstrates a proper hug.

Dear Spawn . . .

Kate stares at the word, then scratches it out hard with a pencil. She wads up the paper and starts over—

It's odd that I don't know your name since suddenly I can't stop thinking about you. I have forced you out of my mind for so long, but now, all of the sudden, I can't shake you. You're fifteen, and I wonder what your life is like. Where do you live in Rail Road Flat? Did your parents tell you you were adopted? Are your parents kind? Do they love you? Do you love them? Are you happy?

Maybe someday we can meet and, if you want, I can tell you about your mom. I am your—

Kate wads the letter up, tosses it into the trash, and walks to the phones.

There are two phones on the white cinder-block wall of the Calaveras County jail. Kate replaces the sticky receiver, wipes her hand on her pants, and tries the neighboring phone. "Kate Dunnigan," she says to the computerized operator assisting with the collect call.

"Hello, Kate."

"Maureen, hi, how is she?"

"Fine. I just spoke to her, and she is recovering well. The procedure took longer than Dr. Sanchez anticipated, almost six hours, but we were successful."

"What about her mental . . ." Kate doesn't know how to label it—what to call it. "I mean—"

"We won't be able to diagnosis while she is in ICU. Sleep is an essential part of the brain's recovery. Since she will be unable to return to a favorable environment, I have requested that Dr. Sanchez extend her hospital stay by one week, then initiate a rehabilitation program. In the meantime, I will visit her every day and assess her thoughts, feelings, and behavior. Her ability to remember and cope will play a vital role in the recovery process.

"What about the babies?"

"The most incredible thing happened, I felt them kick."

The fetal monitor broadcasts the twins' rapid heartbeats as a sharp pain wakes Em. Attempting to grab the pain, she grabs her belly, but only her left hand is free and now she remembers why. Something is wet and sticky between her legs. *Did I piss the bed? Is it the medication?* More pain hits like a truck rolling from her back to her abdomen and coming to rest in her pelvis. "Oh, owww!" She wants to double over, but can only get halfway. "Help." Wrapping her left arm around herself. "Hey!" No one comes. "Help!" The pain and pressure is unbearable for a moment and then begins to subside. *"Hey!"* Em runs her left hand up and down the side of the bed, searching for the cord with the call button attached. Her cuff slides and bangs against the opposite bed rail as she tries with her right hand to find the call button. "Where is it!" The cord is wedged between the mattress and rail, but Em finds it. Follows the cord with her left hand as far as she can and works the remainder through her fingers until she has the button.

Within thirty seconds, a nurse is in the room. "Yes?"

Em feels her move closer. "Something's happening. There's a lot of bad pain." Em swallows. "I might have wet the bed."

"Oh, that's okay, it happens. Not to worry."

Em feels the nurse pull the covers back. "Oh. Um, I have to get the doctor. I'll be right back."

"What's wrong? What's happening?" Em feels pain and pressure winding up again in her pelvis and tightening in her abdomen.

Breaths are hard and fast and loud. "Emma Lee, I'm Dr. Loredo." A strong light clicks on overhead. "I'm the physician on duty tonight." Em feels his hand on her thigh.

"Can you describe your pain?"

"It hurts like fucking hell. Like crazy pressure." Em squeezes her lower abdomen.

"Okay. It's possible your placenta has detached. Unfortunately, you're hemorrhaging and probably going into premature labor."

"No." The thought of losing her sons overrides the pain. "It's too soon, right?"

"Contact her obstetrician."

"Yes, sir," the nurse says.

"Call Maureen Yamaguchi. I need her."

"Who's Maureen, hon?" the nurse asks.

"My doctor." The pain feels like it's crushing her spine. Em wads up the corner of her blanket, shoves it over her mouth, and screams.

Kate twists the phone cord around her fingers. "The kid's still in the county. Rail Road Flat ain't twenty miles from here. If his folks let us get his DNA, we can prove what Will did and I'm outta here."

"That is fantastic news."

"I don't want to get my hopes up too much, but . . ."

"It sounds encouraging. Kate, hold on." There's silence on the line until Maureen returns. "Kate, the hospital is calling. I should take it."

THIRTY-EIGHT

The smell of BBQ sauce and burgers wafts on the breath of a new voice. "We're going to move you, Emma Lee."

The bed is moving forward, then turning, then backing. Now forward again. Click-clack and the entire bed is rolling.

"I've got the IV."

Em forces her eyes to focus and sees a faceless dark-haired woman next to her. Out the door, passing windows. More doors. Faster and faster down the hall, now stopped at the elevator.

"Are my babies going to be okay?"

"I hope so, hon. I'll pray for them." The faceless dark-haired woman says it like she means it.

"Thank you."

"You have a very good doctor, and you're in the best possible place to give birth."

Give birth? It sounded so good at first. "But they're too little. Right?"

"We have a level-three neonatal intensive care unit here. They have amazing success with preemies."

The elevator dings. Doors open and another contraction hits. Muscles strain and knot. Suddenly, an overwhelming urge to push erupts, and Em leans back against the bed. "Ughhhh!" Gripping the cold metal rails on the bed, she pushes. Another ding and the bed rolls out of the elevator and travels only a short distance before coming to a halt.

"I have Emma Lee Quick," the nurse says, and Em hears the worry in her voice. "Dr. Loredo ordered a bed."

"Room 204 on the right."

The bed is in motion again. Fast. The rush of cool air feels good against Em's sweaty face. Oh *shit!*" The contraction peaks. She clenches her jaw—throws her head to the side. Muscles trembling as she spreads her knees and lets go of an unrepressed scream.

The wool blanket feels like a hideaway as Kate wiggles under it and yawns. After last night on a cement floor, sleeping in the bunk bed is divine. Below is the new girl, Elizabeth. Tall and slender with long blonde hair. She could easily pass for twelve or thirteen and reminds Kate of a prepubescent Em. Kate listens to the rhythm of the girl breathing, then stretches and searches for gratitude. With a smile, she thinks, *Em is okay. Maybe even sane. I've got the money to hire good lawyers. That lawyer today, what a conniving bastard—Eddie Manetti. Why would someone name their kid Eddie Manetti? It's mean, but it probably forced him to defend himself at an early age—like that song, "A Boy Named Sue." Kids are cruel. He's probably married. No, divorced. Definitely divorced— twice. He's not that good looking. But he is smart. How'd he get so smart? Prison maybe. He sure did smell good. Maybe because he didn't shower and had to compensate with cologne. He'll get the boy's DNA. Then they'll know the truth. Shit. They'll all know the truth. All the hell poor Em's been through. But they'll blame me. Not the deviant father. Never. It's always the mother's fault. The murdering mother. Sounds like the name of a bad movie. Oh well, fuck them. Fuck them all. Only thing that matters is Em and those babies.*

"They're coming. Where's her doctor?" someone says in a hushed voice as they gently lift Em's feet into the stirrups.

"You can do this, hon. You just go ahead and push those babies out now." It's the dark-haired nurse, and she takes Em's left hand. "Squeeze my hand. It's okay." Every muscle quakes as Em pushes. "Push hard and squeeze hard as you can."

"She's crowning." The hushed voice sounds worried.

"Good job, hon." The nurse cradles Em's hand with both of hers. "Take a break now. Just breathe, okay? Nice and deep and slow."

Em takes deep breathes and sees a figure standing just inside the door. She forces her focus on the person but can't make him or her out.

"Maureen?"

"I'm right here."

"The boys are coming, and it's too soon. They're too little." Em begins to cry.

Maureen moves next to Em. "They may have to undergo extra care, but—"

"When the doctor arrives, you'll have to go," someone says.

The hushed voice rebukes. "If she's her birth coach, she can stay. She *is* your birthing coach, right, hon?" The nurse holding Em's hand squeezes it twice.

"Yes, I need her."

The nurse releases Em's free hand, and Maureen takes over. "I will do my best," she whispers.

Another contraction sets in. "It's starting again. Oh God." Em tightens her grip on Maureen's hand.

"How are we doing?" Dr. Loredo steps between Em's legs.

"Talk to her," the nurse instructs Maureen. "Just reassure her."

"Have you considered any names yet?" Maureen asks.

"Huh?" Em looks at Maureen's face and can make out a full smile. "Maureen, tell me to breath, or relax, or something! Shit!"

"Oh. I am not very good at this."

The contraction is strong along with the urge to push. Em digs her heels into the stirrups, tucks her chin to her chest, and bears down. Tightening every muscle deep inside until she can feel the pressure of a head on the verge of release.

"Okay. Very nice. Push now. Hard as you can until I tell you to stop," Dr. Loredo instructs with a calm, quiet candor.

Em gathers her strength, takes a deep breath, and pushes with all her might until the little head leaves her body. Shoulders slide out with little effort. The release of pain and pressure and exhaustion force Em to go limp as Dr. Loredo holds a tiny thing in his hands. "It's a boy." He methodically passes him to the nurse, who is waiting with a warm towel. Both nurses go to work. Suctioning fluid from his mouth and nose. Weighing, wiping, clamping, clipping, and measuring the little body. His cry is as delicate as his body. The size of a beanie baby, Em thinks. No, she must be wrong. Her eyes are unreliable, and now they're causing objects to appear smaller than normal.

"You did it, hon! You did it! It's a beautiful little baby boy!" The nurse shows Em her son from across the room.

"I can hardly see him. Is he okay?" Em looks to Maureen. "Is he okay, Maureen?" Maureen releases Em's hand, steps away, and crashes at the foot of the bed. "Maureen?"

"I think she fainted, hon. It happens."

"Oh my God." Another contraction hits, peaks, and subsides all while a new nurse helps Maureen into a wheelchair. "Maureen?"

"I am so sorry." Maureen's labored breath. "I am not suited for this. I should have known better."

With her heels pressing hard into the stirrups, Em tucks her chin to her chest, clutches the bed rails, and prepares to deliver her second son.

THIRTY-NINE

Saturday morning prisoners are painting and prepping their unfortunate faces for visitation. By ten a.m., family and friends have waited in long lines to be scrutinized and searched before making contact with the incarcerated woman in their life. Shannon relived the entire painful process, step by horrifying step, to Kate, who was pleasantly surprised that her mother had made the effort. The drive from San Francisco to San Andreas should have been reason enough not to come. *So why? What does she want?* That familiar twinge of suspicion rears its ugly head, but Kate buries it.

A wall of plexiglass separates citizens from riffraff. A toddler bangs his chubby fist against the fake glass. "Mama, Mama!" He bawls and reaches for his mother. Arching his back and throwing his entire body her way. On the wrong side of the glass, his mother's mascara runs like black tears down her bronze cheeks. The guard reprimands the little boy with an understanding smile and a wagging finger.

"I don't blame you," Shannon says, avoiding Kate's narrowing eyes.

Kate tenses and crosses her legs. Confessing to murder and explaining her entire defense to her mother felt good for a moment.

Shannon glances at Kate, then smooths her plaid skirt. "Given the circumstances, I may have done the same."

A split-second satisfaction comes over Kate. Then, something kicks in, like when you see a familiar face, and Kate recalls that Shannon always pets the dog before she kicks it. "You didn't come here to patch things up or see if I was okay, did you, Shannon?" Calling her mother by her first name always pinched a nerve.

"I pray for you, Katherine. Every night—on my knees." Her voice becomes sharp.

"Well, you can stop 'cause it ain't workin'."

"I can pray for whomever I choose!" Shannon, gruff as any angered good Catholic can be. She fingers the gold crucifix hanging at her breast. It seems to soothe her. "I've handled the arrangements for Patrick's funeral. They *finally* completed the autopsy and the coroner has released his remains. It's just sinful making us wait so long. I had to pay the mortuary five hundred dollars to transport him to the funeral home. *Five hundred dollars.* What a racket."

"When's the service?"

"Monday."

"This Monday?"

"Yes." Shannon's lips purse as she crosses her arms. Preparing for battle.

"You be sure and let everyone know I send my love." Kate stands as every bit of her tightens.

"Besides sending your love—could you send a check?"

"There it is!" Kate feels the sick relief of being right.

"Funerals aren't cheap. And, since Patrick saw fit to leave his entire estate to you . . ." Shannon stands, facing Kate. "It's only fitting, since your daughter—"

"Shannon! You best stop." Kate slams her fists on the counter. "I knew you'd never come here just to see how I was doin'." Kate fights back tears. "Not even ask, how's the food here? Are you getting any sleep? How are you getting along with the other prisoners? Nope. Couldn't even pretend to give a shit that I have two black eyes and a busted nose!" Kate hates the disappointment taking over. Hates that Shannon can still get to her after all these years. Forming a lump in her throat. Stinging her eyes. "I'll pray for *you*, Shannon."

"I'd prefer a check."

Kate leans into the plexiglass. "When the funds are available, I'll pay for the funeral. The entire fucking thing. Keep your money, old woman—and take it with you straight to hell." Kate swallows her tears as she passes prisoners who are no doubt loved and truly missed by their poverty-stricken people on the opposite side of the glass. Envy makes her want to punch something, someone. A vending machine stands in for Shannon, and Kate punches it as hard as she can without slowing down. Pain fires from her fist to her shoulder and cures the hurt inside.

Nearing the pay phones, Kate concentrates on her breath. Forcing calm as she closes her eyes and leans against the wall. In less than five minutes, Kate is cool enough to call Maureen collect.

"Kate?"

"Hi, Maureen. Sorry to call so early. I just wanted to tell you my mother has planned Pat's funeral for Monday. *This* Monday. I can't believe she—"

"Kate!" Maureen interrupts. "There was a complication with Em. She went into premature labor and gave birth late last night."

"Jesus—are the babies . . ."

"Both boys. They are in the neonatal intensive care unit. They are extremely premature, but Dr. White is working with a specialist who has a terrific track record. They are receiving the best possible care."

Kate won't consider not having the twins. Can't consider it. They die—she dies. "Boys, huh. Grandsons." She forces a smile, and it seems to make her feel better for a fraction of a moment.

"Patrick and Joseph."

The names are like a kick to her gut. "You're kidding me?" Part of her wants to cry—break down completely. She laughs.

"I seldom kid."

Kate leans against the wall. Laughing. "Don't you think that's funny?" Kate's laughter teeters on hysterical. "Not funny ha-ha, but funny. Like fucked-up kind of funny. Right?"

"What I think is irrelevant. Em does not see it the way you or I do. These were people she loved and lost. Not her victims. She may or may not ever comprehend her actions, and it certainly was not the time or place for a therapeutic discussion."

"Patrick and Joseph." Kate nods, reining in her laughter and wiping away tears. Wondering if she should try to catch Shannon and give her the good news. She pictures the baby boys—their tiny bodies—cradling and cuddling them. That sweet newborn baby smell. She loves them already. "I gotta get outta here."

"This may sound harsh, but to be perfectly honest, giving birth buys Em more time. She can remain hospitalized rather that incarcerated."

"I bet she's scared to death. Can I call her?"

"I think so. I would like to get a read on her reaction to you. I'm meeting with Dr. White at ten o'clock, and then I will see Em. Call me at eleven, and if she is receptive, you can speak to her."

"Really? I'll pay you back for all these collect calls. I'm sure they ain't cheap."

"Please don't concern yourself with that. And, Kate, I *am* sorry about Pat's funeral arrangements. Perhaps it's better this way."

"If anyone else had arranged the funeral, I'd be grateful."

"It is one less issue for you to deal with right now. Be grateful."

Micro-preemies is what the specialist labeled the boys. Patrick weighs in at exactly two pounds, and Joseph tips the scales at one pound, fourteen ounces. From what Em could see, they were like baby birds that had fallen from their nest too soon. The size of a squirrel. Breastfeeding wasn't an option. It will take some time before the preemies will develop the coordination to suck and swallow. They partake of mama's milk via a feeding tube, one of the NIC unit nurses had said so.

Breast milk has extra nutrients—Em knew it was true with mares and foals and had to be true with her boys. Antibodies that babies, especially premature babies, need. "Colostrum, right?"

"Exactly. Pumping your breasts will stimulate production." The lactation consultant, Dora or Laura, sounds like she's hearing impaired. Between the meds and the masses of nurses and doctors in and out of the room, what did a name matter? Em hasn't the energy to care. Dora or Laura rolls a machine next to Em's bed. "Mama's milk is much easier to digest than formula. And we can freeze what we don't use." Dora or Laura unties the back of Em's cotton gown. "Let's slide your arm out." The handcuff clacks. Dora or Laura sees Em's right wrist is cuffed to the bed. "Oh."

Em uses her free hand to pull her gown below both breasts. "Take your pick."

"Okay. Well. Okay." Dora or Laura wipes Em's nipples down with an antibacterial wipe and turns on the pump. It sounds like a vacuum cleaner on the fritz. The woman places a nipple guard, then a suction cup with a small bottle attached to it against Em's left nipple. It grabs hold, then another on the right. The tug begins. The drag and release is similar to the milking machines used at dairies, Em thinks. The stimulation sets off a tingle, an odd sexual sensation, and Em worries why.

"When can I see them?" Em asks over the arousal and vibrating pump.

"You'll have to ask your doctor. I would think as soon as you're out of recovery. But I'm not sure." The woman adjusts Em's left breast inside a clear plastic nipple guard.

"Hello?" Maureen knocks on the door and cracks it. "It's Maureen."

"Come in," Em says over the humming of the machine.

"You may want to give us about ten minutes." Dora or Laura steps to the door in front of Maureen.

"Oh, of course." Maureen steps back. "I'm sorry."

"No!" Em yells. "Maureen."

"I'll just wait outside."

"Thank you." Laura or Dora shuts the door.

"Can she please come in."

"Soon as we're done. It won't take long, I promise. Look. You're lactating!" The woman's excitement over milk production seems abnormal. "Look at that!"

"Yeah." Em could see the milk. It was blurry, but she could see it. Milk filling little bottles. "Oh my God. I see it." Her eyes were clearing. "I can see it." Em's excitement fuels Dora's or Laura's, and the woman claps. Em sees the woman's smiling face. "You have braces."

"Yes." The woman's smile fades.

In less than ten minutes the lactation consultant has her equipment and her milk and is working her way out the door. "I'll be back in a few hours."

"Thank you."

As soon as the woman clears the door, Maureen pokes her head in. "I can see you!" Em spouts.

Maureen stops just inside the door. "Clearly?"

"Better than before."

"How many fingers am I holding up?" Maureen makes a piece sign.

"Two."

"Yes!" Maureen rushes to Em's side and hugs her. "Terrific. Just terrific."

"I can't wait to see my babies."

"They won't be able to leave the NIC unit for a while, so it will depend on your recovery, which seems to be going fantastic." Maureen pulls the chair from the corner up next to Em.

"I had a dream last night," Em says as she adjusts her sagging gown back over her shoulder. "It was so real." Maureen lifts and tightens Em's gown, then reties the back. "I was here. In this room, in this bed. The doctor came in and unwrapped my bandage. My head was bald and there was a big bulge in the center of my forehead." Em presses her fingers to the center of her bandaged forehead. "The bulge moved around under my skin like it wanted out." Maureen sits on the edge of the bed. "It had a tail—like an organism you'd see under a microscope or something."

"A flagellate."

"It starts squirming and twisting out of my forehead like smoke. Then it becomes this ghost-looking creature. Floating up higher and higher until it started thrashing in the air, like it wants to leave but it can't 'cause its tail is stuck in my head. I tried to scream, but you know how in dreams nothing ever comes out?" Maureen nods with a look of uncertainty.

"How did the dream end?"

"It finally came loose and floated away. I think it represents that my demons have left." Em doesn't dare share the entire dream. The full truth. That, in fact, her father appeared in the dream and pulled the demon's tail from her head. Then killed it with a hatchet. It's just a dream, and her father's appearance in it is perfectly normal subconscious residue, she hopes. "Now my eyes are getting better. Do you think it could be a sign?"

"I would certainly like to believe so. What matters is what you believe. Do you know who Plato was?"

"I heard of him. He was a philosopher or something?"

"That's right. In Ancient Greece. He was extremely intelligent. I studied his writing, and he believed that the capacity of dreaming was given by the gods to man so that he might have some apprehension of truth."

Em thinks a while. "I'll go with that."

Maureen's cell ding-dongs, and she pulls the phone from her coat pocket. "Hello? Yes." She waits.

Em reaches a cup of water from the nightstand and fills the silence with gulps.

"Kate. Hold on please." Maureen touches her cell screen and leans into Em. "How do you feel about talking to your mother?"

"She's on the phone?"

"Yes."

"Does she wanna talk to me?"

"Yes. But you do not have to speak to her if you're not ready."

"I want to." Em puts the water back on the stand. Maureen pokes the screen and unmutes it, then pokes it again, putting Kate on speaker.

"Kate, I'm here with Em. You're on speakerphone."

"Hi, Mom."

"Hi, sweetie. How are you?"

Em hesitates. The flowery tone of Mom's voice soothes her like the sweet scent of lavender. "I'm okay. How are you? Where are you?"

"I'm fine. I hear I have grandsons."

"Yep. Joseph and Patrick." She imagines the tiny beings alone in incubators. Wanting to be held. Crying for their sick mother who is cuffed to a bed.

"I can't wait to see them. And you."

"Me too." A burst of dread sucks at Em. Like falling down a mine shaft. "Mom?"

"Uh-huh?"

"Mom?" At the bottom of the mine, timbers are cracking and she realizes in a moment she will be trapped forever. "Mom!" Em begins to cry. Panic making it hard to breathe.

"Em?"

Maureen sets her hand on Em's shoulder. "What is it, Em?"

Em only shakes her head—sobbing. Both hands in fists like it hurts. Tears soaking her pain-filled face.

"Em? Try and tell us. Are you—"

"Mom! I can't—" Her entire body stiffens.

"Take deep breaths. Focus on oxygen filling your lungs," Maureen instructs. "Feel yourself calming with each release.

Deep breath in." Maureen breathes with Em. "There. And slowly release. One more time." Slow and methodical, Em and Maureen breathe together until the hysteria softens.

"I love you, Em." Kate clears her throat. "I love you more than anything in this world."

"You shouldn't." Em shakes her head.

"Well, I do."

"Em? It's important to understand what you are feeling."

"I want to go home." The words burst from Em's gut. "Please. I wanna go home so bad. I miss my mom—and Joe. I wanna be home with Joe and my mom and my babies like a normal family, and now it's never gonna happen!" The truth is too much, and Em slams the back of her head into the pillow. "Please take me home. I'll be good, Mom, come get me. Please!"

"Kate, perhaps you can call me later?"

"I'll try. I love you, Em. Don't you give up. We're in this together. We have to stay strong for those boys. They need us."

"Goodbye, Kate." Maureen disconnects the call.

"Mom!"

"Em, Em, listen to me please." Maureen wraps Em's hand with both of hers. "Em, you are in the midst of a breakdown. Do you understand?"

"No shit, Maureen." Her eyes swim in tears as she sobs.

"This is when breakthroughs occur! After a *breakdown*! *You* are making progress, believe it or not." Maureen smiles and pumps Em's hand. "I am going to ask you a few simple questions. No need to overthink or explain them. Understand?"

Em nods and wipes her snotty nose on her shoulder, and Maureen hands her a cup of water. After a few gulps, Maureen sets the cup back on the bed stand.

Now, you fill in the blanks. I feel disappointed because—" Maureen waits for Em to answer.

Em takes a moment. "Because I can't be home with my babies and Joe and my mom." Hot tears line her face.

"I feel frustrated because—"

"The same thing. I can't be home with my babies."

"I feel angry because—"

"I can't go home!" Em's face stiffens.

"I feel afraid because—"

Em looks up. Doesn't want to answer.

"Em? I feel afraid because?"

"Because of my dad." Em shakes her head. "I'm afraid he might come back. And I'm kind of afraid he might not."

"That is understandable. He has been your security."

Em nods.

"One more, okay? I feel ashamed because—"

"Because . . . because, my dad loved me more than he loved my mom," Em whispers.

FORTY

The cell feels like a sauna. Burning Kate up from the inside out. Sleep is impossible. Perspiration coats her entire body. *Is this it? The beginning of the end? The dreaded change.*

"Elizabeth, are you hot?" Kate asks her lower bunkmate.

"Hell ya!" She laughs and Kate's still not sure about the room temperature. She closes her eyes and drops her shoulders, feels the tension leave.

"One therapist said I might be a nymphomaniac. They have to label you, write something in your file, or it's like they're not doing their job. I do like sex. It makes me feel good. What's wrong with that? Do you like sex, Miss D?" Elizabeth asks Kate—middle-aged inmate, killer, mother of a murderer, and new grandma that can't remember if she likes sex or not. It hasn't been an option for quite a while—or a priority.

"Don't be embarrassed, Miss D. Guys talk about it all the time. Why shouldn't we?"

"I like it just fine. I'm really tired and need to get some sleep."

"Orgasms are better than sleeping pills."

"Okay. Good night."

"Really. You shouldn't let your flower wither. You really shouldn't." The girl pops her head up to Kate's bunk. "Want me to water it for you?"

"*What?* No." Kate rolls over.

"Then you should water it yourself, at least once a day." Elizabeth shakes the bunks as she situates herself back in bed.

"Worry 'bout your own damn garden." Kate hates the girl's comprehension of her flower. *It's not withered, not yet, just a bit wilted. Maybe I should water it myself.* Uninvited visions of Eddie Manettie. His hand touching her. His finger sending that spark, but before Kate can seduce herself, Elizabeth begins to moan and the bunk begins to shudder. A threesome is not part of Kate's fantasy—she pulls the blanket over her head and tries to think of something else. Something good. Something bad. Anything. Pizza. Elizabeth gets louder, and Kate wonders when she became a prude. Completely out of touch with her own sexuality.

Two is Kate's number. Number one was not invited and number two was Will. She decides then and there that the first chance she gets, she's going to fuck someone. Anyone. A one-night stand before she shrivels up.

"Ahhh!" Elizabeth spurts. "Ahhh!" Then, like a jack-in-the-box, her head springs up to Kate. "Just kidding! Hahaha! Gotcha, right?"

Kate looks over her shoulder at the laughing girl. "Yep. You got me alright. Now, can we *please* go to sleep?"

"Okay." The girl disappears. "Good night, Miss D."
"Good night."

Deep in a medicated dream, Em feels Joe tugging on her. Trying hard to pull her up and out of bed by her hands, but she's limp and heavy with sleep. *"Come on, Em. Get up. Come with me."*

Suddenly, it's as if someone pulled the bottom out of Em's world. The sensation of falling takes only a moment, and Em is standing among quaking aspens. Watching Joe from a distance—sleeping with the innocence of a child in his bedroll. Devil's Nose glows in the moonlight above the meadow, and an unknown dread hits Em hard. She runs to Joe barefoot and in her hospital gown, but a sharp wind holds her back. *"Joe!"* He doesn't wake. *"Joe!"* Em drops to her hands and knees and crawls to him. *"Joe. I'm here."*

"Come to bed." Joe folds the bedroll back and makes room for Em.

"I'm so tired," she says, snuggling against his chest. *"And I missed you so much. Where've you been?"*

"You know I've been right here. Waiting for you." Joe kisses her forehead. *"I'm glad you came."*

His lips are warm and tender and feel like heaven when Em kisses them. He wraps his arms around her and for a time smothers the dread seeping in. A long shadow casts across the meadow moving toward them as Em sits up. Terror taking over. *"Joe, something's out there."*

"I know. It's okay. I forgive you." Joe's smile is bigger than any Em has ever seen when blood trickles down his forehead.

"You're bleeding!" She looks for something to stop the blood. Looks around the camp. Looks down to find a bloody rock in her hand.

"Why'd you do it, Em? Why?" Joe's face covered in blood.

"Do what?" Em tries to scream, but can't. She crawls out of the bedroll and runs but doesn't get far as the shadow engulfs her.

Sunday morning brings a chorus of "Amazing Grace" from the recreation room. Kate steps in, attempting to find a book to occupy her time and avoid any and all fights. *Lonesome Dove* is back on the rolling book rack, and Kate grabs it. Stray purple and pink hairs hang like tiny party streamers from the book and remind Kate how shamefully good it felt to beat Mee. *Deep down, I'm an animal—Em never stood a chance.*

"I once was lost but now I'm found . . ." Women singing pulls Kate away from her guilt for a moment. Old habits die hard, and Kate joins in: "Was blind but now I see."

The song ends, and someone calls, "Sit here, Miss D."

"Thanks, I'm just grabbin' a book."

"Come on, Miss D." Tanya's easy voice sounds demanding.

"Yeah, come on, Miss D," Monkey pleads.

"Please," Elizabeth adds.

"What the hell." Kate sits between Tanya and Elizabeth. Monkey and two new faces complete the circle of folding chairs. "Welcome." Tanya's tattooed hand gives Kate's knee two approving pats.

"Let's give thanks." Tanya laces her fingers with Kate's and the new girl's, then closes her eyes. "Dear Lord"— Elizabeth wraps her warm hand around Kate's and it feels nice—"thank you for the many blessings you have bestowed upon us." Kate watches the women with their closed eyes and nodding heads. "Lord, we come to You with broken hearts. Crushed spirits. But You are our rescuer. Your Word is our hope. Our salvation. Revive us, oh Lord. Comfort us in our time of need. Our souls require your breath of life to sustain us. Bless those who mourn, and I pray that You will bless each and everyone here today. Take Kate into your loving arms and keep her and her family close."

Kate squirms in her chair, crosses one leg over the other and bounces a dangling foot. Preposterous fanatics, she thinks. There's no animal as dangerous as the true believer. "Rescue her from the dark cloud of despair and let her delight in your everlasting grace. In Jesus's name we pray, Amen."

"Amen," the congregation repeats.

"Amen," Kate mutters and hugs *Lonesome Dove*, hoping the charade is over and she can return to her cell where Augustus McCrae and Captain Woodrow F. Call will romance her back to the Wild West. When Tanya opens her hymn book, Kate feels the way she does when she realizes that she's been waiting almost ten minutes in the express line with a full cart. "I've got to get going."

"Where?" Tanya stands.

"The hell outta here. Sorry. It's not you, it's just—"

"*Why* do you blame God for your problems?"

"'Cause he can take it."

"Your concept of God is completely muffed," Tanya says as Kate walks out—back to the comforts of alienation.

Gusts of wind throw rain at the window like handfuls of pebbles and stir a deep yearning to be outside. If only Em could reach the window where condensation falls like tears. She imagines herself out in the real world where dead fathers don't haunt daughters and dead husbands don't bleed. She closes her eyes. Thinks of the good part of her Joe dream. The way he felt against her. And wishes he were here with her now or she were there with him. Wherever there is.

"Hello?" Maureen steps in. Her ivory hair gray with rain. She shakes her head, then rubs her bangs in a futile attempt to add style. "It is really coming down out there." She takes her cell out of her soaked jacket and presses a few buttons. "How was your night?"

"Great. I had a dream about Joe. It was so real." Save the bad part.

"Medication often induces vivid dreams."

"He's in a good place. I know that."

"How do you know?" Maureen removes her wet jacket and hangs it over the back of a chair.

"Because I was there with him."

Maureen stops straightening her jacket and looks at Em. Her face tense with concern.

"Don't worry. It was just a dream. I'm not nutso. I wasn't really there, but kind of I was. In a way that let me know everything's good. He's in heaven. His heaven."

Maureen smiles and nods.

"You believe in heaven, Maureen?"

"I do. Just not the kind represented by most religions." She smiles and sits on the bed next to Em. "Your Uncle Pat and I used to debate the subject for hours."

"Guess he didn't convince you."

"No. But it forced us both to dig deeper into our beliefs than we ever would have. He wanted so badly to prove me wrong. Ultimately, I believe he was trying to convince himself."

"I think there's a heaven because I can't imagine Uncle Pat not being there."

Maureen is taken aback and considers it. "That may be the best affirmation that I have ever heard."

Em feels good and now has the nerve to ask, "Can I see my babies?"

FORTY-ONE

In the neonatal intensive care unit, Joseph's and Patrick's world consists of a clear plastic box and warming lights. Their tiny red heels double as pincushions. Breathing tubes connect the boys to ventilators. Wires run from their tiny chests to beeping monitors. "They look like beanie babies," Em says to the security guard and respiratory specialist with one wrist cuffed to a wheelchair. "Can I hold them, with all those tubes?" Em asks Song Lee, the respiratory specialist.

"First, we going to adjust your chair a little." The dainty woman with quick hands reclines Em so that she's on an angle. She maneuvers the wheelchair against the wall, alongside the ventilator, and locks the wheels down. Em's head is heavy and still smothered in bandages as she keeps watch on her precious boys. Hospital security, a sunburned man who looks to be in his late fifties, steps back while Song Lee spreads Em's gown, exposing the top half of her chest but not her breasts. Like she's done it a thousand times, Song Lee steps to the nearest boy sleeping on his stomach and slides her hands under him. With backup from a NIC unit nurse, they cradle the preemie and his tubes, then lie him on

Em's chest. The soft skin-to-skin contact and sweet baby smell stimulate a profound pleasure in Em. An instant bond and affection so strong she's transported to a place where nothing bad has ever happened or ever will.

The NIC unit nurse smiles knowingly. "Is that one Joseph or Patrick?"

"Good question." Em runs two fingers gently up and down the soft new skin on his tiny back.

Song Lee takes a final look at the ventilator, then peeks at the name tag on the baby's thumb-size ankle. "Joseph."

"Hi, little Joe," Em whispers. "I'm your mom and I love you so, so much." She kisses his fuzzy head and wishes Joe were here. Visions of him holding his sons puts a smile on her face. She sees little Joseph fitting perfectly in Joe's big hand. His long fingers cradling the child—keeping him safe. A stubbled smile and hazel eyes full of pride fill Joe's face, then become mangled into an invasive recollection of his face after the accident. Em takes a deep breath. Tries to clear the awful image from her mind. Joe's twisted torso stained with blood stagnates her happiness. Without warning, the memory of her killing Joe returns. Plays unmuted in her mind over and over again. Rock cracking skull. She's suffocating. Her heart racing, about to explode. Gasping for her next breath, her entire body shivers as she feels the weight of the cold, hard rock in her hand—the power it took to slam it into Joe's skull. She looks down at the same hand, her hand, now filled with her warm, soft son. "No."

Both nurses and the security guard turn their heads toward Em.

"I killed him," Em mumbles, squeezing her hand around little Joseph's back. Pressing him into her one last time. Breathing in his scent with long, deep breaths. Memorizing it the best she can.

"Are you okay, Ms. Quick?" Song Lee asks.

"Take him. Please. Something's wrong. Just, take him."

Song Lee checks the ventilator hose. "Everything look good." She appears confused.

Em slides her free hand away from baby Joseph. "I can't be trusted." Joe. *Joe was murdered. It was no accident.* The thought that she could hurt—no, kill him—is unbearable. Her soul is appalled. *What else am I capable of?* "Take him, now!" Em screams and stares at the ceiling, knowing the memory is real. Knowing she cannot be trusted. Knowing she can never be near her beautiful baby boys ever.

At the arraignment, District Attorney Bonnie York concludes with the recent DNA evidence presented to her by Attorney Steven Cline only a half hour ago. Silence fills the courtroom as Judge Barrett sits like God in his high-back leather throne behind a mahogany bench. He adjusts his round glasses on his face and carefully reads the DNA results.

Eddie Manetti leans into Kate and stops her bouncing leg. "He has to set bail. Try and relax," he whispers. But relaxing is impossible when there is no plan B if the judge doesn't set bail. Sitting between Cline and Manetti, Kate wonders if they are the least bit nervous. Do they possess any give-a-shit at all? Or is her case just another job?

Judge Barrett looks up, slides his glasses atop his bowling-ball head, leans forward into the microphone, and inhales. Then stops. What is he waiting for?

"Evidence appears to be in order—so, I find it admissible." Kate takes a deep breath and holds it in as Barrett continues. "Considering the accused pleads not guilty and has no prior record, bail will be set at one hundred thousand dollars with a preliminary hearing scheduled for . . ." Barrett looks to the clerk for available calendar dates, but Kate wants to jump out of her seat and throw her hands in the air. She releases her breath—pumps her fists in a small triumph. Eddie gives her a grin, and she fights the impulse to hug him. Kiss his full Italian-leather-sofa lips. If it weren't for his Calaveras County connections and manipulative know-how, they would have had to wait a month or more to subpoena the child's parents. Eddie knew Pastor Ken Berry. Knew that he had not followed the proper legal procedures before placing the child, a boy now named August Buller, with parishioners who had donated $10,000 to the church a week after receiving the baby. All Eddie had to do was mention the possibility of an illegal baby sale along with the implications that would follow, and the mother was in tears. He guaranteed their son's identity would not be disclosed. He left with a signed consent and a DNA swab sample in less than an hour. With an "urgency" charge of five hundred dollars, he had test results the next day.

"Preliminary hearing is set for July 2." Judge Barrett drops his gavel.

Memories come through as bright and clear as sunshine after a storm, and no matter how she tries, Em cannot stop them.

Saddling her mare. Putting her father's black hat on her head. His rain slicker. Riding in the dark. Watching Joe sleep in the meadow from the cover of aspen trees. The smoothness of the cold rock in her hand. A twig breaking as she approached and Huck barking at her. Barking and bashing Joe's skull. It makes her sick. The ease of it all when your father takes over. She wants to blame him for the brutal attack on Savannah. For killing Uncle Pat. She would never have burned down the only home she'd ever known. Mom was right. It was him. All him. Always. No matter how she tried, Mom could not save her, no one could. He had ruined her years ago.

"Time to pump again." Dora, the lactation specialist, rolls in with her breast-pump cart. Em stares at the wall. "Ms. Quick?" Em is neck deep in her attack on Savanah. The young girl's angelic face as she slept. The weight of the rock as Em lifted it overhead. The way the first blow cratered the forehead. Beating the girl's abdomen sounds like a distant drum that won't stop pounding.

"Ms. Quick, are you okay?" Em hears Dora, but cannot ignore the invasive fact of giving birth to her father's spawn. Sweating and shaking. The pain is real. "I'm going to get a nurse." Dora leaves the breast pump and cart next to Em's bed as Uncle Pat's murder plays out. Em just wants it all to stop, but there is no exit from hell. No way out unless she creates one. Her free hand reaches the breast pump. Feels for a bottle and brings it to her cuffed hand. Shaking and stiff, she removes the plastic nipple guard and brings it to her mouth. Refusing to allow the devil he planted in her to ever damage those boys, she opens her mouth and, with a middle finger, shoves the soft plastic as far down her throat as she can. Then waits. Waits for the nightmare to end.

The day was like any other late-summer day to most folks, but when the sun touches Kate's face, she stops. Closes her eyes and lifts her chin as high as it will go. There's nothing as welcome as sunshine when you've been cold for so long. The sky is a brilliant blue. The grass a vivid green. White roses congregate in luscious blooms outside the county jail, and Kate plucks one. Appreciates and inhales it. She breaks off three more flowers to take to Em and removes the thorns while waiting for Steven Cline.

A horn toots from an approaching red Jeep, and Kate rushes over. Inside, the mix of warm leather, roses, and some new age bebop song on the radio kick Kate's mood up so high, she wants to stick her head out of the window and let a loose a long overdue, *"Woo-hoo!"* She rolls her window down and settles for resting her arm on the door. Letting the wind wash over her as they drive west out of Calaveras County.

"Nice weather." Steven Cline shifts the Jeep into high gear as they hit the two-lane.

"Couldn't be better." Kate taps her fingers with the beat.

"I'd never been to Calaveras before last week. I like it here."

"I'll sell you a ranch." It surprises Kate how quickly a collection of reasons that she should sell the place she thought she could never live without come to mind. From the very beginning, it was Will. The down payment he convinced her to steal from her grandfather's import business. The way the ranch—more than Will—came to occupy her life. Then consume her. Over the years, it took control, and she could never escape. No vacations, ever. Always on the brink of losing the ranch was cliché but true. And for what? Pride of ownership? Looking into the deepest, most honest part of herself, Kate knows that the ranch doesn't matter. It never did. Life would go on just fine, probably better, without it. "I'll sell it to you cheap."

Steven seems to consider it. "I'll mention it to my dad, he's looking for a place to retire. Speaking of which, Ed Manetti tells me Judge Barrett is retiring."

"He doesn't seem old enough." Kate tucks flying hair behind her ears.

"He's not. From what Ed says"—Steven shifts gears—"it's complicated."

"Who will I get for my trial?"

"They haven't assigned a judge yet. Apparently, there aren't many candidates." Steven presses a button on his steering wheel and silences the music. "Kate, there is a way—shit. May I be frank?" He looks to Kate for permission.

"That'd be nice."

"Okay. I'm not going to explain how, or with whom, it's one of those—the less-you-know things—but Ed can get you a deal. For twenty thousand, the DA will drop the charges."

Kate waits for more, but there's isn't any. "How's that legal?"

Steven gives Kate a *do you really have to ask* look.

Kate thinks. Considers the last time she didn't play by the rules. "Boy, that'd be a huge relief, but, I just—" She shakes her head. "Shit like this always comes back."

"Forget I said anything. Just do yourself a favor—you pay whatever bill Ed Manetti sends you. Okay?"

"Maybe." Kate smiles at the thought of dickering with Eddie Manetti again.

A stop at Burger King for a Whopper meal deal and a bathroom break is like winning *Survivor: Calaveras County Jail.* Kate watches the bathroom door shut all on its own. Locks the stall door and sits in complete privacy. The antibacterial soap smells like lemons, and Kate takes a few extra pumps.

A chocolate shake. A Whopper with cheese and a hearty, "Hell yes," when they ask if she'd like to super-size her fries. Gold-colored cardboard crowns stacked in a pyramid on the counter, remind Kate of little Queen Em wearing her crown, eating her kids' meals in the back seat of the pickup— ketchup purposely smeared like lipstick across her face. *That smile.* Kate lifts a crown off the top of the pyramid.

"To go," Steven says as he hands the cashier a twenty, then sucks hard on the straw in his milkshake.

They make good time until the San Francisco–Oakland Bay Bridge where traffic is at a crawl. The delay gnaws at Kate. Anticipation of seeing Em and meeting her grandsons makes sitting still nearly impossible. She wants to get out of the Jeep—run across the bridge. Maybe she'll start jogging. Lose ten pounds and get in shape. Buy one of those jogging strollers you see the young moms with in Golden Gate Park. There's no rule that grandmothers can't push twins in a jogging stroller. *Do they even make them for two?* she wonders.

The drop in temperature is drastic the second Kate opens the Jeep door in front of UC San Francisco at Mission Bay. Steven rolls his window down and asks, "How will you get home?"

"I'll figure it out. Thanks."

"Here, take this." Steven reaches into the back seat and hangs a black Giants sweatshirt out of the window.

Kate accepts it. "Thanks," she says, and slips it over her head, slides the crown on her arm, grabs the roses, and reads the directory. Obstetrics, Gynecology & Perinatal Specialties entrance ahead. Kate follows the arrows through the sliding glass doors with a spring in her step.

After asking about Em's location at the information desk, the hundred-year-old receptionist presses keys and squints at her computer screen. Adjusts her glasses, then makes a call. "I have someone requesting to see Emma Lee Quick." The woman covers the receiver with her hand and looks at Kate. "Are you a relative?"

"Her mom."

"It's the mother," the woman says into the phone. "Okay. Thank you." She hangs up and smiles. "You can take a seat if you like, someone should be right down."

Kate can't sit. The crown hangs from her arm like a magnificent cardboard bangle, and in her hand, the roses are beginning to wilt. They need water and so does she. If only her damned old cell phone wasn't dead or if she had the charger, she could have called Maureen. Saved time instead of waiting for someone to assist her.

"Can you please just tell me where my daughter's room is? Emma Lee Quick. I can find it on my own," Kate asks the old woman.

"I'm sorry, dear, the doctor should be right down. Would you like some coffee or tea?" The woman points to a cabinet in the waiting area.

"Thanks." Kate tries the green tea. Read somewhere that it was good for you. Now's the time to start taking care of myself, she thinks. *Em and the boys are going to need me.* Daydreams of life with Joseph and Patrick and a second cup of tea occupy the wait until Dr. Loredo walks in with his hand out.

"Hello. You are Ms. Quick's mother?"

"Yes." A sudden and sick feeling stabs Kate in the chest.

"I'm afraid I have terrible news. Would you prefer to sit?" He opens his hand toward the seating area.

"No." Kate unconsciously locks her knees and stiffens her spine as sweat tickles her armpits.

"I'm sorry to inform you that at approximately ten a.m. your daughter took her life. Our attempts at resuscitation . . ." Kate doesn't hear the rest. The rest doesn't matter. She's falling through a trapdoor she never imagined was there. A brutal insignificant life gone completely dark.

No one would ever know why she did it. Or that her brain's uncontrollable panic hadn't started for two full minutes, when Em's blood became starved of oxygen and the brain told the rest of her it was dying. *Good,* was her last thought. The plastic nipple guard was lodged so deep in her trachea that the involuntary gag reflex was of no use. Not even the slightest hint of choking or coughing. By the time the nurse arrived, Em had been four minutes without oxygen. Her face was possessed by an alien blue. Her eyes bulged blood red and watered.

"She's choking!" rose from somewhere far below as the room spun and Em felt lighter and lighter as if she were being lifted. Like the Gravitron ride at the Calaveras County Fair, when she spun sideways so fast and was forced off her feet—up into that place where screams are lost in another dimension. Like here, in this hospital room somewhere between scared shitless and having the time of her life. Until a pleasing and peaceful blast of dopamine unleashed by the brain's last effort to survive. She smiled. Closed her eyes and flapped her wings.

FORTY-TWO

Sunlight beamed through the windows and promised warmth and hope in the waiting area when Kate had arrived, but now light has shifted into shadow. Now there is only dark. Time is irrelevant as Kate watches a tiny gray spider crawl a little at a time along the windowsill, then in and out of a crack in the dusty aluminum girder. The pest comes and goes and comes and goes. The Burger King crowns still hang from her wrist. Roses wilted in her hand. Maureen is there, sitting across from her—looking like hell. Pale. Despondent as the captain of a sinking ship who has fully accepted their fate. Their eyes meet.

"You go to Pat's funeral?" Kate mumbles.

Maureen's tired eyes nods yes. "Then this." She laces her fingers on her lap. "I tried to call you."

"Phone's dead." Kate moves into the chair next to Maureen.

"My incompetence is unforgivable." Maureen keeps her eyes down.

"So is mine."

"Em is the fourth patient I've lost to suicide."

"You keep count of the ones you save?"

Tears well in Maureen's eyes. She looks at Kate.

"You got sense enough to know this ain't your fault." Kate puts her hand on top of Maureen's.

"I wanted to help her more than anything in the world, and I failed." Overgrown tears roll down Maureen's cheeks like they'd been yearning to escape for years. "I could not help her."

"No one could. And I love you for trying." Kate puts her arms around Maureen as they cry for what seems like an eternity.

Tears subside, and as if on cue, a woman carrying a big black binder enters. "Ms. Dunnigan, I'm Sonya Fisher and I'm with the organ procurement staff here at the hospital." Kate wipes the snot from her nose with the borrowed sweatshirt, leaving a trail on the black sleeve. "I understand your grieving, but some find comfort in knowing that their loved one's organs will live on by saving a life." Sonya cocks her head—presses her lips together inside her mouth, then finally spits it out. "Unfortunately, time is crucial and—"

"I want to see her. Can I? Can I see her?" Kate interrupts and immediately regrets it.

"Yes, ma'am."

"I'll wait here," Maureen says.

"Like hell you will," Kate snaps and grabs Maureen's hand and holds it tight until she stands. Hand in hand, the women follow Sonya Fisher through the *Hospital Staff Only* door. Onto the elevator, then down, down, down to the basement.

A sharp antiseptic stench hits Kate the moment she walks into the hospital morgue. Death in every direction, behind each stainless-steel drawer. Under a half dozen white sheets. Time stalls. Em lying there. Her bandaged head resting on a cold metal table with a black U-shaped headrest for a pillow. Her blue lips frozen in a sleepy grin and the rest of her covered in a crisp white sheet like a distant landscape of peaks and valleys covered in snow. The bright silence is deafening as a man in magnifying glasses and a lab coat stops examining a cadaver and looks up. Looks at Kate like she's the one being dissected. Pulled apart piece by piece.

Maureen leans against the wall as Kate ignores the man with the magnifying glasses. White petals fall as Kate sets the roses alongside Em and places the crown on her torso. She takes Em's cold hand and kisses it. Smells it. All familiarity gone, only the sting of antiseptic remains. Kate rubs the hand against her own cheek to warm it, then kisses it twice more. Three times. Something cracks loudly like bones breaking, and Kate looks around the room. "What was that?"

"What?" Maureen looks puzzled. They look to the man who is taking notes and not responding.

The expression on Em's face seems different somehow. It's undeniable and absolute satisfaction—almost smug. Kate would know that look anywhere. She'd seen it a million times before. Like when Em did well at rodeos, saved a drop calf, or married Joe. Kate had been proud of her daughter so many times, and this time is no different as an understanding comes to her. Em has shown her the true meaning of mercy.

Joyful laughter bursts from Kate. Quickly, she slaps her

hand over her mouth to stifle the inappropriate emotion and looks at Maureen. Laughter comes up and out like vomit, and Kate can't stop. It's as if someone else is in control. The man glares over his magnifying glasses at Kate as her revelation punctures the dead silence. "Sorry." She looks at him. "I'm sorry." A grin escapes Maureen.

"Sweet baby girl. I'm so proud of you." Kate kisses her cheek, then whispers in her ear, "Don't you be scared. It'll be alright." She takes one last long look and thinks of what remains.

It feels like prophecy. Like God just breathed life into Kate at the sight of those boys—their tiny bodies so delicate. So in need of protection. "You can touch them if you scrub up." The nurse hands Kate and Maureen a gown and points to the sink.

After washing extra, extra well, and tying each other's gowns in place over their clothes, Kate waits while the nurse opens the side of Joseph's incubator. Maureen waits at Patrick's.

"Just watch the tubes," the nurse says as she moves aside and Kate moves up. Reaching her right hand slowly to the boy, Kate offers him an index finger and he takes it. Wraps his miniature fingers around her cut and swollen knuckle. In an instant, that sick hollowness that had resided inside her for so long is gone. Filled with love and gratitude. Suddenly, it all makes sense. She glimpsed at the power of life everlasting and knew she'd been wrong. *This is God*. Not the God forced upon her in childhood—the grantor of wishes or judgmental persecutor. God was not a mental concept to believe in or deny but the reality and miracle of life and love itself.

All the anger, pain, and suffering over the years seem minute compared to this moment. Truly at peace and filled with hope, Maureen reaches into Patrick's incubator and touches his cheek with the back of her finger. The child opens his mouth like a baby bird waiting to be fed and begins to cry. Maureen laughs. "Oh my."

"Did you ever think two pounds could smother all the heartbreak in the world?" Kate smiles with every bit of her being.

EPILOGUE

After a cold San Francisco summer of sampling sushi that never could compare to a thick, juicy steak, Kate spent a dreary fall attending writing classes that caused her work to sound like regurgitated paint-by-number irrelevant bullshit. The cinema was expensive, but the movies were cheap and predictable. Winter was mild, and most mornings, Kate and Maureen tucked the twins into their jogging stroller built for two and took turns pushing them through Golden Gate Park. Maureen took an indefinite leave of absence and by fall had decided to sell the clinic and help Kate rebuild the Calaveras ranch.

Although it is late June, the weather is unseasonably cool. The newly built farmhouse has central heating, but Kate still builds a fire each morning to take the chill off. She never fails to wipe the dust from the blistered eight-by-ten of Em receiving her All-Around Cowgirl buckle that hangs next to the old woodstove along with a dozen rodeo reprints. Pictures of Em and Joe decorate most of the space on the white walls throughout the house.

Daily hikes with Maureen, the twins, and Huck are now

routine. Barking ravens follow like always, but now offer an odd sense of comfort. Being in nature with her grandsons is where Kate finds comfort and feels closest to what she calls God. Watching Joseph throw a rock for Huck or Patrick inspecting a pine cone never goes by unappreciated.

Sunday dinners are now a thing. A customary cause for celebration because Kate and Maureen decided it should be. No more eating over the sink alone for either of them. Ever. Old Hank snores on the porch while Kate holds the screen door open for Roper. Huck barges in as Roper's spurs clack up the steps, then echo across new wood flooring.

"Mmm. Smells like fresh-baked bread in here." Roper lifts little Patrick out of his playpen.

"Maureen made sourdough." Kate sets Joseph, who now weighs in at a whopping fifteen pounds, into his high chair, and Huck sits close by, ready for the toddler to spill.

"Hi, Maureen." Roper carries Patrick to the second high chair and straps him in.

"Roper, how are you?" Maureen proudly sets her veggie lasagna and warm sourdough on the table. "This is Isabelle Garcia and her husband, Tony."

Former Officer Garcia stands up from the table, as does Tony, and they take turns shaking Roper's hand.

"Isabelle was my boss while I was in the pokey." Kate grins.

"What? No way." Roper takes a seat and digs into the basket of warm sourdough.

"Yep, way." Kate attempts to cut the lasagna. "She's retired now. No more cavity probes for her."

"Wait!" Maureen gently stops the spatula until Kate hands it over. "I'll do it." Everyone watches Maureen struggle to measure out equal portions.

"Just cut the son of a bitch before it gets cold." Kate sits at the head of table.

"That's one chore you owe me. Care to curse again?" Maureen cuts the lasagna into perfect squares.

"Sorry." Kate waits for Maureen to sit. When she does, Kate bows her head. "Thank you for this amazing meal, this home and our health, and these *beautiful* boys." Kate looks up at her perfect grandsons. Each of her perfect friends. "I am so very grateful for each one of you."

"Yeah, yeah, we know, we know. Let's eat before we starve." Roper wipes away a tear.

Kate, Maureen, Roper, Isabelle, Tony, Joseph, and Patrick feast.

"This the zucchini you grew?" Kate asks Maureen.

"Yes. The garden is bursting. I put a box together for the community center."

"I can drop it off tomorrow. I have to go to Rail Road Flat," Kate says around a mouthful of lasagna.

"What's in Rail Road Flat?" Isabelle asks.

"August Buller." Kate butters her bread.

"August Buller?" Roper grabs a second slice of lasagna.

"My grandson. He lives in Rail Road." Kate looks at Maureen—waits for a response that doesn't come. "He's sixteen and wants to meet me. And I wanna meet him."

"*Whoa.*" Roper stops eating. "Did you consult the professional first?" He eyes Maureen.

"Is Eddie going with you?" Maureen asks.

"Maybe. Probably. Yeah." Kate grins. "He's picking me up at noon."

"Miss Katherine, are you and Mr. Ed knockin' boots?" Roper exposes his big teeth with a huge smile while helping Patrick load a spoonful of zucchini. Kate's glare dares him to go further.

"I certainly hope so," Isabelle says while Tony rolls his eyes.

"Maureen"—Kate takes a bite—"this lasagna is delicious. Don't you think?"

"That's your grandmama's way of changing the subject." Roper shakes his head at Patrick, and the boy mimics him with his own headshake. "Yeah, she doesn't want to tell us if she's having sex."

"Roper!" Kate says as everyone giggles.

Maureen awkwardly interrupts her own laughter. "The lasagna is quite good. Maybe it's the ricotta. I tried a new brand. And the zucc—"

"*Nope.* I added a few secret ingredients to the sauce while it was simmering." Kate pinches a long noodle and feeds it to Joey like a mama bird.

"You did not." Maureen waits. "What?"

"A bit of bacon grease, some hamburger, and a whole lot a love." Kate sets a second helping on Maureen's plate.

"Amen, sista!" Roper claps and laughs so hard he turns red. "Amen."

"Amen!" Joey's first word fills their home with laughter.

Thank you for reading *Calaveras*. I'd love to hear what you thought of it. Please take a moment to leave a review on Amazon. Just a few words determine the success or failure of an author's work.

Lisa Michelle is the author of several award-winning stories and finds inspiration in many aspects of storytelling. From prose to film, her work appears in the medium best suited to the story. This former rodeo cowgirl and mother of two writes the people and places she knows best.

Find more information or join our crazy fun reading group at: www.LisaMichelle2020.com

Made in the USA
Monee, IL
18 September 2020